看影片學英語

用英語去旅行

TRAVELING IN ENGLISH: A HANDS-ON GUIDE FOR TOURISTS

看影片學英語 用英語去旅行

發 行 人	鄭俊琪
總 編 輯	王琳詔
責任編輯	廖慧雯
英文編輯	Jeff Curran
英文作者	Joseph Schier · Mike Corsini · Michelle Adams · Justin Thibedeau
英文錄音	Michael Tennant · Mandy Roveda
藝術總監	李尚竹
美術編輯	蕭暉璋
封面設計	蕭暉璋
技術總監	李志純
程式設計	李志純 · 郭曉琪
光碟製作	廖苡婷
點讀製作	高荔龍 · 李明爵
出版發行	希伯崙股份有限公司
	105 台北市松山區八德路三段 32 號 12 樓
	劃撥：1939-5400
	電話：(02)2578-7838
	傳真：(02)2578-5800
	電子郵件：service@liveabc.com
法律顧問	朋博法律事務所
印　　刷	禹利電子分色有限公司
出版日期	民國 103 年 6 月　初版一刷
	民國 104 年 11 月　初版三刷
推廣特價	書 + 互動光碟：399 元

看影片學英語
用英語去旅行

TRAVELING IN ENGLISH: A HANDS-ON GUIDE FOR TOURISTS

英語數位學習第一品牌

CONTENTS

PART A 旅遊會話通

PART B 繞著地球玩

旅遊達人 10 大嚴選

旅遊達人私房推薦

旅遊達人季節限定

別怕英文不好，只怕你不踏出那一步，就讓本書帶你用英語去旅行！

　　旅遊的型態很多種，最常見的就是參加旅行團和自助旅行，近年來背包客越來越多，可見想自助旅行的人也與日俱增。但許多人總卡在語言問題遲遲不敢跨出那一步，如果可以善用英語，就有機會跨出暢遊世界的第一步。藉著本書，跟著我們用英語去旅行吧。

　　本書分為兩部份，PART A 將出國會遇到的各種情境分為 12 大主題，收錄行前規劃、接洽旅行社、自助準備、入境、搭機、訂房、住宿、購物、用餐、問路、租車到急難救助等內容，使用最道地的美語及實用的對話，並利用實況影片呈現各種出國時所會面臨的情境。而與旅遊相關的實用句也可以在這個部分學到，例如：我們來安排一趟三天兩夜澳門自由行。Let's plan a three-day package tour of Macau.、新年假期還有兩人房的空房嗎？Are there any double rooms available during the New Year's holiday?。另外還有實戰對話及延伸學習，依序說明如下：

12 大旅遊必備主題

單元標題

動手寫寫看

進入單元學習前可先動筆練習，測試自己的英語實力。

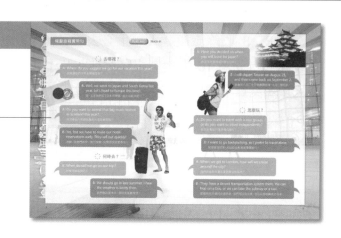

旅遊實用句

以問答方式介紹最
常用的旅遊例句。

實戰對話

由美籍專業老師編寫而
成,用最道地的美語學
習自然的應答。

QR 碼上看

掃瞄圖示可直接觀看,
利用影片學習更有效。

課文朗讀 MP3

數字標示為 MP3 音軌,可聆
聽美籍專業老師正確的發音。

中英對照

提供中文翻譯方便讀者
完整對照。

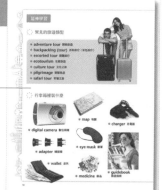

延伸學習

視主題不同而補充圖解字彙
或是旅遊實用句。

　　PART B 收錄旅遊達人一生必去的 25 個旅遊景點，皆為各具特色的城市或國家，分為 10 大嚴選、私房推薦及季節限定三個部分。由專業外師來撰寫旅遊文章，輔以單字例句及文法說明，再依主題補充「從旅遊看文化」、「旅遊小辭典」等相關資訊，讓讀者一邊跟著部落旅遊達人環遊世界，一邊讀出好英文。以下為 PART B 的內容介紹：

25 篇旅遊好文認識各地風俗文化

旅遊好文

藉由文章瞭解各景點的地理環境、風俗文化等面向，培養英文閱讀能力。

旅遊小辭典

補充如當地美食或地名的介紹。

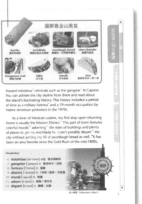

景點特色

介紹該景點特色，搭配賞心悅目的照片，讓讀者彷彿身歷其境。

中文翻譯

建議先閱讀文章
後再搭配參考。

實用單字

文章中的實用單字會以編號標
示，輔以音標、詞性及中文解釋
方便學習。

常用句型片語

補充實用片語與句型，加強
閱讀寫作能力。

除了本書及 MP3 朗讀光碟外，電腦互動光
碟中還有多種功能提供你不同面向的學習。此
外，本書亦附有點讀功能，若你已有點讀筆，
可將光碟中的檔案安裝至點讀筆中即可使用。

希望本書提供你受用的旅遊英語，搭配豐
富又有畫面的旅遊景點，讓你不再為語言隔閡
煩惱，好好享受出國旅遊的樂趣！

系統最低需求

- 處理器 1GHz 以上
- 憶體 1GB 以上
- 全彩顯示卡 1024*768 dpi（16K 色以上）
- 硬碟需求空間 200 MB
- 16 倍速光碟機以上
- 音效卡、喇叭及麥克風（內建或外接）
- Microsoft XP、Win 7 、Win 8 繁體中文版系統
- Microsoft Windows Media Player 9
- Adobe Flash Player 10

光碟安裝說明

❶ 將光碟片放進光碟機。

❷ 本產品備有 Auto Run 執行功能，如果您的電腦支援 Auto Run 光碟程式自動執行規格，則將自動顯現【看影片學英語 用英語去旅行】之安裝畫面。

❸ 如果您的電腦已安裝過本公司產品，如【CNN 互動英語雜誌】或【Live 互動英語雜誌】，您可以直接點選「快速安裝」圖示，進行快速安裝；否則，請點選「安裝」圖示，進行安裝。

❹ 如果您電腦無法支援 Auto Run 光碟程式自動執行規格，請打開 Windows 檔案總管，點選光碟機代號，並執行光碟根目錄的 autorun.exe 程式。

❺ 如果執行 autorun.exe 尚無法安裝本光碟，請進入本光碟的 setup 資料夾，並執行 setup.exe 檔案，即可進行安裝程式。

❻ 如果您想要移除【看影片學英語 用英語去旅行】，請點選「開始」，選擇「設定」，選擇「控制台」，選擇「新增 / 移除程式」，並於清單中點選「觀光旅遊英語通」，並執行「新增 / 移除」功能即可。

❼ 當語音辨識系統或錄音功能失去作用，請檢查音效卡驅動程式是否正常，並確認硬碟空間是否足夠且 WINDOWS 錄音程式可以作用。

❽ 麥克風設定請參照光碟主畫面中的「操作及語音辨識說明」。

❾ 執行光碟時，若遇見某些單元無法播出聲音，請安裝以下這支解碼器：

K-Lite Codec 2.82f 解碼器下載、安裝教學：

http://www.liveabc.com/liveabc_cd/
install_klcodec.asp

請注意！

◎在 Win7 / Win8 系統中安裝互動光碟，如出現【無法安裝語音辨識】訊息：

請依照以下步驟操作：

❶ 進入控制台
  ⓐ 進入「程式和功能」
  ⓑ 解除安裝或變更程式
  ⓒ 移除本書互動光碟軟體
  ⓓ 移除「Microsoft Speech Recognition Engine 4.0 (English)」

❷ 開啟檔案管理員，讀取本光碟，進入資料夾「setup」下。

❸ 按滑鼠右鍵點選「MSCSRL.EXE（語音辨識程式）」，點選「以系統管理員身分執行（A）」來進行安裝。

❹ 重新執行本互動光碟之安裝步驟。

操作說明

光碟安裝後點選「執行」，即進入本光碟的教學課程。依序說明如下：

主畫面

進入主畫面可看到 PART A、PART B、LiveABC
網站、操作説明、索引及離開的圖示。

點選欲學習的課程,進入學習畫面。

目錄

點選「目錄」圖示,會拉
出目錄頁,您可在此選擇
其他課程。

課程學習

影片學習

PART A 可用
影片和文字兩
種學習方式練
習,當您點選
課程名稱後,
將進入本畫
面。

文字學習

PART B 的學
習方式為文字
學習。在文字
學習模式中,
點選課文中任
一句子都可以
聽取正確發音,點選藍字部分則會出現用法説
明和例句,點選「單字解説」則可以學習本課重
要單字、音標、詞性及中譯。

索引

提供課程內容的單字及文法檢索。

LiveABC 網站

點選圖示後可連結到 LiveABC 英文學習網
站,提供豐富的學習資源與訊息。

説明

點選圖示可進入「操作使用説明」及「語音
辨識設定説明」畫面,提供光碟使用及學習
上相關的協助。

課文朗讀 MP3

電腦互動光碟中含有課文朗讀 MP3 的內
容,您可以將光碟放置於電腦中,從「我的
電腦」選擇光碟資料裡 MP3 的資料夾,使
用播放軟體將檔案開啟聆聽 MP3 內容。

功能說明

準備利用點讀筆學習前，請先將互動光碟裡的檔案安裝至點讀筆中，
再點選封面上 點讀筆 圖示，即可進入本書的內容學習。

【如何安裝點讀筆檔案】

1. 將互動光碟放置於電腦中，
   從「我的電腦」點選光碟
   機，按右鍵以「檔案總管」
   開啟光碟資料。

2. 找到光碟中「點讀筆」資料
   夾中的檔案（*.ecm），解
   壓縮到點讀筆的「BOOK」
   資料夾裡，即完成安裝。

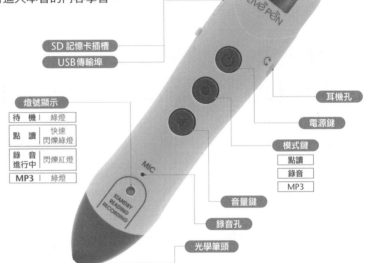

SD 記憶卡插槽
USB傳輸埠
耳機孔
電源鍵
模式鍵　點讀　錄音　MP3
音量鍵
錄音孔
光學筆頭
MIC

燈號顯示	
待　機	綠燈
點　讀	快速閃爍綠燈
錄　音進行中	閃爍紅燈
MP3	綠燈

錄音卡

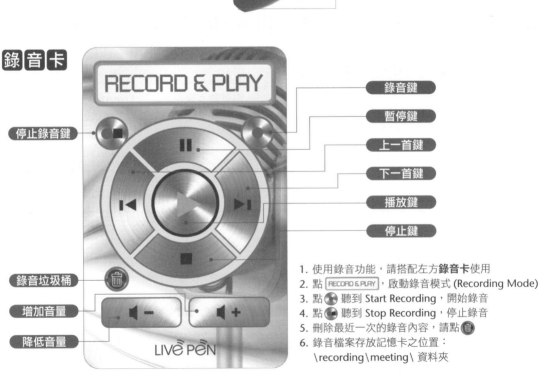

RECORD & PLAY

停止錄音鍵
錄音鍵
暫停鍵
上一首鍵
下一首鍵
播放鍵
停止鍵
錄音垃圾桶
增加音量
降低音量
LIVE PEN

1. 使用錄音功能，請搭配左方**錄音卡**使用
2. 點 RECORD & PLAY ，啟動錄音模式 (Recording Mode)
3. 點 🔵 聽到 Start Recording，開始錄音
4. 點 🔴 聽到 Stop Recording，停止錄音
5. 刪除最近一次的錄音內容，請點 🗑
6. 錄音檔案存放記憶卡之位置：
   \recording\meeting\ 資料夾

音 樂 卡

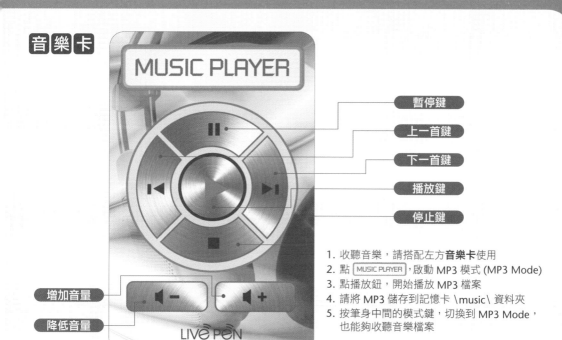

1. 收聽音樂，請搭配左方**音樂卡**使用
2. 點 MUSIC PLAYER ，啟動 MP3 模式 (MP3 Mode)
3. 點播放鈕，開始播放 MP3 檔案
4. 請將 MP3 儲存到記憶卡 \music\ 資料夾
5. 按筆身中間的模式鍵，切換到 MP3 Mode，
   也能夠收聽音樂檔案

本 書 用 法　　點 PLAY ALL 圖示，即播放整篇對話或文章的發音。

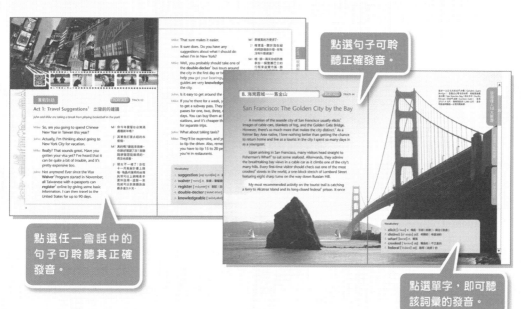

點選句子可聆聽正確發音。

點選任一會話中的句子可聆聽其正確發音。

點選單字，即可聽該詞彙的發音。

PART A
旅遊會話通

出國旅遊會面對許多不同的狀況，如何處理問題及達到最好的溝通，才能有趟完美的旅程。PART A 收錄最常見的 12 個主題，提供旅遊實用句、實戰對話及多元的延伸學習內容，讓你出國旅行一路順風。

Unit 1

規劃旅遊行程
Planning a Vacation

動手寫寫看

1. 這一次你最想去哪裡玩？

2. 你什麼時候有假可以去峇里島玩呢？

3. 你想跟團還是自由行？

4. 今年秋天，你想去京都賞楓嗎？

5. 我們來安排一趟三天兩夜澳門自由行。

參考答案請見 p. 338

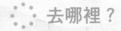

去哪裡？

A: Where do you suggest we go for our vacation this year?
你建議我們今年去哪裡度假？

B: Well, we went to Japan and South Korea last year. Let's head to Europe this time!
嗯，去年我們去了日本和韓國，這次去歐洲吧！

A: Do you want to attend that big music festival in Scotland this year?
你想參加今年蘇格蘭的大型音樂節嗎？

B: Yes, but we have to make our hotel reservations early. They sell out quickly!
想啊，但我們得早一點訂旅館，房間很快就會售完！

何時去？

A: When should we go on our trip?
什麼時候去旅行？

B: We should go in late summer. I hear the weather is lovely then.
我們應該夏末去。那時天氣最理想。

A : Have you decided on when you will leave for Japan?

你決定什麼時候出發去日本？

B : I will depart Taiwan on August 25, and then come back on September 2.

我會在八月二十五號離開台灣，九月二號回來。

怎麼玩？

A : Do you want to travel with a tour group, or do you want to travel independently?

你想跟團旅行還是獨自旅行？

B : I want to go backpacking, so I prefer to travel alone.

我想當背包客，所以我比較喜歡單獨旅行。

A : When we get to London, how will we cruise around the city?

我們去倫敦時要怎麼遊覽這個城市？

B : They have a decent transportation system there. We can hop on a bus, or we can take the subway or a taxi.

那裡有很完善的交通系統。我們可以搭公車，也可以搭地鐵或計程車。

PLAY ALL   TRACK 02

Act 1: Travel Suggestions[1]　出發前的建議

John and Mike are taking a break from playing basketball in the park.

Mike: So, are you going to spend Chinese New Year in Taiwan this year?

John: Actually, I'm thinking about going to New York City for vacation.

Mike: Really? That sounds great. Have you gotten your visa yet? I've heard that it can be quite a bit of trouble, and it's pretty expensive too.

John: Not anymore! Ever since the Visa **Waiver**[2] Program started in November, all Taiwanese with e-passports can **register**[3] online by giving some basic information. I can then travel to the United States for up to 90 days.

M：你今年要留在台灣過農曆新年嗎？

J：其實我打算去紐約市度假。

M：真的嗎？聽起來很棒。你辦好簽證了沒？我聽說辦簽證挺麻煩的，而且也很貴。

J：現在不一樣了！自從十一月免簽計畫上路後，有晶片護照的台灣民眾可以上網填基本資料註冊。這麼一來我就可以到美國旅遊最多達九十天。

Mike: That sure makes it easier.

John: It sure does. Do you have any suggestions about what I should do when I'm in New York?

Mike: Well, you probably should take one of the **double-decker**[4] bus tours around the city in the first day or two. That will help you get your bearings, and the guides are very **knowledgeable**[5] about the city.

John: Is it easy to get around the city?

Mike: If you're there for a week, you'll want to get a subway pass. They offer day passes for one, two, three, or seven days. You can buy them at the subway stations, and it's cheaper than paying for separate trips.

John: What about taking taxis?

Mike: They'll be expensive, and you'll have to tip the driver. Also, remember that you have to tip 15 to 20 percent when you're in restaurants.

M：那樣真的方便多了。

J：確實是。關於我在紐約時該做些什麼,你有沒有什麼建議?

M：嗯,頭一兩天你或許應參加一個雙層巴士的行程來遊覽市區。那將有助你熟悉環境,而且導遊對整座城市瞭若指掌。

J：在市區裡活動方便嗎?

M：如果你要在那裡待一個星期,你會需要地鐵通行票。他們有賣一日、兩日、三日,或是七日的通行票。你可以在地鐵站買到這種票卡,它比分別買單程票便宜。

J：那搭計程車呢?

M：計程車很貴,而且你還得給司機小費。還有,記得你到餐廳吃飯時,得付百分之十五至二十的小費。

Vocabulary

1. **suggestion** [səgˋdʒɛstʃən] *n.* 建議;暗示

2. **waiver** [ˋwevə] *n.* 放棄;棄權證書

3. **register** [ˋrɛdʒəstə] *v.* 登記;註冊

4. **double-decker** [ˋdʌbəlˋdɛkə] *n.* 雙層巴士

5. **knowledgeable** [ˋnɑlɪdʒəbəl] *adj.* 知識淵博的

【註】
visa waiver 並不是真正的免簽,全世界除了與美國相鄰的加拿大和墨西哥之外,所有來自 VWP(Visa Waiver Program)名單上國家、欲前往美國旅遊的旅客都必須先上網註冊並繳交規定的費用後,才能赴美旅遊。

John: I'll make a mental note of that, definitely.

Mike: You really should read up on what you want to do before you get to New York. You'll definitely want to visit the Empire State Building, check out Central Park, go to the **Metropolitan**[6] Museum, and maybe see a show on Broadway.

John: What about hotels? Are they expensive?

Mike: Very expensive compared to Taiwan. There are some **hostels**[7] you can stay at, and a few cheaper hotels. You'll have to book ahead of time, though, as they fill up quickly.

J：我一定會記得要給小費的。

M：你到紐約前真的要就你想做的事好好做功課。你一定要去參觀帝國大廈、逛逛中央公園、去大都會博物館，或許也去百老匯看場表演。

J：那飯店呢？會不會很貴？

M：跟台灣比是很貴。那裡有一些你可以住宿的旅社，還有幾間比較便宜的旅館。不過你要事先訂房，因為它們很快就會客滿了。

Language Spotlight

get one's bearings 熟悉環境

bearing 意為「方位；方向感」，get one's bearings 引申表示「熟悉環境」之意。

- I was totally lost when I arrived in London, but once I got my bearings, I was fine.

  剛到倫敦時，我完全分不清楚東西南北，但熟悉環境後就適應了。

Vocabulary

6. **metropolitan** [ˌmɛtrə`palətən] *adj.* 大都會的

7. **hostel** [`hastl] *n.* 旅社（尤指青年旅社）

實戰對話

 PLAY ALL   TRACK 03

Act 2: Final Preparations   行前準備

*John is calling a travel **agency**[1] to find out about vacation packages for New York City.*

Agent: Good morning, Plus Travel Agency. How can I help you today?

John: Hello, I'm calling about the package deal you're offering for New York City over the Chinese New Year. I noticed that all of them are for two people traveling together, but I'm going **solo**[2] on this trip.

Agent: Well, all of the hotel accommodations are for two people. However, we can give you a slight discount on the rooms as you will be alone, and we'll only charge for a single plane ticket.

A： 早安，Plus 旅行社您好。有什麼我能為您效勞的嗎？

J： 妳好，我是打來詢問你們提供的農曆新年期間的紐約套裝行程。我注意到那些行程全都是兩人同行的，但是我只有自己一個人要去。

A： 嗯，所有的飯店住宿都是雙人房。不過由於您是一個人，我們在房價上可以給您一點折扣，而且我們只會收一張機票的錢。

23

John: I'd also want to stay an extra two days, if possible.

Agent: I can rearrange the flight, but you'll have to find a hotel for the extra two days. Let me look into the flights and call you back.

John: Great! My name is John Lee, and my number is 2578-2626. (Pause) OK! Bye!

(John hangs up the phone. He sits down at his computer and starts looking up information. Later, he makes a call to the United States.)

Clerk: Regency Hostel, Carrie speaking.

John: Hi, Carrie. I found your hostel online, and I have a few questions about it before I make a **reservation**.[3] If I'm staying in one of the bunk rooms with other people, how can I make sure my luggage is safe?

Clerk: We provide all guests with a key to a personal **locker**.[4] However, we're not responsible for your **belongings**,[5] so I'd suggest not traveling with valuable items.

John: That shouldn't be a problem. Are **toiletries**[6] and towels provided, or do I have to bring my own?

J：可以的話我還想多待兩天。

A：我可以重新替您安排班機，但是您必須自行找另外兩天的住宿飯店。我幫您查查班機再回電給您。

J：太好了！我叫李約翰，我的電話號碼是2578-2626。（停頓）好！掰！

（約翰掛上電話。他在電腦前坐下來並開始查資料。稍後，他打電話到美國。）

C：Regency 旅社，我是凱莉。

J：嗨，凱莉。我在網路上找到你們這家旅社，我在訂房前有幾個問題。如果我要和其他人一起住上下舖房，我要怎麼確保我的行李安全無虞？

C：我們提供所有旅客個人寄物櫃的鑰匙。不過我們不負責保管您的財物，所以我建議不要帶貴重物品旅行。

J：那應該不成問題。有提供盥洗用具和毛巾嗎？還是我得自己帶呢？

Clerk: Towels are provided for $10, $5 of which acts as a deposit. We don't provide any toiletries, but there is a **vending machine**[7] in the lobby where you can buy them.

John: Perfect! I'll book online and see you in a few weeks, then.

C： 毛巾要收十美元，其中五塊是押金。我們並未提供任何盥洗用具，不過你可以在大廳的販賣機購買。

J： 好極了！我會上網訂房，過幾週後見囉。

Vocabulary

1. **agency** [ˈedʒənsi] *n.* 代辦處；經銷處
2. **solo** [ˈsolo] *adv.* 單獨地　*adj.* 單獨的
3. **reservation** [ˌrɛzəˈveʃən] *n.* 預訂；保留
4. **locker** [ˈlɑkə] *n.* 寄物櫃
5. **belongings** [bɪˈlɔŋɪŋz] *n.* 所有物（作此義時常用複數）
6. **toiletries** [ˈtɔɪlətriz] *n.* 盥洗用品（作此義時常用複數）
7. **vending machine** [ˈvɛndɪŋ] [məˈʃin] *n.* 販賣機

常見的旅遊類型

* **adventure tour** 探險旅遊
* **backpacking (tour)** 自助旅行（背包旅行）
* **escorted tour** 跟團旅行
* **ecotourism** 生態旅遊
* **culture tour** 文化之旅
* **pilgrimage** 朝聖旅遊
* **safari tour** 狩獵之旅

行李箱裡裝什麼

* **digital camera** 數位相機

* **map** 地圖

* **charger** 充電器

* **adapter** 轉接頭

* **eye mask** 眼罩

* **wallet** 皮夾

* **medicine** 藥品

* **guidebook** 旅遊指南

Unit 2

✈ 旅行社英語
Dealing with a Travel Agent

動手寫寫看

1. 我想訂兩張到關島的機票。

2. 到新加坡最便宜的機票是多少錢?哪一家航空公司?

3. 我們的預算不多,最好不要超過五萬。

4. 新年假期還有兩人房的空房嗎?

5. 我想更改班機時間。

參考答案請見 p. 338

訂機票

A: Hi. Could you help me book a ticket to Los Angeles, please?
嗨，可以幫我訂一張到洛杉磯的機票嗎？

B: Sure, no problem. When do you plan on going?
當然沒問題。你計畫何時出發？

A: I need one round-trip ticket to Tokyo for the fifteenth of April, please.
請給我一張四月十五號去東京的來回機票。

B: Sure. Do you need a hotel room or a car?
好，您需要訂飯店或租車嗎？

行程推薦

A: I would like to go to Europe, but I don't know where exactly.
我想去歐洲，但不知道去哪裡好。

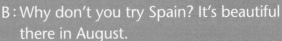

B: Why don't you try Spain? It's beautiful there in August.
何不試試西班牙？那裡八月很漂亮。

A: I would like the package deal. Does it include meals?

我想訂套裝行程。有含餐嗎？

B: Yes. It includes complimentary breakfasts at the hotel.

有，這行程有包含飯店早餐。

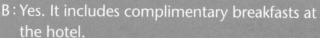 費用討論

A: How much are you looking to spend on this vacation?

你想要花多少錢在這次假期上？

B: Our budget is about NT$100,000. Is that enough for a family of three?

我們的預算大約台幣十萬。夠一家三口出遊嗎？

A: Two round-trip tickets and three nights at a hotel will cost you only NT$85,000.

兩張來回機票加三個晚上的住宿只需要台幣八萬五。

B: I also need to rent a car. How much would that be?

我還需要租一台車。那要多少錢？

Act 1: Booking a Flight 訂購機票

A customer is booking a flight at a travel agency.

TA: Travel **Agent**[1]   C: Customer

TA: Good morning. Welcome to Global Vacations Travel Agency. What can I do for you today?

C: I need to book a flight to New York for next month.

TA: That shouldn't be a problem. On what dates will you be traveling?

C: I need to leave on the 5th of November and return on the 15th.

TA: OK, let me check the fares and **availability**.[2] Do you need a direct flight?

TA： 早安，歡迎光臨「全球假期旅行社」。今天您需要什麼樣的服務呢？

C： 我要訂一張下個月飛往紐約的機票。

TA： 沒問題。您要哪一天出發呢？

C： 我要在十一月五號出發、十五號回來。

TA： 好的，我確認一下票價和機位。您要直飛班機嗎？

C: Oh, now that you mention it, I'd actually like to stop over in Tokyo for one night if possible. I have a friend there whom I'd like to visit.

TA: That should be **doable**.³ So, let me confirm the dates. You'd like to fly to Tokyo on the 5th and continue on to New York on the 6th. Is that correct?

C: Yes, and actually, I'd like to fly with NorthJet Airlines if possible. I collect frequent-flier miles with them, and I'm just a few thousand miles away from gaining **elite**⁴ member **status**.⁵

TA: No problem. Just a moment. I'm checking now. *(Typing into the computer)* NorthJet does have some **remaining**⁶ seats on the dates you've requested, but the fare is a bit higher than some of the other airlines.

C: How much is the difference?

C： 既然你提了，如果可能的話，我其實是想在東京停留一晚，去拜訪那兒的一位朋友。

TA： 這應該是可行的。所以，讓我先跟您確認日期，您想要五日飛往東京，然後六日再接著飛往紐約。對嗎？

C： 是的，事實上，如果可以的話，我想要搭北方航空的班機。我有累積他們的哩程點數，我還差幾千哩就可以獲得尊榮會員的資格了。

TA： 沒問題，請稍後一下。我現在正在確認。（正在輸入電腦）北方航空的班機在您希望出發的日期上的確還有一些空位，但是票價比其他家航空公司稍微貴了一點。

C： 貴多少？

Vocabulary

1. **agent** [ˋedʒənt] *n.* 仲介人；代理商（travel agent 是指「旅行社業務員」）

2. **availability** [əˌveləˋbɪlətɪ] *n.* 可獲得性；可用性

3. **doable** [ˋduəbəl] *adj.* 可做的；可執行的

4. **elite** [eˋlit] [ɪˋlit] *adj.* 菁英；精華

5. **status** [ˋstætəs] *n.* 身分；地位；狀態

6. **remain** [rɪˋmen] *v.* 剩餘；留下；保持（remaining [rɪˋmenɪŋ] 為現在分詞作形容詞用，指「剩餘的」）

TA: *(Looking at computer)* Well, the lowest fare I'm showing with another airline is NT$30,000, but NorthJet's lowest fare is $33,000.

C: Oh well. I still think it's worth it to pay the higher fare for NorthJet. Once I'm an elite member, I can get a lot of free **perks**[7] on future flights.

TA: So, you'd like me to reserve the flight on NorthJet?

C: Please.

TA: Very well, I'll just need to get some information from you, then.

TA：（看著電腦）嗯，我這裡顯示另一家航空公司最低票價是新台幣三萬元，但北方航空的最低票價是三萬三。

C：喔，我還是覺得可以多付一點搭北方航空的。一旦我成為尊榮會員，以後搭機就可以享有免費優惠。

TA：所以您需要我幫您保留北方航空的機位嗎？

C：麻煩你。

TA：好，那麼我還需要您提供一些資料。

Language Spotlight

now that 既然……

now that 為連接詞，用來引導副詞子句。

- Now that the new highway is finished, I can drive to work much faster.

  新的高速公路已經完工，我開車上班就更快了。

continue on + (to + 地點) 繼續前往（某地）

類似的用法還有 continue on + to V. 表示「接續……（中斷後接續）」；continue + V-ing 則表示「繼續……（不中斷）」。

- After stopping at a restaurant for lunch, we continued on to the city in our car.

  在一家餐廳停留用了午餐後，我們繼續開車前往市區。

Vocabulary

7. **perk** [pɜk] *n.* 額外的待遇（作此義恆用複數）；津貼

PLAY ALL   TRACK 06

Act 2: Planning a Honeymoon[1] Getaway 計畫蜜月旅行

A man is booking a honeymoon vacation at a travel agency.

TA: Travel Agent   C: Customer

TA: Hello. Welcome to Global Vacations Travel Agency. How can I help you?

  C: Hi! I'm getting married in a couple of months, and I need to plan a honeymoon vacation.

TA: Well, congratulations! Do you have any particular **destination**[2] in mind?

  C: Nowhere specific, but it must be somewhere romantic. Somewhere with a beach would be nice.

TA: Are you looking for somewhere domestic or international?

TA: 哈囉，歡迎光臨全球假期旅行社。您需要什麼服務呢？

  C: 嗨，我再過幾個月就要結婚了，我想要計畫蜜月旅行。

TA: 這樣啊，恭喜您！您心裡有特別的地點嗎？

  C: 沒有特定地點，但是一定要是浪漫的地方。有海灘的地方應該不錯。

TA: 您想找國內還是國外的旅遊點呢？

C: International. This is a once-in-a-lifetime event, so I plan to **splurge**.[3]

TA: OK, how about Bali? We currently have some package deals that are great for couples. It's quite a romantic place.

C: Yes, it is, but actually my **fiancée**[4] has been to Bali a couple of times. I'd like to take her somewhere new.

TA: All right. Has she been to the Philippines or Malaysia? There are some great beach **getaways**[5] in those places, too.

C: Yeah, she's been pretty much all over Southeast Asia. I was thinking somewhere a bit more out-of-the-way.

TA: Hmm, well, perhaps the Caribbean, then?

C: The Caribbean? That sounds more like it.

TA: In that case, I can highly **recommend**[6] Aruba. I've been there twice, and it has some of the most **spectacular**[7] beaches in the world.

C: Sounds great! Tell me more!

TA: Let me get you a **brochure**[8] of a wonderful **all-inclusive**[9] **resort**[10] that I've personally stayed at. Your fiancée will love it!

C： 國外的。這是一生一次的大事，我可以多花一點錢。

TA： 好的，峇里島如何？我們現在有一些很適合情人的特惠專案。那裡是相當浪漫的去處。

C： 是沒錯。但事實上我未婚妻去過峇里島幾次。我想帶她去別的地方。

TA： 好吧，那麼她曾去過菲律賓或馬來西亞嗎？那裡也有幾個很棒的海灘度假地點。

C： 沒錯，但她幾乎東南亞都跑遍了。我在想可以去比較特別的地方。

TA： 嗯，那麼或許可以考慮加勒比海？

C： 加勒比海？聽起來很像我要的。

TA： 如果這樣的話，我十分推薦阿魯巴島。（編按：委內瑞拉西北方的小島，為荷蘭的自治國。）我去過那兩次，而且那裡有一些世界上最漂亮的海灘。

C： 聽起來很棒！多提供我一些資訊吧！

TA： 我先給您我曾住過的一間很棒的度假中心的介紹手冊，裡頭吃住玩樂應有盡有。您的未婚妻一定會很喜歡的！

Language Spotlight

have . . . in mind　想著……；心裡盤算……

字面意思是「心裡想著某事」，也可引申為「心中有某種想法」的意思。

- I have a great new restaurant in mind if you'd like to go out to eat with me tonight.

  如果你今晚想要跟我去外頭用餐，我想到一間很棒的新館子。

once-in-a-lifetime　一生一次的；彌足珍貴的

此為副詞片語 once in a lifetime 加上連字號而成的複合形容詞。

- High school graduation is a once-in-a-lifetime moment for students all over the world.

  高中畢業對世界各地的學生來說是一生難忘。

- This type of opportunity only comes by once in a lifetime, so I think we should take it.

  這樣的機會一輩子只會發生一次，所以我覺得我們應該要好好把握。

out-of-the-way　奇特的；不尋常的

同義　out-of-the-ordinary、unusual

- When I walked into the room, I didn't notice anything out-of-the-ordinary.

  我走進房間時沒有注意到任何不尋常的事情。

Vocabulary

1. **honeymoon** [ˋhʌnɪ‚mun] *n.* 蜜月；蜜月假期

2. **destination** [‚dɛstəˋneʃən] *n.* 目的地；終點

3. **splurge** [splɝdʒ] *v.* 揮霍（金錢）

4. **fiancée** [fi‚ɑnˋse] *n.* 【法語】未婚妻（fiancé [fi‚ɑnˋse] 指「未婚夫」）

5. **getaway** [ˋgɛtə‚we] *n.* 短期假期；遠離塵囂的好去處

6. **recommend** [‚rɛkəˋmɛnd] *v.* 推薦；建議

7. **spectacular** [spɛkˋtækjələ] *adj.* 壯麗的；壯觀的

8. **brochure** [broˋʃur] *n.* 小冊子

9. **all-inclusive** [‚ɔlɪnˋklusɪv] *adj.* 全部包括的；囊括一切的

10. **resort** [rɪˋzɔrt] *n.* 度假勝地；度假飯店

 歐美著名的旅遊景點

United States 美國

* **Yellowstone National Park** [ˈjɛloˌston] [ˈnæʃənəl] [pɑrk] 黃石公園
* **Mt. Rushmore** [maʊnt] [ˈrʌʃˌmɔr] 羅什摩爾山（美國總統山）
* **Statue of Liberty** [ˈstætʃu] [ˈlɪbəti] 自由女神像
* **Hollywood** [ˈhɑliˌwʊd] 好萊塢
* **Golden Gate Bridge** [ˈgoldən] [get] [brɪdʒ] 金門大橋
* **Niagara Falls** [naɪˈægərə] [fɔlz] 尼加拉大瀑布

Europe 歐洲

* **Stonehenge** [ˈstonˌhɛndʒ] （英）史前巨石堆
* **Big Ben** [bɪg] [bɛn] （英）大笨鐘
* **Arch of Triumph** [ɑrtʃ] [ˈtraɪəmf] （法）凱旋門
* **Eiffel Tower** [ˈaɪfəl] [ˈtaʊə] （法）艾菲爾鐵塔
* **Neuschwanstein Castle** [nɔrˈʃvanˌstaɪn] [ˈkæsəl] （德）新天鵝堡
* **Mont Blanc** [ˌmonˈblɑn] （法）白朗峰
* **Leaning Tower of Pisa** [ˈlinɪŋ] [ˈtaʊə] [ˈpɪzə]/[ˈpɪsɑ] （義）比薩斜塔
* **Colosseum** [ˌkɑləˈsiəm] （義）羅馬競技場
* **Acropolis** [əˈkrɑpələs] 希臘神廟（衛城）

Unit 3

✈ 自助旅行英語
Let's Go Backpacking

動手寫寫看

1. 背包旅行的好處就是想去哪就去哪。

2. 到加州自助旅行最好要租車。

3. 我們要不要冒險一下，搭地鐵去？

4. 我計畫在舊金山停留三天，有沒有什麼必看的景點？

5. 到大阪旅行，有可以推薦的通行券嗎？

參考答案請見 p. 338

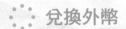
兌換外幣

A: Here are some bills that I need to exchange.
我需要兌換一些鈔票。

B: OK. Would you like large or small bills?
沒問題，您需要大面額還是小面額的鈔票？

A: What is your exchange rate for US dollars?
你們美元的匯率是多少？

B: The current rate is ten local dollars to one US dollar.
現在的匯率是本地貨幣十元換一塊美金。

旅遊資訊

A: Do you know of any cheap places to stay at in Bali?
你知道峇里島有什麼便宜的住宿地方嗎？

B: Yes, there are many reasonably priced hostels near the beach.
有啊，海灘附近有很多價位合理的旅社。

A : Where can I buy a subway pass?

我可以在哪裡買地鐵通行券？

B : You can buy one at any subway station. They offer 2-day and 3-day passes.

你可以在任一個地鐵站購買。他們提供兩天和三天的通行券。

 行前討論

A : Where do you carry your money when you go backpacking?

你去背包旅行時都把錢放在哪裡？

B : To be safe, I carry traveler's checks. I never keep much cash on me.

安全起見，我會用旅行支票。我身上不帶太多現金。

A : What are some must-see places for backpacking?

哪些地方是自助旅行一定要去的？

B : The temples in Angkor Wat are stunning.

吳哥窟的廟宇很令人讚嘆。

PLAY ALL　TRACK 08

Act 1: Money Exchange　兌換外幣

June and Chris are backpacking and on a tight budget. Having arrived in a new country, they figure out how to get from the airport to a hotel. First, they approach a money exchange counter in the airport.

Chris: Excuse me. What's your exchange rate for US dollars?

Clerk: Cash or traveler's checks?

Chris: I'd like to exchange a one-hundred-dollar traveler's check.

Clerk: One hundred US dollars can be exchanged for four thousand one hundred and thirty of the local **currency**.[1]

C：不好意思，請問一下美金的匯率是多少？

J：是換現金還是旅行支票呢？

C：我想換一張一百元的旅行支票。

Cl：一百元美金可以兌換本地幣值四千一百三十元。

Chris: Is there a service charge on traveler's checks?

Clerk: Yes. We charge 2 percent.

Chris: *(Hands the clerk the traveler's check)* OK. Here is the check and my passport.

June: I think I'd rather **withdraw**[2] money from the bank machine. Is there an ATM around here?

Clerk: Yes. There is one to your left. *(To Chris)* Here is your cash. Please sign this **receipt**.[3]

Chris: *(Signs)* Thank you. Wow, June, look at this—four thousand! I'm rich in this country!

June: Chris, be careful! You won't be rich for long if you let all the **pickpockets**[4] in the airport see your money!

Chris: Oh, you're right. *(Puts his money away)*

C：換旅行支票的話要收手續費嗎？

Cl：是的，我們收百分之二的手續費。

C：（把旅行支票遞給服務人員）好的，這是支票和我的護照。

J：我想我寧可去銀行的機器領錢。這附近有自動櫃員機嗎？

Cl：有的，您左邊就有一台。（對克里斯說）這是您的現金，請在這張收據上簽名。

C：（簽名）謝謝。哇！瓊，妳看看——四千塊錢！我在這個國家是有錢人！

J：克里斯，小心！如果你讓機場裡所有的扒手都看到你的錢的話，你也有錢不了多久的！

C：喔，妳說的對！（把他的錢收起來）

Vocabulary

1. **currency** [ˈkɝənsi] *n.* 貨幣

2. **withdraw** [wɪðˈdrɔ] *v.* （從銀行帳戶）提領（款項）

3. **receipt** [rɪˈsit] *n.* 收據

4. **pickpocket** [ˈpɪkˌpɑkət] *n.* 扒手

June: OK, so we're all **set**,[5] then. We've got money, our passports—

Chris: Passport? . . . Oh no! Where's my passport? Oh, yeah! The exchange counter.

June: I think I need to exchange my travel partner!

J： 好囉，所以我們都準備好了。我們有錢、護照——

C： 護照？……糟了！我的護照呢？喔，對了！在外幣兌換櫃台那裡。

J： 我想我得換個旅行夥伴！

Language Spotlight

backpacking 背著簡便背包旅行

backpack 作名詞用時，意思是「背包」；用作動詞用時，其中一個意思是背著簡便的背包去旅行。許多年輕人，尤其是學生喜歡背起簡單的行囊就去旅行，而 backpacker 便是指這些背著簡便行李去旅行的人。

• After college, Marco backpacked around Europe.
  大學畢業後，馬克背著簡便背包到歐洲旅行。

on a tight budget 預算很緊

tight budget 的意思是「預算很拮据；手頭很緊」，所以當你做某件事，只有很有限的錢可以使用，就可以說是 on a tight budget。

補充 on a shoestring 意思與 on a tight budget 相似，都是指「用很少錢（做某事）」，兩者可互換，但以 on a tight budget 較常見。

• The young couple decorated their new house on a tight budget.
  那對年輕夫妻在裝潢新居時預算很緊。

Vocabulary

5. **set** [sɛt] *adj.* 做好準備的

實戰對話

PLAY ALL　TRACK 09

Act 2: Tourist Information 旅客資訊

Before leaving the airport, June and Chris explore their travel options.

June: I can't believe we're finally here! Where should we go first?

Chris: I don't know. Do you want to stay in the city for a few days or head straight to the beach?

June: Let's go to the **tourist information booth**[1] to get more information.

(At the booth)

J：我真不敢相信我們終於到這裡了！我們應該先去哪兒呢？

C：不知道。妳想在城裡待個幾天，還是直接到海邊去？

J：咱們去遊客資訊中心多拿一些資料吧。

（在遊客資訊中心）

June: Excuse me. Do you have a copy of the train and bus schedules?

Clerk: Where would you like to go?

June: Well, we want to go diving, elephant trekking, kayaking—

Chris: And parasailing and bungee jumping—

June: And we'd like to see some temples and beautiful beaches.

Clerk: Let me show you some brochures.

June: *(Looking at brochures)* These tours look great . . . but expensive. We're traveling on a shoestring.

Clerk: *(Showing June a map)* Then, I suggest these islands—they're popular with backpackers for their nice beaches and cheap **accommodations**.[2]

June: Wow! Palm trees and bungalows!

Clerk: Bungalows here range from twelve to fifty dollars a night.

Chris: *(Showing June a brochure)* Hey, look at this! For four thousand, we can stay at a five-star **luxury** resort on our own private beach for a week!

June: Four thousand? Is that it?

J：請問一下，妳有火車與巴士的時間表嗎？

Cl：兩位想要去哪裡呢？

J：嗯，我們想要去潛水、騎大象、划獨木舟——

C：還有玩拖曳傘和高空彈跳——

J：還有我們想去看一些廟宇和美麗的海灘。

Cl：我拿一些小冊子給兩位看看。

J：（看著小冊子）這些遊覽行程看起來都很棒……但是滿貴的。我們的旅行預算很緊。

Cl：（在一張地圖上指給瓊看）那麼我建議去這些小島——這些地方的海灘很美，而且住宿很便宜，所以很受自助旅行者的歡迎。

J：哇！有棕櫚樹和小木屋！

Cl：這裡的小木屋一晚十二元到五十元不等。

C：（給瓊看一本小冊子）嘿，妳看這個！只要花四千元，我們就能在私人海灘上的五星級豪華度假飯店住一個星期！

J：四千塊錢？就這樣嗎？

Clerk: Uh-huh. But the prices in that brochure are in US dollars.

Chris: Oh! Of course! So, what were you saying about those cheap bungalows?

Cl：嗯，但是那本小冊子裡列的是美金。

C：喔！當然！那麼，你剛說的那些便宜小木屋是怎麼回事？

Language Spotlight

luxury vs. luxurious 豪華的

luxury 是名詞，但有時也作形容詞用，意思雖與形容詞 luxurious 一樣，都是「豪華的、舒適的」，但是含意卻不同。當把 luxury 作形容詞用時，是用來指這樣東西的「樣式、等級」，例如 a luxury hotel（高級的飯店）、a luxury car（豪華型的轎車）。而以 luxurious 來形容某物時，則是指這樣東西是「很舒適的；很豪華的；很奢侈的」。

- One night at the luxury hotel will cost you over NT$10,000.
  住在奢華旅館一晚會花費台幣一萬元以上。
- We spent a luxurious vacation on an island in Europe.
  我們在歐洲的一個島上度過一個舒適的假期。

Vocabulary

1. **tourist information booth** [ˋtʊrɪst] [ˌɪnfɚˋmeʃən] [buθ]
   遊客資訊中心
2. **accommodation** [əˌkɑməˋdeʃən] *n.* 暫時的住所（作此義時常為複數）

* **go surfing**
衝浪

* **go diving**
潛水

* **go snorkeling**
浮潛

* **go jet-skiing**
騎水上摩托車

* **go kayaking**
划獨木舟

* **go white-water rafting** 泛舟

* **go hang gliding**
玩滑翔翼

* **go parasailing**
玩拖曳傘

* **go skiing**
滑雪

* **go snowboarding**
玩滑雪板

* **go bungee jumping**
高空彈跳

* **go cycling**
騎腳踏車

Unit 4 ✈ 機場英語
Airport English

動手寫寫看

1. 可以看一下你的護照和登機證嗎？

2. 你的行李超重了。你得額外付費。

3. 請給我靠走道的座位好嗎？

4. 我可以帶這個包包上飛機嗎？

5. 我們等得兩個小時，去貴賓室坐一下吧。

參考答案請見 p. 338

旅遊出境

A: Do you have any bags that you need to check?

你有行李要托運嗎？

B: I have one suitcase to check and one carry-on.

我有一個手提箱要托運，一件隨身行李。

A: It appears that your 7:40 a.m. flight to Hong Kong has been delayed.

您要搭乘早上七點四十分前往香港的班機似乎誤點了。

B: That's not good. It means I'll miss my connecting flight.

那可不妙。這表示我會錯過我的轉機。

A: Jasmine Airlines Flight 320 to Los Angeles is now boarding at Gate 12.

傑斯敏航空飛往洛杉磯的三二〇號班機現在正在十二號登機門登機。

B: Come on! We need to rush over to the gate. They're boarding now.

快點！我們要趕快到登機門。他們在登機了。

入境通關

A : What is the purpose of your visit?
你來訪的目的是？

B : I am here on vacation with my family.
我和我的家人來度假。

A : How long will you be staying?
你會停留多久？

B : I am going to stay for two weeks.
我預計停留兩個星期。

A : Do you have anything to declare?
你有什麼東西要申報嗎？

B : No. I have brought very little with me.
沒有，我沒帶什麼東西。

PLAY ALL　TRACK 11

Act 1: Carry-on Confusion 隨身行李新規定

Kelly and Fred are taking a trip to Los Angeles. Their bags are being inspected by a security officer before they check their luggage.

SO: Security Officer

SO: Please place your bags on the table.

Kelly: Here you are.

SO: Thank you. Are these the bags that you will be checking through to Los Angeles?

Kelly: Yes, they are.

Fred: I'm planning on taking this backpack as a carry-on.

*(The security officer starts going through the **contents**[1] of Kelly's bag.)*

SO： 請把行李放在桌上。

K： 給你。

SO： 謝謝。這是你們去洛杉磯要托運的行李嗎？

K： 是的。

F： 我打算把這背包當作隨身行李。

（安檢人員開始檢查凱莉袋裡的東西。）

SO: OK, this bag should be all set.

Kelly: Before we check this bag, though, you should make sure you don't have anything that's not allowed on the plane in your backpack, Fred.

Fred: I don't have anything dangerous in here. It's just my change of clothing, some shampoo, toothpaste, and my **cologne**.[2] Oh, and a bottle of water for the plane.

SO: With the new security **regulations**,[3] you're not allowed to take **containers**[4] of liquid holding more than three **ounces**[5] in your carry-on bag. You should **transfer**[6] your shampoo and other liquids into the checked bag.

Kelly: And don't you have your shaving kit as well?

Fred: Come to think of it, I do. But it shouldn't cause a problem.

SO：好了，這袋應該沒問題。

K：不過，佛萊德，我們檢查這件行李之前，你應該確認你的背包裡沒有機上違禁品。

F：這裡沒有放什麼危險的東西。只有我的換洗衣物、洗髮精、牙膏和我的古龍水。喔，還有一瓶要在飛機上喝的水。

SO：新的安檢規定是，不得在隨身行李中攜帶超過三盎斯的罐裝液體。你應該把洗髮精和其他液體放進托運行李中。

K：而且你不是還有帶刮鬍組嗎？

F：這樣一說我才想起來，我的確有帶。可是應該不會有問題吧。

Vocabulary

1. **content** [ˋkɑnˌtɛnt] *n.* 內容（物）

2. **cologne** [kəˋlon] *n.* 古龍水

3. **regulation** [ˌrɛgjəˋleʃən] *n.* 規定；法令

4. **container** [kənˋtenə] *n.* 容器

5. **ounce** [aʊns] *n.* 盎斯（約為 28.35 公克）

6. **transfer** [ˋtrænsfə] *v.* 轉移；調動

Kelly: Your nail **clippers**[7] are in there, and they probably have one of those little knives on them.

Fred: Oh, no! You're right.

SO: That will definitely need to be checked through. No sharp objects, **box cutters**,[8] knives, or scissors are allowed in your carry-on bag.

Fred: In that case, I may as well just check this bag through. But first, let me grab my novel.

K：你的指甲刀在裡面，可能上面有小刀。

F：糟了！妳說得對。

SO：那一定要用托運的。隨身行李裡不可以攜帶尖銳的物品、美工刀、刀子或是剪刀。

F：那樣的話，我不如也托運這件行李好了。不過我先把小說拿出來。

Language Spotlight

come to think of it 這樣一想；經你這麼一說

用在突然記起或了解某件事時，並帶出接下來要講的話，有「說到這裡我才想到」的意思。

- I'm pretty sure Terry will make it to the party. Come to think of it, he should already be there.

  我很確定泰瑞會參加派對。說到這，他應該已經到了。

may/might as well + 原形動詞　不妨……；不如……

might as well（勸告或建議用語）語氣要比 may as well 更委婉。

- We might as well clean the house, seeing that it's supposed to be pouring rain all day.

  看來整天都會下大雨，我們來打掃家裡。

- There's nothing that I want to watch on television tonight, so I may as well go to bed.

  今晚沒有我想看的電視節目，所以不如上床睡覺。

Vocabulary

7. **clipper** [ˋklɪpə] *n.* 剪具（常用複數）（nail clippers 為「指甲剪」）

8. **box cutter** [bɑks] [ˋkʌtə] *n.* 美工刀

PLAY ALL   TRACK 12

Act 2: Cruising[1] through Customs 合法通關

*Kelly and Fred have arrived in Los Angeles and are going through **customs**.*[2]

CO: Customs Officer

Fred: Did you fill out the customs **declaration**[3] form?

Kelly: Of course! I filled it out on the plane.

Fred: OK, then, let's head over to customs.

CO: Hello. May I see your passports and your declaration form, please?

Kelly: Here they are.

CO: You have nothing to declare? What items do you have in the larger bag?

F：妳填好海關申報單了嗎？

K：當然有！我在飛機上填好了。

F：好，那我們去通關。

CO：你們好。麻煩出示護照和申報單。

K：在這裡。

CO：你們沒有東西要申報嗎？你們那個比較大的袋子裡有什麼東西？

53

Kelly: The only thing of real value in the bag is my camera. Other than that, there are my clothes, shoes, and a few small gifts.

CO: How much are the gifts worth?

Kelly: Less than fifty dollars.

CO: What are they?

Kelly: Let's see. There is a stuffed bear for my niece, a hat for my nephew, and a wooden toy for my other nephew.

CO: You didn't bring any fruits or vegetables with you, did you?

Fred: We didn't bring any food at all.

CO: What is in the smaller bag?

Fred: Just clothing, shampoo, and other **personal**[4] items.

CO: And what is the purpose of your visit?

Kelly: We're just here for vacation. We're planning to visit family and to take a trip to the Grand Canyon.

CO: It should be beautiful at this time of year. You're all set. Enjoy your vacation.

K & F: Thanks a lot!

K： 袋子裡唯一的貴重物品就是我的相機。除此之外，還有衣服、鞋子和一些小禮物。

CO： 這些禮物價值多少錢？

K： 不到五十美元。

CO： 是什麼東西？

K： 我看看。有給我姪女的熊熊玩偶、給我侄子的帽子，還有給另一個侄子的木製玩具。

CO： 你們應該沒有帶水果或蔬菜吧？

F： 我們完全沒有攜帶任何食物。

CO： 比較小的袋子裡裝什麼？

F： 就是衣服、洗髮精和一些個人用品。

CO： 那麼兩位此行的目的是？

K： 我們只是來度假的。我們打算去探視家人，然後去大峽谷旅遊。

CO： 現在這個時節應該很漂亮。你們沒問題了。祝你們假期愉快。

K&F： 謝謝你！

Language Spotlight

fill out/in 填寫（表格、文件）

fill out 和 fill in 都可用來指填寫表單、文件等，前者多用於美語中，而 fill in 則用於英式英語中。

用法 fill out/in + N.、fill N./ 代名詞 + out/in

- Please fill out your name, address, and telephone number on this form.

  請在這張表格上填寫你的名字、地址和電話號碼。

- After filling in what he thought were the correct answers, the boy handed in his test.

  這名男孩填下他認為的正確答案之後，便交卷了。

Vocabulary

1. **cruise** [kruz] *v.* 緩慢巡行；巡航
2. **customs** [ˋkʌstəmz] *n.* 海關
3. **declaration** [ˏdɛkləˋreʃən] *n.* 申報；宣布（動詞為 declare [dɪˋklɛr]）
4. **personal** [ˋpɝsnəl] *adj.* 私人的；個人的

延伸學習

出境程序

Step 1 check in 辦理登機報到

Step 2 check baggage 托運行李

Step 3 report to passport control 證照查驗

Step 4 go through security 安全檢查

Step 5 board aircraft 登機

常見行李種類

隨身行李

* **handbag** 手提包
* **backpack** 背包
* **purse** 女用包
* **briefcase** 公事包

拖運行李

* **duffel bag** 圓筒狀行李袋
* **suitcase** 手提箱
* **rolling/roller bag** 行李箱

Unit 5

機上英語
In-Flight English

動手寫寫看

1. 不好意思，可以跟你換位子嗎？

2. 我可以在飛機上使用筆電嗎？

3. 我應該怎麼填這張表格？

4. 你若需要幫忙的話，可以按呼叫鈕。

5. 請將餐盤收起來，因為我們即將降落。

參考答案請見 p. 339

機上服務

A: Would you like the spaghetti or the beef with rice?
您要義大利麵還是牛肉飯？

B: I'll take the beef with rice. And can I have some wine?
我要牛肉飯。另外我可以來點酒嗎？

A: Excuse me, I would like to buy some duty-free goods.
不好意思，我想買一些免稅品。

B: Sure. What would you like to buy?
沒問題，您要買什麼？

A: Could you please tell me what the in-flight movie will be?
可以告訴我什麼時候才會播放機上電影嗎？

B: We will be showing *Captain America* right after we serve breakfast.
早餐供應完後就會播放《美國隊長》了。

機上狀況

A: Sir, you'll need to put your carry-on in the overhead compartment.

先生，您必須將隨身行李放在艙頂置物箱。

B: OK, just a minute. I need to take my book out.

好，等一下，我得把我的書拿出來。

A: Ladies and gentlemen, the captain has just turned on the fasten seat belt sign.

各位女士先生，機長已開啟繫上安全帶的指示燈。

B: Oh, no. I really have to use the bathroom.

糟糕，我真的很想去洗手間。

A: What am I going to do during this eleven-hour flight?

我要怎麼打發這十一小時的飛行啊？

B: You could listen to one of the music stations on the plane. Or you could read the in-flight magazine.

你可以選一台機上播放的音樂電台收聽。或者你可以看看機上雜誌。

PLAY ALL　　TRACK 14

Act 1: EZ Check-In 搭機登機輕鬆 GO

Sam is sitting by the aisle when Fay arrives. Holding her many duty-free shopping bags, she takes the seat next to Sam.

Sam: So you're the one we've been waiting for! Did some last-minute shopping, I see.

Fay: Yeah, I got stuck in a long **line**[1] at the duty-free shop. It was almost as long as the line at the check-in counter!

Sam: Next time you should try the e-check-in machine. It saves you a lot of time! *(Flashback shows Sam using e-check-in.)* I chose my seat there. And you can also buy your ticket and get your boarding pass there, too.

S：原來妳就是我們一直在等的人！看來是搶在最後一分鐘買了些東西。

F：是啊，我被困在免稅店大排長龍的隊伍裡。那一排隊伍幾乎跟登機櫃台前排的隊伍一樣長！

S：下次妳應該試試電子化登機。可以讓妳省很多時間！（畫面倒敘到山姆使用電子化來辦理登機。）我就是用那機器選位子的。妳也可以透過那個機器買票和取得登機證。

Fay: I saw those machines at the check-in, but I didn't know how to use them.

Sam: They're pretty **self-explanatory**.[2] You just follow the directions on the screen.

Fay: It would have been nice to skip that line. *(Flashback shows Fay waiting in a long line.)* I could have spent more time shopping!

Sam: Actually, you can just use the e-shopping online. So you don't have to face the crowds, or the **pushy**[3] salespeople. That's what I did!

Fay: Hmm . . . that does sound **handy**.[4] I'm Fay, by the way. You are?

Sam: Sam. Nice to meet you! Oh! Here we go!

Fay: But . . . I missed the safety demo! I'm not ready!

F：我在辦理登機手續時有看到那些機器，不過我不知道怎麼用。

S：那些機器還滿容易使用的。妳只要跟著螢幕上的指示就行了。

F：可以不用大排長龍會很不錯。（畫面倒敘到菲在排隊。）我就可以多花一點時間購物了！

S：事實上，妳可以使用線上電子購物。那妳就不用面對人群或那些強迫購買的推銷員了。我就是這麼做的！

F：嗯……聽起來很方便。對了，我是菲，你是？

S：山姆，很高興認識妳！喔，我們出發了！

F：可是……我錯過搭機安全示範了！我還沒準備好！

Vocabulary

1. **line** [laɪn] *n.* 行列；排列
2. **self-explanatory** [ˌsɛlfɪkˋsplænəˌtɔri] *adj.* 無需解釋的；意思清楚的
3. **pushy** [ˋpuʃi] *adj.* 強求的
4. **handy** [ˋhændi] *adj.* 便利的

Sam: Uh . . . is this your first-time flying, by any chance?

Fay: How did you guess? *(She **fumbles**[5] with her seat belt, trying to **buckle**[6] it.)*

S：呃……妳可能是第一次搭飛機吧？

F：你怎麼猜到的？（她摸索著找安全帶，試著將它扣上。）

Language Spotlight

by any chance 也許；可能

在詢問或提出請求時，可用 by any chance 來表達謙恭禮貌，可放在句首、句尾或插入句中。

- By any chance, do you have a pen I could borrow?
  你有可能可以借我一支筆嗎？

- Do you, by any chance, have any green tea?
  你有沒有碰巧有綠茶呢？

Vocabulary

5. **fumble** [ˈfʌmbəl] *v.* 摸索；搜尋
6. **buckle** [ˈbʌkəl] *v.* 扣住

實戰對話　　　　　　PLAY ALL　TRACK 15

Act 2: How May I Help You?　我能為您服務嗎？

*Fay is **munching**[1] on some nuts and looking nervously around the plane.*

FA: Flight Attendant

Sam: Well, that takeoff wasn't so bad, was it?

Fay: I survived. Hey, do you have any water left? These nuts are salty.

Sam: Let's ask the **flight attendant**[2] for some. Just push this button.

(Sam shows Fay the call button. She pushes it.)

FA: Yes? How may I help you?

Fay: May I have some more water, please?

S：嗯，飛機起飛狀況還不錯，對吧？

F：我撐過來了。嘿，你還有沒有水？這堅果好鹹。

S：我們跟空服員要吧，按這個鍵就可以了。

（山姆指著服務鈴給菲看。她按下服務鈴。）

FA：是的，我能為您服務嗎？

F：可以請妳給我一點水嗎？

FA: Certainly. Just a moment.

Sam: *(Notices Fay **wiggling**[3] around, trying to get comfortable)* What's wrong now?

Fay: I'm freezing! I packed my sweater in my suitcase.

Sam: Well, the flight attendant may have a blanket for you . . .

(Fay jumps on the call button again.)

FA: Yes? What can I do for you?

Fay: Could I have a blanket, please? It's a bit chilly in here.

FA: Of course. Anything else?

Fay: I'm a bit hungry.

FA: Dinner will be served in about an hour. I'll get you another snack.

Fay: I always eat when I'm nervous.

(Fay is in the bathroom fixing her hair. An announcement comes on.)

FA: Attention passengers. We are entering an area of **slight**[4] **turbulence**.[5] Please return to your seats and buckle your seat belts.

Fay: Hurry. Let me in!

FA： 沒問題，請稍等。

S：（注意到菲左右扭動，試著讓自己舒適）現在又怎麼了？

F： 我冷死了！我把毛衣裝在行李箱裡了。

S： 那，空服員可能可以給妳一條毯子……

（菲毫不猶豫地又按了鈴。）

FA： 是的，請問我能為妳做什麼？

F： 請給我一條毯子好嗎？這裡有點冷。

FA： 當然好，還需要什麼嗎？

F： 我有點餓了。

FA： 晚餐約一小時後供應。我拿別的點心給妳。

F： 我緊張的時候就會一直吃東西。

（菲在洗手間整理頭髮。廣播聲響起。）

FA： 各位乘客請注意，我們正進入輕微亂流區。請回到座位上並繫好安全帶。

F： 快，讓我進去！

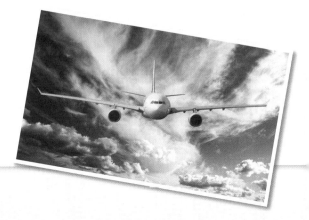

Sam: Don't be **ridiculous**.[6] It's just a bit **bumpy**.[7]

Fay: Where's that throw-up bag? I don't feel so good.

Sam: *(Handing her the bag)* Just relax. It will be over in a . . . there. See? No more bumps.

Fay: Phew. Thank God that's over. Now if I can just get some sleep . . .

S：別鬧了。只是一點顛簸而已。

F：嘔吐袋在哪？我覺得不太舒服。

S：（拿袋子給她）放輕鬆，很快就結束啦……看，不顛了。

F：呼。感謝老天爺這一切結束了。如果現在能睡一會兒就好了……

Language Spotlight

now if I can (just) . . . 如果現在能……

在這裡 if 引導條件子句，後方應會再接主要子句，例如：if it rains tomorrow, (then) I will not go hiking。但在口語中，此句型後面常不接主要子句，由條件子句就可了解說話者的意思。例如本篇對話中：Now if I can just get some sleep (, everything will be all right.)。

• Now if I can only find my car keys.
  只要我能找到我的車鑰匙就好了。

Vocabulary

1. **munch** [mʌntʃ] *v.* 咯吱地咀嚼；津津有味的咀嚼（作不及物用時，之後接 on 再接受詞）

2. **flight attendant** [flaɪt] [əˈtɛndənt] *n.* 空服員

3. **wiggle** [ˈwɪgl] *v.* 扭動；擺動

4. **slight** [slaɪt] *adj.* 輕微的

5. **turbulence** [ˈtɜbjələns] *n.* 亂流

6. **ridiculous** [rəˈdɪkjələs] *adj.* 荒謬的；可笑的

7. **bumpy** [ˈbʌmpi] *adj.* 顛簸；氣流多變的

機場廣播

- Passengers of Flight 965, please be advised that your flight is being delayed thirty minutes due to the previous flight's late arrival time. The new departure time is scheduled for 9:05 p.m.

  九六五號班機的乘客請注意，因為前班班機誤點，您的班機將會延誤三十分鐘，新的起飛時間預計在晚間九點○五分。

- Because of an approaching thunderstorm, all flights have been grounded. We apologize for the delay.

  因為即將到來的大雷雨，所有班機已經停飛。我們為耽誤各位行程向您致歉。

- Attention, please. Passengers of United 535 bound for New York: Your departure gate has been changed. Your flight is now departing from Terminal 2, Gate 5B.

  聯合航空五三五號班機飛往紐約的旅客請注意：您的登機門已經更改，班機將改到第二航廈的 5B 登機門。

機上廣播

- Attention passengers. We are entering an area of slight turbulence. Please return to your seats and buckle your seat belts.

  各位乘客請注意，我們正進入輕微亂流區。請回到座位上並繫好安全帶。

- We are just approaching over Chicago. We should be touching down at Chicago O'Hare International Airport in approximately 15 to 20 minutes for an on-time arrival.

  我們快到芝加哥了，大約再過十五到二十分鐘，我們就會準時降落在芝加哥歐海爾國際機場。

- Current weather is sunny with a few scattered clouds, and the temperature is approximately 25 degrees Celsius.

  目前的天氣是晴朗有雲，氣溫大約是攝氏 25 度。

Unit 6

旅館英語
Finding a Home Away from Home

動手寫寫看

1. 我想多住一天，不知道還有沒有空房？

2. 我有在網路上訂房，也付了訂金。

3. 請問雙人房房間可加床嗎？

4. 麻煩你明天早上七點打電話叫我起床。

5. 可以用無線上網嗎？

參考答案請見 p. 339

登記住宿實用句

訂房詢問

A: Hi. Welcome to the Sunshine Hotel. How can I help you?
嗨，歡迎光臨陽光飯店。我能為您服務嗎？

B: I have a reservation. My name is Tim Daniels.
我訂了一個房間。名字是提姆‧丹尼爾斯。

A: Would you like a single room or a double?
您需要單人房還是雙人房？

B: I'll take the double room with an ocean view.
我要有海景的雙人房。

A: How many nights will you be staying with us?
您預計要住幾天？

B: I'll be staying for three nights.
我會住三天。

櫃台服務

A: Are there any good restaurants near the hotel?
飯店附近有不錯的餐廳嗎？

B: There is a great Italian place nearby. Would you like me to call you a cab?
附近有間很棒的義大利餐廳。需要我幫你叫計程車嗎？

A: Could I have some help carrying my bags to my room?
可以幫我把袋子送到房間嗎？

B: Certainly. Our bellboy, Alan, can help you with that.
當然，我們的行李員艾倫會幫你送。

A: I'd like to take a city tour. Can you arrange for that?
我想要到市區觀光，你能幫我安排嗎？

B: There are a number of tours you can take. Let me give you some brochures.
這裡有許多行程可供選擇。我拿些手冊給您。

PLAY ALL   TRACK 17

實戰對話

Act 1: Checking into a Hotel 登記入住

Jeff and Lisa Miller have arrived at a hotel and are checking in.

R: Receptionist

R: Good morning. How can I help you?

Jeff: Hello! My wife and I would like to find out about room availability and rates. We'd like a room with a king-sized bed.

R: We're pretty full right now, but let me see if any guests will be checking out today. *(Checks her computer)* Ah, yes. We have a king room that will be opening up this afternoon.

Lisa: And how much is the room rate per night?

R：早安,兩位需要什麼服務呢?

J：哈囉!我和我太太想要詢問是否有空房和價格。我們想要一間特大雙人床的房間。

R：我們現在幾乎客滿,但讓我看看是不是有客人今天會退房。(確認電腦)啊,有了,我們下午就有間特大雙人床空出來了。

L：那一晚的房價是多少?

R: Let's see. For the king room, the rate is $185 per night, and that includes all taxes. The room comes with a **complimentary**[1] **continental**[2] breakfast each morning from six to nine o'clock.

Jeff: That sounds pretty good to me. What time would we be able to check in?

R: The room will be available after two o'clock.

Jeff: OK. Do you accept credit cards?

R: Yes, sir. We accept Visa, Mastercard, and American Express.

Lisa: Is it possible to see the room first?

R: You can, but it will have to be after housekeeping has cleaned the room. I can show you a similar room that has two single beds, though.

Lisa: (*Shrugs*)[3] That should be all right. (*To Jeff*) Don't you think so?

Jeff: I'm sure the rooms are all pretty similar. That's fine.

R：我看看，特大雙人床的房間價錢是一晚一百八十五元，包含所有稅金。房間並附贈歐式早餐，用餐時間每天早上六點到九點。

J：聽起來很不錯。我們什麼時候可以登記入住？

R：房間要兩點以後才可使用。

J：沒問題。你們收信用卡嗎？

R：有的，先生。我們有收威士、萬事達和美國運通卡。

L：我們能不能先看看房間呢？

R：可以的，但必須等清潔人員打掃過房間後。不過，我可以帶您看另一間有兩張單人床的類似房型。

L：（聳聳肩）應該也可以。（對傑夫說）你覺得好不好？

J：我相信這些房間都差不多。我是沒問題。

【註】
continental breakfast 指「歐陸式早餐；歐式早餐」，通常包括簡單的麵包、水果和咖啡等。

Vocabulary

1. **complimentary** [ˌkɑmpləˋmɛntəri] *adj.* 附贈的；讚美的

2. **continental** [ˌkɑntəˋnɛntl̩] *adj.* （大寫）歐陸的；大陸的

3. **shrug** [ʃrʌg] *v.* （表疑惑、無奈的）聳肩

R: OK. Let me grab the key, and I can show you the room.

Lisa: Great!

(The receptionist finds a key, and they walk over to the elevator.)

R: Would you also like to take a quick look at the indoor pool?

Jeff: Sure! *(To Lisa)* I'm glad we brought our **bathing suits**[4] along!

R：好的。我去拿鑰匙，然後就帶兩位去看房間。

L：太棒了！

（櫃台人員找到鑰匙後一起走到電梯旁。）

R：你們想不想快速參觀一下室內泳池？

J：當然好！（對麗莎說）很高興我們有帶泳衣來！

Language Spotlight

check in 登記入住；報到

check in 表示「在（飯店、機場）辦理入住、報到手續」，亦可作及物用，check sb in 或 check in sb 則指「替某人辦得入住、搭機手續。」

- Let's check in at the hotel first so that we don't have to carry our luggage around town.

  我們先到旅館登記入住，這樣就不用提著行李逛市區了。

Vocabulary

4. **bathing suit** [ˈbeðɪŋ] [sut] *n.* 泳衣（= swimsuit）

實戰對話

PLAY ALL　TRACK 18

Act 2: A Helpful Concierge 待客之道

Kevin is a guest at a hotel. He has gone to the concierge to ask some questions.

C: Concierge

C: Good afternoon, Mr. Simmons. How can I help you?

Kevin: Hi! I wanted to find out if there are any exercise **facilities**[1] in the hotel.

C: Yes, sir. There is an exercise room on the second floor. *(Pointing)* On the ground floor, just down that hallway, is the swimming pool.

Kevin: That sounds wonderful. Are towels provided?

C：午安，西蒙斯先生。您需要什麼服務嗎？

K：嗨！我想要知道旅館裡是否有運動設施。

C：有的，先生。二樓有健身房。（用手指）地面層則有游泳池，沿著走廊走過去就是。

K：聽起來不錯。有提供毛巾嗎？

C: They are. You don't need to bring one from your room, and there is also a dressing room with lockers for your **convenience**.[2]

Kevin: That sounds perfect! How late is the exercise room and pool open?

C: The exercise room is open 24 hours. You can use your key card to **access**[3] it. The pool opens at 6 a.m. and closes at 10 p.m.

Kevin: Wonderful. *(Looks at his watch)* I should be able to get some dinner and then have a swim before bed. Oh, one other thing—I need to get a few shirts **laundered**[4] and ironed. How long does it take to get them back?

C: If you drop your laundry bag off before 8 a.m., it will be done by that same evening. Anything dropped off later than that won't be ready until the following day.

Kevin: That shouldn't be a problem. I can drop them off tomorrow morning. Are there any restaurants in the area that you can recommend?

C：有提供。您不必從房間帶毛巾過去,那裡也有附置物櫃的更衣室,方便您使用。

K：聽起來很完美!健身房和泳池開放到多晚?

C：健身房是二十四小時開放,您可以使用門卡直接進入。游泳池則是早上六點開放到晚上十點。

K：太棒了。(看一下手錶)我應該可以先用晚餐,然後睡前再去游個泳。喔,還有一件事,我有幾件襯衫需要洗燙。要多久才可以取回?

C：您若在早上八點前將洗衣袋送出,當天晚上就會洗好。八點以後放的衣物則要到隔天才會好了。

K：那應該不成問題。我明天早上就會拿出來。這個地區有沒有什麼餐廳是你會推薦的?

C: *(Hands him a sheet of paper)* This is a map with a list of various restaurants close by. Most of them are walking distance from here. If you like barbecue, I'd suggest Baron's Steak House, which is about five minutes' walk down the road.

Kevin: Barbecue it is, then. Thanks for your help.

C: It's been my pleasure. Enjoy your dinner!

C：（給凱文一張紙）這張地圖上有列出附近各式各樣的餐廳。多數都在走路可到的距離。如果您喜歡烤肉，我會推薦拜倫牛排館，只要沿著這條路走五分鐘就到了。

K：那就吃烤肉吧。謝謝你的幫忙。

C：我的榮幸。祝您用餐愉快！

Language Spotlight

drop off 順便把某物送到（某地）

deop off 在此是字面意思，指順便把某物放在某地。另外常見的意思還有「在途中留下某事物；讓某人下車」。

用法 drop + 名詞 / 代名詞 + off、drop off + 名詞

反義 pick up

- Erin needs to drop off her car at the auto repair shop before she goes to work in the morning.
  愛琳早上出門上班前得先將她的車送到修理廠去。

Vocabulary

1. **facility** [fəˋsɪlətɪ] *n.* 設備；設施

2. **convenience** [kənˋvinjəns] *n.* 方便；便利

3. **access** [ˋækˌsɛs] *v.* 接近；進入

4. **launder** [ˋlɔndə] *v.* 洗燙（衣物）

延伸學習

常見的旅館房間種類

房型：

* **single room** 單人房
* **business/executive suite** 商務套房（包含臥房與小客廳）
* **double room** 雙人房（通常包括一張雙人床或兩張單人床 twin beds）
* **honeymoon suite** 蜜月套房
* **presidential suite** 總統套房
* **dorm room** （青年旅館的）通鋪房

床型：

* **queen-size bed** 雙人床
* **king-size bed** 加大雙人床

五星級飯店名稱這樣唸

* **The Continental Hotels** [ˌkɑntəˋnɛntḷ] 洲際酒店
* **Four Seasons Hotels** 四季酒店
* **Hyatt Hotels and Resorts** [ˋhaɪ͵ɑt] [rɪˋzɔrts] 君悅飯店
* **Hilton Hotels and Resorts** [ˋhɪltṇ] 希爾頓飯店
* **Le Meridien** [ləˌmeˋrɪdiən] 美麗殿酒店
* **Mandarin Oriental Hotels** [ˋmændərɪn] [͵oriˋɛntḷ] 東方文華酒店
* **Peninsula Hotels** [pəˋnɪnsələ] 半島酒店
* **Ritz-Carlton Hotels** [ˋrɪtsˋkɑrltən] 麗池卡登酒店
* **Sheraton Hotels and Resorts** [ˋʃɛrətṇ] 喜來登飯店

Unit 7

住房英語
Staying in a Hotel

動手寫寫看

1. 我房間的空調好像有問題。

2. 你安排的房間沒有打掃乾淨,我可以換一間嗎?

3. 隔壁房的人吵得我睡不著。

4. 我需要住房費用明細。

5. 我可能把房間鑰匙弄丟了。

參考答案請見 p. 339

住宿問題

A: My television isn't working properly. I am getting only one channel.

我的電視故障了，只有一個頻道可以看。

B: Our hotel repairman is on his way.

我們飯店的維修人員已經前去處理了。

A: Hello? This is Jack Williams in Room 540. Could you please send up some towels?

你好。我是五四〇號房的傑克·威廉斯。可以幫我拿幾條毛巾過來嗎？

B: We will send those up right away, sir.

先生，我們現在馬上送過去。

A: Are there any messages for me?

有人留言給我嗎？

B: I can check. What is your room number?

我可以查一下，您是幾號房？

辦理退房

A: I'd like to check out.
我要退房。

B: No problem. Your name and room number, please.
好的。請給我您的大名和房號。

A: Do you have a shuttle service to the airport?
你們有機場接駁服務嗎?

B: Yes. The shuttle bus runs to the airport once every thirty minutes.
有,機場接駁車每三十分鐘都有一班。

A: May I go back to my room to look for something?
我可以再回房去找個東西嗎?

B: I think the housekeeping staff has already cleaned the room. What were you looking for?
我想客房清潔人員已經清理過房間。您要找什麼呢?

PLAY ALL   TRACK 20

Act 1: Accidentally[1] Locked Out 意外被反鎖在外

Dennis is in his hotel room ordering room service over the phone.

Dennis: Hi, this is Dennis Murphy in Room 822. I'd like to order some room service if it's still available.

Clerk: It is available until 10 p.m. What would you like to order?

Dennis: I think I'll just have a **club sandwich,**[2] some fries, and an iced tea.

Clerk: OK, your order will be brought to your room in 20 to 30 minutes.

(The room service waiter shows up at Dennis's room.)

D：嗨，我是八二二號房的丹尼斯·莫菲。如果還有供餐的話，我想要點一些客房服務。

C：到晚上十點為止都有供餐。您想要點什麼呢？

D：我想我只要一份總匯三明治、薯條和冰茶。

C：好的，您點的餐大約會在二、三十分鐘後送到您的房間。

（客房服務人員出現在丹尼斯房外。）

Waiter: Room service! Hello, sir. Where would you like me to put the tray?

Dennis: Over on the desk will be fine, thanks.

Waiter: *(Puts down the tray)* OK, sir. If you could just sign for this. When you are finished with your dinner, you can just leave the tray outside your door.

Dennis: Great! Thanks!

*(Dennis has finished his meal. He is dressed in a **bathrobe**[3] and slippers. He turns on the water to take a bath, then goes back into the room and dials the front desk.)*

Dennis: Hello, I'd like to arrange for a wake-up call at 6:30 tomorrow morning for Room 822. Great! Thank you so much!

(He remembers the room service tray. As he places the tray on the floor outside his room, his door locks behind him.)

Dennis: Oh, no! And I'm dressed in a bathrobe!

(Dennis is at the front desk of the hotel.)

W：客房服務！您好，先生。您想要我把托盤放在哪裡？

D：放在那個書桌上就好，謝謝。

W：（放下托盤）好的，先生。麻煩您簽一下這個。您用完餐後，只要把托盤放在門外就可以了。

D：好極了！謝謝！

（丹尼斯用完餐。他穿著浴袍和拖鞋，放水準備洗澡，然後走進房間打電話給櫃台。）

D：喂？我想要安排明天早上六點半叫八二二號房起床的電話。太好了！非常謝謝你！

（他想起客房服務的托盤。當他把托盤放在房門外的地板上，房門鎖上了。）

D：糟了！我還穿著浴袍！

（丹尼斯在飯店櫃台。）

Vocabulary

1. **accidentally** [ˌæksəˋdɛntli] *adv.* 意外地；無意間
2. **club sandwich** [klʌb] [ˋsændˏwɪtʃ] *n.* 總匯三明治
3. **bathrobe** [ˋbæθˏrob] *n.* 浴袍

Dennis: Hi. I'm a little bit embarrassed, but I locked myself out of my room when I put out my room service tray. I need another key for Room 822.

Clerk: OK. Can I have your name, please?

Dennis: It's Dennis Murphy.

Clerk: Do you have any **identification**,[4] sir?

Dennis: No. My wallet's in my room, but I need to hurry—the bathwater's running!

Clerk: Let me get a staff member to let you into your room. You'll just have to show him your ID when you get there. It's hotel policy that is strictly for your protection.

D：嗨。我有點難為情，我把客房服務的托盤放到外面時，把自己反鎖在門外了。我需要八二二號房的備份鑰匙。

C：好的。可以請您告訴我您的大名嗎？

D：我是丹尼斯·莫菲。

C：先生，您有身分證明文件嗎？

D：沒有，我的錢包在房間裡，但我得快點——浴室的水正開著！

C：我找一位工作人員讓您進入房間。您進房時只需要向他出示您的身分證件。這是我們飯店為了保護您所定的規定。

Vocabulary

4. **identification** [aɪˌdɛntəfəˋkeʃən] *n.* 身分證明（作此義時可簡稱為 I.D.）

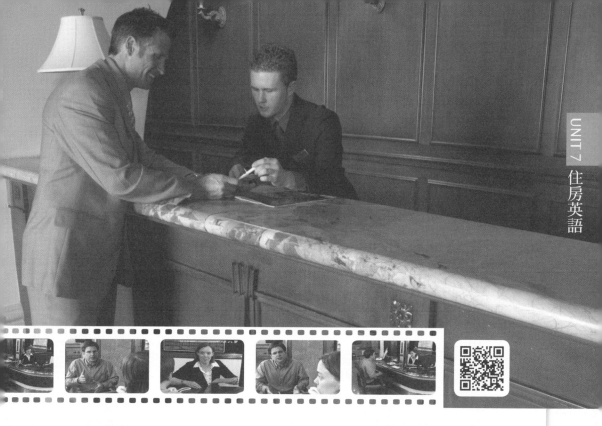

實戰對話

PLAY ALL　　TRACK 21

Act 2: Checkout Time 辦理退房

Dennis is checking out of his hotel room. He is carrying one suitcase and a carry-on bag.

Clerk:	Good morning, sir. Are you checking out?
Dennis:	Good morning. Yes, I am.
Clerk:	OK. What is your room number?
Dennis:	Room 822.
Clerk:	There is a room service meal on your bill and a few other charges. Do you want to put everything on the credit card you gave on check-in?

C：先生，早安。您要退房嗎？

D：早安。對，我要退房。

C：好的。您的房間號碼是幾號？

D：八二二號房。

C：您的帳單上有一份客房服務以及一些其他的費用。您要用登記入住那張信用卡支付所有的費用嗎？

Dennis: Can I see the **bill**[1] first? I only ordered one meal. This restaurant bill that was charged to my room isn't mine. I didn't even check in until five in the afternoon.

Clerk: I'm very sorry, Mr. Murphy. Let me **remove**[2] that charge.

Dennis: That's OK. Then just put everything else on my card.

Clerk: Will do. Was everything else OK during your stay here?

Dennis: It was fine. Thanks.

Clerk: OK, here is your receipt. Do you need a **shuttle**[3] to the airport?

Dennis: I will later on. How often do they leave?

Clerk: During the morning, they leave every half hour. In the afternoon, they leave every hour at half past.

Dennis: OK, that will work out fine. I'd like to take the 4:30 shuttle to the airport. In the meantime, I wanted to do a little bit of shopping in the city, for my flight isn't until this evening. Could I leave my bags here for a few hours?

D：我可以先看一下帳單嗎？我只點了一份餐。這個記在我房間上的餐廳帳單不是我的。我下午五點才登記入住。

C：我很抱歉，莫菲先生。我來把這筆款項刪除。

D：沒關係。那其他的就用我的信用卡來付。

C：好。您住房期間其他一切都還好嗎？

D：很好。謝謝。

C：好的，這是您的收據。您需要到機場的接駁車嗎？

D：我晚一點會需要。多久會有一班呢？

C：上午是每半個小時一班。下午則是每半點時發一次車。

D：好，這樣可以。我要搭乘四點半開往機場的接駁車。在此期間，我想到市區買一些東西，因為我的飛機晚上才起飛。我可以把我的包包留在這裡幾個小時嗎？

Clerk: Sure. We have a locked luggage room for our guests. How many bags did you want to leave?

Dennis: Just my suitcase and my carry-on bag.

Clerk: OK, let me get a **claim ticket**[4] for you, and you'll be all set.

Dennis: Thanks! I **appreciate**[5] it!

C：當然可以。我們有為客人準備的上鎖行李房。您要放幾件包包在這裡？

D：只有我的手提行李和隨身行李。

C：好的，我拿行李牌給您，這樣就可以了。

D：謝謝！我很感謝。

Language Spotlight

in the meantime 在此期間；與此同時

同義 meanwhile、in the meanwhile、meantime

meantime 和 meanwhile 皆可作名詞和副詞使用。

• Tina took a nap, and in the meantime I watched television.
蒂娜小憩了一下，在此期間我則看了電視。

be all set 準備就緒；一切妥當

set 在此作形容詞用，指「準備好的」。

• I called the mechanic, and your car is all set to be picked up.
我打過電話給技工，你的車已經弄好、可以去取了。

Vocabulary

1. **bill** [bɪl] *n.* 帳單

2. **remove** [rɪˋmuv] *v.* 移除；拿掉

3. **shuttle** [ˋʃʌt!] *n.* 穿梭兩地間的車輛（火車、巴士等）

4. **claim ticket** [klem] [ˋtɪkət] *n. phr.* 領回票；（行李）提取票

5. **appreciate** [əˋpriʃɪͺet] *v.* 感謝；欣賞

延伸學習

旅館常見的設施及服務

* **cable TV** 有線電視
* **pay TV** 付費電視
* **Wi-Fi** 無線上網服務
* **safe-deposit box** 保險箱
* **swimming pool** 游泳池
* **spa** 水療休閒中心
* **gym** 健身房
* **lounge bar** 酒吧
* **business center** 商務中心
* **conference center** 會議中心
* **butler** 管家服務
* **laundry service** 洗衣服務
* **car rental** 租車服務

客房裡常見的問題

* **The window won't open.** 窗戶打不開。
* **My door doesn't lock.** 我的房門不能上鎖。
* **My room doesn't have hot water.** 我房間沒熱水。
* **I can't call out.** 我沒辦法打外線。
* **The lamp won't turn on.** 燈不會亮。
* **The toilet is clogged.** 馬桶塞住了。

Unit 8

購物英語
Let's Go Shopping

動手寫寫看

1. 這雙鞋多少錢？

2. 我可以試穿這件嗎？

3. 我買兩件可以算便宜一點嗎？

4. 這是要送朋友的，可以幫我禮品包裝嗎？

5. 這幾件物品可以幫我結帳嗎？

參考答案請見 p. 339

選購商品

A: Does this T-shirt come in any other colors?
這件 T 恤有其他顏色嗎？

B: The T-shirt also comes in blue, pink, and gray.
這件 T 恤還有藍色、粉紅色和灰色。

A: Are the items in this area on sale?
這區商品有特價嗎？

B: All of these items are buy one, get one free.
這裡所有的商品都買一送一。

 殺價與結帳

A: Can you lower the price a little?
可以算便宜一點嗎？

B: The towel is sixty dollars, but I can sell you two for one hundred dollars.
毛巾一條六十元，但我可以賣你兩條一百。

A : I have seen it cheaper in other places.
我在其他地方看過比這便宜的價錢。

B : I can go down to $300, but that's my final offer.
我可以降到三百元，但那是我最後出價了。

退稅與換貨

A : I'm a foreign visitor. Can I get a refund on the tax?
我是外國旅客。我可以退稅嗎？

B : Yes, you can get a refund at the airport when you leave.
可以，您可以在機場離境時退稅。

A : What's your return policy?
請問你們的退換貨規定是什麼？

B : You can return items within seven days for a cash refund.
七天內退貨可以退還現金。

PLAY ALL　TRACK 23

實戰對話

Act 1: Beyond Her Budget 超出預算

*Kate and Brad notice a **vendor**[1] selling an **assortment**[2] of hats.*

Kate: Hey! Let's stop here for a minute. I need a new hat.

Brad: Take your time. Maybe I should get one, too.

Kate: *(Tries on a hat and looks at Brad)* How do you like this one?

Brad: It's OK, but I think this one is more your style. *(Grabs a different hat and hands it to her)*

K：嘿！我們在這裡停一下。我需要一頂新帽子。

B：慢慢看吧。也許我也該買一頂。

K：（試戴一頂帽子然後看著布萊德）你覺得這頂怎麼樣？

B：還不錯，但我覺得這頂比較適合妳。（拿起另一頂遞給她）

Kate: *(Takes off the first hat and tries on the second)* Hmm. This is the latest style, but I don't think it suits me. It's too big for my head. Oh, what about this one? It's so cute! *(Tries it on)*

Brad: Yeah, that hat is **definitely**³ you!

Vendor: It looks great on you. Have a look for yourself. *(Holds up a mirror)*

Kate: Yes, I like it. How much is it?

Vendor: That is a high-**quality**⁴ hat made with **mosquito repellent**⁵ material. It's a **steal**⁶ at eight hundred NT dollars.

Kate: Oh, that's quite a bit more than I was hoping to spend.

Vendor: Well, for such a beautiful lady I can knock a hundred dollars off the price.

K：（拿下最先戴的帽子，試了第二頂）嗯，這是最新的款式，但我覺得不適合我，它太大了。喔，這個怎麼樣？這好可愛！（試戴）

B：對耶，這頂最適合妳！

V：妳戴起來很好看。妳自己看看。（舉起鏡子）

K：我喜歡，這頂多少錢？

V：那是含有驅蚊材質的高級帽子，便宜賣妳八百就好。

K：喔，這超出我的預算太多了。

V：嗯，像妳這麼漂亮的小姐我可以再減一百塊。

Vocabulary

1. **vendor** [ˈvɛndɚ] *n.* 小販；攤販

2. **assortment** [əˈsɔrtmənt] *n.* 各式種類

3. **definitely** [ˈdɛfənɪtli] *adv.* 肯定地；當然

4. **quality** [ˈkwɑləti] *n.* 品質

5. **mosquito repellent** [məˈskito] [rɪˈpɛlənt] *n. phr.* 驅蚊劑；防蚊液

6. **steal** [stil] *n.* 以極低價買的東西；便宜貨

Kate: That's still more than I can afford at the moment. I don't want to spend more than five hundred.

Vendor: I can probably drop the price by another fifty dollars, but I'm afraid that's as low as I can go.

Kate: Six hundred and fifty is still a lot. I really need to think about it.

K：我現在還是買不起。我不想花超過五百塊。

V：我或許可以再降五十塊，不過這恐怕是我的底價了。

K：六百五十還是很貴。我真的得再考慮一下。

Language Spotlight

beyond one's budget 超出某人的預算

反義 outside of one's budget

反義 within one's budget

- I never buy first-class plane tickets because they are beyond my budget.

  我從沒買過頭等艙的機票，因為超出我的預算。

- I want to buy a new coat, but I need to find one that's within my budget.

  我想買一件新外套，但得找到在我預算內的。

knock/take + 金額 + off 降價

同義 drop/lower the price by + 金額

- If you can knock/take $20 off, I'll buy the dress.

= If you can drop/lower the price by $20, I'll buy the dress.

  如果你能降價二十美元，我就會買這件洋裝。

實戰對話

PLAY ALL   TRACK 24

Act 2: Let's Make a Deal 達成交易

Kate and Brad are still standing by the hat vendor. Kate is deciding whether to buy a hat.

Brad: Well, while you're deciding on the hat, let's **check out**[1] the toys they're selling over there.

Kate: *(Laughs)* What are you, ten years old?

Brad: They're not for me! One of my nephews has a birthday coming up.

Kate: *(Teasing)*[2] You sure seem to have a lot of nephews.

(They walk over to the vendor selling electronic toys.)

B：好吧，妳在考慮要不要買時，咱們到那邊看看賣玩具的。

K：（笑）你是怎樣，十歲小孩嗎？

B：這不是買給我自己！我有個侄子生日快到了。

K：（取笑）你的侄子還真多。

（他們走到賣電動玩具的攤位旁。）

Brad: Check out these **remote control**[3] cars! I would have a **blast**[4] with one of these in my apartment . . . you know, for when my nephews visit.

Kate: Of course you would. Actually, they do look like they're a lot of fun.

Brad: How much for one of the toy cars?

Vendor: They're five hundred NT dollars each, or two for nine hundred.

Brad: Do they come with batteries?

Vendor: They sure do, and they're **rechargeable**.[5]

Brad: Hmm. How about I give you eleven hundred for three of them?

Kate: You're going to buy three?

Brad: I really do have a lot of nephews!

Vendor: Make it twelve hundred and you've got a deal. It's good for you and good for me.

Brad: *(Thinks about it for a second)* OK, it's a deal.

(Brad hands the vendor some money.)

Kate: I wonder if I should still buy that hat.

Brad: While you're deciding, I'm going to go test one of these cars in the park across the street.

(The vendor hands Brad a bag with the cars in it. Brad walks away smiling.)

B：看看這些遙控車！我家裡有台這種玩具一定會很好玩。妳知道的，就是我侄子來的時候。

K：當然囉。其實看起來的確很好玩。

B：這一台玩具車要多少錢？

V：一台五百塊，兩台九百。

B：有附電池嗎？

V：當然有，而且是充電式的。

B：嗯，三台算一千一怎麼樣？

K：你要買三台？

B：我真的有很多個侄子嘛！

V：一千二就成交。你開心，我也開心。

B：（考慮了一下）好，成交。

（布萊德將錢給了小販。）

K：我還在想是不是要買那頂帽子。

B：趁妳還在考慮，我先到對街的公園試車。

（小販將裝了車子的袋子拿給布萊德，布萊德笑著走開。）

Language Spotlight

come up 發生；靠近

come up 也常被用來指「（問題、意見等）提出；出現」。

- With the elections coming up, most of the commercials on television are political advertisements.

  隨著選舉接近，電視上大多數的廣告都是政治廣告。

- During the meeting, the question about hiring new employees never even came up.

  這次會議中完全沒有提到關於雇用新員工的問題。

it's a deal 成交；一言為定；就這麼辦

此用法也可以省略，直接說 deal。

- A: If you let me borrow your bicycle, you can use my computer to play video games.

  如果你借我腳踏車，就能用我的電腦打電玩。

- B: It's a deal. /Deal.

  就這麼說定。

Vocabulary

1. **check out** v. 【俚】看看；試試

2. **tease** [tiz] v. 取笑；戲弄

3. **remote control** [rɪˋmot] [kənˋtrol] n. 遙控器

4. **blast** [blæst] n. 【俚】狂歡、極開心的經驗或場合

5. **rechargeable** [riˋtʃɑrdʒəbəl] adj. 可再充電的

 用英語詢問退稅事宜

《詢問退稅限制》

- Could I get a tax refund for this?
  請問這個可以退稅嗎？

- A: How much do I have to spend to get a tax refund?
  我要買多少錢的東西才能退稅？

  B: You have to buy at least 125 euros' worth of items.
  你最少得買一百二十五歐元的商品。

《詢問辦理方式》

- A: How do I claim/get a tax refund?
  我要如何申請退稅？

  B: All you have to do is purchase items above a minimum threshold, and you get the refund.
  只要購買商品超過最低門檻就可以退稅。

《詢問受理地點》

- A: Where can I apply for a tax refund?
  要在哪裡申請退稅？

  B: You can apply for a tax refund at the tax refund counter.
  你可以在退稅櫃檯申請退稅。

- A: Could you tell me where the tax refund counter is?
  能否告訴我退稅櫃檯在哪裡？

  B: It's next to the information counter.
  在服務台旁邊。

《詢問相關細節》

- May I have a tax refund form?
  可以給我一張退稅申請單嗎？

- A: How much of a refund will I get?
  能退給我多少錢？

  B: Your refund will be 10 percent of the total purchase.
  你可以獲得購買總額百分之十的退稅。

【註】
各地的退稅規定不同，有些國家甚至沒有退稅制度。在此為歐洲較常見的退稅情況。

Unit 9

餐廳英語
Dining Out

動手寫寫看

1. 我要一張非吸煙區的位子，最好可以靠窗。

2. 份量有多大？

3. 有什麼推薦的菜色嗎？

4. 能不能幫我把這道菜打包？

5. 我們要買單。

參考答案請見 p. 340

點餐用餐實用句

候位

A: How much longer do we have to wait?
我們還要等多久?

B: There are three parties ahead of you.
您前面還有三桌客人。

點餐

A: Good evening. I'm your waiter, Phil. Are you ready to order?
晚安。我是你們的服務生菲爾。你們準備好要點餐了嗎?

B: Yes. My wife would like the salmon, and I'll have the roasted chicken.
對。我太太要點鮭魚,而我要烤雞。

A: This place looks good, but everything is in French.
這間餐廳看起來不錯,但全都是法文。

B: Let me ask the waitress if she can speak English.
我來問問服務生會不會講英文。

⬭ 用餐狀況

A: This isn't what I ordered. I wanted the house special.

這不是我點的菜。我要的是招牌特餐。

B: I'm sorry. Let me get you the correct order right away.

很抱歉。我馬上替你們送正確的餐點過來。

A: Would you like to try any desserts?

請問你們要試試甜點嗎？

B: No, thank you. We're stuffed! We'll just take the check, please.

不用了，謝謝。我們已經飽了。請幫我們買單。

⬭ 結帳

A: Would you like separate checks?

你們要分開付嗎？

B: Yes, we're going Dutch, thanks.

對，我們要各付各的，謝謝。

PLAY ALL　TRACK 26

Act 1: So Many Choices　難以抉擇

John and Lisa walk into a restaurant for dinner.

Hostess: Good evening, folks. How many are in your party?

John: Hi. We have a reservation for two at seven thirty under the name John Thompson.

Hostess: Ah, yes. We have a nonsmoking table for two by the window for you. This way, please.

(They walk to the table.)

H：晚安，兩位好。請問幾位用餐？

J：妳好。我們用約翰·湯普森的名字訂了兩個七點半的位子。

H：噢，有的。我們在非吸菸區為您留了一個靠窗的兩人桌。這邊請。

（他們走向座位。）

John: *(Taking hold of the chair)* Let me get that for you.

Lisa: Why, thank you. You're such a gentleman.

John: Well, I'm trying my best.

(John sits down. He and Lisa start reading the menus.)

Lisa: Mmm. The baked **mussels**[1] sound really good for an **appetizer**.[2]

John: They do, but you know I can't eat shellfish. I think I'll just have some soup to start.

Lisa: We should find out what the specials are. Oh, here comes our waiter.

Waiter: Good evening, **madam**,[3] sir. Can I get you a drink before your meal?

John: Yes, I'd like a glass of red wine, please.

Lisa: Just ice water for me will be fine. Are there any specials this evening?

J：（拉椅子）讓我幫妳。

L：喔，謝謝。你真是個紳士。

J：嗯，我盡力而為。

（約翰坐了下來。他和麗莎開始研究菜單。）

L：嗯。烤蚌殼似乎是很好的開胃菜。

J：的確是，不過你知道我不能吃貝類。我想我還是從湯開始好了。

L：我們應該問一下今天有什麼特餐。哦，我們的服務生來了。

W：小姐，先生，您們好。餐前需要為兩位準備飲料嗎？

J：好啊，請給我一杯紅酒。

L：我要一杯冰開水就好。今天晚上有什麼特餐嗎？

Vocabulary

1. **mussel** [ˈmʌsəl] *n.* 蚌（shellfish [ˈʃɛlˌfɪʃ] 指「貝類」）

2. **appetizer** [ˈæpəˌtaɪzə] *n.* 開胃菜

3. **madam** [ˈmædəm] *n.* （對女士的尊稱）夫人；太太

Waiter: There are. Tonight we have roasted **sea bass**,[4] lightly **breaded**,[5] with a butter and lemon sauce. It comes with pan-roasted vegetables and **new potatoes**.[6]

Lisa: That sounds really good to me!

John: It does, but I've got my heart set on a steak. Yet, there are so many **side dishes**[7] to choose from. I'll probably need a few more minutes to look at the menu.

Waiter: Take your time. Meanwhile, I'll get your drinks and bring you some dinner **rolls**.[8]

W：有的。今晚我們有烤鱸魚，外層裹上些許麵包屑，再加上奶油檸檬醬汁。附餐是有香煎烤蔬菜和小顆馬鈴薯。

L：聽起來很合我的胃口！

J：是啊，不過我已經決定要吃牛排了。但是有太多配菜可以選擇。我大概還需要幾分鐘看一下菜單。

W：您慢慢來。在此同時，我先將您的飲料和餐包送過來。

Vocabulary

4. **sea bass** [si] [bæs] *n.* 鱸魚

5. **bread** [brɛd] *v.* 覆以麵包屑

6. **new potato** [nu] [pəˋteto] *n. phr.* 小馬鈴薯（= baby potato）

7. **side dish** [saɪd] [dɪʃ] *n.* 配菜；附菜

8. **roll** [rol] *n.* 小圓麵包

實戰對話

PLAY ALL   TRACK 27

Act 2: A Little Surprise 甜蜜的驚喜

John and Lisa have just received their dinners at the restaurant.

John: Hmm. This steak looks awfully rare. I wanted it well-done.

Lisa: I can see the waiter. Let me flag him down.

(Lisa waves to the waiter, who walks to their table.)

Waiter: Is everything all right?

John: Unfortunately, I think my steak is **undercooked.**[1] I wanted it well-done.

J：嗯。這牛排看起來太生了。我點的是全熟的。

L：我看到服務生了。我叫他過來。

（麗莎對著走向他們桌子服務生招手。）

W：一切都還好嗎？

J：很遺憾，我想我的牛排沒有煮熟。我點的是全熟的。

Waiter: My goodness! I **apologize**,[2] sir. I must have accidentally marked your order as medium. Let me have the **chef**[3] put another steak on the **grill**[4] for you right away.

John: Actually, you can just have him cook this one a little bit longer.

Waiter: Right away, sir.

(The waiter takes the plate with the steak and walks away. A few minutes later, he returns with it.)

Waiter: Here you are, sir. Once again, my apologies for the mistake.

John: Not a problem at all. Do you need anything, honey?

Lisa: I think I'd like a glass of white wine, after all, to go with my fish.

Waiter: I'll get that for you immediately. Is everything else OK?

John: Maybe just some more butter for the rolls, and then we'll be all set.

Waiter: Coming right up.

(John and Lisa have now finished their meal, and John is looking at the bill.)

John: There seems to be a mistake. There's a piece of cake on this bill that we didn't order.

Lisa: Let me take a look. *(Takes the **slip**[5] from John)* You're right. That shouldn't be there . . . or should it?

W：天哪！十分抱歉，先生。我一定是不小心寫成五分熟了。我馬上請廚師再重新烤一份牛排給您。

J：其實你把這塊拿回去讓他煮久一點就可以了。

W：馬上辦，先生。

（服務生把裝有牛排的盤子收走。幾分鐘後，他端著盤子回來。）

W：先生，您的牛排來了。我再次為我犯的錯道歉。

J：一點都沒關係。親愛的，妳需要什麼嗎？

L：我想我還是來杯白酒來搭配我的魚好了。

W：我立即為您送上。其他方面都還可以嗎？

J：或許再給我們一些塗麵包用的奶油就可以了。

W：馬上來。

（約翰和麗莎已經用完餐，而約翰正在看帳單。）

J：這裡似乎有錯。帳單上有一筆蛋糕，但是我們沒有點。

L：讓我看看。（從約翰那裡接過帳單）你說得對。應該沒有……或應該有呢？

(The waiter walks up with a slice of cake with a lit candle on it.)

Waiter: Here you are, sir. Happy birthday!

Lisa: Happy birthday a few days early, dear. I wanted to surprise you, so I ordered it when I went to powder my nose.

John: That was nice of you, honey . . . and **sneaky**!⁶ Thanks!

（服務生拿著一塊點著蠟燭的蛋糕走過來。）

W：先生，這是給您的。生日快樂！

L：親愛的，提早了幾天，生日快樂。我想給你個驚喜，所以我去補妝時點了蛋糕。

J：親愛的，妳真貼心⋯⋯或者說真狡猾！謝謝妳！

Language Spotlight

flag down 揮手攔下

用法 flag down + N.、flag + N./ 代名詞 + down

flag 作動詞指「揮手；揮旗」。

- Thomas flagged down a taxi to take him to the airport.
  湯瑪士招了一輛計程車去機場。

coming right up 馬上來

原句應為 It's coming right up. ，但口語中常省略主詞與 be 動詞。

- A: Could I get a towel to use after I go swimming, please?
  我游完泳可以給我一條毛巾嗎？
- B: Absolutely, sir. Coming right up.
  沒問題，先生。馬上來。

Vocabulary

1. **undercooked** [ˋʌndɚˏkʊkt] *adj.* 未煮熟的
2. **apologize** [əˋpɑləˏdʒaɪz] *v.* 道歉；認錯
3. **chef** [ʃɛf] *n.* 廚師；主廚
4. **grill** [grɪl] *n.* 烤架
5. **slip** [slɪp] *n.* 紙條（在此指「帳單」）
6. **sneaky** [ˋsniki] *adj.* 偷偷摸摸的；鬼鬼祟祟的

《催促上菜》

- We've been waiting for a long time, but our order hasn't come yet.
  我們已經等很久了，但是我們點的菜還沒來。

- Is there a problem in the kitchen? We've been waiting almost 45 minutes.
  廚房裡有什麼問題嗎？我們已經等了差不多四十五分鐘了。

- I came here and ordered earlier. Why did you serve other tables first?
  是我先來、先點菜的。為什麼你先上其他桌的菜？

《抱怨餐點》

- There is something in my soup.
  我的湯裡有東西。

- This dish is tasteless/ too salty.
  這道菜沒味道 / 太鹹了。

- The meat is still raw/undercooked/ too tough.
  這塊肉還是生的 / 沒煮熟 / 太硬了。

- This steak is well-done. I wanted it rare/medium-rare/medium/ medium-well.
  這塊牛排是全熟的。我要的是一分熟 / 三分熟 / 五分熟 / 七分熟的。

Unit 10

✈ 問路英語
Asking for Directions

動手寫寫看

1. 我完全迷路了。請問最近的地鐵站在哪裡？

2. 從這裡到美術館最好的方法是什麼？

3. 火車站是往這條路走嗎？

4. 我要回美麗殿酒店。我應該往哪個方向走？

5. 請問有地方可以停車嗎？

參考答案請見 p. 340

 行人問路

A: Is it possible to walk there from here?
從這裡走路到得了那邊嗎？

B: Sure. It will only take about 15 minutes.
可以啊。只需要十五分鐘左右。

A: Excuse me. Do you know how to get to the botanical gardens?
抱歉，你知道植物園要怎麼走嗎？

B: I do, but it's pretty difficult. Let me draw you a map.
知道，不過蠻難說明的，我畫張地圖給你好了。

 駕駛問路

A: Could you tell me where the nearest gas station is?
請問最近的加油站在哪裡？

B: Just keep going straight until you reach Beach Street, then take a left.
只要一直走到畢區街，然後左轉。

A: Park Avenue is closed for some reason. Is there a detour I can take?

公園大道不知為何封閉了，要怎麼繞道？

B: Get on Route 6 North and drive for about 10 minutes until you reach Exit 3.

六號公路北上，大約開十分鐘到三號出口。

搭乘大眾運輸

A: OK. According to this sign, we can take bus number 905 to the arena.

嗯，根據標示，我們可以搭九〇五公車去運動場。

B: That's perfect. How often does it come around?

太好了。多久有一班車？

A: How do I get to the Metropolitan Museum?

請問要怎麼去大都會美術館？

B: Take the blue line going downtown and get off at 67th Street.

搭藍線往市中心的方向，在六十七街下車。

PLAY ALL TRACK 29

實戰對話

Act 1: Taking a Shortcut 走捷徑

John and Lisa are in an unfamiliar city trying to find a museum.

Lisa: Are you sure we're going the right way?

John: No. I think we're lost. Let's ask someone for directions.

(They walk over to a woman sitting on a park bench.)

Lisa: Excuse me, ma'am. We're trying to find the Museum of Modern Art. Do you happen to know where it is?

L：你確定我們走的方向對嗎？

J：不對。我想我們迷路了。我們找個人來問路吧。

（兩人走向一名坐在公園長椅上的女子。）

L：不好意思，小姐。我們在找「現代藝術博物館」。您知道它在哪裡嗎？

Woman: Yes, I do. The most **straightforward**[1] way to get there is to walk up this street, which is Park Street. You'll go about three blocks and then take a left on Beech Street. From the **intersection**,[2] it's about a 20-minute walk.

John: That's not too bad.

Woman: However, there is a shortcut that's a little more difficult.

Lisa: Not to worry. I have a paper and pen in my purse, so I can write the directions down. *(Pulls out paper and pen from her purse)*

Woman: Actually, let me draw you a quick map. OK, here's where we are now. What you'll want to do is cross the street. Take a right and walk to that **convenience**[3] store. Once you're there, take a left into the alley.

Lisa: Got it.

W：我知道啊。到那裡最直接的方法就是沿著這條公園街往前走。你們會經過約三個路口，然後在「山毛櫸街」左轉。從那個路口，走二十分鐘左右就到了。

J：聽起來還好。

W：不過，有個稍微複雜點的捷徑。

L：不用擔心。我包包裡有紙筆，我可以把路線寫下來。（從她包包裡拿出紙筆）

W：事實上，我幫你們畫個大概的地圖好了。好，這是我們現在的位置。你們要越過這條街。右轉然後走到那間便利商店。你們一到那裡就左轉進巷子裡。

L：了解。

Vocabulary

1. **straightforward** [ˌstretˋfɔrwɚd] *adj.* 直接的；坦率的
2. **intersection** [ˋɪntɚˌsɛkʃən] *n.* 交叉口；十字路口（T-intersection 指「T 字形路口」）
3. **convenience** [kənˋvinjəns] *n.* 便利

Woman: The alley will **curve**[4] around the buildings to the left, so you'll think you are going in the wrong direction, but you're not. Just keep walking until the alley ends in a T-intersection, and take a left.

Lisa: OK, left at the T.

Woman: Follow that alley until you reach a **dead end**[5] at a small park. Just walk through the park until you get to a brick wall. There you will find a gate. Go through it, and you'll be in another alley. Take a right, and that brings you to a main road, which is Beech Street. From there, you'll see the museum right across the street.

John: You got that, Lisa?

Lisa: Sure do. Thanks for the help!

W：那條巷子會順著建築物向左彎，所以你們會以為走錯方向了，但其實沒有。只要一直走到巷子底的 T 字形路口，然後左轉。

L：好，在 T 字路口左轉。

W：順著那條巷子走到盡頭有座小公園。穿過公園後你們會看到一面磚牆。你們會在那裡看到一道門。走出那個門後你們會進到另一條巷子裡。右轉，然後你們就會回到大路上了，那裡就是山毛櫸街。你們從那裡會看到博物館就在對面。

J：麗莎，妳聽懂了嗎？

L：當然。謝謝妳的幫忙！

Vocabulary

4. **curve** [kɜv] *v.* 彎曲；依曲線行進

5. **dead end** [dɛd] [ɛnd] *n.* 死路

實戰對話

PLAY ALL   TRACK 30

Act 2: Using Public Transportation 搭乘大眾運輸工具

John and Lisa have left the museum. They now have to get to the city's main train station.

John: Do you want to just hop in a taxi to get to the train station?

Lisa: *(Looks at her watch)* We have plenty of time before our train leaves, so we should take the subway or a bus.

(They walk over to a bus stop.)

John: Hmm. I can't figure out where we want to go. *(Turns to a man at the bus stop)* Pardon me. Do you know which bus to take to get to the main train station?

J：妳想不想搭計程車去火車站？

L：（看了看她的錶）離我們要搭的火車還有很多時間，所以我們應該搭地鐵或公車。

（他們走到公車站。）

J：嗯。我搞不清楚我們要去哪裡。（轉向站在公車站的男子）抱歉。您知道去火車站要搭哪一路公車嗎？

113

Man: There are no buses that run directly from here to there. You'll have to **transfer**[1] at least twice.

Lisa: In that case, is there a subway station nearby?

Man: There's one about a 25-minute walk from here. Just walk up to that **stoplight**[2] and take a right. Walk two blocks until you get to Green Avenue. Cross to the other side of the street, take a left, and the station will be about 100 meters up on the right.

John: Do you want to walk?

Lisa: My feet are pretty sore, actually.

Man: Probably the best thing to do then is to take the number 52 bus. Get off at the South Station stop. There, you can jump on the subway. Take the blue line heading towards the main station.

Lisa: That sounds more like it.

John: Are there a lot of **souvenir**[3] shops around the main station? I wanted to buy a few small gifts for my parents.

M：這裡沒有直達那裡的公車。你們至少要轉兩次車。

L：那樣的話，這附近有地鐵站嗎？

M：離這裡步行約二十五分鐘的地方有一個。走到那個紅綠燈後右轉。走過兩個路口到葛林大道。過馬路到另一邊，左轉，然後車站在離那裡大概一百公尺遠的右手邊。

J：妳想用走的嗎？

L：其實我的腳蠻酸的。

M：那麼最好的辦法可能就是搭五十二路公車。在「南站」那站下車。你們可以在那裡搭地鐵。搭藍線前往火車站。

L：聽起來好多了。

J：火車站週邊的紀念品店多嗎？我想買些小禮物給我父母。

Man: At the main station, there really aren't that many, but when you get off the bus at the South Station stop, there are lots of little shops close by. Just get off the bus, walk past South Station, and you can **browse**[4] in any of the little shops in the alleys. They're easy to find—just follow the people.

Lisa: Thank you so much!

Man: It's my pleasure.

M：其實市火車站附近沒那麼多。不過你們在「南站」那站下車時，附近有很多小店。你們只要下公車、走過「南站」，就可以隨意逛那些巷子裡的小店了。它們很好找，跟著人群走就對了。

L：非常謝謝你！

M：這是我的榮幸。

Language Spotlight

in that case 在那種情況下；那樣的話
此為獨立副詞片語，通常置於句首。

同義 if that's the case、that being the case

- A: Peter will probably want to stay home this weekend.
  彼得這個週末可能要待在家。
  B: If that's the case, I'll find someone else to play tennis with.
  如果是那樣的話，我只好找別人來跟我打網球了。

Vocabulary

1. **transfer** [ˋtrænsfɚ] *v.* 換車；轉換

2. **stoplight** [ˋstɑpˏlaɪt] *n.* 紅綠燈、交通號誌燈（英式英語中用 traffic light）

3. **souvenir** [ˋsuvəˏnɪr] *n.* 紀念品

4. **browse** [braʊz] *v.* 隨意觀看；隨便翻閱

位置表達法

- B is kitty-corner from E.　　　　　　B 在 E 的斜對角。
- A is across from E.　　　　　　　　A 在 E 的對面。
- D is next to E.　　　　　　　　　　D 在 E 隔壁。
- C is down the road from E.　　　　　C 在 E 往下走的位置。
- G is in front of H. / H is behind G.　G 在 H 前面 / H 在 G 後面。
- G is on the right of F. / F is on the left of G.　G 在 F 右邊 / F 在 G 左邊。
- H is around the corner from F.　　　從 F 轉個彎過去就是 H。

Unit 11

✈ 租車英語
Renting a Car

動手寫寫看

1. 你們有車可以租嗎？

2. 這部車可以坐幾個人？

3. 我必須把車開回同一個地點歸還嗎？

4. 如果我晚一個小時還車，你們要收多少錢？

5. 請幫我檢查胎壓，如果有需要就替我打氣。

參考答案請見 p. 340

租車

A: What kind of car would you like to rent?

您想租哪種車？

B: I'm traveling solo, so I don't need much space. I think I'll go with a compact.

我一個人旅行，所以不需要太多空間。我想租小型車就好了。

A: I need to see your license and registration, miss.

小姐，我需要看一下妳的駕照和行照。

B: Here you go.

在這裡。

費用與保險

A: How much will you charge for one day?

一天要多少錢？

B: You have to pay $35 for the first day, and $30 for each day after that.

第一天要付三十五元，之後每天是三十元。

A : Would you like to purchase additional liability insurance? It provides full coverage in case of an accident.

您要另外購買責任險嗎？萬一發生意外可以有全額理賠。

B : No, thanks. My platinum card provides automatic insurance for car rentals.

不用，謝謝。我的白金卡會自動提供租車險。

還車事宜

A : Do I have to fill up the car with gasoline when I return it?

還車時需要把油加滿嗎？

B : You can either pay for the gas now and bring it back empty, or just fill up the tank before you drop it off.

您可以現在付油錢，然後把油用完再還車，或者是在還車前把油加滿就好。

A : Do you offer a drop-off service?

你們有提供異地還車服務嗎？

B : Yes, and there is no charge for it.

有，而且不另外收費。

 PLAY ALL　　TRACK 32

Act 1: Taking Care of the Paperwork 辦理租車手續

*Alan is talking with a clerk inside a car **rental** [1] agency about renting a car.*

Alan: I need to rent a car for the next five days.

Clerk: That shouldn't be a problem. We have plenty of cars available. Do you know what type of car you would like? We have compacts, subcompacts, midsize cars, and compact minivans.

Alan: I think a compact minivan is what I'm looking for, as I will be with a few friends.

A：接下來的五天，我需要租一台車。

C：沒問題。我們有許多車子可以提供。您知道您想要的車型嗎？我們有小型房車、超小型車、中型車和小型休旅車。

A：我想我要找的是小型休旅車，因為我會和幾個朋友同行。

Clerk: OK, then. May I have your driver's license and credit card, please?

Alan: Sure, here they are. Here is my international driver's license as well.

Clerk: All right, these should be fine. Do you have **insurance**[2] already?

Alan: I believe I'm covered automatically through my credit card, but let me get the basic **liability**[3] insurance just in case.

Clerk: OK. Let me input the rest of your information. Meanwhile, this is the selection of cars we have. Unfortunately, all of the Mazda5 cars have been rented. However, we have all other compact minivans available.

Alan: Great! Hmm, so many cars to choose from. I think I'll go with the Toyota Wish.

Clerk: Fine choice. OK, so this is the daily rental rate, and this is the total for five days' worth of insurance.

C：好的。可以給我您的駕照和信用卡嗎？

A：當然，在這裡。還有我的國際駕照。

C：好了，這些應該沒問題。您已經投保了嗎？

A：我相信我的信用卡會自動幫我投保，但是我還是保個基本責任險以防萬一。

C：好的。我來把您其他的資訊輸入電腦。您在這段時間可以看看我們所有的車款。很不巧，所有的馬自達 5 都租出去了。不過我們其他所有的小型休旅車都還有。

A：太棒了！嗯，好多車可以選。我想我要一台豐田 Wish。

C：不錯的選擇。好的，這是日租金，而這是五天的保險費用。

Vocabulary

1. **rental** [ˋrɛntl̩] *n.* 出租；租金 *adj.* 出租的
2. **insurance** [ɪnˋʃʊrəns] *n.* 保險
3. **liability** [͵laɪəˋbɪlətɪ] *n.* （法律）責任；義務

Alan: That seems fine. Will I need to fill up the tank with gas before I return the car?

Clerk: Not to worry, you can drop it off empty if you choose.

Alan: Great. Oh, do I have to drop the car off at this location? I might be doing some traveling by plane from another city in about five days.

Clerk: You can drop the car off at any of our rental locations. Let me get you a map and a list of where our other offices are.

A：看起來還可以。我還車前需要把油加滿嗎？

C：不用擔心，您還車時油箱沒油也沒關係。

A：太好了！對了，我需要開回來這裡還車嗎？我五天後可能會從其他城市搭飛機去旅行。

C：您可以在我們任何一處租車地點還車。我拿張地圖和我們其他營業據點的位置一覽表給您。

Language Spotlight

plenty of 許多的

plenty of 後面可接複數名詞與不可數名詞。

- We have plenty of time to make it to the airport, so there's no need to hurry.

  我們有充裕的時間去機場，所以不需要這麼趕。

Act 2: Dealing with Problems 處理行車狀況

Alan is in a hotel parking lot, and his rental car won't start. He calls the rental company.

TTD: Tow Truck Driver

Clerk: ABC Rental Car. How can I help you?

Alan: Hi, this is Alan Burns. I've rented a car for the week, and I am currently at the hotel I stayed at last night. Unfortunately, the car won't start this morning.

Clerk: OK, Mr. Burns. Let me pull up your file. OK, I've got it. You have rented a Toyota Wish.

Alan: That's correct.

C：ABC 租車公司您好，很高興為您服務。

A：嗨，我是艾倫·伯恩斯。我這個禮拜租了一台車，現在人在昨晚住宿的飯店。不幸的是，今天早上車子無法發動。

C：好的，伯恩斯先生。讓我把您的檔案叫出來。有了，我看到了。您租的是一台豐田 Wish。

A：沒錯。

Clerk: And what seems to be the problem?

Alan: I think the battery is dead. When I try to start the car, nothing happens.

Clerk: OK. Tell me where your location is, and I'll send a tow truck right over.

Alan: I'm at the Marriot Hotel on 24 High Street.

Clerk: That's perfect. We have a tow truck in that area right now. If you could pop the **hood**[1] on the car, it'll make it easier for him to find you. He should be there within ten minutes.

Alan: Thanks for your help!

(The tow truck driver has arrived, and they are talking next to the car, the hood of which is open.)

TTD: Good morning, Mr. Burns. I've been told the car won't start?

Alan: Yes. When I put the key in the **ignition**,[2] nothing happens.

TTD: May I have the keys, please?

Alan: Sure.

TTD: Yes, the battery is dead. I noticed that the lights were left on.

Alan: I must have turned them on, but I arrived here in daylight, so I mustn't have noticed they were still on.

C：請問車子有什麼問題？

A：我想是電瓶沒電了。我試著發動車子，但是沒有任何反應。

C：了解。告訴我您的位置，我將馬上派一台拖吊車過去。

A：我在高街二十四號的萬豪酒店。

C：太好了。我們正好有台拖吊車在附近。如果您把引擎蓋打開，就可以讓他更容易找到您。他應該會在十分鐘內抵達。

A：謝謝妳的幫忙。

（拖吊車司機已抵達，他們在車子旁說話，引擎蓋是打打開的。）

TTD：早安，伯恩斯先生。我聽說這台車無法發動。

A：是的。我插入鑰匙要發動車子，卻沒有反應。

TTD：我可以借一下鑰匙嗎？

A：沒問題。

TTD：沒錯，電瓶沒電了。我注意到燈沒有關。

A：我一定把它們打開了，因為我到這裡的時候是大白天，所以我一定沒有注意到它們還亮著。

TTD: Not a problem. Let me get my **jumper cables**,[3] and I'll get this started for you in no time.

Alan: Thank goodness!

TTD：沒關係。我去把充電電線拿過來，我馬上替您發動。

A：謝天謝地！

Language Spotlight

in no time 立刻

in no time 表示「馬上；不久」，意思接近於 soon。

- The doctor says Rex will be feeling better in no time.
  醫生說瑞克斯馬上就會好轉。

Vocabulary

1. **hood** [hʊd] *n.* 引擎蓋

2. **ignition** [ɪɡˋnɪʃən] *n.* 發動（裝置）；點火開關

3. **jumper cables** [ˋdʒʌmpɚ] [ˋkebəlz] *n.* 跨接電纜
   （指「連接兩車電池的一對充電電線」）

汽車種類知多少

* **compact**
　[ˋkɑmˌpækt] 小型車

* **subcompact**
　[ˋsʌbˋkɑmˌpækt] 超小型車

* **tow truck**
　[to] [trʌk] 拖吊車

* **compact minivan**
　[ˋmɪniˌvæn] 小型休旅車

* **compact SUV**
　小型運動休旅車

* **midsize car**
　[ˋmɪdˌsaɪz] 中型車

圖片 / Wikipedia:Rudolf Stricker/Rudolf Stricker/Thomas doerfer/S 400 HYBRID/Rene/Thesupermat

自助加油 6 步驟

STEP 1 Turn off your engine and remove your gas cap.
熄火然後打開油箱蓋。

STEP 2 Insert a credit card or a bank card in the slot.
把信用卡或金融卡插到狹槽中。

STEP 3 Choose the kind of gas you want.
選擇你要的汽油種類。

STEP 4 Insert the nozzle in the tank and lift the handle on the pump. Then squeeze the lever on the nozzle to begin pumping.
把油槍管插到油箱孔裡，再拉起加油機上的把手。然後用力握住油槍上的壓桿就可以開始加油了。

STEP 5 When the gas has finished pumping, return the nozzle to its holder and replace the gas cap.
加油機停止加油後，把油槍管放回架上，蓋上油箱蓋。

STEP 6 Press the button to print your receipt.
按下按鈕列印收據。

Unit 12

急難救助英語

Travel Emergency

動手寫寫看

1. 我的皮夾被偷了。

2. 失物招領處在哪裡？

3. 我需要一份遺失證明。

4. 我朋友生病了。這附近有醫院嗎？

5. 有人受傷了。請叫救護車。

參考答案請見 p. 340

PLAY ALL　TRACK 34

●●● 遺失物品

A: I've lost my passport. What should I do?
我的護照掉了，我該怎麼辦？

B: Go to the US embassy so that they can help you get a new one.
去美國大使館，他們會幫你弄一本新的。

A: I think I left one of my bags on the plane.
我想我把一個袋子留在飛機上了。

B: I'll check for you. Could you leave your contact information?
我幫您查一下。可以留下您的聯絡資料嗎？

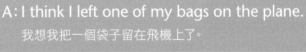

A: My credit card has been stolen.
我的信用卡被偷了。

B: You have to call and cancel your card.
你得打電話跟取消卡片。

意外狀況

A: I have been in a car accident, and my friend is hurt. I need help!

我發生車禍而且我朋友受傷了。我需要幫忙！

B: Don't worry, sir. An ambulance is on its way.

先生，不要擔心。救護車已經在路上了。

A: I would like to report a crime.

我要報案。

B: Certainly. Take a seat, and an officer will come and get all the details from you.

好的，坐一下。有警官會來問你所有的細節。

A: I got separated from my friend and can't find her. Could you please make an announcement for me?

我和朋友走散了、找不到她，可以幫我廣播嗎？

B: May I have your attention, please. Will Kate Wang please come to the information desk? Your party is waiting for you.

請大家注意，可以請王凱特小姐到服務台嗎？妳的朋友在等妳。

Act 1: An Unfortunate Theft[1] 不幸遭竊

Tom and Cecilia are on vacation. They've just finished lunch at a café, and Cecilia notices her purse is missing.

Cecilia: What am I going to do? Everything was inside my purse—my passport, credit cards, traveler's checks, and all my cash.

Tom: OK, just stay calm. The first thing we need to do is talk to the police. If someone has your purse, he might just take the cash and **ditch**[2] the rest of it nearby.

C：我該怎麼辦？我所有的東西都在包包裡——護照、信用卡、旅行支票和所有現金。

T：好，冷靜點。我們當務之急就是報警。如果有人拿了妳的包包，他可能只會拿走現金，然後把其他東西丟在附近。

Cecilia: There's a security guard in that building over there. Let's see if he can help.

(They walk over to the security guard.)

Tom: Excuse me, sir, but my wife's purse has been stolen.

Guard: Did you see who did it?

Tom: We didn't see anything. We had lunch at the café, and now her purse is gone.

Guard: Let me call the police for you immediately.

Cecilia: What a **nightmare**[3] this is!

(The security guard makes and finishes the call.)

Guard: You know, there are security cameras that we can look at when the police get here. It might give them a quick **lead**.[4]

Cecilia: In the meantime, I need to call the credit card companies and cancel my cards, but my cell phone is gone, too.

C：那邊那棟大樓有個警衛。我們去看看他能不能幫我們。

（他們走向警衛。）

T：先生，不好意思，我太太的包包被偷了。

G：你們有看到是誰偷的嗎？

T：我們什麼都沒看到。我們在餐館吃午餐，然後現在她的包包不見了。

G：我馬上幫你們報警。

C：這真是場惡夢啊！

（警衛打完電話。）

G：嗯，警察來的時候我們會有監視器畫面可以看。那可能可以立即提供他們線索。

C：同時我還需要打電話到信用卡公司去取消我的卡片，但我的手機也被偷了。

Vocabulary

1. **theft** [θɛft] *n.* 偷竊；竊盜
2. **ditch** [dɪtʃ] *v.* 丟棄；拋棄
3. **nightmare** [ˈnaɪtˌmɛr] *n.* 惡夢；夢魘
4. **lead** [lid] *n.* 線索；頭緒

Guard: You can get an international calling card over at that convenience store, and there is a **pay phone**[5] out front.

Tom: You just stay here and wait for the police. I'll go get the card.

Cecilia: OK. *(Tom walks away and Cecilia turns to the guard.)* Sir, do you know where the closest Canadian **embassy**[6] is? I'm going to need to get my passport replaced.

Guard: I don't, but I'm pretty sure the police will know. They should be here any minute now.

G：妳可以在那邊那間便利商店買到國際電話卡，店外面就有付費公用電話。

T：妳在這裡等警察。我去買電話卡。

C：好。（湯姆離開，西西莉亞轉向警衛。）先生，你知道最近的加拿大大使館在哪嗎？我得重辦護照。

G：我不知道，但我確定警察會知道。他們應該馬上就到了。

Language Spotlight

(at) any minute/moment (now) 隨時；馬上

同義 very soon、(at) any time、any second

- We should get out to the platform, as the train should be here any minute now.
  火車隨時就要進站了，我們應該去月台上了。

Vocabulary

5. **pay phone** [pe] [fon] *n.* 付費公用電話

6. **embassy** [ˋɛmbəsi] *n.* 大使館

實戰對話

PLAY ALL   TRACK 36

Act 2: A Medical Problem 遺失藥物

*Tom and Cecilia are back in their hotel room. Cecilia is looking through her **toiletries**[1] bag for her **medication**.[2]*

Rec: Receptionist

Cecilia: Oh, no! Even the pills I need were in my purse! I have to take the **antibiotics**[3] for two weeks, or my sickness will come back.

Tom: We'll have to go find a pharmacy. Did you bring your **prescription**[4] with you?

Cecilia: I did, but I don't think a pharmacist will accept it in this country.

C：喔，糟了！連我的藥都在包包裡！我必須吃兩個星期的抗生素，否則病會復發。

T：我們得去找藥局。妳有把處方箋帶在身上嗎？

C：有，但我想這裡的藥劑師不會接受。

133

Tom: In that case, we should head over to an emergency room at a hospital. You can see a doctor and describe what the problem is. Let me go downstairs and talk with someone at **reception**[5] to find out where the hospital is.

(Tom leaves the hotel room and walks to reception.)

Rec: Good afternoon, sir. What can I do for you?

Tom: My wife and I have a little problem. We need to find a hospital.

Rec: Is it an emergency, sir? If so, I can call an **ambulance**[6] right away.

Tom: No, it's not that urgent. You see, my wife's purse was stolen, and her medication was in it. She needs to get a replacement.

Rec: I'm very sorry to hear about that. We've dealt with this situation before, though. Does your wife have the original prescription from her doctor?

Tom: Yes, she does.

Rec: OK, then. About two blocks from here is a small clinic. Two doors down from it is a large pharmacy. You should be able to see a doctor, and if necessary, he can give you a local prescription that you can then take to the pharmacy.

T：那樣的話，我們應該去醫院的急診室。妳可以看醫師，並且向他描述妳的病情。我下樓去找櫃台人員，看醫院在哪裡。

（湯姆離開飯店房間，走向櫃台。）

Rec：午安，先生。有什麼我能為您效勞的嗎？

T：我太太和我出了點麻煩。我們需要找一家醫院。

Rec：先生，是緊急狀況嗎？如果是的話，我可以馬上叫救護車。

T：不是，沒那麼緊急。是這樣的，我太太的包包被偷了，而她的藥在裡頭。她需要替代藥物。

Rec：我很遺憾聽到這種事。不過我們之前處理過這種狀況。你太太有帶醫生開立的原處方箋嗎？

T：有，她有帶。

Rec：那好。離這裡兩個路口的地方有間小診所。小診所隔兩戶就是間大藥局。你們可以先去看醫生，必要的話，他會開給你們這裡的處方箋，你們再拿去藥局就可以了。

Tom: Thank goodness! Do you know if the pharmacy and clinic take credit cards? I doubt they will accept my wife's health insurance.

Rec: They do, sir. Now, let me show you how to get to the clinic on this map.

T： 謝天謝地！你知道藥局和診所收不收信用卡？我不認為他們會接受我太太的醫療保險。（編按：在美國等國家若無醫療保險的話，醫療費用將相當高昂，故湯姆才會詢問可否使用信用卡。）

Rec： 他們收信用卡，先生。現在，我在這張地圖上告訴你診所怎麼去。

Language Spotlight

if necessary 如果必要的話；必要時

if necessary 是由 If it is necessary . . . 而來，但一般會用 if necessary，也可以用 when necessary 和 where necessary。

- I can lend you some money at the end of this month if necessary.

  必要的話，這個月底我可以借你一些錢。

Vocabulary

1. **toiletry** [ˈtɔɪlətri] *n.* 旅行所準備的盥洗用品（常用複數）

2. **medication** [ˌmɛdəˈkeʃən] *n.* 藥物

3. **antibiotic** [ˌæntɪbaɪˈɑtɪk] *n.* 抗生素

4. **prescription** [prɪˈskrɪpʃən] *n.* 處方箋；藥方

5. **reception** [rɪˈsɛpʃən] *n.* 接待處；接待（此為英式英語說法，在飯店是指「櫃台服務」，即美式英語中的 front desk / reception desk）

6. **ambulance** [ˈæmbjələns] *n.* 救護車

求救

- Thief! 有小偷！
- Help! 救命！
- Fire! 失火了！
- Dial 911! 快打一一九！
- Call the cops! 快叫警察！
- My friend has been robbed! 我朋友被搶了！
- Please do something about it. 請想想辦法。
- I have a terrible problem. 我有個麻煩的問題。

自保

- I don't want any trouble. I'll do whatever you say.
  我不想惹麻煩。你說什麼我都照做。

- OK. Here you go.
  好，這些都給你。

狀況詢問

- Does anyone know CPR?
  誰會心肺復甦術？

- How long will it take to issue a new one?
  請問補發新卡要多久？

- Is it necessary for me to have a prescription
  to get medicine?
  拿藥需要處方箋嗎？

- Where's the emergency?
  緊急出口在哪裡？

- Can I use your cell phone?
  我能借用你的行動電話嗎？

- Excuse me. May I go first?
  抱歉，可以讓我先嗎？

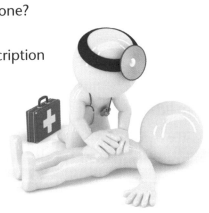

PART B

繞著地球玩

世界各地迷人的旅遊景點非常多，PART B 收錄旅遊達人一生必去的 25 個地方，圖文並茂，並精選單字及搭配中文翻譯，讓你用英文環遊世界。

清水舞台為清水寺的著名景點
圖片 / Wikipedia: Oilstreet

1. 京都的千年風華

PLAY ALL　TRACK 37

Kyoto: The Heart and History of Japan

It is fall in Kyoto, and red maple[1] leaves move in the breeze and scatter[2] sunshine on the streets and ancient wooden buildings. Even though red and gold cover the city in fall, each season brings its own bright colors to Kyoto. In winter, snow turns the city white. Spring's pink cherry blossoms warm Kyoto's streets, and the greens of summer seem to glow. These colors make a beautiful setting for Kyoto's rich history and traditions.

圖片 / Melody

名列世界文化遺產的金閣寺（又名「鹿苑寺」）二、三樓牆面貼滿金箔，在湖水的映照下顯得金碧輝煌。

圖片 / Rachel

Kyoto was the capital[3] of Japan for 1,200 years, and even now it is the spiritual[4] heart of Japan. This city's long history can be seen in ancient customs[5] practiced today. Likewise, beautiful wooden houses and temples show visitors that the past is very much alive.

The lovely buildings in Kyoto are matched by the city's natural beauty. Spring brings millions of visitors to view the cherry blossoms.[6] One of the most popular spots for this is Philosopher's Walk. The path runs beside a canal[7] and is lined with cherry trees. Their branches are heavy with delicate[8] pink and white blossoms in the spring.

Vocabulary

1. **maple** [ˋmepəl] *n.* 楓樹
2. **scatter** [ˋskætə] *v.* 撒；散布
3. **capital** [ˋkæpətl] *n.* 首都；首府
4. **spiritual** [ˋspɪrɪtʃʊəl] *adj.* 精神上的；心靈的
5. **custom** [ˋkʌstəm] *n.* 風俗習慣；慣例
6. **cherry blossom** [ˋtʃɛri] [ˋblasəm] *n. phr.* 櫻花
7. **canal** [kəˋnæl] *n.* 溝渠；運河
8. **delicate** [ˋdɛlɪkət] *adj.* （顏色）柔和的；雅緻的

【註】
英文中的 cherry trees 可以指觀賞用的櫻花樹，也可指櫻桃樹，兩者雖屬於同科同屬的植物，但並不相同。觀賞用的櫻花可分為單瓣和複瓣兩種，單瓣會開花結果，稱為「櫻花果」，但汁液偏酸，鳥類非常喜愛，人類則不食用；而複瓣多半不結果。至於櫻桃樹也會開花，稱為「櫻桃花」，花色為白色或粉色，常見的品種有甜櫻桃（sweet cherry）和酸櫻桃（sour cherry）。

The temples of Kyoto offer another kind of beauty to visitors. The Temple of the Golden Pavilion in northwest Kyoto is one of the most popular in the city. If you can fight your way through the crowds,[9] you'll see a temple covered in gold leaf and shining as bright as the sun. Outside the pavilion, a pond and Japanese gardens add to the beauty.

People who look for Zen simplicity[10] visit Ryoanji Temple to see the most famous Zen rock garden in Japan. Some visitors prefer a beautiful city view to a view of rocks, so they stop by Kiyomizu Temple. This temple's waterfall offers a cool drink to go with the amazing view from its cliffs.

【從旅遊看文化】

Philosopher's Walk 即「哲學之道」，據傳是因為日本哲學家西田幾太郎常在此散步而得名，為京都著名的散步小徑，尤其在櫻花盛開時節，遊客更是絡繹不絕。

Zen 即「禪」的音譯，Zen rock garden 指「禪花園」，又稱為「枯山水」，多見於禪寺之中，是指利用石頭、白砂和盆栽等，在狹小的空間中呈現大山大水的樣貌。

nightingale 指「夜鶯」，nightingale floor（鶯聲地板）是日式寺廟或城堡中常用的防盜設計，只要有人踩到地板上，就會牽動埋在底下的金屬片而發出聲響。

清水寺仁王門

京都小檔案

千年古城京都多年來一直是日本的政治、經濟及文化中心。紫式部的《源氏物語》、三島由紀夫的《金閣寺》等名著都是以京都為背景。此外，京都景色秀麗，每年還有三大祭典：五月的葵祭、七月的祇園祭及十月的時代祭，充分展現地方色彩和傳統風情，有機會到京都可不要錯過囉！

*There is more to Kyoto than beautiful temples. Nijo Castle also draws tourists. This 400-year-old castle was struck by lightning and suffered fires, but it still displays[11] wealth and power. Each room is rich in wood carvings[12] and gold designs. As visitors walk through the halls,[13] they hear birdsong. The floors, called "nightingale floors," were made to tweet like birds with every step. This way, no one could sneak[14] up on palace[15] guests.

The Gion district[16] is another landmark[17] in Kyoto. In the teahouses on these streets, geisha have performed traditional arts for hundreds of years. Even now, visitors to this district can catch sight of geisha in brightly colored kimonos.

Vocabulary

9. **crowd** [kraʊd] *n.* 人群
10. **simplicity** [sɪm`plɪsəti] *n.* 簡樸；簡單
11. **display** [dɪ`sple] *v.* 展示；展現
12. **carving** [`kɑrvɪŋ] *n.* 雕刻品；雕刻圖案
13. **hall** [hɔl] *n.* 走廊；走道
14. **sneak** [snik] *v.* 偷溜；偷偷地走（sneak up on 是指「偷偷挨近……」）
15. **palace** [`pæləs] *n.* 宮殿
16. **district** [`dɪstrɪkt] *n.* 地區、區域；行政區
17. **landmark** [`lænd͵mɑrk] *n.* 地標

Another way to connect[18] with ancient Kyoto is by watching a traditional Kyomai dance performance. Kyomai dance movements are very controlled, but they also express strong emotions.[19] Visitors can pay a little extra and enjoy a tea ceremony[20] before the show. The tea ceremony is a true taste of Japanese culture. It takes focus and a peaceful heart to perform this 500-year-old tradition.

Kyoto's food also opens a door to the past. The dishes focus on tofu and fresh, seasonal vegetables. Many feel that the gentle flavors of Kyoto dishes are the origin[21] of Japanese cuisine.[22]

In Kyoto, the past and present flow together like movements in a Kyomai dance: with grace,[23] control, and beauty. People usually come to this city to view autumn's maple leaves or spring's cherry blossoms. However, Kyoto's temple buildings, traditional arts, and delicate food will capture the heart in any season.

【從旅遊看文化】

身著華麗和服（kimono [kɪˋmono]）、化著豔妝的藝妓（geisha [ˋgeʃə]）是京都的特色之一。藝妓是指用歌舞或樂器演奏來娛樂賓客的女性藝人。在日本，要成為藝妓必須經過多年嚴格訓練，以求精通舞蹈、歌曲乃至禮儀、茶道（tea ceremony）等技藝。不過現在京都各地都有「藝妓變身館」，由專業化妝師幫遊客盛裝打扮，讓你可以化身為美美的藝妓，留下美麗的回憶。

Vocabulary

18. **connect** [kəˋnɛkt] *v.* 連結；聯繫
19. **emotion** [ɪˋmoʃən] *n.* 情感；情緒
20. **ceremony** [ˋsɛrəˏmoni] *n.* 儀式；典禮
21. **origin** [ˋɔrədʒən] *n.* 起源；來源
22. **cuisine** [kwɪˋzin] *n.* 菜餚；烹飪（方法）
23. **grace** [gres] *n.* 優雅

嵐山的傳統人力拉車

圖片 / Rachel

京都的千年風華

在入秋的京都，紅色的楓葉在微風中飄動，且將陽光撒落在街道和古老的木造房屋上。雖然秋天時紅色和金黃色覆蓋了整個城市，每個季節仍為京都帶來特有的明亮色彩。冬天的白雪將城市化為銀白一片。春天的粉紅櫻花溫暖了京都的街道，而夏天的綠地似乎在閃閃發光。這些色彩為京都豐富的歷史和傳統提供了美麗的背景襯托。

京都曾是日本的首都達一千兩百年之久，即使現在仍是日本的精神核心。這座城市的悠久歷史可以在今日仍奉行的古老習俗中見到。同樣地，美麗的木造房屋和廟宇向遊客展示著那些過往依舊非常活躍。

京都的自然美景足以和城裡迷人的建築物相較量。春天帶來數百萬的遊客來欣賞櫻花。最受歡迎的賞櫻地點之一就是哲學之道。這條步道沿著一條溝渠延伸，兩旁種滿了櫻樹。春季時，樹枝上都開滿了柔和的粉紅色和白色的櫻花。

京都的寺廟則提供遊客另一種美景。位於京都西北邊的金閣寺是城裡最受歡迎的寺廟之一。如果你能奮力穿過擁擠的人群，就會看到一座覆蓋著金箔的寺廟，猶如太陽般閃亮。在金閣寺外，一座池塘和美麗的日式庭園為此地增添一分美麗。

想要尋求禪宗簡樸精神的人則會參觀龍安寺，看看日本最有名的「枯山水庭院」。有些遊客比較喜歡美麗的市景勝於岩石景色，所以他們會去造訪清水寺。這座寺廟的瀑布提供清涼的飲水以及從懸崖上所看到的令人讚嘆的景色。

京都不只有漂亮的寺廟而已。二條城也吸引了觀光客。這座有四百年歷史的城堡曾被閃電擊中，也曾遭到祝融肆虐，但仍然展現出財富及權力氣息。每間房間都有許多的木雕品及黃金設計品。遊客穿過走廊時，他們會聽到鳥鳴聲。這些地板稱為「鶯聲地板」，被設計成每踏一步就會發出像鳥鳴般的啾啾聲。這樣一來，就沒有人能偷偷接近宮殿裡的賓客了。

祇園區是京都的另一個地標。在街道上的茶館裡，數百多年來藝妓表演著傳統的技藝。即使在今日，來到此區的遊客們還能看到穿著豔麗和服的藝妓身影。

另一種和古京都連繫的方法是欣賞一場傳統的京舞表演。京舞的動作很節制，但也表現出強烈的情感。遊客可以再多付一點錢，在舞蹈開始前欣賞一場茶道表演。茶道是日本文化的精髓之一，需要專注和平靜的心才能表演這項有五百年歷史的傳統技藝。

京都的食物也開啟了通往過去之門。這些菜色主要是豆腐和新鮮的時蔬。許多人覺得京都菜的溫和滋味就是日本料理的起源。

在京都，過去和現在就像京舞的動作——優雅、克制和美麗一樣綿綿不斷。人們造訪這個城市通常是為了欣賞秋季的楓葉或春季的櫻花，但是京都的寺廟建築、傳統技藝和精緻的食物在任何季節都能抓住人心。

1. alive vs. live 「活的」不一樣

alive 指「活躍的；活著的、現存的」，文中用 the past is very much alive 表示「過去的事物依舊非常活躍」。另一個相似的字 live [laɪv] 作形容詞時也表示「活著的」，但用法略有不同：

	alive	live
詞性	只作形容詞	可作形容詞 還可作副詞，指「現場實況地」
注意	只能作補語用，常放在 be 動詞或連綴動詞之後	作形容詞時一定要放在名詞前

- Tyler was in a car accident, but he is alive.
  泰勒發生了車禍，但他還活著。

- My cousin keeps a live snake in her house.
  我表弟在家裡養了一條活生生的蛇。

- You can watch the concert live on TV.
  你可以在電視上看那場演唱會的實況轉播。（live 在此作副詞用）

2. fight your way through the crowds 奮力穿過人群、擠出一條路

fight one's way 字面上指「（某人）努力走出自己的路」，後面常接介系詞片語來表示所穿越或面對的對象，例如文中的 through the crowds 表示「穿越重重人群」。

- Jessica fought her way through the trees to get to the river.
  潔西卡奮力穿過了樹林去到河邊。

3. suffer 的用法

在文中作及物動詞，指「遭受（災難等）；忍受（不愉快的事）」，後面接所遭遇的苦難、痛苦等，通常是外來因素造成的磨難。

- A: Let's come back when this place is less busy.
  我們等這裡比較不忙的時候再來吧！

  B: Good idea. I don't want to suffer the long lines.
  好主意，我不想忍受大排長龍。

- After years of suffering hardship, Tom felt that his life was finally getting a little better.
  湯姆辛苦幾年之後，覺得生活終於逐漸有些好轉了。

補充 suffer 還可作不及物動詞，指「受苦、受折磨；患病」，之後接 from，再接受苦的原因，如 suffer from poverty（受貧窮之苦）、suffer from high blood pressure（受高血壓之苦）。

- Richard suffers from a bad heart.
  理查深受心臟毛病所苦。

4. **catch sight of + N.**（突然或剎那間）看見、發現⋯⋯

sight 在此指「景象」，catch sight of . . . 表示「突然看到⋯⋯；不經意瞥見⋯⋯」。

- I caught sight of the movie star as she got out of her car.
  我在那位電影明星下車時瞥見了她的身影。

5. **open a door to + N.** 提供⋯⋯的機會

open a/the door to + N. 字面上表示「開啟通往⋯⋯之門」，引申指「提供⋯⋯的機會；使⋯⋯可能發生」。

- Good grades can open the door to a bright future.
  好成績讓你有機會擁有光明的未來。
- Kevin's sweet words opened a door to Melissa's heart.
  凱文的甜言蜜語開啟了梅麗莎的心扉。

Sentence Patterns

* **There is more to Kyoto than beautiful temples.**

句型 there is more (to sb/sth) than . . .（某人或某事）不只是⋯⋯

- There is more to Tom than you would think. He's actually a highly skilled pianist.
  湯姆不只是你想的那樣。他其實是一位琴藝精湛的鋼琴師。
- There is much more to Paris than just the Eiffel Tower and the Louvre.
  巴黎不是只有艾菲爾鐵塔和羅浮宮而已。

Paris: City of Lights, City of Love

Ah, the City of Lights! It was night and I was taking a taxi into the heart of the French capital. Paris has earned many names over its long and eventful[1] history, and I quickly understood why this particular name stuck.

Heading toward my hotel on the Champs-Élysées, I watched the world pass outside my window. The sparkling[2] view of the most photographed street in the world took my breath away. Lights from designer[3] shops glowed agreeably,[4] while ahead shone the noble Arc de Triomphe, or Arch[5] of Triumph.[6]

I was here to visit my friend and fellow football fan, Jean. We met at the World Cup in Germany the previous summer, and he had invited me to experience life in his grand city.

"I hope you slept well," said Jean when he met me at the hotel the next morning. "There is much to see your first day!"

位於巴黎市中心的羅浮宮（the Louvre）收藏超過三萬件的藝術品

凱旋門（Arc de Triomphe）位於戴高樂廣場（Place Charles de Gaulle）中央

He wasn't joking. After a quick breakfast of coffee, cheese, and baguettes,[7] we were off to our first stop, the Louvre. Perhaps the most famous museum in the world, the Louvre is home to works every art lover knows. Everywhere I looked, there was a da Vinci, a Monet, or a Matisse. The small *Mona Lisa* smiled out at us, as if to say, "Welcome to Paris."

Vocabulary

1. **eventful** [ɪˋvɛntfəl] *adj.* 多事的；充滿變故的
2. **sparkling** [ˋspɑrkəlɪŋ] *adj.* 閃閃發光的；有氣泡的
3. **designer** [dɪˋzaɪnɚ] *adj.* 名牌設計師設計的；時尚的
4. **agreeably** [əˋgriəbli] *adv.* 愜意地；一致地
5. **arch** [ɑrtʃ] *n.* 拱門；拱形
6. **triumph** [ˋtraɪəmf] *n.* 勝利
7. **baguette** [bæˋgɛt] *n.* 法國長棍麵包

147

The next day, we hopped on the Métro and headed for the city's number one landmark, the Eiffel Tower. At the base of the massive[8] steel structure, we were met by Jean's girlfriend, Simone, and her cousin, Josette.

From the top, Josette pointed out some of Paris's other landmarks. *Next to us was the Seine River, which divides the city. The Left Bank lay along one side, and Josette said it was the traditional home of the city's artists and writers.

A writer myself, I was keen[9] to learn more. Josette offered me a tour. We left Jean and Simone behind and set off on rented bicycles. Along the banks of the Seine we spotted[10] artists painting the riverside scene, just as Monet once did.

At one of the cafés along the river, we stopped for lunch. It was easy to imagine philosophers and writers gathering here. I could picture them passionately[11] discussing the important questions of their generation.

After lunch, we biked up the hill known as Montmartre. At the top lay the Basilique du Sacré-Cœur, or Church of the Sacred[12] Heart. In the shadow of this beautiful church, we looked out over the city. Josette slipped her hand in mine. As the sun set over the Seine, I thought of Paris's other nickname: the City of Love.

位於巴黎市北郊蒙馬特區的聖心堂（Basilique du Sacré-Cœur）

Jean, Simone, and Josette met up with me again the next morning. Typical Parisians[13]—fashionable and stylish[14]—they would be perfect shopping companions.[15] Fashion houses like Chanel and Louis Vuitton represent the best of Paris fashion. However, I was not exactly rich enough for such luxury. So, my hip[16] friends took me to some of the city's more affordable[17] markets.

Vocabulary

8. **massive** [`mæsɪv] *adj.* 巨大的；大規模的

9. **keen** [kin] *adj.* 熱切的；渴望的

10. **spot** [spɑt] *v.* 察覺；注意到

11. **passionately** [`pæʃənətli] *adv.* 熱情地；激昂地

12. **sacred** [`sekrəd] *adj.* 神聖的

13. **Parisian** [pə`rɪʒən] *n., adj.* 巴黎人；巴黎人的

14. **stylish** [`staɪlɪʃ] *adj.* 時髦的；流行的

15. **companion** [kəm`pænjən] *n.* 同伴；伴侶

16. **hip** [hɪp] *adj.* 流行的；時髦的

17. **affordable** [ə`fɔrdəbəl] *adj.* 負擔得起的

As we pushed our bicycles through the crowds of shoppers at one outdoor market, I felt I had found the true heart of Paris. Street performers, food sellers, and fragrant[18] flower carts created an environment uniquely[19] Parisian. A meeting place of many cultures, Paris is special among all French cities. Cultures from North Africa to Southeast Asia can be found in the city's many open-air markets. In Paris, life itself is a work of art.

A few days later, my adventure was at an end, and my bags were much heavier. They were loaded with new clothes and souvenirs.[20] My friends helped me carry them to the airport. *Although sad to leave, I was able to smile about the great memories I was taking home with me. Paris had given me so much during my short stay: art, history, friendship, and even romance.[21] Josette gave me a light peck[22] on the cheek and waved good-bye. I would be back.

巴黎景點這樣念

Centre Pompidou [ˈpɑmpɛˌdu] 龐畢度中心
Arc de Triomphe [ˈɑrk də trɪˋɔmf] 凱旋門
Basilique du Sacré-Cœur
[ˌbɑsɪlɪk dju ˋsɑkreˌkɚ] 聖心堂
Montmartre [ˌmɔnˋmɑrtrə] 蒙馬特區
the Louvre [ˋluvɚ] 羅浮宮

Vocabulary

18. **fragrant** [ˋfregrənt] *adj.* 芳香的
19. **uniquely** [juˋnikli] *adv.* 獨特地；唯一地
20. **souvenir** [ˌsuvəˋnɪr] *n.* 紀念品
21. **romance** [roˋmæns] *n.* 浪漫；羅曼史
22. **peck** [pɛk] *n.* 輕吻；輕啄

【從旅遊看文化】

為保存法國美食的原汁原味，法國政府在全國各級學校和大學的自助餐廳（cafeteria）裡禁止使用番茄醬（ketchup），因為番茄醬被他們視為一種文化威脅（cultural threat）。但薯條（French fries）搭配番茄醬時倒是個例外。

巴黎——愛與光明之都

啊，光明之都！夜暮低垂，我正搭著計程車前往法國首都的市中心。巴黎在其悠久且多事的歷史中有過許多名字，而我很快就明白「光明之都」這個特別的名字為何得以沿用至今。

在前往位於香榭大道上飯店的途中，我望著車窗外飛馳過的景物。這條全世界最常被拍攝的街道閃耀的景色令人屏息。時尚名店的燈火齊放，而宏偉的凱旋門則在前方閃耀著。

我是來拜訪跟我一樣是足球迷的朋友吉恩。我們去年夏天在德國舉行的世界盃上認識，他邀請我到他居住的這座大城市來體驗生活。

「希望你有睡好，」吉恩第二天早上跟我在飯店碰面時這麼説。「第一天有很多東西要看呢！」

他可不是説笑的。匆匆用完咖啡、起司和法國長棍麵包後，我們前往第一站羅浮宮。羅浮宮或許是世界上最著名的博物館，所有藝術愛好者所熟知的作品都收藏於此。放眼望去到處都有達文西、莫內或馬蒂斯等偉大畫作。小小的《蒙娜麗莎》畫像對著我們微笑，彷彿在説：「歡迎來到巴黎。」

第二天，我們跳上地鐵前往巴黎最著名的地標艾菲爾鐵塔。在這座巨型鋼鐵建築底下，我們與吉恩的女友席蒙以及她表妹喬瑟碰面。

從塔頂，喬瑟指出了巴黎其他的地標。在我們旁邊的是穿過巴黎的塞納河。「左岸」就位於河的一側，喬瑟説那裡是巴黎藝術家、作家的傳統聚集地。

我本身也是作家，所以很想進一步了解。喬瑟就為我做導覽。我們把吉恩及席蒙拋在後頭，騎著租來的腳踏車就出發了。沿著塞納河岸，我們看到畫家畫著河岸風光，就像莫內過去曾經所做的一樣。

我們停下來到河岸一家咖啡館裡吃中餐。不難想像很多哲學家和作家會聚集在此。我可以想像他們熱烈討論著他們那世代的重要議題。

午餐過後，我們騎上著名的蒙馬特丘，聖心堂座落於丘頂。在這座美麗教堂的屋蔭下，我們眺望這座城市。喬瑟悄悄將手伸到我手裡，夕陽落在塞納河時，我想著巴黎另一個別名：浪漫之都。

隔天早上我又與吉恩、席蒙和喬瑟碰頭。典型的巴黎人——時尚又有型——他們會是最理想的購物夥伴。香奈兒、路易威登等時尚名店最能代表巴黎的時尚。然而，我可買不起那樣的奢侈品。所以，我這些時髦的朋友就帶我到城裡一些較平價的市集。

我們牽著腳踏車穿過一處擠滿購物人潮的露天市場時，我覺得我找到了巴黎真正的核心。街頭藝人、美食攤販及芳香撲鼻賣著花的推車營造出一股獨一無二的巴黎氛圍。巴黎匯集了多種文化，在所有法國城市中獨樹一格。從北非到東南亞的文化都可在城裡許多露天市集中發現。在巴黎，生活本身就是藝術。

幾天後，我的探險旅程接近尾聲，我的包包也變得更重。它們裝滿了新衣服和紀念品。我的朋友們幫我將行李送到機場。離別儘管感傷，但我想到滿載而歸的美好回憶就不禁微笑起來。短暫停留期間，巴黎讓我收穫良多：藝術、歷史、友誼、甚至是浪漫邂逅。喬瑟在我臉頰上輕吻後揮手道別。我還會再回來的。

1. **take sb's breath away**　因驚訝、美麗而喘不過氣

   此片語用來強調某事物極為漂亮或令人大感吃驚。

   同義 leave sb breathless

   - The sunset was so beautiful that it took my breath away.
     夕陽美得令我屏息。

2. **be home to N.**　（某地）擁有……；是……的所在地

   此片語字面意思為「是……的家園」，可譯為「（某地）擁有……；是……的所在地」，可用來指某人居住或出生的房子、城鎮或國家，或用來強調說話者認為某事物是屬於此地，home 在此作不可數名詞用。

   - The island is home to a number of rare birds and plants.
     這座島有一些稀有的鳥類和植物。

3. **as if to say**　好像在說

   as if to say 是由 as if she wanted to say 省略而來，as if 在此作連接詞用，與 as though 意思相同，表示「彷彿；好像」的意思。

   - The man frowned, as if to say that he wasn't going to be able to help us out at all.
     男子皺起眉，好像是在說他無法幫我們任何忙。

4. **leave . . . behind**　將……丟下；遺留下……

   一般會把受詞放在 behind 後面，或移到 leave 和 behind 之間，受詞為代名詞時只能放在中間。

   - I think I left my hat behind at your house, so please give me a call if you find it.
     我想我把帽子留在你家了，如果你找到請打電話給我。

   - If you go out with your friends tonight, don't leave your little brother behind alone at home.
     如果你今晚要和朋友出去，不要把弟弟一個人留在家。

5. **be loaded with**　載滿了……；裝滿了……

   load 可作動詞，表示「使充滿；裝載」。表示「A 裡面充滿、裝滿了 B」的句型為 A + be loaded with + B。

   - Jenny's laptop is loaded with movies to watch on the plane.
     珍妮的筆電裡裝滿了要在飛機上看的電影。

補充 表示「某人在 A 中裝滿了 B」，則用 S. + load + A + with B。

- Jenny loaded her laptop with movies to watch on the plane.
  珍妮在她的筆電裡裝滿要在飛機上看的影片。

Sentence Patterns

主詞補語　　　　　　　　修飾主詞 the Seine River

* <u>Next to us</u> was the Seine River, which divides the city.

本句為主詞補語提前的倒裝句。主詞補語如 V-ing、p.p. 或介系詞片語移至句首時，主詞與動詞必須倒裝，且主詞與動詞的單複數需一致。

- Written on the wall was a message, which warned us not to open the door.
  牆上寫了個訊息，警告我們別開那扇門。

* Although sad to leave, I was able to smile about the great memories I was taking home with me.

本句可還原成：Although I was sad to leave, I was able to smile . . .

句型 Although/Though + S. + be + adj., S. + V.
Although/Though + adj., S. + V.

although/though 所引導的副詞子句與主要子句的主詞相同時，可省略副詞子句中的主詞與 be 動詞。

- Although I was happy to win the award, I refused to smile onstage.
= Although happy to win the award, I refused to smile onstage.
  雖然很高興贏得獎項，我仍拒絕在台上展露笑容。

The Spirit of Santorini

Set in the southern Aegean Sea, Santorini offers travelers the quintessential[1] Greek island experience. Filled with whitewashed[2] villages and famous blue-domed[3] churches, the island draws visitors in to walk the ancient streets that are paved with stones. The stunning sea views and dramatic cliff[4] faces make Santorini a must-see on any traveler's wish list.

The island offers a host of attractions for visitors. For those interested in history, Santorini has several archaeological[5] sites to visit. Black-sand beaches await those who just want to kick back and relax. The quaint[6] villages around the island have windmills, art galleries, and plenty of great places to get lost while exploring.

聖托里尼北端的依亞鎮擁有世界最美麗的落日

聖托里尼小檔案

位在希臘東南方二百公里的愛琴海（Aegean Sea）上的聖托里尼由火山環組成，在西元前三千六百多年時曾發生大爆發，考古學家推測這間接促成了克里特島（Crete）上米諾斯（Minoan）文明的滅亡。聖托里尼目前人口約一萬五千人，本島是弦月形的狹長島嶼，藍白相間的房屋和白色風車伴著綿延不絕的海景，構成浪漫滿點的絕美畫面。

Vocabulary

1. **quintessential** [͵kwɪntə`sɛnʃəl] *adj.* 精華的；典型的
2. **whitewash** [`hwaɪt͵waʃ] *v.* 粉刷成白色（文中 whitewashed 為過去分詞作形容詞用，指「刷白的」）
3. **dome** [dom] *n.* 圓頂；穹頂
4. **cliff** [klɪf] *n.* 懸崖；峭壁
5. **archaeological** [͵ɑrkɪə`lɑgɪkəl] *adj.* 考古學的
6. **quaint** [kwent] *adj.* 古色古香的

155

Some people love Santorini so much that they decide to get married there. The island is also a popular destination[7] for honeymooners from around the world. Wherever you go in Santorini, love seems to be in the air. The beauty of the surroundings[8] only adds to the romance.

Santorini serves up some excellent cuisine as well. Thanks to the island's volcanic[9] soil, the cherry tomatoes grown there are said to be the tastiest in the Mediterranean. Santorini is also famous for its wine, known to be the best in Greece, and visitors can stop by the local vineyards[10] for free samples.

依亞鎮的鐘台讓人有種和諧的寧靜感

Santorini wasn't always so serene.[11] It was once the site of one of the largest volcanic eruptions[12] in recorded history, some 3,600 years ago. A later eruption in 1866 became part of the world's literature when it was witnessed by Captain Nemo and his crew in the novel *Twenty Thousand Leagues*[13] *under the Sea*. Fortunately for visitors today, the last volcanic eruption on Santorini occurred in 1950, and the volcano has been quiet

Vocabulary

7. **destination** [ˌdɛstəˈneʃən] *n.* 目的地
8. **surroundings** [səˈraʊndɪŋz] *n.* 環境（恆用複數）
9. **volcanic** [vɔlˈkænɪk] *adj.* 火山的
10. **vineyard** [ˈvɪnjəd] *n.* 葡萄園
11. **serene** [səˈrin] *adj.* 寧靜的
12. **eruption** [ɪˈrʌpʃən] *n.*（火山）爆發
13. **league** [lig] *n.* 里格（古長度單位，一里格約 3.9 到 7.4 公里之間）；聯盟

聖托里尼的錫拉夏島（Thirasia）
圖片 / Flickr: lyng883

since then. The adventurous can climb the volcano and even take a dip in the natural hot springs found there.

*As a result of all this volcanic activity, the main island of Santorini is crescent[14] shaped, with a string of smaller islands forming a circle nearby. This unique layout[15] provides for unlimited vistas[16] and spectacular sunsets. Most visitors head to the village of Oia in northern Santorini to take in an uninterrupted[17] view of the sun as it slowly sinks below the horizon. Sunset has become a social activity of sorts in Santorini, with photographers snapping away as others enjoy sundowners[18] or a special dinner on a terrace[19] against this wonderful backdrop.[20]

Santorini is a very special place that will leave you with wonderful romantic memories. This Aegean gem[21] born of a volcano awaits all those who are lucky enough to visit.

Vocabulary

14. **crescent** [ˈkrɛsn̩t] *n.* 新月;弦月
    （crescent shaped 意為「弦月形的」）
15. **layout** [ˈleˌaʊt] *n.* 安排;設計;佈局
16. **vista** [ˈvɪstə] *n.* 景觀;前景
17. **uninterrupted** [ˌʌnˌɪntəˈrʌptəd] *adj.* 不被中斷的;
    （景色）一望無際的、一覽無遺的
18. **sundowner** [ˈsʌnˌdaʊnɚ] *n.* 日落小酌（英式口語）
19. **terrace** [ˈtɛrəs] *n.* 露天平台;梯田
20. **backdrop** [ˈbækˌdrɑp] *n.* 背景;襯托
21. **gem** [dʒɛm] *n.* 寶石;珍品

【從旅遊看文化】

希臘（Greek）禁止女性遊客參觀古蹟（ancient site）時穿著細跟高跟鞋（stiletto heels），因為細跟鞋的壓力集中在一個點，可能會讓古蹟的地面造成損害。不過，觀光旅遊時當然還是穿著舒適好走的鞋比較適合。

聖托里尼——美景佳餚的浪漫邂逅

聖托里尼島坐落於在愛琴海南端，帶給遊客們經典的希臘島嶼體驗。這座島上遍布著粉刷上白牆的村落和著名的藍色圓頂教堂，吸引遊客走進舖滿石子的古老街道。絕美的海景和斷崖絕壁讓聖托里尼成為所有旅人夢想清單上的必遊之處。

這座島嶼提供遊客許多景點。對那些對歷史感興趣的人來說，聖托里尼有一些考古地點可去參觀。黑沙海灘等著那些只想要好好放鬆休息的人造訪。全島各處的古樸村莊裡有風車、藝廊，還有許多讓你探訪時會流連忘返的好地方。

有些人非常喜愛聖托里尼，甚至決定在那裡完成終身大事。此島也是世人的熱門蜜月地點。在聖托里尼，無論你走到哪裡，空氣中似乎都瀰漫著愛情。周遭的美景只是增添浪漫氣息。

聖托里尼也有一些美味的佳餚款待你。多虧島上的火山土壤，那裡種植的櫻桃番茄據說是全地中海最甜美的。聖托里尼同時也以希臘最棒的葡萄酒聞名，遊客們可以到當地的葡萄園免費試飲。

聖托里尼並非總是如此寧靜。這裡在大約三千六百年前，曾是史上其中一處規模最大的火山爆發地點。近期一八六六年的爆發成了世界文學《海底兩萬浬》小說中尼莫船長和船員們親眼目睹的事件。對現今遊客來說幸運的是，聖托里尼島最後一次的火山爆發發生在一九五〇年，而火山在那之後就平靜了下來。愛探險的人可以攀爬火山，甚至泡一泡當地的天然溫泉。

由於火山活動的結果，聖托里尼的主要島嶼為弦月形狀，周圍還有一串較小的島嶼環繞著。這種獨特的分布造就了美不勝收的景色以及壯觀的落日餘暉。多數遊客會前往聖托里尼北部的依亞鎮，欣賞太陽緩緩落入海平面時，一望無際的美景。觀賞夕照在聖托里尼已算是社交活動，攝影師們不斷按下快門、其他人則是在這樣美麗的背景襯托下，於露天平台上享受「日落小酌」或是來頓特別的晚餐。

聖托里尼是個極為特別的地方，能留給你浪漫美好的回憶。這顆火山形成的愛琴海寶石等著那些幸運兒到此一遊。

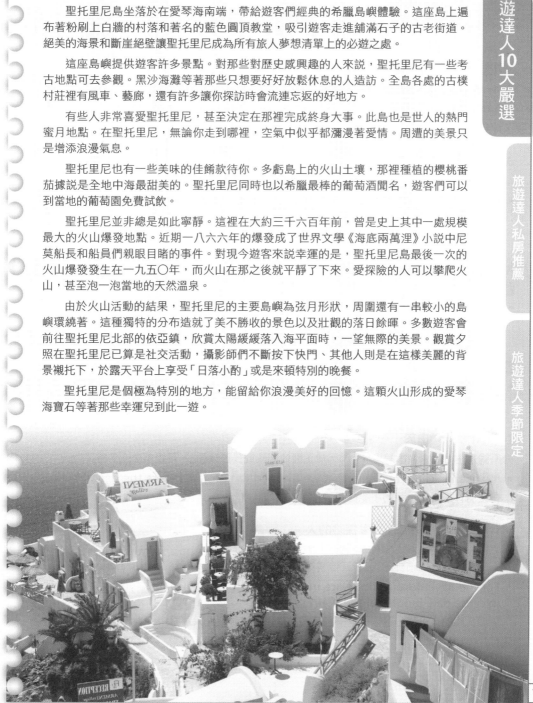

島上居民在貧瘠的山坡上建造了一棟棟美麗的房子，彩色圖騰與鮮豔的花朵交織成一片美麗的景象。

1. **draw in** 吸引；使參與

   用法 draw sb in, draw in sb

   draw in 作及物動詞時，表示「使某人參與、捲入；吸引某人」的意思。

   - A good storyteller can draw in listeners with the power of his voice.
     一個很會講故事的人，可以用他聲音的力量來吸引聽眾。

2. **a host of** 許多；大量的

   host 在此作名詞，指「大量」，a host of 後面接可數複數名詞。

   - When the man went to get tested at the clinic, he was found to have a host of diseases.
     男子到診所接受檢查時，他被診斷出有許多疾病。

3. **kick back** 放鬆

   同義 take it easy

   - Jason just wants to kick back this weekend, so I doubt he'll want to go on a hike with us.
     傑森這個週末只想要休息，所以我懷疑他會想要跟我們一起去爬山。

   補充 kickback 回扣

   - The buyer at the company demanded that its suppliers pay him a kickback.
     該公司的採購人員向供貨商要求回扣。

4. **thanks to** 由於……；多虧……

   介系詞片語 thanks to 常用於「歸因於正面的因素或表達感謝」，可置句中或句首。

   - It was thanks to your help that we finished the project before the deadline.
     由於有你的幫忙，我們才能在期限內完成這項計畫。

5. **the adventurous** 愛探險的人

   用法 the + adj. 表示「代表具有此形容詞特性的全體」，故 the adventurous 表示「具有冒險精神的人」，其他常見的用法包括 the rich（富人）、the poor（窮人）。

   - For the adventurous, there are many hiking trails that will take you deep into the dark jungles of the country.
     對愛探險的人來說，這個國家有許多登山步道可以帶你深入叢林中。

6. **N. + of sorts** 勉強稱得上的……；算是……

[同義] N. + of a sort

- Watching football on television on Thanksgiving Day is a tradition of sorts in the United States.
  在感恩節看美式足球賽的電視轉播在美國算是一項傳統。

Sentence Patterns

* **As a result of all this volcanic activity, the main island of Santorini is crescent shaped, with a string of smaller islands forming a circle nearby.**

[句型] with + O. + O.C.

此用法用來表示主詞或主要子句的附帶狀況，通常與主要子句之間有逗號隔開。受詞補語可以是 V-ing（與受詞的關係為主動，如本句的 forming）、p.p.（與受詞的關係為被動）、形容詞或介系詞片語。

- With the storm quickly approaching, the campers looked for shelter.
  由於暴風雨迅速接近，那些露營的人尋找遮蔽處。
- Alex showed up to class with his hair still wet from swimming.
  艾力克斯游完泳後，頭髮還是濕的就來上課。

[片語] as a result of + N./V-ing 由於……；因為……

- As a result of drinking and driving, James was injured in a car accident.
  由於酒駕，詹姆士出車禍受傷了。

A Rome Holiday

　　We've all heard the phrase, "When in Rome, do as the Romans do." What better advice could there be for anyone taking a vacation there? If you're traveling to the city known as Roma to its residents,[1] become a temporary Roman—do as the locals do, and you'll fall in love with this fascinating[2] city.

巴洛克風格的羅馬建築

羅馬的西班牙台階（Spanish Steps）是歐洲最長且最寬的階梯，與西班牙廣場相連接，階梯頂端為山上天主聖三教堂（Trinità dei Monti）。

When in Rome . . . Feast[3]

Food is something near and dear to the hearts of all Italians, and Romans say that their cuisine is the best in all of Italy. Keep in mind that most restaurants in Rome don't even open for dinner until after 7 p.m., and locals often sit down to eat around 9 p.m. While pasta is certainly an Italian dish, it'll probably just be the first course. Your second course might be grilled scampi, abbacchio (roast lamb), or even a crispy fried artichoke. Remember to save room for a heavenly[4] dessert, such as tiramisu.

If your stomach starts to rumble[5] before dinner, go for a gelato. This is ice cream, Italian style. The owner of my favorite gelateria[6] in Rome is fiercely[7] proud of his gelato, and he allows no cones or toppings at his shop. Customers simply get a spoon, a paper cup, and a scoop of the best gelato in the world. Who could ask for more?

種類豐富、口味綿密的義式冰淇淋（gelato）

Vocabulary

1. **resident** [ˈrɛzədənt] *n.* 居民
2. **fascinating** [ˈfæsəˌnetɪŋ] *adj.* 迷人的
3. **feast** [fist] *v.* 盡情享用
4. **heavenly** [ˈhɛvənli] *adj.* 極好的；天堂般的
5. **rumble** [ˈrʌmbəl] *v.* 隆隆作響
6. **gelateria** [ˌdʒɛlɑˌtɛˈrɪɑ] *n.* 【義】冰淇淋店
7. **fiercely** [ˈfɪrsli] *adv.* 猛烈地；極度地

When in Rome . . . Roam[8]

I like exploring Rome on foot because you never know what you'll see next. Once I turned a corner and came face-to-face with the two-thousand-year-old Colosseum. Though it was originally built in AD 70 to seat 50,000 spectators,[9] this ancient amphitheater[10] was almost empty the day I explored it. *I couldn't help but think of *Gladiator* and imagine myself doing battle in front of a roaring crowd.

西斯汀禮拜堂（Sistine Chapel）內的壁畫：創造亞當

Another time I explored the Pantheon. It is Rome's best preserved[11] classical building, and I lost myself in its beauty. Constructed[12] in AD 125 as a temple to the Roman gods, the Pantheon has been a Christian church since the seventh century. It remains as spectacular[13] today as when it was first built.

納佛那廣場（Piazza Navona）

羅馬競技場（Colosseum）

Vocabulary

8. **roam** [rom] *v.* 漫遊；遊蕩
9. **spectator** [ˋspɛkˏtetɚ] *n.* 觀眾
10. **amphitheater** [ˋæmfəˏθiətɚ] *n.* 競技場；圓形露天劇場
11. **preserve** [prɪˋzɝv] *v.* 維護；保存
12. **construct** [kənˋstrʌkt] *v.* 建造
13. **spectacular** [spɛkˋtækjəlɚ] *adj.* 壯觀的；精彩的

義大利美食小辭典

Main Courses

pasta [ˋpɑstə] 義大利通心麵
grilled scampi [grɪld] [ˋskæmpi] 烤蝦
abbacchio [ɑˋbɑkjo] 【義】香烤小羊排
fried artichoke [fraɪd] [ˋɑrtəˏtʃok] 炸朝鮮薊

Desserts And Drinks

tiramisu [ˏtɪrəˋmisu] 【義】提拉米蘇
gelato [dʒɛˋlɑto] 【義】冰淇淋
cappuccino [ˏkæpəˋtʃino] 卡布奇諾咖啡
espresso [ɛˋsprɛso] 義式濃縮咖啡

As you stroll[14] through Rome's streets, however, stay alert.[15] The traffic is chaotic,[16] the drivers are aggressive,[17] and the scooters are everywhere. Always be ready to dodge a buzzing Vespa!

The best way to remain on your toes is to take frequent coffee breaks. Grab a table at one of the cafés lining a public square, like the Piazza Navona. Here, you are actually sitting on history, since this piazza was built on the site of a first-century stadium. Just remember that cappuccino is a breakfast drink in Rome, so order an espresso instead.

When in Rome . . . Reflect[18]

I once spent an afternoon in Rome sitting on the Spanish Steps and soaking up the atmosphere[19] by watching people. One thing I noticed was how well dressed all the locals were, and it made me feel seriously underdressed[20] in my jeans and T-shirt. So, dress up a bit, or do a little shopping for the latest Italian fashions.

萬神殿（Pantheon）大廳上方的穹頂

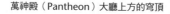

Vocabulary

14. **stroll** [strol] *v.* 散步；閒逛
15. **alert** [əˋlɝt] *adj.* 警覺的
16. **chaotic** [keˋɑtɪk] *adj.* 混亂的
17. **aggressive** [əˋgrɛsɪv] *adj.* 挑釁的；有進取心的
18. **reflect** [rɪˋflɛkt] *v.* 沈思；反省；反射
19. **atmosphere** [ˋætməˏsfɪr] *n.* 氣氛；大氣
20. **underdress** [ˏʌndəˋdrɛs] *v.* 過於簡樸地打扮

聖天使堡（Castel Sant'Angelo）入口有十二座天使雕像

Since religion plays an important role in daily life in Rome, a visit to the Vatican is a must. The Vatican is actually a separate country and is the government capital of the Catholic[21] Church. Walking through Saint Peter's Basilica, I thought of its importance to the one billion Catholics worldwide. Inside the Sistine Chapel, I was fascinated by the beautiful ceiling painting that Michelangelo completed in 1512. I spent much of my time just gazing[22] at *The Creation of Adam*.

I must admit that there is one touristy[23] thing I do whenever I'm in Rome. On my last day in the city, I always throw a coin into Trevi Fountain. Legend has it that by doing this, a visitor is sure to return someday. *While I'm not superstitious,[24] Rome is an incredible[25] city that is worth visiting again and again. I figure, why take any chances?

特萊維噴泉（Trevi Fountain）

聖彼得大教堂（Saint Peter's Basilica）

【從旅遊看文化】

你想品嚐義式冰淇淋（gelato）的美味嗎？但千萬不要邊走邊吃！因為羅馬、佛羅倫斯（Florence）和威尼斯（Venice）都立法禁止觀光客在歷史遺跡（monument）附近飲食。如果被抓到，你可能必須付一筆鉅額罰款（a heavy fine）。還有，在威尼斯也禁止餵食鴿子（pigeon）以減少這些鳥類的數量。因為鴿子如果在脆弱的建築物上築巢，他們的爪子和排泄物（droppings）容易損壞建築物的表面。

Vocabulary

21. **Catholic** [ˋkæθlɪk] *adj., n.*
    天主教的；天主教徒
22. **gaze** [gez] *v.* 凝視
23. **touristy** [ˋturəsti] *adj.* 觀光客喜歡的
24. **superstitious** [͵supəˋstɪʃəs] *adj.* 迷信的
25. **incredible** [ɪnˋkrɛdəbəl] *adj.* 不可置信的；美妙極的

羅馬假期

大家都聽過「入境隨俗」這句話。對到居羅馬度假的人來說，還有什麼比這個更好的建議呢？如果你到這個當地人稱 Roma 的城市旅遊——就入境隨俗暫且當個羅馬人吧，你會愛上這個迷人的城市的。

置身羅馬……大快朵頤

美食是所有義大利人最重視的事，而羅馬人宣稱其美食是全義大利最棒的。記住，羅馬大部分的餐館都在晚間七點之後才開始供應晚餐，而且當地人通常到九點左右才入座用餐。雖然義大利麵是正統的義式料理，但它或許只是第一道菜而已。第二道菜可能是烤蝦、香煎小羊肉，或甚至是酥脆的炸朝鮮薊。記得留點肚子吃點有如天上佳肴的甜點，像是提拉米蘇。

如果晚餐前你的肚子已開始咕嚕咕嚕叫，就去嚐點「吉拉多」吧。這是義式冰淇淋。我在羅馬最喜歡的冰淇淋店的老闆對自家冰淇淋可是相當自豪，他的店裡不提供甜筒或在上面加料。客人只會有湯匙、紙杯，以及一球人間極品的冰淇淋。有此美味夫復何求？

置身羅馬……恣意漫遊

我喜歡走路探訪羅馬，因為你永遠不會知道接下來映入眼簾的會是什麼。有一次我在拐了個彎後，出現在眼前的是有兩千年歷史的「羅馬競技場」。儘管在西元七〇年建造時可容納五萬名觀眾，這個古代競技場在我參觀當天卻幾乎空無一人。我不禁想起了電影《神鬼戰士》，想像自己在鼓譟的群眾面前浴血奮戰。

還有一次我參訪了「萬神殿」。這是羅馬保存最完善的古典建築，美得令人渾然忘我。建於西元一二五年的萬神殿是祭祀羅馬諸神的神廟，從第七世紀後已成為基督教教堂。直至今日它仍保留了當初建造時的磅礡面貌。

然而，漫步羅馬街頭時，要提高警覺。這裡的交通混亂，駕駛人橫衝直撞，而且到處都是摩托車。隨時都要準備好閃避疾馳而過的偉士牌機車！

維持體力的最佳方式是時常停下來休息喝杯咖啡，在「納佛那廣場」這樣的露天廣場周邊選一家咖啡店找張桌子。這個廣場建於西元一世紀的競技場遺跡之上，所以在此，你其實已融入歷史之中。不過要記得卡布其諾咖啡在羅馬是早餐飲品，所以改點義式濃縮咖啡吧。

置身羅馬……沈思回想

我曾經在羅馬花了一個下午坐在「西班牙階梯」上，看著來往人群，沈浸在那樣的氛圍中。我注意到當地人打扮入時，反而是我這身牛仔褲與 T 恤打扮太隨便。所以，稍作打扮，或是逛街買點義大利最新流行精品。

既然宗教在羅馬日常生活中扮演重要角色，那麼「梵諦岡」便絕不能錯過。梵諦岡實際上是另一個國家，而且是天主教教廷的首府。走進聖彼得大教堂，我想起了它在全世界十億天主教徒心中的份量。在「西斯汀禮拜堂」裡，米開朗基羅在一五一二年所完成的美麗天井畫令我深深著迷，光是《創造亞當》這幅作品我就凝視了許久。

我得承認每當造訪羅馬時，我會做一件觀光客會做的事。在羅馬的最後一天，我總會丟一枚硬幣進「許願池」裡。傳說遊客這麼做的話，將來一定會再回到羅馬。儘管我不是那麼迷信，但羅馬的確是個值得一遊再遊的迷人城市。所以我想，何不一試？

1. **near and dear** 深得人心的；極重要的

near and dear 也可形容「關係密切的」，如 my near and dear friend。

- The Queen of England is near and dear to the hearts of the British.
  英國女王深得英國民心。

2. **lose oneself in . . .** 迷失在……；忘情於……

此用法表示「沈浸在……（某種氣氛、情緒等）中；因某事而忘我」。

同義 be lost in . . .

- Lisa lost herself in a romance novel and ended up reading until well past midnight.
  莉莎沈浸在言情小說當中，結果一直看到深夜。

3. **on one's toes** 有警覺的；機敏的

on one's toes 有一說是源自賽跑時踮起腳尖準備聽到槍聲就起跑，常搭配 keep、remain、stay 等動詞。

- To avoid accidents, drivers always have to stay on their toes.
  駕駛人必須時時保持警覺以免發生車禍。

4. **a must** 必須做的事；不可缺少的事物

sth is a must 是口語用法，must 作名詞用，表示「必要的事物；必須做的事」。

- For most people in the United States, owning a car is a must.
  對大部分住在美國的人來說，擁有一部車是必要的。

5. **legend has it that** 傳說……

在此句型中，it 為 has 的虛受詞，真正的受詞為 that 子句。類似的用法還有：

句型 Rumor has it + that 子句　謠傳……

　　　Tradition has it + that 子句　有……的傳統

　　　Word has it + that 子句　傳言……

- Legend has it that on moonlit nights, ghosts walk the halls of the castle.
  傳說在月夜裡鬼魂會在城堡的走廊上四處徘徊。

Sentence Patterns

* **I couldn't help but think of** *Gladiator* **and imagine myself doing battle in front of a roaring crowd.**

   句型 can't (help) but + V.
   　　　不得不；必然

   亦可寫作 cannot (help) but、could not (help) but，but 之後接原形動詞。

   * We couldn't help but hear our neighbors yelling at each other.
     我們迫不得已聽著鄰居在吵架。

   句型 imagine + (sb/oneself) + V-ing
   　　　imagine + that 子句 /wh- 子句
   　　　想像……

   * Margaret imagined herself living as a princess in a beautiful castle.
     瑪格莉特想像自己是住在美麗城堡裡的公主。

   * Can you imagine how Sarah must have felt when she found out her dog had been hit by a car?
     你可以想像莎拉知道她的狗被車撞後會有什麼反應嗎？

* **While I'm not superstitious, Rome is an incredible city that is worth visiting again and again.**

   用法 be worth N./V-ing　值得

   * Skiing is a fun sport that is worth a try /trying if you get the chance.
     如果有機會，滑雪是值得嘗試、好玩的運動。

   延伸學習 ▶ 表示「值得、配得上」還有以下常見用法：

   be worthy $\begin{cases} \text{of N./V-ing} \\ \text{to + V.} \end{cases}$

   * Stanley is worthy of respect because he is one of the most honest people I know.
     史丹利值得尊敬，因為他是我認識的人之中最誠實的其中一個。

   * The brave soldier was worthy to lead the other soldiers into battle.
     這名英勇的軍人領導其他士兵上戰場當之無愧。

Dreaming of Spain

What do Hemingway, Picasso, and Gaudí have in common? Spain! I'm a fan of all three people, and a trip to Spain became one of my life goals.

After years of planning, I finally began my dream trip in Pamplona, Spain. Every July 6, this town's streets become dangerous when the San Fermín festival combines[1] the running of the bulls, made famous in a Hemingway novel, with fireworks[2] and food. I joined in one local tradition by sampling tapas. These are small dishes that come in an endless variety, but my favorite was a plate of olives[3] and salty cheese. When I was invited to run with the bulls, though, I politely declined.[4] Those more courageous[5] than I stood in the street dressed in red. Then, twenty bulls charged around the corner, and runners fell beneath their hooves. I was glad I was sitting out this tradition.

奎爾公園（Park Güell）內的高第住宅博物館（Casa Museu Gaudí） 圖片 / Wikipedia: Jordiferrer

巴特婁之家（Casa Batlló）造型特殊，又稱「骨頭之家」 圖片 / Flickr: Francisco Diez

Vocabulary

1. **combine** [kəm`baɪn] *v.* 結合
2. **firework** [`faɪrˌwɜk] *n.* 煙火（作此義時常用複數形）
3. **olive** [`ɑlɪv] *n.* 橄欖
4. **decline** [dɪ`klaɪn] *v.* 婉拒；減少
5. **courageous** [kə`redʒəs] *adj.* 勇敢的；英勇的

171

【從旅遊看文化】

位於巴塞隆納的聖家堂
（Sagrada Família）是高第最著
名的作品，也是全球唯一未完工便
列入世界遺產（heritage）的建
築，動工至今已逾一百年，目
前仍在興建中。

蘇菲亞美術館（Reina Sofía Museum）前兩座設計感十足的透明電梯　圖片 / Wikipedia: Luis García

After Pamplona's insanity,[6] I headed to Madrid. In the quiet Reina Sofía Museum, I marveled[7] at Picasso's paintings, including the famous antiwar *Guernica*. Following Picasso's footsteps, I also visited the Prado Museum to view the art that had inspired[8] him. My Madrid Card allowed access to over fifty museums, so I also learned about the history of the city and walked the halls of a real palace.

Flamenco drew me to Granada in the south. A week of dance lessons showed me how challenging and tiring the flamenco rhythm[9] can be. However, the passionate guitar music kept drawing me to my feet to dance "just one more song."

Vocabulary

6. **insanity** [ɪnˋsænəti] *n.* 瘋狂
7. **marvel** [ˋmɑrvəl] *v.* 對……感到驚異
8. **inspire** [ɪnˋspaɪr] *v.* 賦予……靈感；激勵
9. **rhythm** [ˋrɪðəm] *n.* 節奏；節拍

聖佛明節每年吸引許多冒險愛好者
圖片 / Wikipedia: budgetplace

173

Saying good-bye to my classmates, I headed to Buñol for La Tomatina festival. Locals covered their shop fronts with plastic sheets while trucks loaded with tomatoes pulled into town. By 11:00 a.m., I was standing in a red river, covered in slime,[10] and throwing tomatoes as hard as I could! At the end, I made friends with my former targets, and they hosed me down on my way out of town.

Finally, it was time to pay tribute[11] to the imaginative[12] architect Gaudí in Barcelona. Inspired by nature, Gaudí used curved[13] stone, twisted sculptures, and colorful mosaics to make the city magical. My favorite, Casa Batlló, looks like an organic[14] creature covered in scales.[15] *Its bone-like pillars,[16] oval windows, and wavy[17] walls assured me that there are no straight lines in this building.

*While I was sitting on Barcelona's beach on my final night in Spain, a local insisted on buying me a drink. I realized that what made my journey so memorable[18] wasn't just the colorful culture. It was also the generous hospitality[19] of the people in Spain.

【從旅遊看文化】

西班牙人的作息時間很特別，午餐是中午兩點到三點之間，晚餐則是九點到十點。有時晚餐後還會續攤到酒吧（bar）喝點小酒。如果是週末，大家就會玩到半夜或隔日清晨才回家。

Vocabulary

10. **slime** [slaɪm] *n.* 爛泥（在文中指「番茄糊」）

11. **tribute** [ˈtrɪbjut] *n.* 敬意；尊崇

12. **imaginative** [ɪˈmædʒnətɪv] *adj.* 有想像力的

13. **curved** [kɜvd] *adj.* 彎曲的

14. **organic** [ɔrˈgænɪk] *adj.* 有機體的；生物的

15. **scale** [skel] *n.* （魚或爬蟲類動物的）鱗片

16. **pillar** [ˈpɪlə] *n.* 柱子

17. **wavy** [ˈwevi] *adj.* 波浪狀的

18. **memorable** [ˈmɛmərəbəl] *adj.* 難忘的；值得懷念的

19. **hospitality** [ˌhɑspɪˈtæləti] *n.* 好客；殷勤招待

布紐爾（Buñol）番茄節　■片 / Wikipedia: Graham McLellan

就愛西班牙

　　海明威、畢卡索和高第的共同點是什麼？就是西班牙！我很喜歡這三個人，去西班牙旅行也成了我畢生的目標之一。

　　經過多年的計畫，我終於在西班牙的潘普隆納展開我的夢想之旅。每年七月六日，在結合因海明威小説而出名的奔牛活動及煙火、佳餚的聖佛明節期間，這個市鎮的街道變得很危險。我品嚐西班牙的餐前小菜參與一項當地的傳統習俗。這些小菜的種類千變萬化，但我最愛的是一盤橄欖配鹹起司。不過當有人邀我與牛群一同奔跑時，我禮貌地拒絕了。那些比我有勇氣的人穿著紅色衣物站在街上。接著，二十隻公牛從街角衝出來，然後奔跑的人倒在牠們蹄下。我很慶幸我沒參加這項傳統。

　　體驗完潘普隆納的瘋狂後，我前往馬德里。在寧靜的蘇菲亞美術館裡，我對畢卡索的畫作讚嘆不已，包含知名的反戰作品《格爾尼卡》。我跟著畢卡索的腳步，也參觀了普拉多博物館，欣賞曾帶給他靈感的藝術品。我的馬德里卡讓我通行五十多座博物館，所以我也了解了這座城市的歷史，以及走過一座真正的皇宮大廳。

　　佛朗明哥吸引我到南邊的格拉納達。一個禮拜的舞蹈課讓我見識到佛朗明哥舞的節奏多麼有挑戰性和有多累。然而，熱情奔放的吉他音樂讓我的雙腳忍不住一首接一首地跳下去。

　　向同學們道別後，我為了要體驗番茄節而前往布紐爾。在一輛輛滿載番茄的卡車駛入小鎮時，當地人用塑膠布蓋住店面。到了早上十一點，我站在一條鮮紅的河流中，渾身都是番茄糊，並且使盡力氣丟著番茄！最後，我和剛剛的攻擊目標成了朋友，在我離開小鎮時，他們還用水管幫我沖洗。

　　最後，要向巴塞隆納這位想像力豐富的建築師高第致敬了。高第的靈感來自大自然，他用彎曲的石頭、扭曲的雕塑和色彩繽紛的鑲嵌圖案讓這座城市充滿魔力。我最愛的巴特婁之家看起來就像一隻佈滿鱗片的有機生物。其骨頭造型的柱子、橢圓形的窗戶和波浪狀的牆壁使我確信這棟建築裡面一條直線也沒有。

　　我在西班牙的最後一夜坐在巴塞隆納沙灘上時，一個當地人堅持要請我喝一杯。我瞭解到讓這趟旅程如此令人難忘的不只是多采多姿的文化，還有就是西班牙人的慷慨好客。

畢卡索的知名反戰作品《格爾尼卡》　　圖片 / Flickr: ahisgett

175

1. have . . . in common 有……共同點

要表示「A 和 B 有……共同點」，用法為 A and B have . . . in common。中間的字詞可依程度不同代換如下：

have +	much / a lot	in common	有很多共同點
	something		有一些共同點
	little		幾乎沒有共同點
	nothing		完全沒有共同點

- Sarah and my brother have a lot in common.
  莎拉和我哥哥有很多共同點。

說明 也可寫成 A have . . . in common with B。

- I have little in common with Jane, so we don't have much to talk about.
  我和珍幾乎沒有共同點，所以我們能聊的話題不多。

2. sit out 不參加、暫停（某項活動）

sit out 有兩個意思，本文指的是「不參加或暫停（某項活動）」，另一個則是待在某處等待某件不愉快或無聊的事情結束。

- I am too tired to continue dancing, so I am going to sit this song out.
  我太累了無法繼續跳舞，所以這首歌我就不跳了。

3. anti- 作字首

anti- 作字首時有「反對；抵抗」的意思，常與名詞或形容詞結合，常用字如下：

anti +	aging	老化	=	antiaging	抗老化（的）
	crime	犯罪	=	anticrime	反犯罪（的）
	flu	流感	=	antiflu	抗流感（的）
	shock	震動	=	antishock	避震（的）
	virus	病毒	=	antivirus	防病毒（的）

- The city government is putting some anticrime measures into place to improve safety in the city.
  市政府正在實施一些防止犯罪措施以改善城市的安全。

- I am feeling very sick, so the antiflu medicine doesn't seem to help.
  我覺得很不舒服，所以這種抗流感藥物似乎沒有幫助。

* **Its bone-like pillars, oval windows, and wavy walls** assured **me that there are no straight lines in this building.**

assure 指「（向人）擔保；（使人）安心」時，常用句型為：

$$\text{assure} + \text{sb} + \begin{cases} \text{(that) S.} + \text{V.} \\ \text{of sth} \end{cases} \quad \text{向某人擔保某事}$$

• The salesman assured me that the camera is easy to use.
銷售員向我保證這台相機很容易使用。

• Jenny assured me of her interest in helping decorate for the school dance.
珍妮向我擔保她對幫忙布置學校舞會很有興趣。

補充 assure 指「確保」時，受詞為事物。

• Marcus carefully read over the essay to assure its accuracy.
馬可仕仔細讀過這篇論文以確保其正確性。

* **While I was sitting on Barcelona's beach on my final night in Spain, a local** insisted on buying me a drink.

動詞 insist 常用於強烈要求某人做某事，表示「堅持要求做某事」，句型為：

$$\text{insist} + \begin{cases} \text{on N./V-ing} \\ \text{that S. (should)} + \text{V.} \quad \boxed{\text{常省略}} \end{cases}$$

• Gertrude insisted on wearing her new shoes even though they hurt her feet.
即使新鞋會弄傷葛楚德的腳，她還是堅持要穿。

• Maggie's parents insisted that she do something useful during her summer vacation.
瑪姬的父母堅持要她在暑假做些有益的事。

$\boxed{\text{do 前面省略 should，所以恆用原形動詞}}$

補充 insist that S. + V. 還可指「堅稱……」，此時子句的動詞須隨句意作時態變化。

• Julia insisted that she locked the door.
茱莉亞堅稱她鎖了門。

布拉格的舊城廣場（Old Town Square）仍保有十四世紀的建築風格。位於舊城廣場前面的單尖塔建築即為舊城市政廳
（Old Town City Hall）。 圖片／捷克觀光局

6. 漫步布拉格，恣意想像

PLAY ALL   TRACK 42

Prague: Where Imagination Comes Alive

When I first set foot in Prague, I felt as if I had stumbled[1] into a fairy tale. This feeling isn't unusual because Prague is one of the few cities in Europe that escaped extensive[2] bomb damage during World War II. Today, even the city's medieval[3] architecture is still beautifully preserved.

With buildings in Romanesque, Baroque, and Gothic styles, Prague felt frozen in time. *Nowhere did I feel this more than in the Old Town Square. As I walked along the cobblestone[4] streets, looking down dark

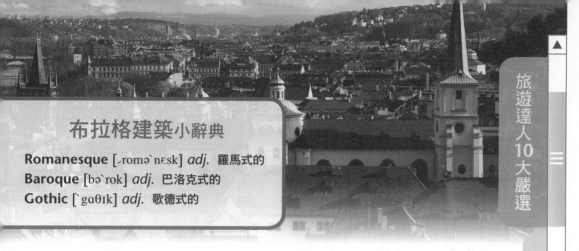

布拉格建築小辭典

Romanesque [ˌroməˋnɛsk] *adj.* 羅馬式的
Baroque [bəˋrok] *adj.* 巴洛克式的
Gothic [ˋgɑθɪk] *adj.* 歌德式的

lanes and gazing up at the spires[5] of churches, I could almost believe it was the seventeenth century.

In front of the Old Town City Hall in Old Town Square is the Astronomical Clock. In use since 1410, this clock's mechanical figures are set in motion hourly, and a skeleton,[6] which symbolizes[7] death, strikes a bell to mark the time. As each new hour approaches, visitors gather to watch the free show.

The Old Town Square is also a place with a variety of small theaters performing concerts, musicals, and other shows. That is why it came as no surprise when a man dressed in a Mozart costume passed me a flyer[8] for a classical music concert later that evening.

Vocabulary

1. **stumble** [ˋstʌmbəl] *v.* 跌跌撞撞地走著；絆倒
2. **extensive** [ɪkˋstɛnsɪv] *adj.* 大規模的；廣泛的
3. **medieval** [miˋdivəl] *adj.* 中世紀的
4. **cobblestone** [ˋkɑbəlˌston] *n.* 鵝卵石
5. **spire** [spaɪr] *n.* 尖塔
6. **skeleton** [ˋskɛlətən] *n.* 骷髏；骨骸
7. **symbolize** [ˋsɪmbəˌlaɪz] *v.* 象徵
8. **flyer** [ˋflaɪə] *n.* （廣告）傳單

市政廳外牆上的天文鐘（Astronomical Clock）

哥德式風格的聖維特斯大教堂（Saint Vitus Cathedral）是捷克最大的教堂，據說登上教堂的西塔可以看見布拉格最美的風景。 圖片／捷克觀光局

From Old Town, I had to cross the Charles Bridge in order to visit Prague Castle. *However, I found myself spending hours crossing—not because it is so long, but because there is so much to see. As I walked, I felt numerous[9] eyes following me, for each side of the bridge is lined with statues of different Catholic saints. The statues began to be placed on the bridge around 1683 and grew to a total of 30 statues by the 1900s.

During the day, the Charles Bridge fills up with artists, street performers, and small stalls[10] selling souvenirs. I liked best to stroll there early in the morning or later at night, as it was a quieter experience that gave me time to enjoy the view of Prague's skyline.[11]

So many fairy tales include a magnificent[12] castle, and Prague Castle is one of the best in the world. Looming[13] over the entire city from its commanding[14] position on top of a hill, this castle has been home to kings, emperors, and presidents since 807. Inside the castle complex is the Saint Vitus Cathedral, which houses the crown jewels of the Bohemian[15] Kingdom.

Down the hill from the castle is an area called the Mala Strana. Known for its stunning[16] Baroque architecture, it is often used as the location for historical films.

Prague does have a New Town, but in this case "new" means something from 1347, when this area of the city was founded. New Town is home to Wenceslas Square. It was once a horse market but now is one of the biggest public squares in Prague. People come here for the entertainment,[17] shopping, and cuisine. It's also famous for its nightlife, which attracts a lot of partygoers.[18]

左：小城區（Mala Strana，又稱為「雷瑟區」(Lesser Quarter）右：查理斯大橋（Charles Bridge）。
圖片 / 捷克觀光局

Vocabulary

9. **numerous** [ˋnumərəs] *adj.* 許多的

10. **stall** [stɔl] *n.* 攤位；亭子

11. **skyline** [ˋskaɪ͵laɪn] *n.* 天際線

12. **magnificent** [mægˋnɪfəsənt] *adj.* 壯麗的；宏偉的

13. **loom** [lum] *v.* 赫然出現；（問題）盤據、揮之不去

14. **commanding** [kəˋmændɪŋ] *adj.* 居高臨下的、視野開闊的

15. **Bohemian** [boˋhimiən] *adj., n.* 波希亞（人）的；波希米亞人

16. **stunning** [ˋstʌnɪŋ] *adj.* 令人震驚的；極美的

17. **entertainment** [͵ɛntəˋtenmənt] *n.* 娛樂；娛樂節目

18. **partygoer** [ˋpɑrtɪ͵goə] *n.* 派對狂歡客

181

Prague is also a city with an intellectual[19] atmosphere. One well-known author, Franz Kafka, was born and raised in Prague, and many believe that the city influenced his writing. In an exhibition entitled[20] *City of K*, his letters and photographs are on display, and they reveal his intimate[21] connection with Prague.

The contemporary[22] writer Milan Kundera also has a close connection with this city. In his famous work *The Unbearable Lightness of Being*, he details the circumstances[23] of artists and intellectuals in the wake of the Prague Spring.

Since the fall of Communism,[24] Prague has opened itself to the world. It is a city that contains a wealth of culture and overflows[25] with beauty. In this well-preserved example of times past, I experienced a vibrant[26] city where the images from fairy tales came to life.

溫瑟拉斯廣場（Wenceslas Square）廣場中央為溫瑟拉斯騎士的雕像，後方則為國家博物館。
圖片 / 捷克觀光局

【從旅遊看文化】

布拉格之春（Prague Spring）為一九六八年一月五日發生於捷克境內的民主運動，當時的捷克斯洛伐克（Czechoslovakia）在共產黨總書記杜布切克（Alexander Dubcek）的領導改革下走向獨立。當時的蘇聯（Soviet Russia, USSR）不樂見此發展，在同年八月以坦克武裝入侵捷克，鎮壓了這場運動。這次軍事入侵引發了十萬多人的難民潮，其中有許多為高級知識份子。

Vocabulary

19. **intellectual** [ˌɪntəˋlɛktʃəwəl] *adj.* 知性的　*n.* 知識份子
20. **entitle** [ɪnˋtaɪtl̩] *v.* 為……命名
21. **intimate** [ˋɪntəmət] *adj.* 親密的；私密的
22. **contemporary** [kənˋtɛmpəˏrɛri] *adj.* 當代的
23. **circumstance** [ˋsɝkm̩ˏstæns] *n.* 情勢；情況（作此義常用複數）
24. **communism** [ˋkɑmjəˏnɪzəm] *n.* 共產主義；共產政體（作此義時須大寫）
25. **overflow** [ˏovɚˋflo] *v.* 充滿；溢出
26. **vibrant** [ˋvaɪbrənt] *adj.* 充滿生氣的；活躍的

漫步布拉格，恣意想像

第一次踏上布拉格時，我感覺彷彿掉入了童話故事的世界裡。這樣的感覺並不奇怪，因為布拉格是歐洲少數躲過二次世界大戰大規模轟炸的城市之一。至今，即使是城裡的中古世紀建築也被完善地保存了下來。

布拉格有羅馬式、巴洛克式和歌德式的建築，彷彿就凍結在時光中。在舊城廣場尤其有這種感覺。當我走在鋪滿鵝卵石的街道上，低頭看見暗巷而抬頭看見的是教堂的尖塔，我幾乎要相信自己身處在十七世紀。

天文鐘就在舊城廣場的舊城市政廳前面。這座天文鐘自一四一〇年啟用，其機器人偶每個整點都會定時運轉，而象徵死亡的骷髏則會敲鐘報時。當接近每一整點時，觀光客便會群聚在此觀賞免費的表演。

舊城廣場也有各式各樣的小劇院上演著音樂會、音樂劇和其他表演。正因如此，那天傍晚一位身穿莫札特服裝的人在發古典音樂會的宣傳單給我時便不足為奇了。

要從舊城區前去參觀布拉格城堡則必須穿越查理斯大橋。然而，我發現光是過橋就花了好幾個鐘頭——不是因為橋很長，而是橋上有太多東西可看。當我走在橋上，總覺得有許多眼睛在看著我，因為橋的兩側陳列著許多天主教聖徒的雕像。這些雕像從西元一六八三年左右開始被放到橋上，到了二十世紀總共已增加到三十座之多。

白天時，查理斯大橋上到處是藝術家、街頭表演，還有販賣紀念品的小攤販。我最喜歡在清晨或是入夜後到那裡散步，因為這是讓我能好好享受布拉格天際線美景的寧靜時光。

許多童話故事裡都有宏偉的城堡，而布拉格城堡是世界上最棒的城堡之一。這座城堡座落在居高臨下的山頭，俯瞰整座城市，自西元八〇七年起這裡就是許多國王、君主和總統的住所。城堡區內有聖維特斯大教堂，裡頭存放著波希米亞王國的皇冠與權杖。

城堡的山腳下這地區稱作「小城區」。此區因美不勝收的巴洛克建築而聞名，常常作為歷史片的拍攝地點。

布拉格也有新城區，只不過在布拉格，這裡所謂的「新」是指此區為西元一三四七年之後所建。溫瑟拉斯廣場就位在新城區。這裡曾是馬匹交易市場，但現在卻成了布拉格最大的公共廣場之一。人們來這裡玩樂、購物及品嚐美食，其著名的夜生活也吸引許多派對狂歡客前來。

布拉格也是個充滿知性氣息的城市。知名作家卡夫卡就是在這裡土生土長，許多人認為這座城市影響了他的寫作風格。一場名為「K 城」的展覽中展出了他的信件與照片，透露出卡夫卡和布拉格之間的緊密關連。

而當代作家米蘭·昆德拉和布拉格也有深厚的淵源。在他的名著《生命中不可承受之輕》當中，他細膩地描繪了藝術家及知識份子在「布拉格之春」事件發生後的處境。

共產主義瓦解後，布拉格向全世界展開了雙臂。這是一個充滿了豐富文化、處處洋溢著美麗的城市。在這個將昔日風華完整保存的城市中，我感受到布拉格活力十足、其景象就如童話故事般栩栩如生。

1. set foot in 踏上、進入（某地）

set foot 表示「抵達、踏上」的意思，之後可接介系詞 in 或 on；set foor in 相當於 enter，之後接地方，set foot on 則與 walk on 意思相同。

- Ken will not set foot in that restaurant anymore because the owner was once rude to him.
  肯恩不會再去那間餐廳了，因為老闆曾經對他粗魯無禮。

2. a variety of 各種各樣的

同義 all kinds/sorts of、all manner of、a wide range of

variety 指「各式各樣；多種多樣」，a variety of 之後可接可數或不可數名詞。

- There are a variety of different lamb dishes available at this restaurant.
  這家餐廳供應各種不同的羊肉料理。

3. be lined with 排列著

line 在此作動詞，指「沿著……排列成行」，要指「（某地）林立著……」，常用 be lined with + N. 表示。

- The beautiful neighborhood had streets that were lined with palm trees.
  這個美麗社區的道路兩旁林立著棕櫚樹。

4. on display 展示；陳列

同義 on show

表示「將……展現出來」時，可以說 put/place sth on display，或用被動表示。

- There are all sorts of tools on display inside the furniture museum.
  在傢俱博物館裡展示各式各樣的工具。
- Kevin put his talent on display at the singing contest.
  凱文在歌唱比賽中展現他的才華。

5. in the wake of 尾隨……之後

本片語亦可寫作 in one's wake。wake 是船在水上行駛時的「尾波；航跡」，通常在距離船尾最近的水面上形成，故此片語意為「隨著……而來」，也可引申為「作為……的結果」。

- Thousands of people lost their jobs in the wake of the factory fire.
  數千人在工廠大火後跟著失業。

6. **a wealth of** **豐富的;大量的**

wealth 原指「財富」,a wealth of 用來形容大量、豐富的事物,而且是有用、好的事物,之後可接可數或不可數名詞。

- The books in the library contain a wealth of knowledge.
  圖書館裡的藏書蘊藏豐富的知識。

7. **come to life** **恢復生機;變得栩栩如生**

字面意思為「甦醒;活了過來」,引申表示某事物「生動起來;變得有趣」,與標題的 come alive 意思相同。

- Some authors write so well that they make their characters come to life.
  有些作家寫作功力非常好,能讓他們筆下的角色活靈活現。

Sentence Patterns

* **Nowhere did I feel this more than in the Old Town Square.**

  句型 Nowhere/Little/Never/Seldom + 助動詞/be動詞 + S. . . .

  ① nowhere 為否定副詞,置於句首時須將助動詞或 be 動詞提前形成倒裝。

  - Little did I know that the train had already departed.
    我壓根不知道火車已經開走了。

  ② 比較級和 nobody、nowhere、nothing 等否定詞搭配使用時,帶有最高級的意思。

  - Nowhere does Henry feel more peaceful than sitting on a quiet beach.
    沒有地方比坐在安靜的沙灘上更讓亨利感到平靜了。

* **However, I found myself spending hours crossing—not because it is so long, but because there is so much to see.**

  句型 not because . . . but because 不是因為……而是因為

  not . . . but . . . 為配對連接詞,用來連接對等的結構,故第二個 because 不可省略。

  - I went home not because I was tired, but because I wanted to watch my favorite television show.
    我回家不是因為我累了,而是因為我想看我最愛的電視節目。

Switzerland—Complexity and Contrasts

Switzerland is a magnet destination for anyone with a camera. Its incomparable beauty ranges from the peaks and valleys of its much-photographed Alpine regions to the charm of old-world cities and towns. It is also a country of fascinating social complexity[1] with four official languages: German, French, Italian, and Romansh. In addition, many Swiss also speak English.

Swiss cities are a mix of ancient charm coupled with state-of-the-art[2] modernity.[3] In Geneva, people can visit the Cathedral[4] of St. Peter that was first begun in the year 1000,

阿爾卑斯山脈（the Alps）綿延瑞士境內，交織成美麗動人的湖光山色。

186

瑞士小檔案

瑞士為聯邦制國家（federal state），由二十六個州組成。其境內有阿爾卑斯山脈（the Alps）、馬特洪峰（Matterhorn）、世界文化遺產少女峰（Jungfrau）等，再加上冰河地形所構成的壯麗美景，使瑞士成為觀光勝地。除了旅遊業外，鐘錶等精密機械工業及金融業也都是該國的主要產業。由於瑞士為中立國，近兩百年來不曾捲入戰爭，因此紅十字國際委員會（International Committee of the Red Cross, ICRC）、世界貿易組織（World Trade Organization）等都將總部設在瑞士。

or check out the United Nations complex[5] that was built in the 1930s. The city boasts[6] over 30 museums and has more surface area devoted to parks and gardens than any other Swiss city. Geneva also has the famous Jet d'Eau, a fountain on Lake Geneva that shoots water 70 meters into the air. For visitors looking at it up close, a change in wind direction can soak them to the bone!

Zurich is the largest city in Switzerland and another city that draws many tourists. Although often thought of as a banking center, Zurich is also known as the "portal[7] to the Alps," as it lies close to the many ski resorts in the mountains. It consistently[8] scores very high on quality-of-living surveys and is one of Europe's premier[9] places to live.

Vocabulary

1. **complexity** [kəm`plɛksəti] *n.* 複雜性；錯綜性
2. **state-of-the-art** [`stetəvði`ɑrt] *adj.* 最先進的
3. **modernity** [mə`dɜnəti] *n.* 現代性；現代化程度
4. **cathedral** [kə`θidrəl] *n.* 大教堂；主教座堂
5. **complex** [`kɑm͵plɛks] *n.* 綜合大樓；綜合建築群
6. **boast** [bost] *v.* 擁有（值得驕傲的事物）；誇耀
7. **portal** [`pɔrtl] *n.* 入口；大門
8. **consistently** [kən`sɪstəntli] *adv.* 一貫地；一致地
9. **premier** [prɪ`mɪr] *adj.* 最好或最重要的

Basel is the Swiss city I hold most dear, though, for I lived there for a year with my husband. It is a city of contrasts,[10] ranging from its Old Town with the dominant[11] Basel Münster built in the 13th century to a city hall dating to the 16th century. Its more contemporary[12] role is as host to some of the world's leading pharmaceutical[13] companies, banks, and the now-famous Art Basel international art show.

Outside of its cities, Switzerland has much more to offer. Being such a mountainous[14] country, it is loved by skiing and hiking enthusiasts[15] worldwide. Probably the best-known mountaintop is the Matterhorn,

蘇黎世（Zurich）是瑞士境內最大的城市，優美的市容吸引來自全球觀光客的目光。

大噴泉（Jet d'Eau）又稱「日內瓦噴泉」，是當地著名的觀光地標，它建於一八八六年，原是為了舒緩發電廠水壓問題而將日內瓦湖的湖水抽出。湖水高速噴入天際的景色搭配水花撞擊湖面的巨響，形成令人震撼的畫面。

旅遊達人10大嚴選

旅遊達人私房推薦

旅遊達人季節限定

Vocabulary

10. **contrast** [ˈkɑnˌtræst] *n.* 對比

11. **dominant** [ˈdɑmənənt] *adj.* 居高臨下的；顯著的

12. **contemporary** [kənˈtɛmpəˌrɛri] *adj.* 當代的；同時代的

13. **pharmaceutical** [ˌfɑrməˈsutɪkəl] *adj.* 製藥的；配藥（學）的

14. **mountainous** [ˈmaʊntənəs] *adj.* 多山的；如山般巨大的

15. **enthusiast** [ɪnˈθuziˌæst] *n.* 熱衷者；對……狂熱者

which lies on the border between Switzerland and Italy. This iconic[16] stone peak has four faces that point to all four points of the compass,[17] and it can be seen from the famous ski resort town of Zermatt.

For travelers in Switzerland today, there is plenty to see and do. Visitors can stay in châteaus,[18] get treatments in ultramodern[19] spas, or have romantic weekends in inns that are accessible only by horse-drawn carriage. Getting around from town to town on the Swiss Rail[20] is quite easy, and the trains are always on time. If you're looking for a fun European getaway,[21] Switzerland has everything you could ask for.

馬特洪峰山腳下的策馬特（Zermatt）是歐洲著名的滑雪勝地，一年四季都非常美麗。

【從旅遊看文化】

如果有一列火車遲到了，瑞士人的解讀有兩種：一是這列火車不是瑞士製造，二是火車上的時鐘不是瑞士製造。可見瑞士是個守時的民族，重視時間觀念，不僅因為它是個造錶的國家，而是做手錶的人會比手錶還來的準時。

Vocabulary

16. **iconic** [aɪˋkɑnɪk] *adj.* 代表性的；符號的
17. **compass** [ˋkʌmpəs] *n.* 指南針；羅盤
18. **château** [ʃæˋto] *n.* 【法文】城堡
19. **ultramodern** [ˏʌltrəˋmɑdən] *adj.* 超現代的
20. **rail** [rel] *n.* 鐵路；鐵軌
21. **getaway** [ˋgɛtəˏwe] *n.* 短期假期；逃離

中文翻譯　美景、文化兼容並蓄的國度——瑞士

　　對任何有相機的人來說，瑞士是個極具吸引力的目的地。其無與倫比的美景包括時常入鏡的阿爾卑斯山脈的山峰和山谷，以及迷人的傳統歐洲城鎮等。該國有四種官方語言：德語、法語、義大利語，以及羅曼什語，其社會多元性也相當令人嚮往。此外，許多瑞士人也會說英語。（編按：瑞士的中部及東部通行瑞士德語，西部通行瑞士法語，南部提契諾州通行義大利語，東南部格勞賓登州則通行印歐語系的羅曼什語。）

　　瑞士的城市融合了古老的魅力與先進的現代感。在日內瓦，人們可以參觀始於西元一千年的聖彼得大教堂，或是去瞧瞧建於一九三〇年代的聯合國大樓。這座城市坐擁三十幾間博物館，且專用於公園和綠地的表面積也為全瑞士之最。日內瓦還有知名的「大噴泉」（又稱為「日內瓦噴泉」），這座位於日內瓦湖上的噴泉向高空噴水達七十公尺。對那些近距離觀賞噴泉的遊客來說，風向一改變可是會讓他們全身溼透！

　　蘇黎世是瑞士最大的城市，也是另一座吸引許多觀光客的城市。雖然蘇黎世常被視為金融中心，但很多人也都知道它是「阿爾卑斯山的入口」，因為它緊鄰許多山區的滑雪勝地。蘇黎世在生活品質調查中向來名列前矛，同時也是歐洲最適合居住的城市之一。

　　不過，我最珍愛的瑞士城市還是巴塞爾，因為我和外子曾在那裡住過一年。那是一座充滿對比的城市，舊城區有建於十三世紀、高聳顯眼的巴塞爾主教座堂，市政府則可追溯至十六世紀。目前，它是一些全球領導品牌的製藥廠、銀行，以及如今名聞遐邇的巴塞爾國際藝術博覽會的所在地。

　　瑞士除了城市之外，還有很多等著你去挖掘。瑞士是個多山的國家，深受來自世界各地滑雪及登山愛好者的喜愛。最有名的山峰大概就是座落在瑞士和義大利交界處的馬特洪峰了。這座具有代表性的岩峰四面分別指向羅盤上的四個方位，從著名的滑雪勝地策馬特便可看見馬特洪峰。

　　如今前往瑞士旅遊的人有許多可觀賞的景點與可從事的活動。遊客可入住城堡、在超現代化設施中做水療，或是在只有搭馬車才能進入的小旅館裡度過浪漫的週末。利用瑞士鐵路系統往返各城鎮相當便利，而且火車從不誤點。如果你正在尋找好玩的歐洲度假地，瑞士能滿足你所有的需求。

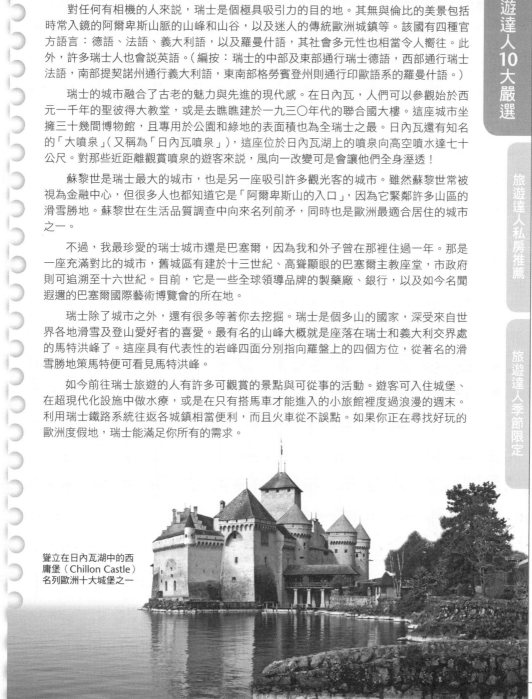

聳立在日內瓦湖中的西庸堡（Chillon Castle）名列歐洲十大城堡之一

1. **in-/un- + V. + -able/-ible** 無法⋯⋯的；難以⋯⋯的

in + compare（比較）+ able = in**compar**able [ˌɪnˈkɑmpərəbəl] adj. 無可匹敵的

in + access（到達） + ible = in**access**ible [ˌɪnɪkˈsɛsəbəl] adj. 無法進入的；無法取得的

un + believe（相信） + able = un**believ**able [ˌʌnbəˈlivəbəl] adj. 令人無法置信的

un + explain（解釋） + able = un**explain**able [ˌʌnɪkˈsplenəbəl] adj. 無法解釋的

- The craftsman is known for his incomparable skill in making watches.
  這名工匠以無可比擬的製錶技術出名。

2. **be coupled with sth** 結合⋯⋯；加上⋯⋯

couple 在此作動詞用，表示「結合；加上」的意思，常用被動來表示。

- Great food coupled with a pleasant atmosphere is what makes this restaurant great.
  美味的食物加上愉悅的氣氛讓這裡成為很棒的餐廳。

3. **devote sth to sth/sb** 將某事專用於⋯⋯；致力於⋯⋯

devote 表示「投入、奉獻」的意思，常用被動來表示。主詞為人時，表示「奉獻、投注心力於⋯⋯」；為物時，表示「專用於⋯⋯的」，如文中用法。

- This room is devoted to Eric's toys and games.
  這房間被用來擺放艾瑞克的玩具和遊戲

4. **to the bone** 徹骨地；（影響）深刻地

to the bone 字面意思是「到骨頭裡」，此為誇飾用法，用來形容到達極致的程度。文中 soak them to the bone 則是形容「使他們全身溼透」。

- By the time the hikers reached the cabin, they were soaked to the bone by the rain.
  在這些登山客抵達小屋時，他們全身都被雨水淋濕了。

  補充 be/feel chilled/frozen to the bone 感到寒冷刺骨
- Without a jacket, I was chilled to the bone as I waited for the bus.
  我在等公車時沒穿夾克，感到冷風刺骨。

5. **hold dear** 珍愛；珍惜

  用法 hold dear + N.、hold + N./ 代名詞 + dear
- Mary holds dear the memories she has about going to school in England.
  瑪麗很珍惜她在英國求學時的回憶。

6. **outside of** 除了……

片語介系詞 outside of 依上下文有兩種意思：

① 除了……還有

同義 in addition to、besides

- Outside of this cake, Lisa also made a lot of delicious cookies.
  除了這個蛋糕，麗莎還做了很多好吃的餅乾。

② 除了……之外

同義 except、except for

- Outside of the boss, no one knows the combination to open the safe.
  除了老闆之外，沒有人知道打開保險箱的密碼。

San Francisco: The Golden City by the Bay

A mention of the seaside city of San Francisco usually elicits[1] images of cable cars, blankets of fog, and the Golden Gate Bridge. However, there's so much more that makes the city distinct.[2] As a former Bay Area native, I love nothing better than getting the chance to return home and live as a tourist in the city I spent so many days in as a youngster.

Upon arriving in San Francisco, many visitors head straight to Fisherman's Wharf[3] to eat some seafood. Afterwards, they admire the breathtaking bay views in a cable car as it climbs one of the city's many hills. Every first-time visitor should check out one of the most crooked[4] streets in the world, a one-block stretch of Lombard Street featuring eight sharp turns on the way down Russian Hill.

My most recommended activity on the tourist trail is catching a ferry to Alcatraz Island and its long-closed federal[5] prison. It once

建於一九三七年的金門大橋（Golden Gate Bridge），是舊金山著名的地標，跨越連接舊金山灣（San Franciso Bay）和太平洋（Pacific Ocean）的金門海峽（Golden Gate）。全長2737.4 公尺，橋墩跨距約 1280 公尺，是全球首座跨幅逾一公里的懸索橋。

旅遊達人10大嚴選

旅遊達人私房推薦

旅遊達人季節限定

Vocabulary

1. **elicit** [ɪˋlɪsət] *v.* 喚起、引起（回應）；探出（訊息）
2. **distinct** [dɪˋstɪŋkt] *adj.* 明顯的；有區別的
3. **wharf** [hwɔrf] *n.* 碼頭
4. **crooked** [ˋkrʊkəd] *adj.* 彎曲的；不正直的
5. **federal** [ˋfɛdərəl] *adj.* 聯邦（政府）的

電纜車（Cable Car）又名「叮噹車」，是早期為適應舊金山特有的山丘地形而發展出的地底纜繩牽引式纜車，在二十世紀初是市區的主要交通工具，現今保留了三條穿越主要旅遊景點的路線。

圖解舊金山美食

burrito
墨西哥捲餅

enchilada
辣醬肉餡玉米捲餅

sourdough bread
酸麵包；天然酵母麵包

clam chowder
蛤蠣巧達湯

Dungeness crab
鄧傑內斯蟹

fajita
法士達

tamale
玉米糕粽

taco
墨西哥玉米（煎）餅

housed notorious[6] criminals such as the gangster[7] Al Capone. You can admire the city skyline from there and read about the island's fascinating history. This history included a period of time as a military fortress[8] and a 19-month occupation by Native American protesters in the 1970s.

As a lover of Mexican cuisine, my first stop upon returning home is usually the Mission District.[9] This part of town features colorful murals[10] adorning[11] the sides of buildings and plenty of places to get my enchilada fix. I can't possibly depart[12] the city without getting my fill of sourdough bread as well. *It has been an area favorite since the Gold Rush of the mid-1800s.

Vocabulary

6. **notorious** [no`torɪəs] *adj.* 惡名昭彰的
7. **gangster** [`gæŋstə] *n.* 幫派份子；流氓
8. **fortress** [`fɔrtrəs] *n.* 堡壘
9. **district** [`dɪstrɪkt] *n.* （特色）區域；行政區
10. **mural** [`mjʊrəl] *n.* 壁畫
11. **adorn** [ə`dɔrn] *v.* 裝飾；使生色
12. **depart** [dɪ`pɑrt] *v.* 離開；出發

漁人碼頭（Fisherman's Wharf）

San Francisco's remarkable[13] natural beauty makes simple walks entertaining.[14] You can take in views of the Golden Gate from above the red-roofed former Army barracks[15] of Fort Mason. You can then go onward to Fort Point, where surfers and sea lions occupy[16] the waters below the most photographed bridge on the planet. Land's End also provides a unique angle looking back at the bridge and bay from cliffs hanging over the Pacific Ocean. Finally, there are the Filbert Steps, which run from the waterfront,[17] up past a line of beautiful homes, to the famous Coit Tower.

Just a few days back in the city make me wonder why I ever left it. To paraphrase[18] the singer Tony Bennett, I can't help but leave my heart in San Francisco.

【從旅遊看文化】

舊金山原本是美國西岸海運門戶,進出的貨物都靠一條濱海高速公路運送,但它的高架設計阻擋了美麗的海景。舊金山大地震(Loma Prieta earthquake)後因為橋樑結構毀損,當時的市長提議拆除,希望利用廣闊的海景吸引觀光人潮。期間雖然歷經抗爭,但最後還是成功讓舊金山成為全美最大的觀光重鎮之一。

左:中國城(Chinatown)、右:藝術宮(The Palace of Fine Arts)
右下:柯伊特塔(Coit Tower),位於電報山(Telegraph Hill)山頂的先鋒公園(Pioneer Park),高約六十四公尺。外觀設計成消防水帶噴嘴的樣子,紀念英勇的消防員。

Vocabulary

13. **remarkable** [rɪˋmɑrkəbəl] *adj.* 顯著的;出色的
14. **entertaining** [ˌɛntɚˋtenɪŋ] *adj.* 具有娛樂性、趣味性的
15. **barrack** [ˋbærək] *n.* 營房;兵營
16. **occupy** [ˋɑkjəˌpaɪ] *v.* 占據;占領;占用
17. **waterfront** [ˋwɔtɚˌfrʌnt] *n.* 濱水區
18. **paraphrase** [ˋpɛrəˌfrez] *v.* 改述;釋義

中文翻譯　　海灣霧城——舊金山

　　一提到舊金山這座濱海城市，通常會喚起人對電纜車（又名叮噹車）、層層濃霧和金門大橋的景象。然而，這座城市之所以獨特還不只這些而已。作為一個在灣區長大的人，能有機會以旅客的身分回到我年少時居住許久的地方，是再開心不過的事了。

　　許多遊客一抵達舊金山，就會直接前往漁人碼頭大啖海鮮。之後，他們會搭乘叮噹車爬上市區眾多山丘的其中一座，欣賞令人嘆為觀止的海灣風景。每一個初次造訪的遊客都應該去看看世界上最彎曲的街道之一，那就是倫巴底街上一段只有一個街區長的九曲花街，其特色是一路從俄羅斯山往下的八個急轉彎。

　　遊覽路線中我最推薦的活動是搭渡輪前往惡魔島及島上那座關閉已久的聯邦監獄。它曾關過像幫派份子艾爾‧卡彭等惡名昭彰的罪犯。你可以從那裡眺望舊金山的天際線，以及閱讀讀惡魔島引人入勝的歷史。歷史上，它曾是軍事堡壘，而且在一九七〇年代曾被北美原住民抗議者佔領了十九個月。

　　身為墨西哥美食愛好者，我一回家鄉的第一站通常是教會區。這一帶有繽紛的壁畫為建築物外牆增添色彩，還有許多餐廳有辣醬肉餡玉米捲餅可以讓我解饞。同樣地，若沒有好好吃夠酸麵包，我也不可能離開舊金山。自從十九世紀中期的淘金熱潮以來，酸麵包就一直是當地居民的最愛。

　　舊金山非凡的自然美景讓簡單的步行變得趣味盎然。你可以從梅森堡紅色屋頂的舊軍營上方飽覽整個金門海峽的風景。接著你可以前往海角堡，這裡就位在全世界最多人拍照的金門大橋底下，海域上到處都是衝浪客和海獅。海角天涯也提供了獨特的視角，讓你從突出太平洋上方的山崖回望金門大橋和海灣。最後還有榛木梯道，它從濱海區一路北上，經過一排美麗的房子，再到著名的柯伊特塔。

　　才回到舊金山幾天就讓我納悶當初為何要離開。改述一句歌手東尼‧班尼特的歌詞，我已情不自禁把心留在舊金山。（編按：東尼‧班尼特（Tony Bennett）一九二六年出生於紐約，為美國知名歌手，其曲風以流行樂、爵士及音樂劇曲目為主。I Left My Heart in San Francisco《心繫舊金山》為他的經典歌曲之一。）

梅森堡（Fort Mason）　圖片／Flickr: BAIA

1. get/have one's fix 解饞

fix 作名詞，表示「一定數量」。原指讓人上癮的毒品的一次注射量，引申為對某物的渴望或需要，文中的 get my enchilada fix 指「解辣醬肉餡玉米捲餅的饞」。

- Don't bother to talk to Angela until she has had her fix of coffee in the morning.
  早上在安潔拉還沒喝咖啡前，別費心去跟她說話。

2. get/eat one's fill （某物）吃個過癮

fill 作名詞，表示「全額；足量」，常用於指某人所想要或所需求的一切。get/eat one's fill (of sth) 則表示「把某物吃個夠」。

- I got my fill of pizza at the birthday party yesterday.
  昨天我在生日派對上吃披薩吃得很過癮。

3. take in 參觀；觀看

take in the sights 指「參觀名勝、欣賞風景」，sight 表示「風景」時常用複數。

- We should take in a movie after we have dinner.
  吃完晚飯後我們應該去看一場電影。

補充

①take in 收留（某人）

受詞為人，可置於 take 和 in 之間或 in 之後。

- The kind old couple took in the poor woman and her child.
  這對好心的老夫婦收留了那名可憐的婦人和她的孩子。

②take in 吸收（訊息、資料等）；理解

受詞為事物，可置於 take 和 in 之間或 in 之後。

- The explanation of the math problem was difficult for the students to take in, so the teacher tried to explain it differently.
  學生難以理解這道數學題的解釋，所以老師試著用別的方式解釋。

③take in 賺取（收入、利潤等）

受詞通常為數額，置於 in 之後。

- The company took in over two million dollars in profit last year.
  這間公司去年獲利超過兩百萬美元。

④take in 欺騙、愚弄（某人）

作此義時常用被動語態，用 be taken in by sb 來表示。

- Jeff was taken in by the salesperson, and now he owns a car that barely runs.
  傑夫被這名業務騙了，現在他的車子幾乎不會動。

Sentence Patterns

* **It has been an area favorite** since **the Gold Rush of the mid-1800s.**

句型

S. + have + p.p. + since +
$\begin{cases} \text{N.（過去時間點）} \\ \text{S. + 過去式動詞} \end{cases}$

從那時起就……；自從……之後

since 可作介系詞或連接詞用，之後要接表過去的時間點或過去式動詞所引導的子句，主要子句則用完成式，表示事情已持續一段時間。在本句中 it 指的是前面提到的 sourdough bread。

• Rose has been dreaming of becoming a superstar since childhood.
  蘿絲從小就一直夢想能成為超級巨星。

• I haven't seen my teacher since I graduated from college.
  自從我大學畢業後我就沒有再見過我的老師了。

補充 It has been + 一段時間 + since . . . 的用法，在英式英語中常用簡單式 It is . . . since . . . 表示。

• It has been two months since Ken saw his parents.（美語）

→It's two months since Ken saw his parents.（英式英語）
  肯恩見到雙親到現在已經過了兩個月。

阿卡特茲島（Alcatraz Island）俗稱「惡魔島（The Rock）」，為距離舊金山灣約二千四百公尺的小島，島上的舊監獄現在已成觀光景點，遊客可入內參觀。這裡曾多次成為好萊塢的電影主題，其中最著名的便是一九九六年由史恩‧康納萊和尼可拉斯‧凱吉主演的《絕地任務》（The Rock）。

圖片 / Flickr: Fmarier

圖片 / San Francisco Convention & Vistors Bureau

莎草紙（papyrus）上的畫作

Egypt: Land of the Pharaohs

As my plane landed at Cairo International Airport, I had to pinch[1] myself to make sure I wasn't dreaming. I was finally fulfilling[2] a lifelong[3] desire and visiting Egypt, the magical land of pharaohs, pyramids, and hieroglyphics.

After landing, I gathered my luggage and left the air-conditioned airport. When I stepped out into the bright sunlight of an Egyptian[4] summer afternoon, the heat hit me like a hammer. It was as if someone

埃及小檔案

四大文明古國之一的埃及有五千多年的歷史。由於氣候乾燥，尼羅河（the Nile）每年六月至十月間河水便上漲氾濫，河水消退後留下肥沃的土壤與生物，因此埃及人將尼羅河視為神明的恩賜，孕育人類最古老的文明。

had turned on a furnace[5] full blast![6] I have spent time in hot places before, but the heat in Egypt—a dry, scorching[7] heat—was something I had never experienced.

I spent my first few days in Cairo. It is a sprawling[8] capital city of more than sixteen million people that sits on the banks of the Nile. Walking the streets, I sampled[9] traditional Egyptian food. Lots of the dishes have foreign influences, and there were plenty of dates, goat cheese, pita bread, and plates of boiled couscous. My favorite meal was lemon-flavored[10] lamb mixed with garlic, onions, and spices, on top of a bed of long-grain rice. *It was a delicious meal that filled me up and gave me the energy to explore the country I'd long dreamt about.

Vocabulary

1. **pinch** [pɪntʃ] *v.* 捏；擰
2. **fulfill** [fʊlˋfɪl] *v.* 完成；實現
3. **lifelong** [ˋlaɪfˏlɔŋ] *adj.* 一輩子的
4. **Egyptian** [ɪˋdʒɪpʃən] *adj., n.* 埃及（人）的；埃及人
5. **furnace** [ˋfɜnəs] *n.* 火爐；暖爐
6. **full blast** [blæst] *adv.* 使盡全力、全速地；極度
7. **scorching** [ˋskɔrtʃɪŋ] *adj.* 炎熱的
8. **sprawl** [sprɔl] *v.* 擴展；延伸（sprawling 為現在分詞作形容詞用，表示「不斷擴張地」）
9. **sample** [ˋsæmpəl] *v.* 品嚐；抽樣檢查
10. **lemon-flavored** [ˋlɛmənˋflevəd] *adj.* 檸檬口味的

製作圓麵餅（pita bread）

I've always loved ancient Egyptian history, and I got to see a lot of it up close at the Egyptian Museum in Cairo. I knew I wouldn't be able to see everything, since the museum has over 120,000 pieces in its collection. As I walked among the artifacts,[11] I was amazed by everything that surrounded me. I saw gold coffins[12] and furniture, enormous statues, boats, chariots, and jewelry. The museum's two floors contain too much to describe.

Walking into one room on the top floor, I was met with the world-famous death mask of King Tutankhamen. For thousands of years, this mask with its divine[13] beard covered the head of the mummified[14] young king. Now, its open eyes stared at me. The mask's gold mouth, nose, and cheeks are polished[15] smooth, surrounded by a headdress containing semi-precious stones like turquoise. The solid gold ears are pierced,[16] and falcon heads decorate the shoulders. A snake and a vulture rise from the forehead, symbolizing Upper and Lower Egypt.

左：圖坦卡門王（King Tutankhamen）的面具上鑲著綠松石（turquoise）的
頭飾，額頭上立著蛇與禿鷹（vulture），肩上則裝飾著獵鷹（falcon）。
下：開羅的埃及博物館（Egyptian Museum）圖片 / C.H. Hsu

埃及吉薩金字塔（The Pyramids of Giza）與人面獅身像（sphinx）

The museum could have held my attention for weeks, yet this beautiful country holds so many treasures outside of the museum. It was time to strike out on an adventure. I had to see one of the Seven Wonders of the Ancient World: the Pyramids at Giza.

Nothing could have prepared me for seeing the Pyramids up close. They are breathtaking, and certainly[17] more impressive than I could have ever imagined they'd be. I spent one whole afternoon just watching the Pyramids change color in the light, from a sandy yellow to a warm brown, and finally to a deep black as the sun set behind me.

Vocabulary

11. **artifact** [ˈɑrtɪˌfækt] *n.* 手工藝品（尤指具有文化和歷史價值者）
12. **coffin** [ˈkɔfən] *n.* 棺木
13. **divine** [dəˈvaɪn] *adj.* 神聖的
14. **mummify** [ˈmʌmɪˌfaɪ] *v.* 將⋯⋯做成木乃伊
15. **polish** [ˈpɑlɪʃ] *v.* 磨光；擦亮
16. **pierce** [pɪrs] *v.* 給⋯⋯穿孔；刺穿
17. **certainly** [ˈsɝtənli] *adv.* 當然

On a different day, I took a step back in time and rode a camel. After climbing into the saddle[18] on the animal's back, I held on for dear life as the camel stood up. I probably didn't look very dashing[19] on my camel ride around the Pyramids and the Sphinx, but at least I didn't fall off!

The sights in Egypt were truly fascinating, and there was also a sound that I came to know quite well. It was the Islamic call to prayer, heard five times each day. Ninety percent of all Egyptians are Muslim, and this songlike call summons[20] them to pray at the nearest mosque. In Egypt, non-Muslims are also allowed to enter these Islamic places of worship,[21] and I was warmly welcomed at the mosque I visited.

Egypt was everything that I thought it would be, and more. Though I left the country with no treasure in my bags, the memories I get to keep are priceless.[22]

埃及文化小辭典

hieroglyphic [ˌhaɪərəˈglɪfɪk] 象形文字
pharaoh [ˈfɛro] 法老
pyramid [ˈpɪrəˌmɪd] 金字塔
sphinx [sfɪŋks] 人面獅身像
headdress [ˈhɛdˌdrɛs] 頭飾
turquoise [ˈtɜˌkɔɪz] 綠松石（土耳其石）

上：路克索神廟（The Temple of Luxor）供奉底比斯三神，在十九世紀時已嚴重損壞，經過一世紀的挖掘和重建才有今日的風貌。右下：位於開羅市區東南方的薩拉丁城堡（Citadel of Salah Al Din）是埃及最大的清真寺。
圖片 / C.H. Hsu

Vocabulary

18. **saddle** [ˈsædl̩] *n.* 馬鞍；鞍
19. **dashing** [ˈdæʃɪŋ] *adj.* 雄赳赳的
20. **summon** [ˈsʌmən] *v.* 傳喚；召喚
21. **worship** [ˈwɝʃɪp] *n.* 禮拜；敬神
22. **priceless** [ˈpraɪsləs] *adj.* 無價的

埃及——法老的國度

　　飛機在開羅國際機場降落時，我不得不捏一下自己，確定我不是在作夢。我終於得償夙願造訪這個法老、金字塔以及象形文字的奇幻國度——埃及。

　　飛機降落後，我收齊行李，離開有空調的機場。當我邁進埃及夏日午後的豔陽下時，熱氣如鐵鎚般襲來，就像是有人將暖爐火力全開。我以前待過炎熱地方，但埃及的熱——那種乾燥的灼熱——可是我畢生頭一遭。

　　剛開始幾天我待在開羅。這個坐落於尼羅河兩岸不斷擴展的城市人口超過一千六百萬人。我走在街上品嚐傳統埃及食物。很多料理都帶有異國風情，有很多的棗子、羊乳酪、圓麵餅以及一盤盤蒸熟的古斯米（又譯作「蒸粗麥粉」）。我最喜歡的一道是加了蒜頭、洋蔥與香料檸檬口味的羊肉，鋪在一盤長米飯上。這美味的一餐可以讓我飽餐一頓，並且有體力探訪這個讓我夢想已久的國家。

　　我一直鍾愛埃及的古老歷史，在開羅的埃及博物館我得以近距離見到許多的歷史。我知道無法看盡所有的東西，因為博物館收藏了超過十二萬件的收藏品。我在這些手工製品間走過時，周圍的每一件都令我驚艷。有黃金打造的棺木和傢具、巨大的雕像、船、單馬戰車以及珠寶。博物館兩層樓的收藏豐富得令人難以形容。

　　走進頂樓的一個房間，我看到舉世聞名的圖坦卡門王的陪葬面具。幾千年來，這個蓄著神聖鬍子的面具覆蓋在這成了木乃伊的年輕國王頭上。如今，它張開的眼睛注視著我。這黃金面具的唇、鼻、臉頰都打亮得相當光滑，並用鑲著像綠松石這類半寶石的頭飾圍繞著。堅實的黃金耳穿了洞，肩上則裝飾著獵鷹頭。額頭上立著蛇與兀鷹，代表著上埃及與下埃及。

　　博物館就可能可以吸引我幾個星期的注意力，但這個美麗的國家在博物館外一樣擁有許多珍寶。該是出發去探險的時候了。我得去參觀古代的七大奇景之一——吉薩的金字塔。

　　這麼近距離觀賞這些金字塔，我不可能事先有心裡準備。它們令人屏息，當然令人震懾得超乎我的想像。我一整個下午就只看金字塔在光線下變幻色彩，從黃沙色轉為暖棕色，然後終於在日落西山後轉為墨黑色。

　　隔日，我體驗古老風情，乘坐駱駝。我爬上駱駝背上的鞍之後駱駝站了起來，我則死命抓緊。或許我坐著駱駝逛金字塔與人面獅身時，看起來並沒有雄赳赳的樣子，但至少我沒有跌下去。

　　埃及的景色真的令人著迷，有個聲音我也逐漸耳熟能詳。那就是伊斯蘭教的祈禱召喚，每天會聽到五次。百分之九十的埃及人是穆斯林教徒，而這聽似歌曲的呼喚召喚他們到最近的清真寺祈禱。在埃及，非穆斯林教徒也可以進入這些伊斯蘭教的膜拜場所，我所參觀過的清真寺都熱情地歡迎我。

　　我能想得到的埃及應有盡有，而且更為豐富。雖然離開這國家時我行李裡並沒有寶藏，但我所珍藏的回憶卻是無價之寶。

1. **on top of a bed of long-grain rice** 在用長米鋪底的上面

on top of 在此表示「在……上面」。a bed of 是指「一層底部食物」，之後會接米、蔬菜之類的食物。grain 意為「穀粒；穀物」，long-grain rice 便是「長形米」。

延伸學習 ▶ on top of 也可用來表示「除……之外；另外」。

- On top of going out to eat, Mary and I also went to see a movie.
  除了出去吃飯，我和瑪莉也去看了電影。

- Hank cooked the dinner, and on top of that, he washed the dishes afterward.
  漢克做了晚餐，除此之外，他後來還洗了碗。

2. **strike out on an adventure** 展開一場探險旅程

strike out 有以下常見的意思：

① 開始；出發

- We should strike out early in the morning if we want to make it to the top of the mountain by noon.
  如果中午前要攻頂，我們應該一大早就出發。

- The explorer struck out to find the ancient city lost somewhere in the dangerous jungle.
  那名探險家出發尋找消失在危險叢林裡的古城。

② （棒球）三振出局

- We thought we were going to win the baseball game until Peter struck out.
  彼得被三振出局之前，我們一直以為會贏得這場棒球比賽。

3. **could have + p.p.** 過去可能

could have + p.p. 表示「過去可能」，用來推測過去事件發生的可能性。而 could not have + p.p. 則表示「過去不可能」，所以 Nothing could have prepared me 意為「我（當時）不可能有心理準備」。

- Few things could have made the old woman happier than seeing her grandchildren.
  沒有什麼事情會比去探望孫子更令這位老太太開心。

延伸學習 ▶ 要表示在現在或未來發生的可能性則用 can/could + V.。

- We should all take our seats, because the teacher could come back at any moment.
  我們都應該坐在位子上，因為老師隨時都可能回來。

4. hold on for dear life 死命抓緊

hold on 意為「抓住；堅持」，若後面有受詞，則須加介系詞 to。而 dear 則表示「寶貴的」，所以 hold on for dear life 就表示因為「害怕危及寶貴生命而繃緊神經或死命抓緊」的意思。

- John held on to his hat when the wind started to blow.
  開始起風時，約翰抓住了帽子。

- The man was found floating in the river, holding on to a log for dear life.
  那名男子被發現在河裡載浮載沈，死命抓著一塊浮木。

延伸學習 ▶ hold on 還有以下常見的意思：

① 堅持；維持（通常接介系詞 to）

- Even though the facts proved otherwise, the people still held on to their beliefs.
  即便事實證明並非如此，人們仍舊這麼相信。

②（電話中的）等待

- Janet told me to hold on while she went to find her purse.
  珍妮要我在她去找錢包時不要掛斷電話。

Sentence Patterns

* It was **a delicious meal that filled me up and gave me the energy to explore the country** I'd long dreamt about.

> 省略 that 的形容詞子句，用於修飾 the country

句型 It is/was + 強調的部分 + that + 剩下的部分

本句是一個分裂句句型，寫法為將句中欲強調的重點（a delicious meal）放在 it is/was 和 that 之間，剩餘的部分放在 that 後面。而分裂句強調部份可為主詞、受詞、介系詞片語、（表時間、地點）副詞片語。

- It was the heavy rain that made the river rise so fast.
  是大雨讓河川水位急速升高的。（強調主詞 heavy rain）

- It was my office that the package was sent to.
  那個包裹是寄到我公司的。（強調受詞 my office）

- It was recently that the news broke about the actress's accident.
  新聞是最近才開始報導那位女演員的意外事故。（強調副詞 recently）

Colorful Cape Town

Cape Town is the most popular travel spot in South Africa. Many tourists visit the Western Cape during the hot, dry summer months. Few realize just how magical[1] it can be during the fall and winter seasons. Winter starts at the end of May and is called the green season. *This is when the area receives most of its rainfall,[2] and the landscape is covered with rich grass. In the evening, the setting sun creates a canvas[3] of warm pinks and reds in the sky.

Table Mountain, which overlooks[4] the city, is a must-see[5] landmark, especially when the winter fog covers it like a tablecloth.[6] Visitors can travel up the mountain by cable car or by hiking one of the trails. Once on the mountain, they can view waterfalls, ruins, and maybe animals roaming the national park.

*Even during winter, Cape Town is a gathering place for those seeking sun, sea, and sand. Many people like to wander[7] through the beach-facing promenade[8] at Camps Bay and enjoy the brilliant view of the sea. One can also visit Clifton, with its four impressive[9] beaches, or head further south to Cape Point. This is where the warm Indian Ocean meets the icy Atlantic.

Vocabulary

1. **magical** [ˋmædʒɪkəl] *adj.* 美妙的；有魔力的
2. **rainfall** [ˋrenˏfɔl] *n.* 降雨；雨量
3. **canvas** [ˋkænvəs] *n.* 油畫；油畫布
4. **overlook** [ˏovəˋluk] *v.* 俯瞰、眺望；高聳於⋯⋯之上
5. **must-see** [ˋmʌstˋsi] *adj.* 必看的（特色景點等）
6. **tablecloth** [ˋtebəlˏklɔθ] *n.* 桌布
7. **wander** [ˋwɑndə] *v.* 漫遊；閒逛
8. **promenade** [ˏprɑməˋned] *n.* 濱海步道
9. **impressive** [ɪmˋprɛsɪv] *adj.* 令人讚嘆的；印象深刻的

For those interested in shopping, dining, or entertainment, head to the Old Biscuit Mill, located in the northeastern section of the city. A fashionable spot, it is home to markets, farm shops, restaurants, and festivals. Further north, another place to get some shopping done is the Victoria and Alfred Waterfront. Here you can also catch a boat tour of Robben Island. The late president Nelson Mandela spent twenty-seven years in prison on this tiny island.

Cape Town is also known for its authentic[10] local cuisine. Infused[11] with the flavors of Southeast Asian spices, which were introduced centuries ago, Cape Malay food is an attraction on its own. *Bobotie*, South Africa's spicy meat loaf,[12] and *koeksisters*, similar to syrup-coated[13] doughnuts, are among the many delicious surprises that await[14] your taste buds.[15]

上：科斯坦伯斯國家植物園（Kirstenbosch National Botanical Garden）位於桌山（Table Mountain）山腳下，是世界七大植物園之一。右：天氣好時，遊客可搭纜車登上桌山（Table Mountain），將開普敦的風光盡收眼底。

地理小辭典

Western Cape 即「西開普省」，是南非九個省分之一，其首府為開普敦（Cape Town）。

the Atlantic 指「大西洋」，也可寫成 the Atlantic Ocean。文中 the warm Indian Ocean 和 the icy Atlantic 分別指溫暖的印度洋環流（阿古拉斯洋流）和冰冷的南大西洋環流（本格拉洋流），兩道洋流在開普角（Cape Point）附近交會。

羅本島（Robben Island）有座當年囚禁曼德拉（Nelson Mandela）的監獄，其歷史意義讓島上遊客絡繹不絕。

Vocabulary

10. **authentic** [ɔˋθɛntɪk] *adj.* 道地的；真正的
11. **infuse** [ɪnˋfjuz] *v.* 注入；灌輸
12. **meat loaf** [mit] [lof] *n.* 肉派；肉餅
13. **syrup-coated** [ˋsɪrəpˏkotɪd] *adj.* 裹了糖漿的
14. **await** [əˋwet] *v.* 等待
15. **taste bud** [test] [bʌd] *n.* 味蕾（常用複數）

南非經典的「雙姐妹酥餅」（koeksisters），為油炸後的麵餅裹上糖漿，口感香甜酥脆。圖片 / Flickr: iferneinez

Cape Town truly deserves[16] its reputation[17] as being one of the top places in the world to visit. Explore one of the colorful suburbs[18] in the City Bowl or visit the Kirstenbosch National Botanical Garden. Cycle through the historic city center or just relax and breathe in the crisp, salty air. It doesn't matter what you do or who you are— Cape Town is welcoming to all.

【從旅遊看文化】

世界設計之都（The World Design Capital，簡稱 WDC），是國際工業設計協會所提出的城市推動計畫，希望透過設計為各城市帶來新活力。開普敦成為二○一四年的世界設計之都，台北則獲選二○一六的代表城市。

上：柏德海灘（Boulders Beach）處處可見黑腳企鵝（Black-footed penguin）。下：舊餅乾磨坊（Old Biscuit Mill）
圖片 / Flickr: iferneinez

THE OLD BISCUIT MILL

E BLOCK

A BLOCK

abode

Vocabulary

16. **deserve** [dɪˋzɝv] v. 應得；值得

17. **reputation** [͵rɛpjəˋteʃən] n. 名聲；聲譽

18. **suburb** [ˋsʌbɝb] n. 近郊、郊區；城郊住宅區（作此義時，常用複數）

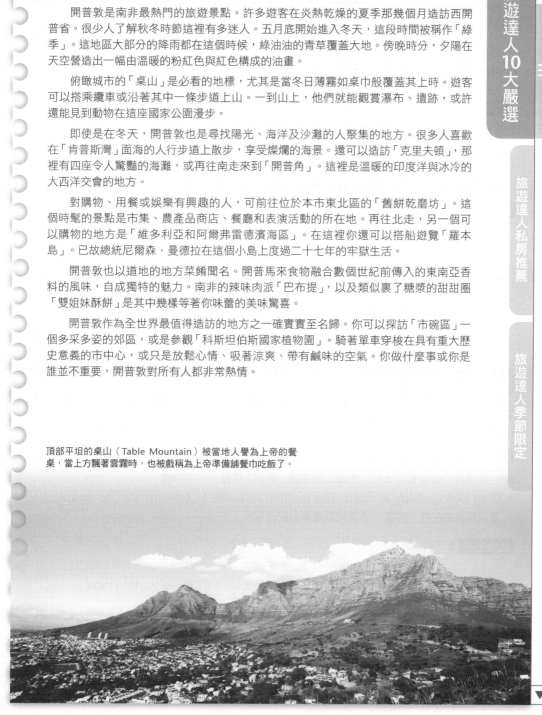

開普敦——繽紛多彩之都

開普敦是南非最熱門的旅遊景點。許多遊客在炎熱乾燥的夏季那幾個月造訪西開普省。很少人了解秋冬時節這裡有多迷人。五月底開始進入冬天，這段時間被稱作「綠季」。這地區大部分的降雨都在這個時候，綠油油的青草覆蓋大地。傍晚時分，夕陽在天空營造出一幅由溫暖的粉紅色與紅色構成的油畫。

俯瞰城市的「桌山」是必看的地標，尤其是當冬日薄霧如桌巾般覆蓋其上時。遊客可以搭乘纜車或沿著其中一條步道上山。一到山上，他們就能觀賞瀑布、遺跡，或許還能見到動物在這座國家公園漫步。

即使是在冬天，開普敦也是尋找陽光、海洋及沙灘的人聚集的地方。很多人喜歡在「肯普斯灣」面海的人行步道上散步，享受燦爛的海景。還可以造訪「克里夫頓」，那裡有四座令人驚豔的海灘，或再往南走來到「開普角」。這裡是溫暖的印度洋與冰冷的大西洋交會的地方。

對購物、用餐或娛樂有興趣的人，可前往位於本市東北區的「舊餅乾磨坊」。這個時髦的景點是市集、農產品商店、餐廳和表演活動的所在地。再往北走，另一個可以購物的地方是「維多利亞和阿爾弗雷德濱海區」。在這裡你還可以搭船遊覽「羅本島」。已故總統尼爾森‧曼德拉在這個小島上度過二十七年的牢獄生活。

開普敦也以道地的地方菜餚聞名。開普馬來食物融合數個世紀前傳入的東南亞香料的風味，自成獨特的魅力。南非的辣味肉派「巴布提」，以及類似裹了糖漿的甜甜圈「雙姐妹酥餅」是其中幾樣等著你味蕾的美味驚喜。

開普敦作為全世界最值得造訪的地方之一確實實至名歸。你可以探訪「市碗區」一個多采多姿的郊區，或是參觀「科斯坦伯斯國家植物園」。騎著單車穿梭在具有重大歷史意義的市中心，或只是放鬆心情、吸著涼爽、帶有鹹味的空氣。你做什麼事或你是誰並不重要，開普敦對所有人都非常熱情。

頂部平坦的桌山（Table Mountain）被當地人譽為上帝的餐桌，當上方飄著雲霧時，也被戲稱為上帝準備鋪餐巾吃飯了。

1. it doesn't matter 不重要；沒關係

matter 作動詞時指「有關；要緊」，it doesn't matter 表示「不重要；沒關係」，後面亦可接名詞子句，表示「……不重要」，此時 it 作虛主詞用。

句型 It doesn't matter + wh-/that/if S. + V.

- It doesn't matter what music you put on as long as it's something lively.
  你放什麼音樂都不要緊，只要是輕快的就好了。

- If it doesn't matter where we eat, then I'd like to make a suggestion.
  如果我們在哪裡吃都沒關係，那我想提個建議。

補充 it makes no difference 表示「沒有差別」，後面也可接名詞子句 wh-/that/if + S. + V. 表示「……沒有差別」。

- It makes no difference if you call him or not because he won't answer the phone.
  你打不打給他沒有差別，因為他不會接電話。

- It makes no difference to me when we leave as long as we don't get there late.
  對我來說何時離開都沒有差別，只要我們不遲到就好。

* This is when the area receives most of its rainfall, and the landscape is covered with rich grass.

句型 This is when . . .　這是……的時候

wh- 疑問詞可引導名詞子句，作為主詞補語，表示「這是……的時候」。

- Greg likes to study at night. This is when he's able to concentrate the most.
  葛雷格喜歡在晚上唸書。這是他最能專心的時候。

延伸學習 ▶ This is where S. + V. 表示「這是……的地方」。This is why S. + V. 可表示「這是……的原因」。

- What do you think of this apartment? This is where I'll live starting next month.
  你覺得這間公寓怎麼樣？這是我下個月開始要住的地方。

- You washed your sweater with hot water, and this is why it shrunk.
  你用熱水洗毛衣，這就是它縮水的原因。

* **Even during winter, Cape Town is a gathering place for those seeking sun, sea, and sand.**

`句型` those who + V.（那些）……的人

在此是省略關係代名詞 who，並將之後的動詞改成分詞來修飾 those，後面動詞為一般動詞時，改為現在分詞 V-ing，如文中句子原為 those who seek . . . ，省略後形成 those seeking . . . ；後面動詞為進行式時，則去掉 be 動詞。

- The presentation will contain useful information for those who are thinking about studying abroad.
- = The presentation will contain useful information for those thinking about studying abroad.

  這場講座會包含實用資訊提供給正考慮出國唸書的人。

`補充` 動詞為被動式（be + p.p.）時，則去掉 be 動詞，保留 p.p.。

- This machine should be used only by those who are skilled in factory work.
- = This machine should be used only by those skilled in factory work.

  這台機器應該只由熟悉工廠作業的人使用。

維多利亞阿爾弗雷德濱海區（Victoria & Alfred Waterfront）

Just Follow the Aroma[1]

For many people, coffeehouses hold a special place in their heart. These establishments[2] give customers much more than just a place to go for a hot cup of aromatic coffee. Rather, coffeehouses serve as meeting places where people can go for good conversation and companionship.[3] In Europe especially, the coffeehouses themselves even have colorful histories.

圖片 / Flickr: Zdenko Zivkovic

花神咖啡館（Café de Flore）位於巴黎聖日耳曼大道（Boulevard Saint-Germain）與聖班諾路（Rue St. Benoit）的交會處，自一八九○年起至今已經有一百多年歷史，過去經常是文人雅客、政治家等名人駐足之地。■片 / Wikipedia: Flore-Alexemanuel

Certain coffeehouses from an earlier time are still famous today because of the writers and artists who were once patrons.[4] In Paris, the Café de Flore and Les Deux Magots are two spots that were frequented by such well-known names as Ernest Hemingway, Pablo Picasso, and Jean-Paul Sartre. Visitors still go to sit at outside tables, sip strong coffee, and imagine they are just a table away from greatness. *While chatting and people-watching, they get to soak up the quintessential Parisian atmosphere as well.

Coffeehouses were also known in the past as hotbeds[5] for intellectual conversation and debate. Some, such as the Café Central in Vienna, can boast just such a history. With its marble pillars that rise up to form the bases for the many high ceiling

Vocabulary

1. **aroma** [ə`romə] *n.* 芳香；（食物的）香味
2. **establishment** [ɪ`stæblɪʃmənt] *n.* （營業的）場所；機構；建立
3. **companionship** [kəm`pænjənˌʃɪp] *n.* 陪伴；友誼
4. **patron** [`petrən] *n.* 顧客、主顧
5. **hotbed** [`hɑtˌbɛd] *n.* 溫床

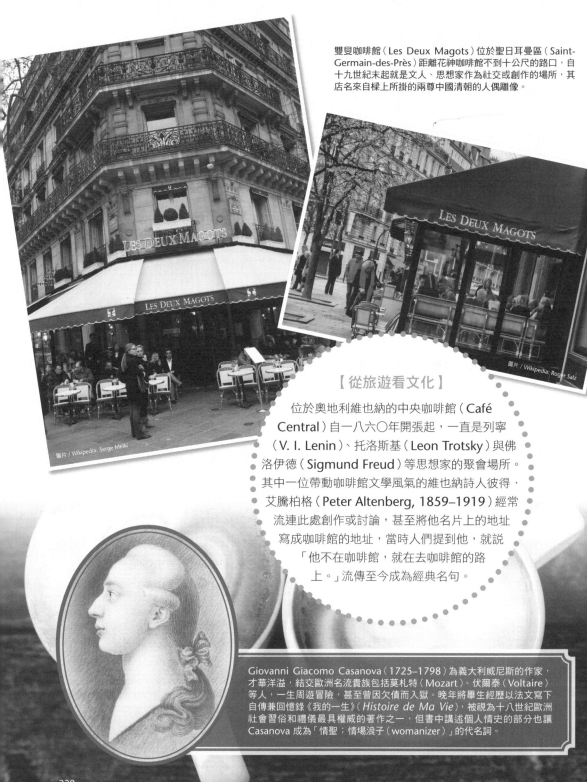

雙叟咖啡館（Les Deux Magots）位於聖日耳曼區（Saint-Germain-des-Prés）距離花神咖啡館不到十公尺的路口，自十九世紀末起就是文人、思想家作為社交或創作的場所，其店名來自樑上所掛的兩尊中國清朝的人偶雕像。

圖片 / Wikipedia: Serge Melki

圖片 / Wikipedia: Roger Salz

【從旅遊看文化】

位於奧地利維也納的中央咖啡館（Café Central）自一八六〇年開張起，一直是列寧（V. I. Lenin）、托洛斯基（Leon Trotsky）與佛洛伊德（Sigmund Freud）等思想家的聚會場所。其中一位帶動咖啡館文學風氣的維也納詩人彼得·艾騰柏格（Peter Altenberg, 1859–1919）經常流連此處創作或討論，甚至將他名片上的地址寫成咖啡館的地址，當時人們提到他，就說「他不在咖啡館，就在去咖啡館的路上。」流傳至今成為經典名句。

Giovanni Giacomo Casanova（1725–1798）為義大利威尼斯的作家，才華洋溢，結交歐洲名流貴族包括莫札特（Mozart）、伏爾泰（Voltaire）等人，一生周遊冒險，甚至曾因欠債而入獄。晚年將畢生經歷以法文寫下自傳兼回憶錄《我的一生》（*Histoire de Ma Vie*），被視為十八世紀歐洲社會習俗和禮儀最具權威的著作之一，但書中講述個人情史的部分也讓 Casanova 成為「情聖；情場浪子（womanizer）」的代名詞。

威尼斯的花神咖啡館在一七二○年開業，英國小說家狄更斯（Charles Dickens）也是座上賓。店外不時有鋼琴、小提琴表演，藝術氣息濃厚。 ■片 / Flickr: Son of Groucho

arches and windows that climb even higher, one can imagine thinking lofty[6] thoughts. Revolutionary[7] thinkers who sipped coffee there are V. I. Lenin, Leon Trotsky, and Sigmund Freud.

Caffè Florian in Venice is one of the longest-established coffeehouses in the world. It is found in the famous Piazza San Marco. Patrons sitting inside are surrounded by deeply-hued[8] walls, paintings, wood carvings, and ornate[9] mirrors. People can enjoy a coffee and take in the cozy,[10] artistic[11] atmosphere of the place as waiters with black vests and white aprons serve them. They can also think about the famous names that were once there, such as Charles Dickens and the notorious womanizer[12] Giovanni Giacomo Casanova.

Vocabulary

6. **lofty** [ˋlɔfti] *adj.* 崇高的；高聳的
7. **revolutionary** [͵rɛvəˋluʃə͵nɛri] *adj.* 革命性的
8. **deeply-hued** [ˋdipliˋhjud] *adj.* 深色的（hued 表「有……顏色的」）
9. **ornate** [ɔrˋnet] *adj.* （裝飾、詞藻等）華麗的
10. **cozy** [ˋkozi] *adj.* 舒適的；愜意的
11. **artistic** [ɑrˋtɪstɪk] *adj.* 藝術的；有藝術天賦的
12. **womanizer** [ˋwʊmə͵naɪzə] *n.* 沈溺女色者；玩弄女性之人

圖片 / Wikipedia: Clayton Tang

圖片 / Wikipedia: DIMSFIKAS

Coffeehouses were also known as places where business took place. One in particular, Jonathan's Coffee-House in London, became known as the spot where people could buy and sell company stocks[13] in the 18th century. As securities trading became more popular, this special coffeehouse eventually[14] became the London Stock Exchange. In the hustling and bustling world of stock trading, it should be little wonder that traders would want to have a bit of caffeine[15] running through their veins.[16]

It is always fun to seek out the places that have a colorful history. Still, there is something to be said for exploring and finding the coffeehouses that are off the beaten track. If you're lucky, you may find a little gem that is on its way to fame.

Vocabulary

13. **stock** [stɑk] *n.* 股票；股份；庫存

14. **eventually** [ɪˋvɛntʃʊəli] *adv.* 最後；最終

15. **caffeine** [kæˋfin] *n.* 咖啡因

16. **vein** [ven] *n.* 靜脈血管；紋理

老咖啡館的記憶拼圖

　　咖啡館在許多人心中佔有一席之地。這些場所讓顧客不只是來喝杯熱熱香醇的咖啡。更確切地說，咖啡館是人們可以暢談、交遊的聚會場所。尤其在歐洲，咖啡館本身甚至有多姿多彩的歷史。

　　一些從以前就存在的咖啡館因為過去曾有作家與藝術家光顧，至今仍聲名遠播。在巴黎，「花神咖啡館」與「雙叟咖啡館」是厄尼斯特·海明威（美國作家，1899–1961）、帕伯羅·畢卡索（西班牙畫家與雕塑家，1881–1973）與尚·保羅·沙特（法國思想家兼作家，1905–1980）等名人經常光顧的兩個地方。至今，顧客仍會坐在戶外的咖啡座啜飲濃郁的咖啡、想像自己與大人物只有一桌之隔。他們可以一邊聊天一邊看著人來人往，同時沈浸在典型的巴黎氛圍當中。

　　過去，咖啡館也是知識性的對話與辯論的溫床。一些咖啡館，像是維也納「中央咖啡館」就以擁有這樣的歷史為傲。店內的大理石柱向上撐起許多挑高的拱形天花板，而窗戶甚至更高，人們可以想像自己正思忖著崇高的思想。在那裡啜飲過咖啡的革命思想家有列寧（蘇聯革命思想家，1870–1924）、里翁·托洛斯基（蘇聯革命家與政治理論家，1879–1940）和席格蒙·佛洛伊德（奧地利精神分析學家，1856–1939）。

　　威尼斯的「花神咖啡館」是目前世界上歷史最悠久的咖啡館之一。它就位在著名的聖馬可廣場。坐在店內的顧客周圍環繞著暗色調的牆面、畫作、木雕和華麗的鏡子。人們可在身穿黑色背心、白色圍裙的服務生送上餐點時享受著咖啡，同時沈浸在舒適、充滿藝術的氛圍中。他們也可以想著曾經造訪過的名人，像是狄更斯（英國小說家，1812–1870）與聲名狼藉的花花公子卡薩諾瓦。

　　咖啡館也是眾所周知的商業場所。尤其是位在倫敦的「喬納森咖啡館」，在十八世紀變成人們得以買賣公司股票的地方。隨著證券交易愈臻普及，這間特別的咖啡館最後變成「倫敦證券交易所」。在股票交易熙攘喧囂的世界中，交易人會需要一點咖啡因在血液中流竄也就不足為奇了。

　　找出那些有輝煌歷史的地方永遠都充滿趣味。而且，探訪找尋那些鮮為人知的咖啡館還是有其吸引人之處：運氣好的話，你可能會在路上發現明日之星。

威尼斯的花神咖啡館（Caffè Florian）圖片 / Wikipedia

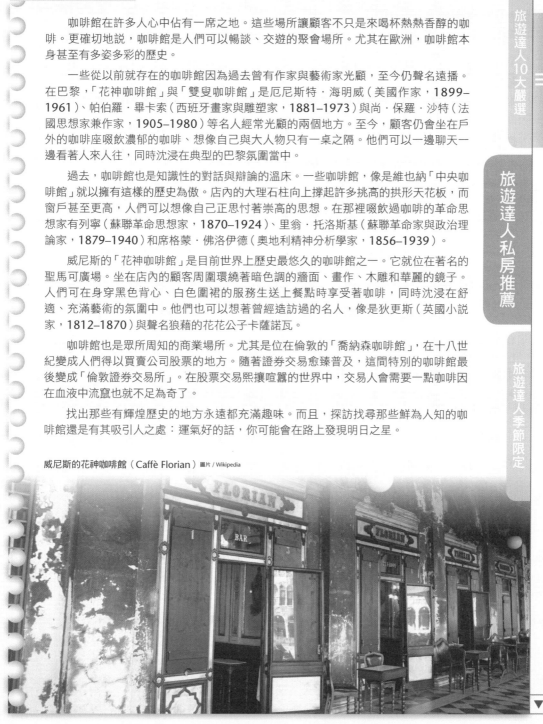

1. serve as 用來當作……

句型 sth + serve as + N.

- The traffic accident yesterday served as a reminder to drive more carefully.
  昨天的車禍可作為要小心駕駛的借鏡。

補充 sb + serve as + 職稱，指「擔任……的職務」。

- He served as the president's bodyguard for five years.
  他擔任總統的貼身侍衛長達五年。

2. hustling and bustling 熙熙攘攘的

形容詞 hustling [`hʌsəlɪŋ] 意為「忙碌的；奔波的」，名詞為 hustle [`hʌsəl]。形容詞 bustling [`bʌsəlɪŋ] 意為「喧囂的；忙亂的」，名詞為 bustle [`bʌsəl]。片語 hustle and bustle 意為「忙碌喧囂」，通常用來指都市忙碌的生活形態。

- You will enjoy the hustle and bustle of the night market once we get there.
  我們一到夜市，你就可以感受到那種熱鬧喧囂。

3. off the beaten track 人跡罕至之地

beaten 在此指「（路）踩出來的；常有人行走的」，off the beaten track 即意為「偏遠的小徑；窮鄉僻壤」。

- The hikers went off the beaten track and made their own way up the mountain.
  登山客踏上人煙罕至的小徑，一路往山上走去。

圖片 / Flickr: Ole Husby

Sentence Patterns

* **While chatting and people-watching, they get to soak up the quintessential Parisian atmosphere as well.**

while 在此作連接詞，表「在……的時候；與……同時」。主要子句與副詞子句的主詞相同時，副詞子句可省略連接詞、主詞與 be 動詞而形成分詞片語。不過有時也會保留連接詞，好讓語意更清楚。

- While Bobby was lost in the foreign city, he remained calm and collected.

→While lost in the foreign city, Bobby remained calm and collected.
  鮑比在國外的城市迷路時，他仍保持鎮靜沉穩。

補充 while 還有另外兩個常見用法：

①表示「而；然而」，用來連接兩個不同的人、事、物。

- The people waiting for the show to start were excited while the actors backstage were nervous.
  等著表演開始的觀眾開始感到興奮，而後台的演員卻緊張得不得了。

②表示「雖然；儘管」，與 although 意思相同。

- While Charlie can't cook, he managed to make dinner for his girlfriend on her birthday.
  雖然查理不會做菜，但他設法在女友生日那天為她煮了一頓晚餐。

威尼斯的花神咖啡館（Caffè Florian）
圖片 / Wikipedia: karlkp

Giethoorn: Where Streets Cannot Be Found

Cruising[1] down the crisscrossing[2] waterways of Giethoorn in the Netherlands, you're greeted with lush[3] grasslands and pink and white water lilies. Old-fashioned thatched[4]-roof cottages seem to float among the grid of canals. Arched wooden bridges connect these little islands while ponds and lakes hide behind thick reeds.[5]

What is missing from this picture? Streets. Giethoorn is a village without streets. There are walking paths, but you won't see any cars. The fewer than 3,000 locals living here instead use water transportation. Some use punts, which are traditional boats pushed by poles, and others move around by motorized[6] water buses.

Giethoorn was founded in 1230 by people fleeing from religious persecution.[7] The first settlers found masses of goat horns from wild goats that died in a flood. The strange sight inspired the name Geytenhoren, meaning "goat horn," which later became Giethoorn. The town became famous in 1958 when the Dutch movie *Fanfare* was filmed there. Tourists who flocked there gave the town its dual[8] nicknames, Venice of the Netherlands and Green Venice.

Vocabulary

1. **cruise** [kruz] *v.* 巡遊；巡航
2. **crisscross** [ˋkrɪsˌkrɔs] *v.* 交叉成十字形（文中 crisscrossing 為現在分詞作形容詞用，指「交錯的」）
3. **lush** [lʌʃ] *adj.* 蒼鬱的；草木茂盛的
4. **thatch** [θætʃ] *v.* 用茅草覆蓋（屋頂）（文中 thatched 為過去分詞作形容詞用法，thatched-roof 表「茅草屋頂的」）
5. **reed** [rid] *n.* 蘆葦
6. **motorize** [ˋmotəˌraɪz] *v.* 為……加上馬達；使機動化（文中 motorized 為過去分詞作形容詞用，指「以馬達驅動的」）
7. **persecution** [ˌpɜsɪˋkjuʃən] *n.* 迫害
8. **dual** [ˋduəl] *adj.* 雙重的；兩個的

羊角村小檔案

距離荷蘭首都阿姆斯特丹（Amsterdam）約一百公里的羊角村禁止車輛進入，居民和遊客只能以船隻或是電動腳踏車當交通工具。此地在冰河時期是位於兩個冰磧丘中間的低地，這種地質條件造成當地土壤貧瘠多沼澤，唯一資源只有地底下的泥煤（peat）。當時在此建村的人為了挖掘泥煤、運輸物資，遂挖出了交錯複雜的運河。村內交織的運河倒映著河上綠意扶疏與溫馨小屋，偶爾船隻或是野鴨划過河中，如此一派悠閒的景致正適合遊客放鬆身心、好好享受。

用篙撐的平底船（punt）是羊角村常見的交通工具　圖片 / Bonnie

The village owes its picturesque[9] look to peat[10] soil, which is mud rich with decomposed vegetation.[11] Peat was dried and burned for heating and cooking, and all this digging resulted in many ponds and lakes. Canals were dug to transport peat, and arched bridges allowed peat boats to pass. This muddy business created Giethoorn's romantic appearance.

The best way to take in Giethoorn's beauty is to hop on an electric whisper boat. As your boat quietly hums along, the peaceful village remains undisturbed. Punting is a unique way to explore if you have strong arms. Navigating[12] your way through the maze[13] of narrow canals can be a challenge, but the scenery is intoxicating.[14]

Tie your boat at the pier[15] and stop by a café for *kopje koffie*. This typical Dutch greeting for guests is a simple

Vocabulary

9. **picturesque** [ˌpɪktʃəˈrɛsk] *adj.* 如詩如畫的
10. **peat** [pit] *n.* 泥煤；泥炭
11. **vegetation** [ˌvɛdʒəˈteʃən] *n.* （統稱）植物；植被
12. **navigate** [ˈnævəˌget] *v.* 航行；駕駛（船隻）
13. **maze** [mez] *n.* 迷宮；複雜難懂的事情
14. **intoxicate** [ɪnˈtɑksəˌket] *v.* 使陶醉或狂喜（文中 intoxicating 以現在分詞作形容詞用，意為「令人陶醉的；醉人的」）
15. **pier** [pɪr] *n.* （突入湖、河、海中的）碼頭

offer of a cup of coffee. Dine in unique restaurants located in charming buildings like a restored[16] mill or an 18th century farmhouse. The chefs whip up delicious meals with local organic produce. *Fanfare* fans should visit the Smit's Paviljoen restaurant, a floating pavilion[17] by Lake Bovenwijde where major scenes were filmed.

Situated in the nature reserve De Wieden, Giethoorn has unspoiled nature that stuns visitors with blossoms in spring and vibrant[18] colors in autumn. Needless to say, water sports like kayaking[19] and sailing are popular here, and in winter, ice-skating in this snowcapped fairy-tale village is a major attraction. If you prefer to stay dry, cycling, golfing, museums, and thatched-roof workshops will keep you busy.

At the end of the day, the cool evening air will encourage you to relax by the fireplace in a cozy cottage. *For an exotic jump back in time, Giethoorn's authentic charm makes it a wonderful place to visit.

Vocabulary

16. **restore** [rɪˋstor] *v.* 復原；修復（文中 restored 為過去分詞作形容詞用，指「已修復的；復原的」）
17. **pavilion** [pəˋvɪljən] *n.* （公園中的）亭；閣
18. **vibrant** [ˋvaɪbrənt] *adj.* （顏色）明亮的；鮮活的
19. **kayak** [ˋkaɪˏæk] *v.* 划獨木舟

中文翻譯　　荷蘭羊角村——如詩如畫水上城

在荷蘭羊角村交錯的水路一路乘船順流而下，迎面而來的是一片綠草如茵以及粉紅與白色相間的睡蓮。傳統茅草屋頂的小屋看起來就好像漂浮在交織的運河上。木頭拱橋連結這些小島，而池塘、湖泊則隱身在濃密的蘆葦之後。

這個畫面少了什麼？是街道。羊角村是個沒有街道的村莊。雖然當地有步行的小徑，不過你看不到任何車子。這裡總數不到三千人的居民都利用水運。有些人會使用平底船，這種船是利用撐篙推進的傳統船隻，有些人則搭乘機動水上巴士來活動。

羊角村是由一群逃避宗教迫害的難民於一二三〇年所建。首批定居者在因洪水溺斃的野羊身上發現大量的羊角。這個奇異的景象就是 Geytenhoren「羊角」這個名字的靈感來源，之後這個名字就演變成 Giethoorn。這座小鎮在一九五八年因為荷蘭電影《軍樂隊》在當地拍攝而聲名大噪。蜂擁而至的遊客給了這座城鎮兩個綽號：「荷蘭威尼斯」以及「綠色威尼斯」。

這座城鎮如詩如畫的景色其實歸因於當地的泥炭，這種土壤富含已分解的植被。泥炭乾燥後供作暖氣和烹調用，也因為挖掘泥炭而造就了許多池塘和湖泊。運河也是開鑿來作運輸泥炭之用，拱橋則讓運送泥炭的船隻能夠通行。這門滿是泥濘的生意創造出羊角村的浪漫風貌。

遊覽羊角村美景的最佳方式就是電動低語船。乘坐的船隻輕聲駛過時，這座祥和的村莊也不會受到打擾。如果你臂力夠強，撐平底木船會是個獨特的觀光方式。要在狹窄如迷宮的運河中駕船可能會是個挑戰，不過這裡的景色會讓你如痴如醉。

把船繫在碼頭，到咖啡館喝杯咖啡吧。（編按：kopje koffie 為荷蘭文的「一杯咖啡」）荷蘭典型的招呼客人方式就是送上一杯咖啡。你可以在獨特的餐廳裡用餐，它們就位在翻修過的磨坊或是十八世紀農舍等迷人的建築裡。主廚會利用當地有機農產品快速做出美味佳餚。《軍樂隊》的影迷則應該去「施密特亭餐廳」，這座餐廳是浮在博溫外德湖上的一座亭子，而那裡正是《軍樂隊》大多數場景的拍攝地。

羊角村位在德威登自然保護區內，它未遭破壞的自然景色，在繁花盛開的春天以及色彩明亮的秋天，都會讓遊客大感驚豔。不用說，划獨木舟、駕駛帆船等水上活動在這裡都很受歡迎，而到了冬季，在這座白雪覆蓋、充滿童話風情的村莊中，溜冰則是遊客最愛的活動。如果你比較喜歡乾爽的活動，騎腳踏車、打高爾夫、逛博物館以及茅草屋頂的工作坊就夠你忙的了。

一日將盡時，涼爽的晚風會讓你想在舒服的小屋裡坐在爐火旁放鬆休息。想來一趟充滿異國風味的復古之旅，充滿真實魅力的羊角村是個值得一遊的好地方。

1. **owe A to B** 把 A 歸功於 B；有 A 是由於 B

owe 是「歸功、歸因於……」的意思。owe A to B 表示「將 A 歸功於 B」。

- I owe a lot to my parents for all that they have done for me in my life.
  我將現在的成就歸功於父母為我所做的一切。

補充

① owing to + N./V-ing　因為……；由於……

- Owing to the bumpy roads, we were not able to drive very fast.
  由於路顛簸不平，我們無法開很快。

② owe + sb + sth　欠某人某物

- Patrick owes his credit card company thousands of dollars.
  派翠克欠信用卡公司數千美元。

2. **whip up**　迅速做好（尤指一頓飯）

whip 除有「鞭打；攪打（奶油等）」的意思，還有「迅速做成」之意，後者常與
up 連用。

- I whipped up a quick breakfast for my friends before we went off on a hike.
  出發去爬山前我為朋友快速做了早餐。

補充　指「激起；煽動（某種情感、激動的情緒等）」。

- News reports about the coming typhoon whipped up public fear.
  關於那個即將來臨的颱風報導引起了大眾的恐懼。

3. **needless to say**　不用說；當然

needless to say 是由 it is needless to say that 省略而來，可放句首或句尾，使用時
需用逗號與句子的其他部分隔開。

- Needless to say, we're going to have a lot of work to do in the coming weeks.
  不用說，我們接下來幾週將有得忙了。

- You will be tired tomorrow if you stay up very late tonight, needless to say.
  如果你今晚熬夜的話，你明天當然會很累。

相似用法

① It goes without saying that S. + V.　不用說，……

- It goes without saying that some people are better at sports than others.
  不用說，有些人的運動細胞就是比其他人好。

② It is obvious that S. + V. 很明顯地，……

　Obviously, S. + V. 顯然地，……

- Obviously, the best way to solve this problem is to talk with the boss.
  顯然地，解決這個問題的最好方法就是去跟老闆談。

Sentence Patterns

* **For an exotic jump back in time, Giethoorn's authentic charm makes it a wonderful place to visit.**

句型 make + O. + O.C. 使……

受詞補語（O.C.）可為形容詞、名詞或介系詞片語，本句受詞 it 指 Giethoorn，O.C. 為名詞片語 a wonderful place to visit。

- The beautiful stars in the sky made it a night to remember.
  夜空中美麗的星星使之成為難忘的一晚。

補充 make it + O.C. + to + V. 使……

此句型中 it 為虛受詞，真正的受詞為後面的不定詞 to + V.。

- The snow and ice make it difficult to climb the mountain.
  下雪和結冰使登山變得很困難。

A Drive through Provence

Paris may be the capital of France, but Provence is its heart. The landscape[1] and culture of this southeastern corner of the country have inspired artists for centuries. Since many of its cities are just a stone's throw away from each other, they can be easily experienced on a delightful[2] road trip.

If you're coming from the north, a convenient entry[3] point to Provence is Avignon, one of France's most beautiful cities. It was home to the popes[4] during the fourteenth century, and its former glory[5] is still visible today from the presence of the Papal Palace. It's the largest Gothic palace in Europe, and you can go inside and get a sense of how the popes lived. Then, take a walk on the nearby bridge to catch an amazing view of the Rhône River and the sand-colored palace walls rising against the city's blue skies.

左：亞維農教皇宮殿被認為是最重要的中世紀哥德式建築之一。右：染匠街（Dyers Street，法文為 Rue des Teinturiers）在十四至十九世紀期間製造業非常活躍，尤以染布業聞名。圖片 / Flickr: David Locke

Not far from the palace is Avignon's main square, lined with open-air restaurants and cafés. After a relaxing meal here, wander south on the city's tree-lined avenues[6] towards Dyers Street, where fabric dyers used to do their trade. This narrow street runs along a canal with ancient waterwheels,[7] and on the opposite side, you can peek[8] into trendy shops and beautiful gardens.

From Avignon, drive around thirty kilometers south to get to Arles. Along the way, stop by St. Remy to visit the twelfth-century St. Paul Asylum, where Vincent van Gogh committed[9] himself after suffering from attacks of mental illness. From his

亞維農教皇宮殿內部華麗的雕飾

Vocabulary

1. **landscape** [ˈlændˌskep] *n.* 風景；自然景色
2. **delightful** [dɪˈlaɪtfəl] *adj.* 令人愉悅的
3. **entry** [ˈɛntri] *n.* 入口；進入權
4. **pope** [pop] *n.* 教皇；教宗
5. **glory** [ˈglɔri] *n.* 光榮、榮耀
6. **avenue** [ˈævəˌnju] *n.* 大道；林蔭大道
7. **waterwheel** [ˈwɔtɚˌhwil] *n.* 水車
8. **peek** [pik] *v.* 窺視；瞥見
9. **commit** [kəˈmɪt] *v.* 把……送進監獄；犯（罪）；做（錯事）

圖片 / Wikipedia: Jean-Marc ROSIER

亞爾競技場（Arles Arena）是世上保存最完善的古羅馬競技場之一。

room in the asylum, Van Gogh painted the wheat fields, flowers, and olive trees that he saw through his window and produced dozens of great works. If you visit Van Gogh's room, you can still see the same landscape that inspired the artist over a century ago.

Once in Arles, you'll be struck by the city's ancient scenery.[10] With magnificent Roman architecture[11] and a network of stone-paved streets, the old part of Arles resembles[12] a living museum. The most important building here is the Arles Arena. Two thousand years ago, thousands of fans came here to cheer on wild-animal-battling gladiators.[13] Today, on the first Monday of July, the arena hosts an exciting bullfight in which men try to remove a ribbon[14] tied around the bull's horns.

Also in July, Arles's ancient theater hosts the Festival of Arles with exhibitions and performances.[15] Not far away, Forum Square is bordered by cafés and offers a peaceful spot for enjoying the golden lights of Arles's summer evenings.

地名小辭典

St. Remy [sent] [rə`mɪ] 聖雷米（法國南部的一個小鎮）
St. Paul Asylum [ə`saɪləm] 聖保羅精神病院
Arles Arena [ə`rinə] 亞爾競技場
Forum Square [`fɔrəm] 論壇廣場
Richelme Square [`rɪʃəm] 里舍姆廣場
Cours Mirabeau [kor] [mɪrɑ`bo] 米拉波林蔭大道

Vincent van Gogh
（文森・梵谷，1853–
1890）為知名後印象派
畫家。梵谷生前在亞爾的
聖保羅精神病院創作出
《星夜》等知名作品。

Heading further south from Arles and driving along stretches of white cliffs and rich fields, you'll arrive in Aix-en-Provence. *Here, you'll see why Provence is known as France's "garden market," as market vendors display fresh produce[16] grown in this region every day of the week. Under large umbrellas on Richelme Square, fruits and vegetables are colorfully displayed, as well as handmade cheeses, sausages, and organic honeys and spices. In the markets, you'll also find Provence's most famous export,[17] lavender,[18] sold in bundles and as cute little souvenir pillows.

Vocabulary

10. **scenery** [`sinəri] *n.* 風景；景色
11. **architecture** [`ɑrkə،tɛktʃə] *n.* 建築
12. **resemble** [rɪ`zɛmbəl] *v.* 與……相似、相像
13. **gladiator** [`glædi،etə] *n.* 戰士、鬥士
    （尤指古羅馬時代與人或動物決鬥來娛樂大眾者）
14. **ribbon** [`rɪbən] *n.* 緞帶；絲帶
15. **performance** [pə`fɔrməns] *n.* 表演；演出
16. **produce** [`prɑdjus] *n.* 農產品
17. **export** [`ɛksport] *n.* 出口（品）
18. **lavender** [`lævəndə] *n.* 薰衣草

艾克斯市場販售各式農產品、
花卉及薰衣草相關產品。
圖片 / Flickr: lamericat、AndyLawson

Besides markets, Aix is also scattered with marble fountains, many of which are found on the Cours Mirabeau, an elegant[19] street decorated with noble buildings. The seventeenth-century Fountain of the Four Dolphins, located on a tree-shaded square, is perhaps the prettiest one of them all. Like other Provence cities, Aix has many narrow lanes separated by graceful[20] squares, and one of the pleasures of visiting this city is to wander around and discover all the hidden sights.

From the papal city of Avignon to the market-filled streets of Aix, Provence provides the perfect route for a road trip in France. The beautiful scenery along the way is an added bonus[21] that makes a July in Provence a magical experience.

Vocabulary

19. **elegant** [ˋɛləgənt] *adj.* 優美的、典雅的
20. **graceful** [ˋgresfəl] *adj.* 典雅的、優雅的
21. **bonus** [ˋbonəs] *n.* 額外的好處；紅利

開車玩遍普羅旺斯

巴黎也許是法國的首都，但普羅旺斯卻是它的心臟。這個位居法國東南角的自然景觀和文化幾世紀以來帶給藝術家靈感。由於普羅旺斯許多城市彼此相距不遠，因此一趟愉悅的公路旅行就能輕鬆體驗這些地方。

如果你從北邊過來，一個進入普羅旺斯方便的地點就是亞維農，它是法國最美麗的城市之一。十四世紀時，亞維農是教宗的駐地，而今從教皇宮殿的存在仍然可見昔日的榮耀。它是歐洲最大的哥德式宮殿，你可以進去感受一下教宗的生活。然後，到附近的橋上走一走，欣賞隆河令人驚豔的美景以及矗立在亞維農藍色天空下的淺棕色宮殿城牆。

離宮殿不遠處是亞維農的主要廣場，四周林立著露天餐館和咖啡館。在這裡享用悠閒的一餐後，可以沿著此城的林蔭大道往南漫步至染匠街，這裡曾是織物染匠做買賣的地方。這條狹小的街道沿著一條有古老水車的運河前進，在運河的另一邊，你可以窺見時髦的商店和美麗的花園。

從亞維農開車往南約三十公里就能到亞爾。沿途可以停駐在聖雷米參觀十二世紀的聖保羅精神病院，文森‧梵谷在承受精神疾病的折磨之後就住在這裡。梵谷從精神病院的病房中畫下了窗外所見的麥田、花朵和橄欖樹，創作出許多偉大的作品。如果你參觀梵谷的病房，仍然可以看到一個多世紀以前賦予這位藝術家靈感的相同景色。

一到亞爾，你會被此城古老的風景打動。宏偉的羅馬建築和縱橫交錯、鋪著石子的街道讓亞爾的古城區宛如一座活生生的博物館。此地最重要的建築是亞爾競技場。兩千年前，數以千計的狂熱者到這裡替與猛獸搏鬥的戰士加油。現今，每年七月的第一個星期一，競技場會舉辦刺激的鬥牛活動，活動中的男子試圖要扯掉繫在公牛角上的緞帶。

同樣在七月，亞爾的古老劇院會舉辦有許多展覽會和表演的亞爾慶典。而在不遠處，論壇廣場周邊的咖啡座則提供一個讓人享受亞爾夏日傍晚金色光暉的寧靜憩點。

從亞爾再往南走，沿著綿延不斷的白色峭壁和豐饒的農田行駛，就會到達艾克斯。在這裡，你將會見識到為什麼普羅旺斯被稱為法國的「花園市場」，因為市場攤販平日每天都會陳列此區所種的新鮮農產品。在里舍姆廣場的大洋傘下陳列著五彩繽紛的各式蔬果，還有手工起士、香腸和有機蜂蜜與香料。在市場裡，你也會找到普羅旺斯最著名的出口品薰衣草，以成束以及小巧可愛枕頭形狀的紀念品來販售。

除了市場之外，艾克斯也遍布著大理石噴泉，其中許多都座落在米拉波林蔭大道上，它是一條由宏偉建築點綴的優美街道。十七世紀的四豚噴泉位於一處林蔭廣場，或許是所有噴泉中最美的。艾克斯就像普羅旺斯的其他城市一樣，有許多由典雅廣場隔開的狹窄巷道，而參觀這個城市的樂趣之一，就是四處閒逛發掘所有隱密的景色。

從教皇城市亞維農到處處都有市集的艾克斯街道，普羅旺斯提供了法國絕佳的公路旅行路線。沿途優美的風景是附加的好處，讓七月的普羅旺斯之旅成為迷人的體驗。

1. southeastern 東南邊的

表示「位在（某方位）的；來自（某方位）的」，可在字尾加上 -ern 形成形容詞，如文中用法。

- Southern Italy is much warmer than northern Italy.
  義大利南部比義大利北部溫暖多了。

延伸學習 各種方向的說法

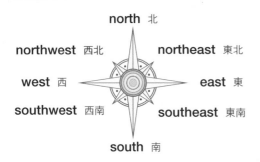

north 北
northwest 西北   northeast 東北
west 西   east 東
southwest 西南   southeast 東南
south 南

2. get a sense of . . . 感受到……；了解……

sense 有「知覺；觀念」的意思，片語 get a sense of + N. 表示「感受到……；了解……」，片語中的名詞也可改用名詞子句，如文中 get a sense of how the popes lived 指「感受教宗的生活起居」。

- Ted wanted to get a sense of what his clients were looking for before starting the project.
  泰德想要在展開這項企劃案前了解他客戶要的是什麼。

3. kilo- 作字首

字首 kilo- 表示「千」，常與長度或重量單位合用，如文中用 kilo- 加上 meter（公尺），kilometer 指「公里」；kilogram 則指「公斤」。

- Molly weighed three and a half kilograms when she was born.
  莫莉出生時有三點五公斤。

補充 與數字相關的字首還有 milli-（千分之一、毫）、cent-/centi-（百；百分之一）。

- Tom has grown four centimeters since last summer.
  湯姆從去年夏天以來長高了四公分。

4. **cheer on sb** 為某人加油、喝采

cheer 表示「喝采；激勵」。

- People who went to watch the race cheered on the runners.
  來觀看比賽的人為跑者加油。

5. **along vs. alone**

這兩個字拼字、發音相似，但詞性、意義有不同：

	along [ə`lɔŋ]	alone [ə`lon]
詞性及意義	介 沿著；順著（文中用法） 副 帶著；一起	形 獨自的；單獨的 副 單獨地；獨自地

- Go along this street and you'll eventually see the barbershop.
  沿著這條街走，最後你會看到那家理髮店。

- Do you mind if I bring my brother along to the party?
  你介意我帶我弟一起參加派對嗎？

- Jeremy was alone when I saw him.
  我看到傑瑞米時，他是獨自一人。

- Dana hates to eat alone in restaurants.
  丹娜討厭獨自在餐廳用餐。

Sentence Patterns

* **Here, you'll see why Provence is known as France's "garden market,". . .**

why 可作表原因的關係副詞，常用 the reason why S. + V. 表示「……的原因」。此句是省略 the reason，why + S. + V. 為名詞子句作 see 的受詞。

- I don't understand why we have to finish all this work before tomorrow.
  我不明白為什麼我們必須在明天前完成這所有的工作。

- No one knows the reason why Charlie decided to change his career.
  沒有人知道查理決定改變職涯的原因。

旅遊達人10大嚴選

旅遊達人私房推薦

旅遊達人季節限定

241

A Journey along the Fairy-Tale Road

Fairy tales bring people on exciting journeys to distant times and places. Many well-known fairy tales were made famous by the Grimm brothers, who traveled across Germany collecting stories that they put into books. Today, the 595-kilometer Fairy-Tale Road in Germany takes visitors on an adventure to discover the origins[1] of some of these tales.

文化小辭典

salad festival（沙拉慶典）最早起源於一七二八年，在每年復活節（Easter）的六十天後舉辦，為期五天，相傳是為了慶祝萵苣（lettuce）傳入該鎮而開始的，此時居民會穿上傳統服飾載歌載舞，舉辦遊行，並準備當地食物來慶祝。

巴特維爾東根（Bad Wildungen）近郊有七矮人雕像和「白雪公主之家」等童話景點。圖片 / Wikipedia

Starting in Hanau, the Grimms' birthplace,[2] visitors head north to Schwalmstadt, where the story of "Little Red Riding Hood" took place. The red caps worn traditionally by little girls here remind us of Little Red Riding Hood's costume.[3] You can see the fairy-tale costume at the regional museum, or during the "salad festival," when people dress up in traditional clothes to celebrate the local culture.

North of Schwalmstadt is the spa[4] town of Bad Wildungen, the setting of Snow White's story. Visitors can see Snow White's house and then soak[5] in the mineral springs or stroll through the town's parks and gardens.

Vocabulary

1. **origin** [ˋɔrədʒɪn] *n.* 起源；由來
2. **birthplace** [ˋbɝθˏples] *n.* 出生地
3. **costume** [ˋkɑstjum] *n.* （某時期、國家、民族特有的）服裝；戲服
4. **spa** [spɑ] *n.* 礦泉療養地；溫泉療養中心
5. **soak** [sok] *v.* 浸泡

Bremen
不來梅

Hamelin
哈梅林

【從旅遊看文化】

十九世紀時，德國的格林兄弟（the Brothers Grimm，或稱 the Grimm brothers）走訪全國各地、收集許多民間故事，集結成為《格林童話》（*Grimms' Fairy Tales*），從此聞名全球。二次大戰後，德國政府為推廣觀光，選出與格林兄弟成長背景或筆下故事相關的城市，連成一條「童話大道」（Fairy-Tale Road），讓遊客有機會身歷其境，體驗童話的神奇氛圍。

Trendelburg
川德堡

Sababurg　薩巴堡

Bad Wildungen
巴特維爾東根

Kassel
卡塞爾

Schwalmstadt
修瓦斯達城

Hamburg

Bremen

Hanau

【GERMANY】

Hanau　哈瑙

Further northeast is Kassel, where the Grimms began studying German literature.[6] It's home to the Brothers Grimm Museum, which contains handwritten[7] books that belonged to the brothers. Another famous attraction[8] here is Wilhelmshöhe Park, with a magnificent palace and water garden.

*Further north, just outside the town of Sababurg, lies a 650-year-old castle. Locals say this is where Sleeping Beauty slept for one hundred years before finally being rescued by a prince's kiss. You could sleep here, too, because the castle is now a hotel, surrounded[9] by a charming[10] park with ancient trees.

圖片 / Wikipedia: Presse03

圖片 / Flickr: moedermens

左：薩巴堡（Sababurg）外牆上蔓生的爬藤為現在的旅館增添浪漫風情
右：位於卡塞爾（Kassel）的格林兄弟博物館
右下：據說觸摸不來梅（Bremen）市政廳前的動物銅像可以帶來好運，
　　　所以驢子的腳被摸得特別光亮！

Vocabulary

6. **literature** [ˈlɪtərəˌtʃə] *n.* 文學（作品）；文獻
7. **handwritten** [ˈhændˌrɪtn̩] *adj.* 手寫的
8. **attraction** [əˈtrækʃən] *n.* 吸引人的地方或事物
9. **surround** [səˈraʊnd] *v.* 圍繞；環繞
10. **charming** [ˈtʃɑrmɪŋ] *adj.* 迷人的

圖片 / Flickr: Allie_Caulfield

245

West of Sababurg is Trendelburg, the setting for Rapunzel's tale. The town's medieval castle is thought to be where the maiden[11] let down her long blond[12] hair so that the prince could climb up and save her.

Another town made famous by the Grimms is Hamelin. The Pied Piper used his music to lure away the rats as well as the children of this town. Today, the children are back, and the rats can be seen mostly[13] in the form of souvenir bakery items.

The final part of the journey takes us to Bremen, where ancient buildings and playful animal statues dot[14] the streets and square. The Fairy-Tale Road ends here, but visitors don't need to be sad. *If they ever want to return to this magical land, a copy of *Grimms' Fairy Tales* can set them on their way.

不來梅如童話般的小店　■片 / Flickr: Allie_Caulfield

川德堡（Trendelburg）附近的「長髮姑娘之家」曾作為故事影集搭景地　■片 / Wikipedia: Presse03

Vocabulary

11. **maiden** [ˋmedn̩] *n.* 少女；未婚女子
12. **blond** [blɑnd] *adj.* （髮色）金的；金髮的
13. **mostly** [ˋmostlɪ] *adv.* 大部分；主要地
14. **dot** [dɑt] *v.* 散布於；點綴

德國童話大道奇幻之旅

　　童話故事帶領人們到遙遠的過去和地方去進行刺激的旅程。許多耳熟能詳的童話故事都是因為格林兄弟走遍德國收集故事集結成書而聞名。今日，德國境內五百九十五公里長的童話大道帶領遊客來趟探險之旅，去發掘其中一些故事的起源。

　　遊客從格林兄弟的出生地哈瑙出發，往北來到修瓦斯達城，這是〈小紅帽〉故事發生的地點。這裡的小女孩傳統戴的紅色帽子讓我們想起小紅帽的服裝。你可以在此區的博物館中看到童話故事裡的服飾，在「沙拉慶典」期間也可看到，此時人們會穿上傳統服飾來歌頌當地的文化。

　　修瓦斯達城北方的水療小鎮巴特維爾東根是〈白雪公主〉故事發生的地方。遊客可以看到白雪公主的家，然後泡一下礦泉浴，或到鎮上的公園與花園裡走一走。

　　再往東北方走就是卡塞爾，格林兄弟在這裡開始研讀德國文學。這裡是格林兄弟博物館的所在地，裡面收藏兩兄弟親手寫的書籍。這裡的另一個知名景點是威廉高地公園，裡面有壯觀的宮殿和水景花園。

　　再往北走，就在薩巴堡鎮外，座落著一座有六百五十年歷史的城堡。當地人說這是睡美人最後被王子的吻拯救前沉睡了一百年的地方。你也可以在這裡過夜，因為這座城堡現在是一間旅館，環繞四周的是一座種著老樹的迷人庭園。

　　薩巴堡西方就是川德堡，即〈長髮姑娘〉的故事地點。這個鎮上的中世紀城堡被認為是那位少女放下她的金色長髮好讓王子可以爬上去救她的地方。

　　另一個因格林兄弟而出名的城鎮是哈梅林。花衣吹笛手曾用他的樂音把這個鎮上的老鼠和小孩拐走。而今孩子們回來了，老鼠則大多可在烘焙紀念品中見到。

　　這趟旅程的最後一段帶我們來到不來梅，當地古老的建築和充滿趣味的動物雕像散布在街道和廣場上。這裡是童話大道的終點站，但是遊客用不著感傷。如果他們想重返這個神奇的國度，一本《格林童話集》就可以帶他們踏上旅程。

不來梅的電箱上畫著四隻主角動物，充滿童趣。圖片 / Wikipedia: Harald Bischoff

哈梅林（Hamelin）的音樂鐘，每天都上演吹笛人的故事。圖片 / Flickr: Allie_Caulfield

1. cap vs. hat 帽子不一樣

	cap	hat
特徵	沒有帽沿（brim）的帽子，常用於特殊用途（如淋浴）或從事特殊工作時戴的帽子	有帽沿的帽子
常見例子	baseball cap 棒球帽 shower cap 浴帽 surgeon's cap 手術帽	top hat 大禮帽 cowboy hat 牛仔帽 hard hat（工地）安全帽

2. belong to 屬於

belong to 有兩種常見用法：

① sth + belong to + sb 某物歸某人所有

- The jacket on the chair belongs to me.
  椅子上那件夾克是我的。

② sb + belong to + 團體、組織 某人是某團體、組織的成員

- Robert belongs to an organization that raises money for orphans.
  羅伯特是一個為孤兒募款團體的成員。

* **Further north, just outside the town of Sababurg, lies a 650-year-old castle.**

此句用的是倒裝句，還原成直述句為：Further north, a 650-year-old castle lies just outside the town of Sababurg。

要說明某建築物座落在什麼地點時，可用主動句型：

sth + lies/sits + prep + 地點

- The ski resort lies next to the mountain.
  那個滑雪度假村座落在山邊。

- The house sits in a quiet neighorhood on the east side of town.
  那棟房子位於小鎮東邊一個寧靜的區域。

延伸學習 也可用以下的被動句型來說明所在位置：

sth + be located/situated + prep + 地點

- The library is located next to the supermarket.
  圖書館位於超市旁。
- Frank's office is situated across the street from here.
  法蘭克的辦公室就在這裡對面。

* **If they ever want to return to this magical land, a copy of *Grimms' Fairy Tales* can set them on their way.**

  ever 的用法如下：

  ① 用在條件句中作強調用，如文中用法。

- If you ever want to borrow my scooter, just ask me.
  如果你想跟我借機車的話，就跟我說吧。

  ② 用在疑問句或否定句中，表示「曾經」，強調過去經驗。

- Have you ever been on a cruise ship?
  你曾經搭過郵輪嗎？
- Toby lives in this apartment, but nobody ever sees him go in or out.
  托比住在這棟公寓裡，但從沒有人看見他進出過。

  ③ 用在比較級和最高級句型中，強調「以往任何時候；至今」。

- Despite his recent injury, the athlete is now running faster than ever.
  儘管最近受過傷，那位運動員現在跑得比以往還要快。
- The best meal I've ever had was in that French restaurant.
  我至今吃過最棒的一餐就是在那間法國餐廳裡。

Destination: London

London is the largest city in Europe, and in many ways, it is also the most unique. It can seem like either a fast-paced modern metropolis[1] buzzing with life and entertainment or an elegant capital that is immersed[2] in tradition. Here, historic monuments, scenic[3] gardens, and world-class museums stand side-by-side trendy[4] restaurants, hip fashion shops, and cutting-edge dance clubs.

Getting around this sprawling city may be a challenge at first, but London's public transportation system is fast and efficient. The Underground, or the Tube as it is commonly called, can get you across the city quickly. If you want a special treat and can spend a little extra, you can also take one of the famed black taxis. The drivers are known for their expert knowledge of the streets and their talkative

Vocabulary

1. **metropolis** [mə`trɑpləs] *n.* 大都市；首都
2. **immerse** [ɪ`mɜs] *v.* 使沈浸；使埋首於
3. **scenic** [`sinɪk] *adj.* 風景的；景致秀麗的
4. **trendy** [`trɛndi] *adj.* 時髦的；流行的

觀光旅遊小辭典

artifact [ˋɑrtɪˏfækt] 文物；藝品

botanical garden [bəˋtænɪkəl] [ˋgɑrdn̩] 植物園

flea market [fli] [ˋmɑrkət] 跳蚤市場；市集

gallery [ˋgæləri] 美術館；藝廊

handicraft [ˋhændɪˏkræft] 手工藝品

monument [ˋmɑnjəmənt] 紀念碑（塔）；歷史遺跡

stall [stɔl] 攤位；亭子

public transportation system [ˏtrænspɚˋteʃən] 大眾運輸系統

underground [ˋʌndɚˏgraʊnd] 地鐵（the tube 可用來指倫敦的「地鐵」）

double-decker bus [ˏdʌbəlˋdɛkɚ] 雙層巴士

personalities. High above the road, London's iconic double-decker buses are another convenient way to travel.

If you want the best view of the city, take a ride on the London Eye, one of the tallest observation[5] wheels in the world. If your budget is small, many museums in London, such as the National Gallery and the British Museum, offer free public access.[6] For the wealth of art and artifacts on display, they are well worth a visit.

Apart from the essential[7] places such as Buckingham Palace and the Tower of London, there is an abundance of things to see located slightly[8] off the beaten path. Camden Markets, for instance, attracts young crowds with its restaurants, pubs, and stalls stacked[9] with handicrafts, alternative[10] fashions, and books. The flea market on Portobello Road in the Notting Hill district is another charming attraction. Here, sellers line

波多貝羅路（Portobello Road）的二手書店
圖片 / Wikipedia: Mark Ahsmann

白金漢宮（Buckingham Palace）

Vocabulary

5. **observation** [ˌɑbzəˋveʃən] *n.* 觀察；觀測
6. **access** [ˋæk͵sɛs] *n.* 管道；通道；途徑
7. **essential** [ɪˋsɛnʃəl] *adj.* 必要的；不可或缺的
8. **slightly** [ˋslaɪtli] *adv.* 稍微地；輕微地
9. **stack** [stæk] *v.* 堆疊；堆放
10. **alternative** [ɔlˋtɜnətɪv] *adj.* 非主流的；非傳統的；替代的

英國皇家植物園「裘園（Royal Botanic Gardens, Kew）」規模龐大，有多種植物溫室及良好的生態環境。

a picturesque, winding road full of colorful houses. If the weather is pleasant, you can also take a walk through Kew Gardens, one of the best botanical gardens in the world.

London's distinctive[11] flavor also comes from a vast[12] immigrant[13] population, which has infused energy and color into the city. In fact, no visit is complete without a stop in Chinatown, and one must have a meal at an Indian or Middle Eastern restaurant. It can be a welcome escape from the traditional street fare[14] of fish and chips.

*No matter how old you are or what your interests are, London offers something fun and exciting for everyone. Whatever you have your heart set on, you are sure to find it in this beautiful British city.

Vocabulary

11. **distinctive** [dɪˋstɪŋktɪv] *adj.* 獨特的；特殊的
12. **vast** [væst] *adj.* 大量的；廣大的
13. **immigrant** [ˋɪməgrənt] *adj.* 移民的
14. **fare** [fɛr] *n.* 飲食；伙食

漫遊英倫

　　倫敦是歐洲最大的城市，在許多方面，它也是最獨特的。它可以是個看似步調快速且充滿生命力和娛樂的現代都會，也可以是個沈浸在傳統的典雅首都。在這裡，歷史古蹟、風景秀麗的園林、世界級的博物館，與時髦餐館、流行時尚的服裝店，和前衛的舞廳並立著。

　　要在這廣闊的城市四處逛剛開始可能是個挑戰，但倫敦的大眾運輸系統快速又有效率。俗稱 Tube 的地下鐵讓您在城裡迅速來往穿梭。如果想有特別的款待，且有能力多負擔一些，您也可以乘坐知名的黑頭計程車。這些司機對專業的街道知識和侃侃而談的個性是眾所皆知的。高高行駛在路上，象徵倫敦的雙層巴士是另一種便利的旅遊方式。

　　如果您想欣賞這座城市最棒的景色，就要搭乘世界最高觀景摩天輪之一的「倫敦眼」。如果您的預算不多，倫敦有許多博物館，如「國家美術館」和「大英博物館」，是讓民眾免費參觀的。豐富的藝術文物展覽非常值得您造訪。

　　除了「白金漢宮」和「倫敦塔」等必遊景點外，在人煙較為稀少之處也有很豐富的東西可以去看看。例如「肯頓市場」的餐廳、酒吧以及堆滿手工藝品、另類時裝和書籍的小攤子，就吸引了年輕族群。「諾汀丘區」波多貝羅路上的跳蚤市場是另一個迷人的景點。小販在這裡綿延成一條如詩如畫的蜿蜒道路，沿途盡是色彩繽紛的房屋。如果天氣舒適的話，您也可以逛逛「裘園」，它是世界上最棒的植物園之一。

　　倫敦獨特的風格也來自其大量的移民人口，為這座城市注入了活力與色彩。事實上，沒有去趟「中國城」就不算真正造訪本地，而且一定要試試印度或中東餐館。這些都是傳統街頭小吃「炸魚配薯條」之外另一種受歡迎的選擇。

　　無論您年紀多大或有什麼興趣，倫敦都能提供大家一些有趣、刺激的事物。不管您心裡所嚮往的是什麼，一定能在這座美麗的英倫之都中找到。

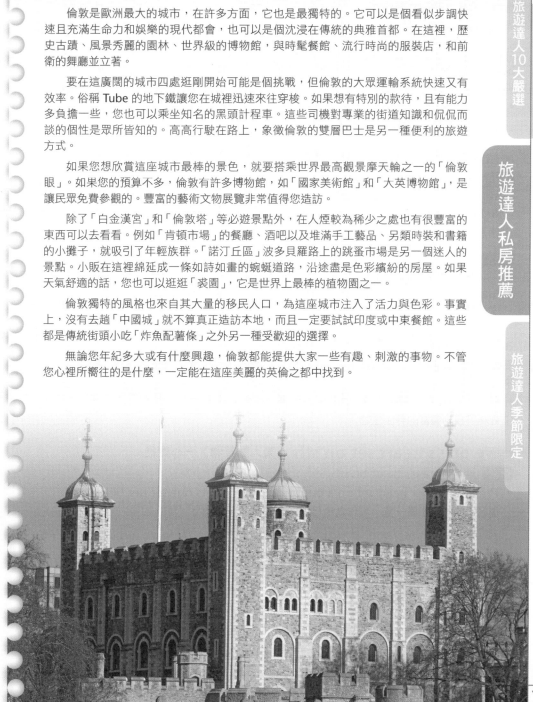

倫敦塔（Tower of London）在一九八八年被列為世界文化遺產

1. **buzz with sth** 充滿（興奮、活動等）

buzz 在此作動詞，本指「（蜜蜂）嗡嗡叫；（機器）唧唧響」，引申為「忙亂；吱吱喳喳地討論」。

- The classroom was buzzing with voices before the teacher showed up.
  老師出現前整個教室鬧哄哄的。

2. **apart from** 除了……之外（還有）

同義 aside from、besides、in addition to

- Aside from the free night at the hotel, the airline paid for our dinner when the flight was canceled
  除了飯店免費住宿一晚外，班機取消後航空公司還請了我們一頓晚餐。

  補充 apart from 還可表示「除了……以外（都……）」，不包括後面的人事物，此時意義同 except for。

- Aside from Jack, all of the students turned in their homework.
  除了傑克以外，其他學生都交作業。

3. **an abundance of** 大量的；豐富的

名詞 abundance [əˋbʌndəns] 指「充沛；豐富」，常用 an abundance of + N. 來形容事物很豐富。

- There is an abundance of wildlife found in the forest.
  森林可找到豐富的野生生物。

4. **have one's heart set on sth** （某人對某物）一心嚮往

同義 get/set one's heart on sth

- The girl has her heart set on a puppy, and she wants one for her birthday.
  那名女孩一心想要一隻小狗作為生日禮物。

Sentence Patterns

* **No matter how old you are or what your interests are, London offers something fun and exciting for everyone.**

No matter + wh- 作連接詞用，可用 wh-ever 代換，用來引導副詞子句。

句型 no matter + wh- + S. + V.
= wh-ever + S. + V.
不管……；無論……

原句可改為 However old you are or whatever your interests are, . . .。而文中下一句的 Whatever you have your heart set on, . . . 亦可改寫成 No matter what you have your heart set on, . . .。

• No matter where we travel to, I want the hotel booked before we get there.
= Wherever we travel to, I want the hotel booked before we get there.
無論我們要去哪裡旅行，我都希望在抵達前先訂好飯店。

圖片 / Wikipedia: Basic LA

6. 玫瑰之城波特蘭

PLAY ALL　　TRACK 52

Summer in the City of Roses

As the sun comes out after a cold, rainy Portland winter, flowers burst into view all over the City of Roses. They perfume[1] the parks and hang in colorful baskets from streetlights.[2] This is the best time of year in my delightful city, and the long summer days allow for plenty[3] of time to enjoy the beauty and fun that Portland has to offer.

One of my favorite things to do on a summer weekend is to go to the Farmer's Market downtown. *The friendly farmers have a lot to display, from berries[4] so sweet that your tongue tingles,[5] to mushrooms[6] picked in the forests and crab caught in the nearby ocean. Better yet, everyone is offering samples, so you can fill up on the freshest foods around.

If I'm still hungry, I stop by something that Portland is quickly becoming famous for: food trucks. I can take a tour of the world's food just by walking from one truck to the next. I may have a sushi[7] snack from one, Mexican pork tacos[8] from the next, and a French dessert from another. Then I carry my

波特蘭小檔案

素有「玫瑰之城」美名的波特蘭（Portland）是美國西北部奧勒岡州（Oregon）的最大城。由於當地氣候適合栽植玫瑰，因此波特蘭處處可見玫瑰花園。除了優美的環境，波特蘭市區規劃良好、適合步行，而且公共運輸效率高，因此常被視為設計良好的模範城市。波特蘭人文氣息濃厚，擁有全世界最大的獨立書店，當地的爵士樂與獨立搖滾音樂也頗負盛名。

Vocabulary

1. **perfume** [pəˋfjum] v. 使充滿香氣
2. **streetlight** [ˋstrit͵laɪt] n. 路燈
3. **plenty** [ˋplɛnti] n. 大量；充足
4. **berry** [ˋbɛri] n. 莓果；漿果
5. **tingle** [ˋtɪŋgəl] v. 感到刺痛的
6. **mushroom** [ˋmʌʃ͵rum] n. 蘑菇；蕈
7. **sushi** [ˋsuʃi] n. 壽司
8. **taco** [ˋtɑko] n. 墨西哥捲餅

街上的市集與美食餐車（food truck）提供波特蘭人（Portlander）嚐鮮的機會。

肥皂箱賽車（Soap Box Derby，derby [ˋdɝbi] 表「比賽；競賽」）源自一九三〇年代的俄亥俄州（Ohio），當時的賽車是用廢棄的肥皂木箱所製成，完全靠地心引力來驅動。

圖片／翻攝自網路

哥倫比亞河是奧勒崗州與華盛頓州的天然邊界，兩岸堅實烏黑的火山岩石經過河水長年累月沖刷，形成今日長達八十英里、深約一千兩百公尺的哥倫比亞河峽谷（Columbia River Gorge）。

treats down to the river and take in the beautiful view of the boats and bridges.

When friends visit me in Portland, we tour rose gardens and art installations[9] in the city and even climb around on an extinct[10] volcano,[11] Mt. Tabor. That's also where the Soap Box Derby takes place every August. For this event, Portlanders build small race cars which are propelled[12] only by gravity.[13] As the tiny cars fly down the steep[14] slope,[15] the cheering people have to laughingly[16] dodge the racers who lose control.

Vocabulary

9. **installation** [ˌɪnstəˈleʃən] *n.* 裝置；設置
10. **extinct** [ɪkˈstɪŋkt] *adj.* （火山）不再活躍的；滅種、不復存在的
11. **volcano** [vɔlˈkeno] *n.* 火山
12. **propel** [prəˈpɛl] *v.* 推動；驅策
13. **gravity** [ˈɡrævəti] *n.* 重力；地心引力
14. **steep** [stip] *adj.* 陡峭的
15. **slope** [slop] *n.* 斜坡；山坡
16. **laughingly** [ˈlæfɪŋli] *adv.* 笑著地；開玩笑地

Portlanders take part in more traditional activities in summer, too. These include watching free movies outdoors, dancing to new bands at music festivals, and buying handmade[17] crafts[18] at street fairs. Portland is also only 90 minutes from the coast and even closer to the Columbia River Gorge. I love watching the sun sink into the ocean behind famous Haystack Rock, or gazing up at Multnomah Falls in the gorge. Oregonians love the outdoors, so it's easy to make new friends on the many hiking trails near the city.

The outdoor beauty and fun of Portland in summer more than makes up for its cold, rainy winters. With unusual sports, tasty food, and a cool art and music scene, Portland is a place that I am proud to call home.

圖片 / Treva Adams

左：在市區的咖啡座可品嚐巫毒娃娃造型麵包，還可與市區的水獺像合影。

下：草垛岩（Haystack Rock）位於波特蘭西部的佳能海灘（Canon Beach）上，由火山岩形成，經過海水侵蝕後成為險礁。

圖片 / Wikipedia: Tiger635

Vocabulary

17. **handmade** [ˋhændˋmed] *adj.* 手工的
18. **craft** [kræft] *n.* 手工藝品（作此義時恆用複數）；工藝

玫瑰之城波特蘭

波特蘭的陽光在寒冷陰雨的冬天過後露臉，「玫瑰之城」到處都看得到綻放的花朵。它們讓公園瀰漫著香氣，在街燈上亦懸掛著五彩繽紛的花籃。這是我所居住的這座怡人城市最棒的時節，而夏季的白天長，讓人有很多的時間享受波特蘭的美景及好玩的事物。

我在夏日週末最愛的活動之一就是逛市區的「農夫市集」。親切的農人展示各式各樣的食物，從甜到讓舌頭有刺刺感覺的莓果，到在森林採集的菌菇和近海捕抓的螃蟹，應有盡有。更棒的是，大家都會提供試吃，因此你在那裡吃最新鮮的食物就能有飽足感。

如果我還覺得餓，我會在波特蘭正迅速成名的東西前停下腳步：美食餐車。我只要走過一台又一台的餐車，就能享受到世界各地的美食。我能從一台車買到壽司，下一台車買到墨西哥豬肉捲餅，再到另一台車買法式甜點。接著我就提著我的點心走到河邊，欣賞船隻與橋樑的美景。

有朋友到波特蘭找我時，我們會去參觀玫瑰花園以及城裡的裝置藝術，甚至到死火山塔伯爾山附近爬山。每年八月也會在那裡舉行「肥皂箱賽車」。波特蘭人為這個賽事，打造只以地心引力作為動力來源的小型賽車。當這些小車從陡峭的斜坡向下俯衝，歡呼的群眾還得一邊笑一邊閃避失控的賽車手。

波特蘭人在夏日也會從事一些比較傳統的活動。包括觀賞免費的露天電影，在音樂祭隨著新樂團的音樂起舞，以及在街頭市集選購手工藝品。波特蘭到海岸也只需九十分鐘的車程，哥倫比亞河峽谷更是近在咫尺。我非常喜歡觀賞太陽在著名的草垛岩後西沉入海，或是凝視峽谷中的蒙諾瑪瀑布。奧勒岡州人熱愛戶外活動，因此很容易在近郊許多的登山步道上結識新朋友。

波特蘭夏日的戶外美景及趣味活動大大彌補了濕冷的冬天。波特蘭不尋常的運動、好吃的食物，以及酷炫的藝術與音樂活動，我以這裡為我的家鄉為榮。

1. **burst into view** 突然出現、顯現

burst 的動詞三態同形，有「突然發生；爆發；爆炸」的意思。burst into 表示「突然……」之意，burst into view 字面意思為「突然進入視線內」，即「突然出現」之意。

- The rainbow burst into view after the heavy shower.
  這場大雨過後，彩虹乍現。

補充 burst into 表示「突然……起來」的意思，常見的搭配如下：

burst into laughter 突然大笑起來	burst into tears 突然大哭起來
burst into flames 突然燃燒起來	burst into song 突然唱起歌來

- The funny dance moves the two people did onstage made the audience burst into laughter.
  那兩人在台上跳的滑稽舞步讓觀眾突然大笑了起來。

2. **allow for sth** 允許……

allow for 除了「允許」外，還有「考慮到、計畫（未來會發生的事）」之意。

- Airlines allow for a small amount of liquid to be brought with you on planes .
  航空公司容許乘客帶少量的液體上飛機。

補充

① allow sb to + V. 允許某人……

- My older sister doesn't allow her children to drink soft drinks that contain too much sugar.
  我姊姊不允許她小孩喝含太多糖的汽水。

② allow for sth 考量到……；將……計算在內

- To get to the mall from my house, it takes about 20 minutes, allowing for traffic.
  從我家到購物中心，考量到交通狀況大約要花二十分鐘。

3. **make up for sth** 補償……；彌補……

make up 之後也可接 to sb，表「彌補某人；向某人賠罪」。

- I made up for the pain I caused my friend by telling him I was very sorry.
  我向我朋友表達最深的歉意以彌補我帶給他的痛苦。

- Kyle will have to make up to his brother for teasing him in front of his friends.
  凱爾得因在朋友面前取笑他弟弟而補償他。

Sentence Patterns

* **The friendly farmers have a lot to display, from berries so sweet that your tongue tingles, to mushrooms picked in the forests and crab caught in the nearby ocean.**

此句為形容詞子句省略為形容詞片語的結構，說明如下：

① so sweet that . . . 可視為由形容詞子句 that/which are so sweet that . . . 省略而來

② picked in the forest 可視為由形容詞子句 that/which are picked in the forest 省略而來

③ caught in the nearby ocean 可視為由形容詞子句 that/which is caught in the nearby ocean 省略而來

形容詞子句簡化時，省略了關係代名詞與 be 動詞，直接以形容詞或分詞來修飾前面名詞。注意，表主動時用現在分詞，表被動時則用過去分詞。

• All of the food (that was) served at this party was catered by the Mexican restaurant.
派對上所供應的食物都是由那家墨西哥餐廳提供的。

• Many of the people waiting for the train did not have luggage with them.
那些在等火車的人有很多都沒有帶行李。

摩達中心（Moda Center）原是玫瑰花園球館（Rose Garden），現為 NBA 波特蘭開拓者隊的主場球館。
圖片 / Wikipedia: Fcb981

265

The Inside Scoop on Boston

"Guidebooks can only get you so far," my friend Vinnie said as I was planning my first trip to Boston. This historical[1] city was his hometown,[2] and he told me to follow his advice for the best Boston experience.

Obeying[3] Vinnie, I headed to the Freedom Trail[4] first. This is a red line that runs 2.5 miles through the oldest parts of the city, so following it is like visiting an outdoor[5] museum. Starting at Boston Common, a beautiful park, the red trail took me past old churches, meetinghouses, and a statue of Benjamin Franklin. I also checked out Faneuil Hall. Some say the American Revolution started in this redbrick[6]

沿著自由步道（the Freedom Trail）可觀賞許多著名的歷史遺跡與波士頓的建築風貌

Vocabulary

1. **historical** [hɪsˋtɔrɪkəl] *adj.* 與歷史有關的

2. **hometown** [ˋhomˋtaʊn] *n.* 家鄉

3. **obey** [əˋbe] *v.* 聽從；遵從

4. **trail** [trel] *n.* 道路；小徑

5. **outdoor** [ˋaʊtˏdor] *adj.* 戶外的

6. **redbrick** [ˋrɛdˏbrɪk] *adj.* 紅磚的

班傑明・富蘭克林雕像（Statue of Benjamin Franklin）

波士頓位於美國東岸的麻薩諸塞州（Massachusetts），創建於一六三〇年，為全美最古老的城市之一，也可說是美國歷史的代名詞，一七七三年在此發生的「波士頓茶葉事件」（Boston Tea Party）引發美國獨立戰爭。波士頓對於殖民與獨立戰爭時的文物一直保存完好，有十六處著名的歷史遺址與十七、十八世紀的建築風貌。波士頓亦是學術重鎮，哈佛、麻省理工學等頂尖名校都在此，文化氣息濃厚。

上：法尼爾廳（Faneuil Hall）原作為市場，但在獨立戰爭爆發前，這棟建築常用於集會討論獨立大業，所以又有「自由的搖籃」（Cradle of Liberty）的別稱。左下：美國憲章號（USS *Constitution*）為美國海軍最古老的船艦，至今仍停泊於波士頓港。右下：麻省理工學院（MIT）麥克勞林大樓的圓頂建築（Maclaurin Building & Great Dome）。

左：歷史悠久的聯合生蠔屋（Union Oyster House）有各式美東傳統海鮮，為美國前總統甘迺迪最喜愛的餐廳之一。右：波士頓公園（Boston Common）為美國最古老的公園，建於一六三四年。

building. Now, you can learn about history there while also getting some great gifts at its many shops.

My hunger finally made me stop shopping and find some food. Union Oyster House is the oldest restaurant in the United States, and Vinnie recommended[7] the clam chowder[8] there. This delicious creamy soup with salty clams and vegetables is one of the most famous dishes of Boston.

After lunch, I followed the red trail to the USS *Constitution*. A crewman[9] showed me around the 215-year-old ship. As I touched the old wood, I was amazed[10] that this piece of history was still floating!

Vocabulary

7. **recommend** [ˌrɛkəˈmɛnd] *v.* 推薦
8. **clam chowder** [klæm] [ˈtʃaʊdə] *n. phr.* 蛤蜊巧達濃湯
9. **crewman** [ˈkrumən] *n.* 船員
10. **amaze** [əˈmez] *v.* 使……驚訝

*After my historical tour of Boston, I headed to Harvard Square for something modern. Harvard University has been around since 1636, but the hip cafés and art events there prove that there is nothing old and dusty about this university. A group of students invited me to the Sunday Parkland Games the next day. These are free activities offered[11] near the Charles River. We made plans to meet at the badminton area and enter a potato sack race.

The sun was setting, so I decided to save the expensive shops of Newbury Street for another day. I wanted to get to the top of the Prudential Tower to have a piece of famous Boston cream pie and watch the lights of Boston come to life. The city looked big and mysterious,[12] but Vinnie's travel advice helped me feel like a local[13] Bostonian[14] coming home.

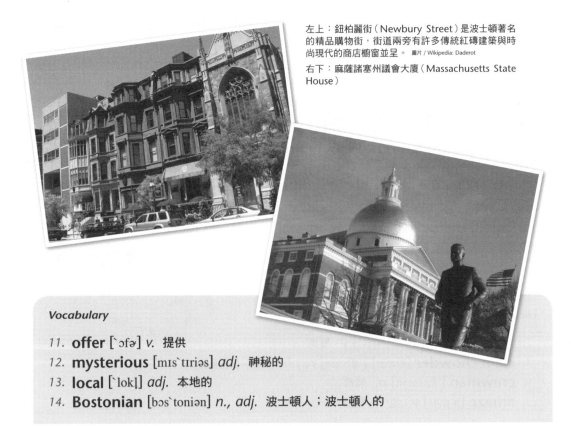

左上：鈕柏麗街（Newbury Street）是波士頓著名的精品購物街，街道兩旁有許多傳統紅磚建築與時尚現代的商店櫥窗並呈。 ■片 / Wikipedia: Daderot

右下：麻薩諸塞州議會大廈（Massachusetts State House）

Vocabulary

11. **offer** [ˈɔfə] v. 提供
12. **mysterious** [mɪsˈtɪrɪəs] adj. 神秘的
13. **local** [ˈlokl] adj. 本地的
14. **Bostonian** [bɔsˈtonɪən] n., adj. 波士頓人；波士頓人的

波士頓「自由」行

旅遊達人10大嚴選

旅遊達人私房推薦

旅遊達人季節限定

　　我正在計畫第一次到波士頓旅行時，我的朋友威尼告訴我：「旅遊指南只能讓妳了解到這麼多。」這座歷史城市是他的家鄉，他要我照著他的意見以獲得最棒的波士頓體驗。

　　我聽從威尼的建議，先前往自由步道。這是一條長二點五英里、穿越此城最古老區域的紅色路線，所以沿著它前進就像參觀一座戶外的博物館。這條紅色步道起點是美麗的波士頓公園，沿途經過古老的教堂、集會所和班傑明・富蘭克林的雕像。我也參觀了法尼爾廳。有人說美國大革命是從這棟紅磚建築物開始的。現在，你可以在那裡學習到歷史，同時也可在其中的許多商店裡買到很棒的禮物。

　　飢餓最後迫使我停止購物、轉而去覓食。聯合生蠔屋是美國最古老的餐廳，而威尼推薦那裡的蛤蜊巧達濃湯。這道有鹹蛤蜊與蔬菜的美味奶油濃湯是波士頓最有名的菜餚之一。

　　吃完午餐後，我沿著紅色步道來到美國憲章號戰艦。一名船員帶我參觀這艘有兩百一十五年歷史的船艦。當我觸碰老舊的木頭，我很驚訝這件歷史物品還浮得起來！

　　在我的波士頓歷史之旅結束後，我前往哈佛廣場去看點現代化的東西。哈佛大學在一六三六年就創立了，但是那裡時髦的小餐館和藝文活動證明了這間大學一點都不老舊，也不枯燥乏味。一群學生邀請我參加隔天的週日運動會。這些是在查理斯河附近提供的免費活動。我們打算在羽球區見面，然後參加跳馬鈴薯袋比賽。

　　太陽要下山了，所以我決定改天再逛鈕柏麗街的昂貴商店。我想到保德信大樓的頂樓來份著名的波士頓奶油派，並觀賞波士頓華燈初上的景觀。這個城市看起來又大又神祕，不過威尼的旅行建議讓我覺得自己像是個返家的波士頓人。

哈佛廣場（Harvard Square）位在劍橋大學城的中心，為當地學生的主要活動場所，街道上充滿書店、咖啡店和餐館。　圖片 / Wikipedia

1. so far 的不同意思

① 指「最多到某個程度」，如文中用法。

- You can only take the train so far. After that, you'll have to get on a bus.
  你只能搭火車到這裡為止。之後的路程，你將得搭公車。

② 指「到目前為止；迄今」。通常指過去某個時間到現在的狀況，所以常搭配完成式使用。

- So far on my trip, I have only bought one gift for my family.
  旅途到目前為止，我只買了一個禮物給我家人。

2. -y 作形容詞字尾

字尾 -y 表示「具有……特質的；……狀態的」，常加在名詞後面形成形容詞，常見例子列舉如下：

cream 乳脂；奶油	➡	creamy	奶油般的
salt 鹽巴	➡	salty	鹹的
dust 灰塵	➡	dusty	滿是灰塵的；枯燥乏味的
sweat 汗水	+y ➡	sweaty	流汗的
taste 滋味；味道	➡	tasty	美味的（字尾是 e 時，常去 e 再加 y）
wit 機智	➡	witty	機智的（重複字尾 t）

- Adding potatoes to soup that is too salty will make the soup taste better.
  在太鹹的湯中加入馬鈴薯可以讓湯更好喝。

- The room has been closed for a long time, so it is very dusty.
  這房間已經關閉很久了，所以滿是灰塵。

3. feel like 感覺好像

feel 在文中作連綴動詞用，之後常接形容詞，表示「感覺……的；給人……的感覺」；或接 like N.，表示「感覺好像……；摸起來如同……」。

- I felt sad when my friend left for the summer, but now I am happy that she is back.
  我朋友去別處過暑假時我感到很難過，但現在我很開心她回來了。

- Jenny felt like a movie star when people took photos of her after the school play.
  當大家在學校戲劇謝幕後幫珍妮拍照時，她覺得自己像是電影明星。

比較 feel like 作動詞時，表示「想要」，之後接 N.、V-ing 或子句，指「想要某物；想要做某事」。

- Do you feel like a walk around the park?
  你想要在公園散步嗎？
- If you feel like watching a movie tonight, please call me.
  如果你今晚想要看電影，請打給我。

Sentence Patterns

* **After my historical tour of Boston, I headed to Harvard Square for** something modern.

形容詞用來修飾由 no-、some-、any-、every- 和 -one、-thing、-body 所組成的代名詞時，形容詞必須置於代名詞後面。文中 . . . but the hip cafés and art events there prove that there is nothing old and dusty about this university 也是同樣用法。

- There is nothing funny about the man falling and getting hurt.
  這名男子跌倒受傷沒什麼好笑的。
- It is easy to find something tasty to eat at the night market.
  在夜市裡很容易找到一些好吃的東西。
- The policeman asked me if I heard anything strange the night before.
  警察問我前一晚是否有聽到任何奇怪的聲音。

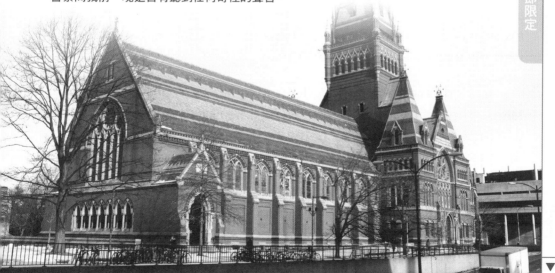

哈佛大學（Harvard University）的 Memorial Hall

273

雲門（Cloud Gate）這座巨大的雕塑品是千禧公園
（Millennium Park）的著名景點。
圖片 / Wikipedia: Tony Webste

8. 漫遊風城芝加哥　　　　PLAY ALL　TRACK 54

Touring the Windy City: Chicago

Filled with art, music, fascinating museums, and impressive architecture, Chicago is a great American vacation destination. I experienced this firsthand[1] when I visited this past summer to vacation with my family.

Touring Chicago is easy to do on foot and with public transportation. The city is famous for its elevated train, called the 'L,' that brings people to many parts of the city. The best thing about the 'L' is that you can get great views as you travel. It weaves around corners and gets surprisingly close to some buildings as it passes.

The area that has many attractions and is the heart of the city is called the Loop. It is an area where the 'L' train loops around and is home to some of the best-known places to visit in Chicago.

芝加哥小檔案

芝加哥位於美國中西部的伊利諾州（Illinois），緊鄰密西根湖（Lake Michigan），人口逾兩百七十萬，是僅次於紐約和洛杉磯的第三大都會區。該城氣候四季分明，終年多風，因此又有「風城」（Windy City）之稱。十九世紀開通的伊利諾密西根運河（The Illinois and Michigan Canal）便利了芝加哥的航運，加上連接各大城市的數十條鐵路交匯於此，以及繁忙的奧黑爾國際機場（O'Hare International Airport），使芝加哥成為美國東西水、陸、空交通運輸的樞紐。

Our first ride on the 'L' brought us to Millennium[2] Park, a beautiful green space on the edge of Lake Michigan. An enormous[3] sculpture,[4] Cloud Gate, greets you as you enter the park. Nicknamed the Bean, it is large enough to walk under. This sculpture acts as a mirror that bends the Chicago skyline with its smooth curves.[5]

Situated next to Millennium Park is the Art Institute[6] of Chicago. It is one of the largest and most beautiful art museums in the world. Housing a world-class selection of art, the museum includes paintings by Monet, Picasso, Matisse, and more. My favorite viewing, however, was of the stained[7] glass windows by Chagall. The cool blue windows were beautiful, and they made me wish I had such artistic[8] ability.

Vocabulary

1. **firsthand** [ˈfɜstˈhænd] *adv., adj.* 直接（的）；第一手（的）
2. **millennium** [məˈlɛniəm] *n.* 千年期；千禧年
3. **enormous** [ɪˈnɔrməs] *adj.* 巨大的；龐大的
4. **sculpture** [ˈskʌlptʃə] *n.* 雕塑品；雕像
5. **curve** [kɜv] *n.* 曲線；彎曲
6. **institute** [ˈɪnstəˌtjut] *n.* （大專）學院；學會
7. **stain** [sten] *v.* 給（玻璃、壁紙等）染色；弄髒
8. **artistic** [ɑrˈtɪstɪk] *adj.* 藝術（家）的；有藝術天賦的

After spending a few hours strolling through the art galleries,[9] we sat down for a fine lunch in the museum restaurant located in an open courtyard.[10] Tables surrounded a pool that had a fountain in its center, and a mother duck and her duckling had made it their home.

Satisfied with our meal, we left the art museum and headed back to an area in the park with a large amphitheater. By chance, we were able to catch a free concert, as the Grant Park Symphony Orchestra was rehearsing[11] for a show. We sat for an hour in the shade and listened to soloists practicing their singing parts while the conductor gave instructions to the orchestra. It made for a relaxing musical afternoon.

On another day, we visited the Museum of Science and Industry. One particularly stunning exhibit there was an actual U-boat, *U-505*, which was captured from the German navy during World War II. We toured the interior[12] of the sub, and it was eerie[13] to think of all the history that had taken place inside it.

We then made a trip to the top of the Willis Tower, once the tallest building in the world. Its Skydeck has glass viewing platforms. Making

左上：夏卡爾（Chagall）創作的藍色彩繪玻璃窗

右上：芝加哥藝術學院（Art Institute of Chicago），創立於一八六六年，包含學校和博物館，為美國知名的私立藝術學院。

右：芝加哥科學工業博物館（Museum of Science and Industry）是一間大型互動式博物館，館內收藏二次大戰遺留下來的潛水艇。

圖片 / Joseph Schier

Vocabulary

9. **gallery** [ˈgæləri] *n.* 藝廊

10. **courtyard** [ˈkɔrtˌjɑrd] *n.* 庭院；中庭

11. **rehearse** [rɪˈhɜs] *v.* 排演；排練

12. **interior** [ɪnˈtɪriə] *n., adj.* 內部（的）；室內（的）

13. **eerie** [ˈɪri] *adj.* 奇怪且可怕的

踏上威利斯大樓（Willis Tower）103 樓的玻璃眺望室，芝加哥風景盡收眼底。圖片 / Joseph Schier

the first step onto the platforms is pretty scary, for you see straight down through the floor—from 103 floors up!

　　*Chicago is where skyscrapers[14] were born, so no trip to this city is complete without an architectural[15] cruise on the Chicago River. Our knowledgeable guide pointed out the different buildings and gave historical anecdotes.[16] From the river were perfect views of many buildings, ranging from older art deco skyscrapers to more modern glass towers.

　　Although we spent an entire week in Chicago, it felt much too short. I will return there someday to revisit[17] the things I fell in love with and to discover more about the city that filled me with wonder.

Vocabulary

14. **skyscraper** [ˋskaɪˌskrepɚ] *n.* 摩天大樓
15. **architectural** [ˌɑrkəˋtɛktʃərəl] *adj.* 建築的
16. **anecdote** [ˋænɪkˌdot] *n.* 軼聞；趣事
17. **revisit** [riˋvɪzət] *v.* 重遊；再訪

【從旅遊看文化】

　　art deco（裝飾風藝術）一字源自法語 Art Decoratifs，常用大寫 A&D 表示。這種建築風格融合多種藝術派別的影響，多採用稀有、貴重的精緻建材，強調裝飾的優雅高貴，同時兼具功能性和現代感。「商業市場」（Merchandise Mart）即為芝加哥常見的「裝飾風藝術」代表性建築之一。

漫遊風城芝加哥

芝加哥充滿了藝術、音樂、引人入勝的博物館以及令人讚嘆的建築，是美國絕佳的度假勝地。我在今年夏天與家人一同度假時，親身體驗了這座城市。

遊覽芝加哥，步行或搭乘大眾運輸工具都很方便。在芝加哥稱為 the 'L' 的高架捷運是出名的，它載送人們到城裡的許多地方。the 'L' 最棒的是能讓你一邊旅行一邊欣賞絕佳景色。the 'L' 穿梭於城市各個角落，列車經過時，車廂與一些大樓的距離之近讓人驚訝。

有許多觀光景點又位於市中心的那個區域稱為洛普區。the 'L' 環繞此區，芝加哥一些最著名的旅遊景點就位在此處。

我們搭 the 'L' 的第一趟旅程來到了千禧公園，這塊優美的綠地就緊鄰密西根湖畔。進入公園時，就會看見一座巨大的雕塑品「雲門」迎接著你。這座綽號「豆子」的藝術品非常大，大到可在底下行走。這座雕塑品就像是一面鏡子，照映著芝加哥的天際線，景色隨其圓滑的曲線而彎曲。

座落在千禧公園旁的是芝加哥藝術學院。它是世界上最大且最美的博物館之一。該館收藏了世界一流的精選藝術品，館藏包括莫內、畢卡索、馬諦斯與其他藝術家的畫作。然而我最喜愛的是夏卡爾的彩繪玻璃窗。冷色系的藍色窗戶很美，它們讓我不由得希望自己也能有那樣的藝術天分。

逛了幾個小時的藝廊後，我們在位於露天庭院的一間博物館餐廳享用了精緻的午餐。餐桌圍繞著一個中間有噴泉的池子，一隻母鴨和小鴨還以此處為家。

酒足飯飽後，我們離開了美術館，回到公園裡的大型圓形露天劇場。我們碰巧聽到了一場免費的演奏會，因為格蘭特公園交響樂團正為一場演出做排演。我們在蔭涼處坐了一個鐘頭，聽著獨唱者練習著他們各自負責的部分，樂團指揮者則指導著管弦樂團。我們就這樣度過了一個樂音繞耳的愜意午後。

另一天，我們造訪了科學工業博物館。其中一項格外酷炫的展示品就是在第二次大戰期間從德國海軍那裡擄獲、貨真價實的 U-505 潛艇。我們參觀了潛艇內部，一想到當時在這裡頭發生的種種歷史，心裡難免感到毛毛的。

後來我們去了威利斯大樓（註：原名為希爾斯大樓（Sears Tower））的頂樓，它曾是世界最高樓。其「天台」有玻璃眺望平台。踏上平台的第一步相當恐怖，因為你能從一百零三層樓高的地方直視地面！

芝加哥是摩天大樓的發源地，因此來到這裡若未坐芝加哥河上的遊輪來趟建築巡禮，就不能算是來過芝加哥。我們博學多聞的導遊指出了許多不同的建築物，並且介紹它們的歷史軼事。從河上能清楚看到許多建築景觀，從年代較久遠的裝飾風藝術摩天大樓到更現代的玻璃高樓都一覽無遺。

雖然我們在芝加哥待了整整一個星期，感覺還是太過短暫。有朝一日我會回到那裡重遊這些我愛上的景物，並且更深入探索這座令我驚嘆不已的城市。

1. **act as . . .** 充當……；作為……

   同義 serve as . . .

   act 在此表示「扮演；充當」的意思。

   - My couch acts as an extra bed when I have guests stay at my house.
     有客人來我家過夜時，這張沙發就當作床用。

2. **by chance** 偶然地；意外地

   同義 by accident、accidentally

   - If you see Kevin by chance, tell him that I am looking for him.
     如果你碰巧看到凱文，告訴他我正在找他。

   比較 by any chance 也許；可能

   在詢問或提出請求時，可用 by any chance 以示禮貌。

   - Do you have Mia's phone number by any chance?
     你是否可能有米亞的電話號碼？

3. **make for** 造就……；成為……

   作此義時，無進行式。

   - Cheese and crackers make for great snacks in the late afternoon.
     起司和餅乾是絕佳的午後點心。

   補充 make/head for + 地點 前往某處

   - The dog made for the bushes when it heard another animal make a sound.
     那隻狗一聽到其他動物發出聲音，便往灌木叢那裡去。

4. **range from A to B** 範圍從 A 到 B；位於 A 與 B 之間

   range 作動詞時可表示「（在一定範圍內）變動、變化」。

   同義 range between A and B

   - My musical tastes range from serious classical music to light jazz.
     我喜好的音樂從純古典樂到輕爵士樂都有。

Sentence Patterns

where 引導的名詞子句作補語用

* **Chicago is** where skyscrapers were born, **so no trip to this city is complete without an architectural cruise on the Chicago River.**

句型 no . . . is complete without + N./V-ing

. . . is not/never complete without + N./V-ing

沒有……就不完整;一定要……才算

此為雙重否定的句型,用來表示肯定的結果。

- For Doris, no meal is complete without a tasty dessert.
→For Doris, a meal is not complete without a tasty dessert.

對陶樂絲來說,每餐一定要有美味的甜點才行。

- A trip to Taiwan is never complete without touring one of the night markets.

沒去逛夜市就不算去過台灣。

芝加哥為摩天大樓的發源地,以高樓構成之錯落有致的天際線聞名於世,這是由於一八七一年市內發生大火後整座城市經過重建,如今才會林立著各式各樣摩登前衛的建築設計。

281

Istanbul: A Turkish Delight

I arrived in Istanbul at the end of a six-month journey through Europe, and I wasn't disappointed. Truth be told, I was a bit overwhelmed when I first walked around the city. With a population of 13 million-plus people, it is one of the largest cities in the world. Istanbul is also one of the oldest, and its roots stretch back to 660 BC. All of this history can be seen in the city's architecture, with ancient

buildings dating from the Roman and Ottoman empires.[1] The old structures can be found among the gleaming[2] office towers and crumbling[3] apartment blocks[4] that are situated side-by-side on the city's streets.

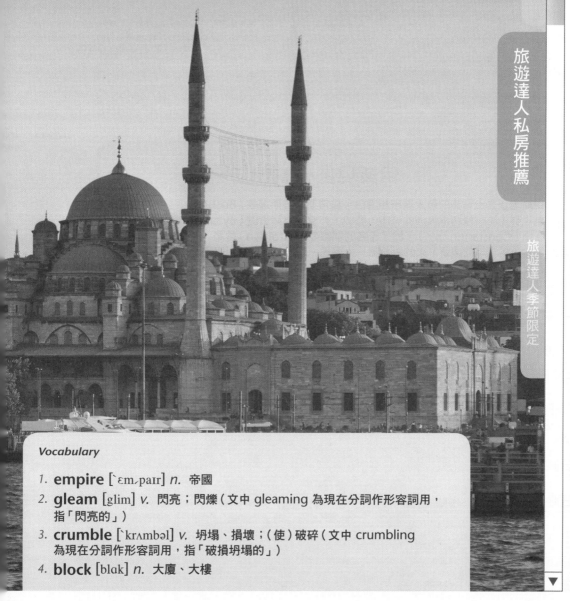

Vocabulary

1. **empire** [ˈɛmˌpaɪr] *n.* 帝國
2. **gleam** [glim] *v.* 閃亮；閃爍（文中 gleaming 為現在分詞作形容詞用，指「閃亮的」）
3. **crumble** [ˈkrʌmbəl] *v.* 坍塌、損壞；（使）破碎（文中 crumbling 為現在分詞作形容詞用，指「破損坍塌的」）
4. **block** [blɑk] *n.* 大廈、大樓

左：大巴札（Grand Bazaar）修建於一四六一年，是世界上最大且最古老的市集之一，其範圍涵蓋數十條街道，令人彷彿置身迷宮（maze）之中。

中、右：聖索菲亞大教堂（Hagia Sophia）融合了伊斯蘭教（Islam）及基督教（Christian）建築，教堂內四處可見以馬賽克磚（mosaic）拼成的基督及聖母圖像。

伊斯坦堡小檔案

伊斯坦堡是土耳其的最大城市和港口，以博斯普魯斯海峽（Bosphorus）為界，成為世界上唯一橫跨兩大洲的城市，歷史上亦曾稱為拜占庭（Byzantium）和君士坦丁堡（Constantinople）。除了著名的鄂圖曼（Ottoman）建築，伊斯坦堡還保有歷史上各個時期遺留下來的古希臘、古羅馬、拜占庭等建築，吸引全球旅客前來，整座城市也在一九八五年被聯合國教科文組織列為世界遺產。

My first stop was the Sultan Ahmet Mosque. This impressive structure is also called the Blue Mosque, for there are thousands of blue tiles[5] covering the inside walls. With six large minarets on the outside, it is widely considered one of the finest examples of classic Ottoman architecture. It is still an active mosque, though, and during the daily times of prayer, only faithful Muslims are allowed in.

I then went to the Hagia Sophia, which shows the city's Christian influences. Built as a church in the sixth century, it was converted into a mosque in the fifteenth century when the city was conquered[6] by the Ottomans. Today, the Hagia Sophia is a museum that holds many Christian mosaics and exquisite[7] Islamic artworks.

Istanbul is a great city for sightseeing[8] and is also blessed with excellent food. My favorite was doner kebab, a type of sliced-lamb sandwich that made for a quick, filling meal as I toured the city. I also stopped in for a snack at the famous Pudding Shop. Back in the 1960s, this was a popular café among travelers taking the overland[9] "Hippie Trail" from Istanbul to India and Asia. It was made popular in the film *Midnight Express*, although today there are more Turkish customers than hippies.

Vocabulary

5. **tile** [taɪl] *n.* 瓷磚；瓦片
6. **conquer** [ˋkɑŋkə] *v.* 戰勝；征服
7. **exquisite** [ɛkˋskwɪzət] *adj.* 精美的；精緻的
8. **sightseeing** [ˋsaɪt͵siɪŋ] *n., adj.* 觀光（的）
9. **overland** [ˋovə͵lænd] *adj., adv.* 經由陸路（的）

*For anyone visiting Istanbul, there is no better shopping place in the city than in the Grand Bazaar.[10] The Grand Bazaar itself is beautiful, with elegant decorated arches and domed buildings that were built in the fifteenth century. With 60 covered streets and 5,000 shops, this bazaar sells jewelry, hand-painted ceramics, carpets, spices, and so much more. I just dove in and wandered around, easily getting lost in the maze. Wanting a souvenir, I haggled[11] over the price of some jewelry and bought it for a good price.

For another perspective[12] on the city, I decided to take a boat trip on the Bosphorus. Munching[13] on some delicious Turkish delight,[14] I gazed out at the cityscape of Istanbul. Straddling[15] the continents of Europe and Asia, Istanbul truly is where East meets West.

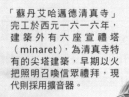

「蘇丹艾哈邁德清真寺」完工於西元一六一六年，建築外有六座宣禮塔（minaret），為清真寺特有的尖塔建築，早期以火把照明召喚信眾禮拜，現代則採用擴音器。

【從旅遊看文化】

土耳其烤肉（doner kebab）是將旋轉架上的烤羊肉、牛肉、雞肉削下切片，加上配料而成的土耳其小吃，常搭配阿拉伯麵包（pita）食用。而我們常說的沙威瑪（shawarma）原是波斯話「烤肉」的意思，引進台灣後作法已改良，與道地的土耳其烤肉不太相同。

Vocabulary

10. **bazaar** [bəˋzɑr] *n.* （尤指中東和印度的）市集

11. **haggle** [ˋhægəl] *v.* 討價還價

12. **perspective** [pɚˋspɛktɪv] *n.* 角度、觀點；思考方法

13. **munch** [mʌntʃ] *v.* 大聲咀嚼（常用 munch on 表示）

14. **Turkish delight** [ˋtɝkɪʃ] [dɪˋlaɪt] *n.* 土耳其軟糖
（delight 表「令人愉悅之事物」，故本文標題語帶雙關）

15. **straddle** [ˋstrædl̩] *v.* 橫跨（邊境、時間、河流等）

中文翻譯　　伊斯坦堡——土耳其感官饗宴之旅

　　我在六個月的歐洲之旅接近尾聲時抵達了伊斯坦堡，它沒有令我失望。說真的，第一次走在城裡時讓我感到有點目不暇給。伊斯坦堡的人口超過一千三百萬人，是世界上數一數二的大城市。伊斯坦堡也是最古老的城市之一，它的起源可以回溯到西元前六六〇年。全部的歷史都能從這座城市的建築物中一窺一二，其古老建築可以追溯到羅馬帝國及鄂圖曼帝國時期。在城市街道上櫛比鱗次排列的閃亮辦公大樓和破損坍塌的公寓大廈之間，可以發現古老的建築構造。

　　我的第一站是「蘇丹艾哈邁德清真寺」。這座令人印象深刻的建築也有「藍色清真寺」之稱，因為內牆覆蓋著成千上萬片的藍色瓷磚。清真寺外頭有六座宣禮塔，普遍被認為是經典鄂圖曼式建築的最佳範例之一。不過，這座清真寺仍在使用中，在每天做禮拜的時刻，只有虔誠的穆斯林得以進入。

　　接著我來到「聖索菲亞大教堂」，那裡展現出該城受到的基督教影響。這裡在西元六世紀建造時是一座教堂，但在十五世紀鄂圖曼土耳其人征服這座城市時把它改成了清真寺。今天，聖索菲亞大教堂是一座擁有許多基督教馬賽克畫作與精緻伊斯蘭工藝品的博物館。

　　伊斯坦堡是個非常適合觀光的城市，它也擁有許多出色的美食。我最喜愛的是土耳其烤肉，那是一種羊肉片三明治，讓我在城裡旅遊時得以快速果腹。我也在著名的「布丁小舖」停下來吃了點心。早在一九六〇年代，這裡就一直是那些行經這條陸路嬉皮大道、從伊斯坦堡前往印度跟亞洲的旅人間相當著名的一間咖啡店。這間店因電影《午夜快車》而走紅，儘管今日土耳其客人比嬉皮還要多。

　　對於任何到伊斯坦堡玩的人來說，城裡沒有一個購物去處比得上「大巴札」。大巴札本身很美，其建築建造於十五世紀，有裝飾優雅的拱門與圓頂。這個市集涵蓋了六十條有棚子的街道、五千間商店，販售珠寶、手工繪製的瓷器、地毯、香料，以及琳瑯滿目的各式商品。我一頭栽進去、到處閒逛，在這個迷宮裡很容易就迷路了。因為想要買紀念品，我和攤販就珠寶售價討價還價，結果以划算的價格買下。

　　為了從另一個角度看這座城市，我決定搭船遊覽博斯普魯斯海峽。我一邊大快朵頤吃著土耳其軟糖，一邊遙望著伊斯坦堡的城市風光。伊斯坦堡橫跨歐亞大陸，是名副其實東西文化的交會處。

1. **truth be told** 老實說、說真的

> 同義 to tell (you) the truth、in truth、to be honest、honestly speaking、frankly speaking

- The movie looks like it will be fun to watch, but truth be told, it has gotten terrible reviews.
  那部電影看起來好像滿好看的,但老實說,它的評論很糟。

2. **be blessed with** 享有……;有幸得到……

bless 在此作動詞表「祝福;保佑」之意,be blessed with 帶有「得天獨厚、有幸得到……」的意思。

- San Diego is blessed with some of the best weather in the world.
  聖地牙哥得天獨厚擁有世界上數一數二的好天氣。

3. **stop in** 短暫停留

> 同義 stop by、drop in/by

此片語表「在前往某地的途中短暫停留」,stop in 及 drop in 尤指「進入屋內拜訪」。

- Let's stop in and see your family when we are visiting the city next week.
  我們下星期去那座城市玩時順道去看看你的家人。

4. **dive in/into** (興致勃勃地)開始做某事

動詞 dive 表「跳水、急速俯衝」,過去式與過去分詞為 dove 或 dived; dive in 有「立即栽入、投入某事」之意。

- I don't know where to start cleaning the apartment, so let's just dive in and start working on it.
  我不知道打掃公寓要從哪裡開始,所以我們就直接開始打掃吧。

Sentence Patterns

* **For anyone visiting Istanbul, there is no better shopping place in the city than in the Grand Bazaar.**

> 句型 there + be 動詞 + no + N. + 形容詞比較級 + N. + than
> 沒有什麼比……更……
>
> 本句型用比較級來表達最高級的意思。

- There is no better place to see dolphins than off the southern coast of the island.

    沒有比這座小島的南方外海更適合看海豚的地方了。

補充 nothing、no one、no (other) 皆有否定意義，用於比較時可表達最高級的意思。

Nothing	
No one	+ be 動詞 /V. + 比較級 + than . . .
No (other) + N.	

- Nothing is more interesting than spending a day with this intelligent man.

    沒有什麼事比跟這位聰明的男子共度一天更有趣的了。

- No one is more likely to take home the prize than Erin.

    沒有人比艾琳更有可能把獎項帶回家了。

- No other person in the room could speak French better than Pierre.

    在這個房間內沒有人的法文能說得比皮耶好。

右：布丁小舖（PuddingShop）曾是旅人們來往歐亞大陸時必定造訪的著名咖啡店。 ▓片/ Wikipedia: Sandstein

下：以博斯普魯斯海峽（Bosphorus）為界，伊斯坦堡分成歐洲與亞洲兩部分。 ▓片/ Wikipedia: Nevit Dilmen

Xinjiang: A Different Look at China

For modern travelers, Xinjiang can seem like an unexplored[1] land. Many first-time visitors to China flock to major cities like Beijing or Shanghai, or to the mountain wonderland[2] of Tibet. However, more and more people eager[3] for a taste of the unknown are heading west to experience Xinjiang, China's only heavily Islamic region.

A journey through Xinjiang, a vast region in the northwest of China, can feel like a trip through the centuries. Time seems to stop when you watch a row of camels walk away from the oasis[4] town of Dunhuang into an endless sea of sand. The same feeling returns when you view the ruins[5] of Jiaohe, once a lively trading city on the ancient Silk Road. Then, taking in the colorful silks, street foods, and the sound of people bargaining[6] in the markets of Hotan, one senses that the ancient way of life remains strong in this area.

Indeed, many cities of modern Xinjiang were key stops on the Silk Road, a trade route[7] that ran from modern-day Xian all the way to the Middle East. Explorers[8] such as Alexander the Great returned from their Silk Road journeys with tales of exotic[9] foods, faces, and landscapes.

Food can serve as a window into a culture, and this is certainly true in Xinjiang, which has a huge variety[10] of interesting foods. Dishes found in the region are influenced[11] by both Central Asian and traditional Chinese cuisines.

Vocabulary

1. **unexplored** [ˌʌnɪkˋsplɔrd] *adj.* 未經探勘的
2. **wonderland** [ˋwʌndəˌlænd] *n.* 仙境；極美之地
3. **eager** [ˋigə] *adj.* 渴望的；熱切的
4. **oasis** [oˋesəs] *n.* 綠洲（複數形為 oases [oˋesiz]）
5. **ruin** [ˋruɪn] *n.* 廢墟；遺跡（作此義時常用複數）
6. **bargain** [ˋbɑrgən] *v.* 討價還價
7. **route** [rut] *n.* 路線；道路
8. **explorer** [ɪkˋsplɔrə] *n.* 探險家
9. **exotic** [ɪgˋzɑtɪk] *adj.* 富異國情調的；外來的
10. **variety** [vəˋraɪəti] *n.* 多樣化
11. **influence** [ˋɪnˌfluəns] *v., n.* 影響

圖片 / Flickr: DPerstin

由左至右：交河故城（the ruins of Jiaohe）是中國唯一保有漢代城市遺跡的文物保護區。
位於天山山脈博格達峰的天池，湖水清澈如鏡，被喻為「天山明珠」。
新疆位居絲路要衝，地處乾燥，地理環境特殊。
在路邊燒烤羊肉串的小販。

As in Central Asia, bread and tea are part of almost every meal. Hand-pulled noodles such as *laghman* show the influence of what we usually think of as Chinese food. *Laghman* dishes usually combine beef, bell peppers,[12] and tomato. *Another popular food in Xinjiang is *zhua fan*, a rice-based dish cooked usually with mutton and carrots, which is meant to be eaten with the hands.

Xinjiang has much to offer to street-food lovers. In addition to delicious lamb kebabs, one of the region's most unique snacks is a shaved-ice dish that includes yogurt, grape syrup, and honey. However, Xinjiang is perhaps best known for the fruits it produces. The *hamigua* (cantaloupe,[13] in English), which got its Mandarin name from the Xinjiang town of Hami, as well as the area's honeydew melons,[14] watermelons, and grapes are incredibly[15] sweet. Many of these fruits are also produced in Turpan, where abundant[16] sunshine and high temperatures create the perfect condition for fruits to grow.

Xinjiang is a largely Muslim area, and it is home to diverse[17] ethnic groups. The facial[18] features of the majority[19] Uygur population appear more Central Asian than Chinese. Uygur men and women follow the traditional Muslim style of dress. Some women cover themselves from head to toe, with only their eyes visible.[20]

圖片 / Flickr: DPerstin

圖片 / Mike Corsini

圖片 / Wikipedia: Mizu Basyo

A 拉麵（laghman，文中特指新疆手工拌麵）
B 烤羊肉串（lamb kebab）
C 刨冰（shaved-ice）
D 抓飯（zhua fan，伴有羊肉及紅蘿蔔）
E 鮮甜的西瓜（watermelon）試吃

Vocabulary

12. **bell pepper** [bɛl] [ˋpɛpɚ] *n.* 青椒；甜椒

13. **cantaloupe** [ˋkæntəˌlop] *n.* 哈密瓜

14. **honeydew melon** [ˋhʌniˌdju] [ˋmɛlən] *n.* 香瓜

15. **incredibly** [ɪnˋkrɛdəbli] *adv.* 極為、十分；不可思議地

16. **abundant** [əˋbʌndənt] *adj.* 充足的；豐沛的

17. **diverse** [dəˋvɝs] *adj.* 迥異、不同的；各式各樣的

18. **facial** [ˋfeʃəl] *adj.* 臉部的

19. **majority** [məˋdʒɔrəti] *n.* 大多數

20. **visible** [ˋvɪzəbəl] *adj.* 可看見的

圖片 / Flickr: jgn

圖片 / Flickr: kaba

圖片 / Mike Corsini

圖片 / Mike Corsini

圖片 / Flickr: DPerstin

宗教人文小辭典

Tibet [tə`bɛt] 西藏
Islamic [ɪs`læmɪk] 伊斯蘭的
Muslim [`mʌzləm] 穆斯林、回教徒；伊斯蘭教的
Uygur [`wigɚ] 維吾爾族（的）（也可拼成 Uighur 或 Uigur）
mosque [mɑsk] 清真寺
Ürümqi [ʊ`rumtʃi] 烏魯木齊（新疆第一大城）

In keeping with Islamic customs, no pork is served in Uygur-owned restaurants. Calls to prayer are heard throughout the day as believers go in and out of local mosques.

A good way to get a feel for the culture of Xinjiang's local ethnic groups is to visit one of the markets. The Erdaoqiao Market in Ürümqi used to be a trading post between China, Russia, and Central Asia. Now, it has hundreds of stalls selling Uygur items, including carpets, copperware, jewelry, and musical instruments. At night, the market is lit up with colorful lights, and people go there to enjoy the food, folk[21] music, and dance.

A vast land with borders[22] extending from Russia to India, Xinjiang is truly unique. First-time visitors to this region will be stunned by its natural and ethnic landscape and come to appreciate China's cultural diversity.

Vocabulary

21. **folk** [fok] *adj.* 民間的；民俗的
22. **border** [`bɔrdɚ] *n.* 邊界

圖片 / 王蔚蓮

新疆行——看見不一樣的中國

對現代的旅客來說，新疆似乎像是一片未經探勘的土地。許多第一次到中國的遊客湧入北京或上海等大城市，或是到西藏的高原祕境。然而，愈來愈多渴望對未知世界一探究竟的人往西去體驗新疆風情，它是中國唯一具有濃厚伊斯蘭文化的地區。

穿過中國西北部廣大地區的新疆之旅感覺可能像是穿越世紀的旅行。當你看著一排駱駝從綠洲城鎮敦煌離開，走進一片茫茫無盡的沙漠時，時間似乎停止了。當你觀賞交河故城時，相同的感覺又油然而生，這座故城曾是古代絲路上一座活躍的貿易城。然後，觀看那繽紛的絲綢、街頭的食物和人們在和闐市場討價還價的聲音，讓人感覺古老的生活方式在這地區仍然根深蒂固。

的確，現代新疆的許多城市曾是絲路的主要驛站，絲路是從現代西安一路到中東地區的貿易路線。像是亞歷山大大帝等探險家從絲路旅程回去時帶回了異國食物、面孔和風景的故事。

食物可以用來了解一個文化，在新疆也的確如此，這裡有各式各樣饒富趣味的食物。在這地區找到的菜色同時受到中亞和傳統中國菜餚的影響。

正如在中亞，麵包和茶幾乎是每餐必備的食物。拌麵之類的手拉麵則顯示出我們習以為的中國食物的影響。拌麵通常搭配牛肉、青椒和番茄。另一道新疆常見的食物是抓飯，這道菜以米食為基底，通常加上羊肉和紅蘿蔔一起煮，吃的時候應該用手抓。

新疆有很多東西可以滿足喜歡路邊攤食物的人。除了美味的烤羊肉串，當地最獨特的小吃之一就是含有優格、葡萄糖漿和蜂蜜的刨冰。然而，新疆最著名的也許是所出產的水果。中文名稱源自新疆哈密市的哈密瓜（英文叫作 cantaloupe），以及當地出產的香瓜、西瓜及葡萄都極為甜美。這些水果許多也產自吐魯番，那裡充足的陽光和高溫創造出十分適合水果生長的條件。

新疆主要是回教地區，也是各種不同民族的家園。這裡的多數民族維吾爾人的外貌特徵看起來比較像中亞民族，而比較不像漢人。維吾爾族的男女遵循傳統穆斯林服飾的風格。有些女人把自己從頭到腳包起來，只看得見眼睛。維吾爾族人遵循伊斯蘭習俗，所經營的餐廳不供應豬肉。信眾在當地的清真寺進進出出，召喚祈禱的聲音整天不絕於耳。

感受新疆當地民族文化的一個好方法就是參觀市集。位於烏魯木齊的二道橋市集曾是中國、俄羅斯和中亞之間的貿易站。現在，它有數百個攤位販售維吾爾族商品，包括地毯、銅器、珠寶和樂器。晚上，五彩繽紛的燈光點亮了市集，人們到那裡盡情享受食物、民俗音樂和舞蹈。

新疆幅員廣大，邊界從俄羅斯延伸到印度，確實是個特別的地方。初次到此地的遊客對其自然與民族景觀驚嘆不已，並進而欣賞中國文化的多元性。

1. **all the way** 一路（作為強調用）；一直、自始至終

可指「全部；自始至終；一直」，在此是強調距離，指「一路……」，之後可接副詞或 to + 地方。

- We drove all the way from New York to California.
  我們一路從紐約開車到加州。

延伸學習

① be on the way 在路上；在途中

- The store is on the way, so I don't mind stopping in.
  路上會經過這間店，所以我不介意順道進去。

② out of the way 地處偏遠

- We don't go to that movie theater often because it's too out of the way.
  我們不是很常去那家電影院，因為它離大家都知道的地方很遠。

2. **in addition to** 除了……之外

in addition to 為片語介系詞，之後可接名詞或 V-ing。其他意思、用法相同的介系詞還有 besides、apart from、aside from 等。

- In addition to computers, this company also makes cell phones.
- = Apart/Aside from computers, this company also makes cell phones.
  除了電腦之外，這間公司也製造手機。
- Besides studying harder, Russ also promised to help more around the house.
  除了更努力唸書之外，羅斯也答應多幫忙做家事。

3. **used to** 曾經、過去習慣……

S. + used to + V. 表示「主詞曾經、過去習慣做某事」，強調過去經驗，暗示現在已經不做了，如文中用法。

- I used to go fishing, but not anymore.
  我以前會去釣魚，但現在不再去了。

延伸學習

① S. + be + used to + N./V-ing 主詞習慣於……

- Sandra is used to going to bed late.
  珊卓拉習慣晚睡。

② sth + be used + to V. 某物被用來做某事（為被動語態）

- The cloth was used to clean the table.
  這塊布是擦桌子用的。

Sentence Patterns

* **Another popular food in Xinjiang is *zhua fan*, a rice-based dish cooked usually with mutton and carrots, which is meant to be eaten with the hands.**

  句型 sth + be meant + $\begin{cases} \text{to V.} \\ \text{for N.} \end{cases}$

    某事物應該要、注定……

  mean 可表示「意圖；打算」，之後接 to V.，且沒有進行式用法。要表示「注定要；應該要」，通常用被動語態，如文中用法。

- This food is meant to be cooked, not eaten raw.
  這種食物應該要煮熟吃，不是生吃。

- These books are meant for adults, not children.
  這些書是給大人看的，不是給小孩看的。

  補充 要表示「某人打算、計畫做某事」，句型為：sb + mean to V.。

- I mean to get the work done by this afternoon.
  我打算今天下午把工作做完。

  此句型還有「某人故意做某事」的意思。

- I'm sorry. I didn't mean to hurt your feelings.
  對不起。我不是故意要傷害你的感情。

Celebrating a Gift of Blossoms

Sunlight streams through soft pink and white petals. As far as the eye can see, the blossoms glow like jewels[1] against the dark tree limbs. It is cherry blossom season, and your thoughts probably immediately jump to Japan. However, the colorful scene described is in Washington, DC, and it's just in time for the National Cherry Blossom Festival.

Washington's beautiful cherry trees do have a link to Japan. In 1912, Tokyo gave the first trees to the American capital city. They were a sign of friendship between the two countries. More trees were given and planted over the years. Now, when spring hits DC, over 3,700 cherry trees on the grounds of the Washington Monument[2] and in West and East Potomac Parks burst into bloom. *Many are Yoshino flowering cherry trees, which are known for the beautiful fragrance[3] of their blossoms.

華盛頓特區小檔案

正式名稱：Washington, District of Columbia

由來：為了紀念美國開國總統喬治‧華盛頓（George Washington）和
新大陸發現者克里斯多福‧哥倫布（Christopher Columbus）

人口（2013）：約六十五萬人

面積：一百七十七平方公里

區分：美國西岸的華盛頓州稱為 Washington State 或 state of
Washington

Vocabulary

1. **jewel** [ˋdʒuəl] *n.* 寶石；首飾（作此義時常用複數形）
2. **monument** [ˋmɑnjəmənt] *n.* 紀念碑
3. **fragrance** [ˋfregrəns] *n.* 香氣

華盛頓哥倫比亞的特區的地標——華盛頓紀念碑（Washington Monument）

【從旅遊看文化】

和日本贈樹一樣，法國也曾經送了個大禮給美國，那就是矗立在紐約埃利斯島（Ellis Island）上的自由女神像（Statue of Liberty），迄今已超過一世紀。這是法國政府為慶祝美國獨立（American Revolution）100 週年，在一八八六年所送的賀禮，除了表達美國人民爭取民主自由的理想，也象徵兩國的友誼。

In honor of the cherry blossoms and Japanese culture, DC puts on a two-week festival in late March and early April. The celebration kicks off with an opening ceremony[4] featuring[5] Western and Japanese performing artists and fun activities for the whole family. For two weeks, you can enjoy time under the flowering trees and welcome spring to DC.

The National Cherry Blossom Festival has a mix of events and activities to choose from. There are traditional tea ceremonies, Japanese film screenings, and a popular street festival. A taste of high-society life can be had at the Grand Ball, where the US Cherry Blossom Queen is chosen from over sixty young women. You can see her again in the festival's parade, along with eye-catching floats,[6] balloons, and marching[7] bands.

櫻花節遊行充滿各式表演隊伍,熱鬧非凡。節慶活動中也會選出年度櫻花皇后。圖片 / Flickr: jeri gloege

Vocabulary

4. **ceremony** [ˋsɛrəˌmoni] *n.* 典禮;儀式
5. **feature** [ˋfitʃɚ] *v.* 以……作為號召;以……為特色
6. **float** [flot] *n.* 花車
7. **march** [mɑrtʃ] *v.* 行進;行軍(現在分詞 marching 當形容詞,指「行進中的」)

301

If you'd rather do something more active than watch a parade or shop at a street festival, sign up for the Cherry Blossom Ten Mile Run. You'll pass some of the nation's greatest monuments and flowering cherry trees as you compete for $40,000 in prize money. There's also the Cherry Blast Art and Music Dance Party. It gives you two nights to get your groove[8] on and get exposed[9] to some of DC's newest and coolest art.

These events are only the tip of the activity iceberg[10] at the National Cherry Blossom Festival in Washington, DC. There are fashion shows and academic[11] contests[12] as well. Most of all, this festival celebrates the beautiful cherry trees that clothe[13] the American capital city in frothy[14] pink and white for spring.

Vocabulary

8. **groove** [gruv] *n.* 音樂韻律；節奏
9. **expose** [ɪkˋspoz] *v.* 使接觸到
10. **iceberg** [ˋaɪsˌbɝg] *n.* 冰山
11. **academic** [ˌækəˋdɛmɪk] *adj.* 學術的；學校的
12. **contest** [ˋkɑntɛst] *n.* 競賽
13. **clothe** [kloð] *v.* 使披上；覆蓋
14. **frothy** [ˋfrɔθi] *adj.* 輕軟精緻的

華盛頓特區櫻花節

陽光從淡粉紅色與白色的花瓣間灑落。目光之所及，如寶石一般的花朵靠在深色樹幹閃閃發光。這是櫻花季，而你的思緒可能立刻想到日本。然而，這裡所敘述的繽紛景色是在華盛頓特區，而此刻正是感受美國櫻花節的時候。

華盛頓特區的美麗櫻花樹確實和日本有關連。一九一二年，東京將第一批樹木送給這個美國首都。它們是兩國之間友誼的象徵。多年來有更多的樹木被贈送與栽種。現在，當春天降臨華盛頓特區時，華盛頓紀念碑地面和西波多馬克河公園與東波多馬克河公園內有超過三千七百株的櫻花樹盛開。許多是吉野櫻花樹，它們以其花朵美妙的香氣而聞名。

為了紀念櫻花與日本文化，華盛頓特區在三月底與四月初舉辦一場為期兩週的節慶。慶祝活動以一場開幕典禮揭開序幕，以西方與日本表演藝術家還有闔家皆宜的趣味活動為號召。兩週期間，你可以享受在開滿花朵的樹下的時光，並歡迎春天來到華盛頓特區。

美國櫻花節有各種節目和活動可供選擇。有傳統茶藝儀式、日本電影放映會和一場很受歡迎的街頭慶典。在盛裝舞會上可一嚐上流社會生活的滋味，美國櫻花皇后會在那裡從六十多名年輕女子中被選出。你可以在節慶的遊行中再度看見她，一同遊行的有引人注目的花車、氣球與行進樂隊。

如果你寧可做些比看遊行或在街頭慶典購物更有活力的事，就報名參加櫻花樹十英里長跑活動吧。當你為四萬元獎金競賽時，將會經過美國一些最偉大的紀念建物及開滿花的櫻花樹。還有櫻花藝文展暨音樂舞蹈派對。它將讓你兩個晚上隨著音樂擺動，並接觸華盛頓特區一些最新、最酷炫的藝術。

這些活動只是華盛頓特區的美國櫻花節在各項活動裡的一小部分。那裡也有時裝秀和學術競賽。最重要的是，這個節慶歡慶了在春天將美國首都披上輕軟精緻的粉紅與白色的美麗櫻花樹。

1. blossom vs. flower 「花」也有不同

blossom 和 flower 當名詞時都指「花朵」，但類型不太一樣：

	blossom	果樹結果前開的花，如櫻花、梅花
	flower	長在植物莖上的花，如玫瑰
	bloom	總稱（花），特別指觀賞用的花

- The blossoms fell from the trees and made colorful piles on the ground.
  花朵從樹上掉落，在地上形成了色彩繽紛的花堆。
- The book says that this yellow flower is called a daffodil.
  書上說這種黃色花朵叫作水仙花。
- Many flowers grow in spring, but some bloom even in winter.
  很多花在春天生長，但有些甚至在冬天也會開花。

2. as far as the eye can see 視力範圍內；就目光所及

此副詞片語中，eye 多用單數形。

- In the valley, there were wildflowers blooming as far as the eye could see.
  放眼望去，山谷中遍地野花盛開。

3. kick off 開始；開幕

此原為足球用語，指「開球」，後來亦引申作「（活動）開始；開幕」之意。名詞寫作 kickoff。

- The weeklong festival was kicked off with a speech by the mayor.
  為期一週的節慶活動由市長的演講揭開序曲。

4. as well 也

as well 為副詞，置於句末，前面不需逗點。

- I put your jacket in the closet. Your shoes are in there as well.
- = I put your jacket in the closet. Your shoes are in there, too.
  我把你的夾克放在衣櫥裡。你的鞋子也在那裡面

> 用 too 可加或不加逗點

補充 as well as 可作介系詞和對等連接詞用，表示「還有；以及」。當連接兩個名詞時，強調的是第一個名詞，故連接的事物為主詞時，動詞須配合前面的名詞。

- Doris says that her new boyfriend is smart as well as funny.
  陶樂絲說她的新男友很聰明也很有趣。

- The cat, as well as the dogs, is lying on the sofa right now.
  那隻貓以及那些狗現在正臥在沙發上。

5. **most of all 最重要的**

此副詞片語放句首時，用來帶出說明事情最重要的部份。

- Ernie likes his job because it makes him think. Most of all, he really likes his coworkers.
  爾尼喜歡他的工作因為那使他思考。最重要的是，他很喜歡他的同事。

補充 此片語也可放句尾，表示「尤其是」。

- All of the cookies are good, but I like the coconut cookies most of all.
  所有餅乾都很好吃，但我尤其喜歡椰子餅乾。

Sentence Patterns

* **Many are Yoshino flowering cherry trees, which are known for the beautiful fragrance of their blossoms.**

which 可用來引導關係子句，用來修飾其前面的名詞，如文中用法。

- The little girl always carries a small blue doll, which she calls Sugar.
  那個小女孩總是帶著一個她稱為蜜糖的藍色小玩偶。

句型 S. + be known for + N. 以某特色而聞名

此句型表示某人事物「以某特色而聞名」，known 也可以 famous 代換。

- The city is known/famous for its beautiful parks and the trees that line its streets.
  這城市以其美麗的公園和林立街道兩旁的樹木聞名。

Slip and Slide: High-Speed Fun at the World's Water Parks

Summer days are long and hot. Sooner or later, everyone feels like taking a dip[1] in some cool water. If you're not a fan of the beach, then spending a day at a water park may be the answer. All around the world, these parks offer fun and excitement[2] for all ages.

Water parks come in all shapes and sizes, but two of them stand out from the rest because they're huge! The first one is Tropical Islands, the largest water park on the planet. *Located in Germany, this 66,000-square-meter park has the world's biggest indoor[3] rain forest and Europe's largest sauna. It also has a pool that's almost the size of ten basketball courts.

Second in size is World Waterpark in Alberta, Canada. It contains[4] a giant wave pool and seventeen waterslides. It even has three new thrill slides. On each one of them, guests go into a glass capsule,[5] and then the floor beneath[6] them drops, sending the riders on a speedy[7] journey. One of the slides even does circles in the air before sending riders into the pool.

「世界水上樂園」（World Waterpark）的刺激滑水道，滑行時速高達六十公里。

「熱帶島嶼」（Tropical Islands）水上樂園讓遊客在室內體驗雨林風情。
圖片 / Wikipedia: Resort

Vocabulary

1. **dip** [dɪp] *n.* 浸；沾
2. **excitement** [ɪkˋsaɪtmənt] *n.* 刺激；興奮
3. **indoor** [ˋɪnˏdɔr] *adj.* 室內的
4. **contain** [kənˋten] *v.* 包含；裝有
5. **capsule** [ˋkæpsəl] *n.* 膠囊式座艙；膠囊
6. **beneath** [bɪˋniθ] *prep.* 在……之下；在……下面
7. **speedy** [ˋspidi] *adj.* 迅速的

遊樂設施小辭典

wave pool [wev] [pul] *n. phr.* 造浪池

waterslide [ˈwɔtɚˌslaɪd] *n.* 滑水道

thrill slide [θrɪl] [slaɪd] *n. phr.* 刺激滑水道

roller coaster [ˈrolɚ ˌkostɚ] *n.* 雲霄飛車

water coaster [ˈwɔtɚ ˌkostɚ] *n. phr.* 水上雲霄飛車（搭乘機動車輛穿過許多水池區，或搭乘橡皮艇等滑過高低落差水道的遊樂設施）

「海灘樂園」（Beach Park）
的極限滑水道挑戰遊客的膽量。
圖片 / Flickr: Noel Portuga

Other water parks around the world can get your heart racing, too. One of them is Noah's Ark,[8] located in Wisconsin, USA. *This park has dozens of rides, including a popular four-lane mat race that winds through a twisting[9] tunnel.[10] Another is a combination[11] of waterslide and roller coaster. Riders slide down in a raft,[12] and rushing water pushes them back up again. At half a kilometer in length, it's the country's third longest water coaster.

Interesting water parks can also be found in South America. For example, Brazil's Beach Park has a ride called the Insano. Here, guests show their courage[13] by sliding at a speed

「挪亞方舟」（Noah's Ark）為全美最大的水
上樂園，遊樂設施包羅萬象，可闔家同歡。
圖片 / Noah's Ark Family Park

圖片 / Noah's Ark Family Park

Vocabulary

8. **Noah's Ark** [ˋnoəz] [ɑrk] *n. phr.* 挪亞方舟（源自《聖經・創世記》）

9. **twist** [twɪst] *v.* 扭曲、蜿蜒曲折；盤繞（現在分詞 twisting 作形容詞，指「曲折的」）

10. **tunnel** [ˋtʌnl̩] *n.* 隧道；地道

11. **combination** [ˌkɑmbəˋneʃən] *n.* 結合；組合

12. **raft** [ræft] *n.* 橡皮艇；木筏

13. **courage** [ˋkɝɪdʒ] *n.* 膽量；勇氣

【從旅遊看文化】

除了刺激的水上樂園，另一種主題性的樂園也很吸睛，例如「樂高水上樂園」（LEGOLAND Water Land），除了一般的水上遊樂設施，還可以在水中大玩樂高積木、乘坐用積木打造的汽船、欣賞各式樂高公仔，是樂高迷不可錯過的水上樂園。

圖片 / Flickr: Loozrboy

of 105 kilometers per hour from a height of fourteen floors. For part of this five-second journey, the sliders are even airborne.[14]

Water parks are always competing[15] to offer the largest space or the best rides. If you want to relax[16] in a wave pool and also slide at high speeds, then a water park has what you're looking for. The next time you find yourself near one, go in and have some fun!

Vocabulary

14. **airborne** [ˈɛrˌbɔrn] *adj.* 浮在空中的；空運的
15. **compete** [kəmˈpit] *v.* 競爭；對抗
16. **relax** [rɪˈlæks] *v.* 放鬆；休息

高速滑水樂——全球特色水上樂園

夏季的白天漫長又炎熱。大家遲早會想要在涼爽的水裡泡一泡。如果你不喜歡海灘，那麼在水上樂園度過一天也許是個法子。在世界各地，這些樂園為所有年齡層的人提供樂趣和刺激。

水上樂園包羅萬象、各種形狀和大小都有，但其中有兩個樂園把其他都比下去，因為它們占地廣大！第一個是「熱帶島嶼」，全球最大的水上樂園。這座六萬六千平方公尺大的樂園位於德國，擁有全世界最大的室內雨林區以及歐洲最大的蒸氣浴場。它還有一座將近十個籃球場大的泳池。

位於加拿大艾伯塔省的「世界水上樂園」面積居次。它有一個巨大的波浪池和十七條滑水道。它甚至有三條新的刺激水道。在其中任一條水道裡，遊客坐進玻璃膠囊中，然後他們下方的地板會向下墜落，將乘客送上高速旅程。其中一個水道在把乘客送進池子前甚至會在半空中繞圈圈。

世界上其他的水上樂園也會讓你心跳加速。其中之一是位於美國威斯康辛州的「挪亞方舟」。這個水上樂園有許多遊樂設施，其中包括一個熱門的、穿過蜿蜒隧道的四線道滑水墊競賽。另一項設施則結合了滑水道和雲霄飛車。乘客坐在橡皮艇裡往下滑，猛烈的水流會把他們再往上推。這個水上雲霄飛車有半公里長，是全美第三長的。

南美洲也可找到有趣的水上樂園。舉例來說，巴西的「海灘樂園」有一個稱為「瘋狂世界」的遊樂設施。在這裡遊客可從十四層樓高的地方以時速一百零五公里的速度往下滑，展現他們的膽量。在這五秒鐘的歷程中，滑水客甚至有段時間會浮在空中。

水上樂園總是競相提供最大的空間或最棒的遊樂設施。如果你想在波浪池中放鬆一下以及想搭乘高速滑行的遊樂設施，那麼水上樂園裡有你在找的東西。下次你發現附近有個水上樂園時，就進去玩個痛快吧！

「毒蠍之尾」（The Scorpion's Tail）讓遊客以接近垂直的角度下水，管道曲折迂迴，歡樂刺激。
圖片 / Noah's Ark Family Park

1. stand out 突出；出色、顯眼

stand out 後面可接介系詞（against、among、as、from、in 等）＋ 名詞，表示「在⋯⋯（情形）下變得顯著、醒目」。stand out from the rest 就是「比其他的出色；出類拔萃」的意思。

- If you want to stand out from everyone else, you need to dress or act differently from them.
  如果你想要與眾不同，就需要穿得或表現得跟其他人不一樣。

2. 尺寸的用法

要表示某事物的長度、寬度或高度等，有兩種方式：

> 句型　sth + be + 數字 + 單位 + in + length/width/height
> 　　　sth + be + 數字 + 單位 + long/wide/high
> 　　　長度／寬度／高度⋯⋯

- The building is over thirty meters in height.
- = The building is over thirty meters high.
  這棟大樓高度超過三十公尺。

> 句型　a + length/width/height + of + 數字 + 單位
> 　　　長度／寬度／高度⋯⋯

- At a length of six meters, John's new boat is quite big.
  約翰的新船相當大，有六公尺長。

* **Located in Germany, this 66,000-square-meter park has the world's biggest indoor rain forest and Europe's largest sauna.**

當對等子句的主詞相同時，可將連接詞及一個主詞省略，並將一個動作改為分詞形式，形成分詞構句。以此句為例，依步驟說明如下：

> 步驟一　刪除相同的主詞與連接詞

- This ~~66,000-square-meter park~~ is located in Germany, ~~and~~ this 66,000-square-meter park has . . .

　　　　　　　刪除相同主詞　　　　　　　刪除連接詞

步驟二 原句為被動語態 is located，故刪除 be 動詞，保留過去分詞 located。

刪 is，保留過去分詞

- i̶s̶ located in Germany, this 66,000-square-meter park has . . .
- →Located in Germany, this 66,000-square-meter park has . . .

補充 原句若為主動語態，則將動詞改為現在分詞。

- Sleeping deeply, Victor didn't hear his brother come into the room and take a book.
  由於維克托睡得很沉，他沒聽到他哥哥進房間拿走一本書。

* **This park has dozens of rides, including a popular four-lane mat race that winds through a twisting tunnel.**

include 表示「包括；包含」，基本用法為 A include B（A 包括 B；B 包含在 A 之內）。

- The cost of the hotel includes breakfast.
  飯店費用包含早餐。

補充 要表示「……，包含某人事物在內」，可用：

　　　　S. + V., including N./V-ing（文中用法）

　　　　S. + V., N./V-ing included

- Four girls are going to the party, including Amy and Sara.
  有四個女孩要去參加派對，包括愛咪和莎拉在內。

- All swimmers must wear a swimming cap to go in the pool, children included.
  所有泳客進入泳池時都必須戴泳帽，包含小孩在內。

北海道支笏湖（Lake Shikotsu）畔長滿板谷楓、山楓、椴樹，秋天時無論在湖岸觀景台或遊船上都可欣賞紅葉美景。

3. 全球秋色之美

PLAY ALL　　TRACK 59

A World Full of Color

One of the most beautiful sights during fall is a tree full of leaves that have changed from the joyful[1] green of summer to red and gold. It looks like the trees put on their fanciest[2] clothes for one final party before they sleep for the winter.

Some of the most impressive trees for pretty fall colors are Japanese maple trees. These trees originally came from Hokkaido, and they still put on a show there every fall. The Lake Shikots Autumn Foliage Festival in October gives people an excuse to go outside and enjoy the beauty. They can also relax in an outdoor hot spring and watch the red leaves float down around them.

慶典小辭典

Lake Shikotsu Autumn Foliage Festival 常譯為「支笏湖紅葉祭」，此慶典常搭配太鼓表演、農產品特賣等活動。

Oktoberfest 指德國慕尼黑的「十月節」，亦常稱作「啤酒節」，是當地一年中最盛大的活動。

圖片 / Flickr: 46137

Japan isn't the only place to enjoy the autumn colors. In Germany, the changing trees act as the perfect setting[3] for the castles of the Rhine Valley.[4] Even the grapevines of the area get in on the act by adding their own golden[5] colors. They make a beautiful natural[6] decoration[7] for Germany's famous fall festival of Oktoberfest.

萊茵河谷（Rhine Valley）兩岸有許多古色古香的城堡，此圖為高琴古堡（Cochem Castle）。

Vocabulary

1. **joyful** [ˈdʒɔɪfəl] *adj.* 充滿喜悅的；令人高興的
2. **fancy** [ˈfænsi] *adj.* 華麗、別緻的；時髦昂貴的
3. **setting** [ˈsɛtɪŋ] *n.* 背景；環境
4. **valley** [ˈvæli] *n.* 溪谷；山谷
5. **golden** [ˈgoldən] *adj.* 金色的；黃金的
6. **natural** [ˈnætʃərəl] *adj.* 自然的；天然的
7. **decoration** [ˌdɛkəˈreʃən] *n.* 裝飾；裝潢

美國佛蒙特州（Vermont）的聖約翰學院（St. Johnsbury Academy）落葉繽紛

Although most people associate[8] England with rain, the Lake District in the north is known for its fall beauty. The Lake District has hills covered with a plant called heather, and it can change to red and yellow when the weather gets chilly.[9] These colors are mirrored[10] in the many lakes there, doubling[11] the beauty.

Over in the United States, the state of Vermont is a great place to take a drive in the fall. Some even call this area "Fall's Color Capital." You won't be disappointed[12] as you drive down lanes[13] lined with trees in bright yellow and orange. With its covered bridges and homemade apple cider offered at stands beside the road, this area certainly provides some of the best autumn drives.

上：卡薩羅馬古堡（Casa Loma）
左：阿岡昆公園（Algonquin Park）

【從旅遊看文化】

加拿大的多倫多（Toronto）也是
欣賞楓葉的絕佳景點，著名的賞楓
景點有卡薩羅馬古堡（Casa Loma）、
西恩塔（CN Tower）及阿岡昆公園
（Algonquin Park）。除了賞楓，還
可以品嚐美味的楓糖餅乾及楓糖漿
（maple syrup）。

Vocabulary

8. **associate** [əˋsoʃɪˏet] *v.* 把……聯想在一起
9. **chilly** [ˋtʃɪlɪ] *adj.* 寒冷的；有寒意的
10. **mirror** [ˋmɪrɚ] *v.* 反映；反射
11. **double** [ˋdʌbəl] *v.* 變成兩倍；使加倍
12. **disappointed** [ˏdɪsəˋpɔɪntɪd] *adj.* 失望的；沮喪的
13. **lane** [len] *n.* 車道；巷弄

楓糖漿小辭典

每年三、四月間，白雪漸融、大地回春之際，楓糖漿生產季節也正式開始。楓糖漿主要集中在加拿大東部的魁北克省（Quebec），加拿大每年出口逾九百萬公升的楓糖漿，其品質皆受到該國食品檢驗局的監督，評鑑標準分為三個等級、五種顏色，品質由高至低分別為：加拿大第一級（極淺琥珀色、淺琥珀色、中等琥珀色），加拿大第二級（琥珀色），以及加拿大第三級（深琥珀色）。

The colors of fall are shining bright in October, and we've mentioned only a few of the many places you can enjoy them. Perhaps the leaves are changing right near you. The only way to find out is to get outside this fall and hunt for your own autumn leaves before winter blows them away.

秋冬是美國的蘋果盛產季，果園常將新鮮蘋果製成 apple cider，即未經去核、過濾的蘋果汁。除可冰涼飲用，加熱後配上肉桂（cinnamon）也別有一番風味。圖片 / Flickr: Waldo Jaquith

中文翻譯

全球秋色之美

秋天最美的景色之一就是樹木的茂密枝葉從夏季那令人愉悅的綠色變成了紅色和金色。這景象看來就彷如樹木在冬眠前為了參加最後一場派對而換上最華麗的衣裳。

優美的秋色中令人印象最深刻的一些樹木便是日本的楓樹了。這些樹木源自北海道，每年秋天，它們仍在那裡上演展示秀。十月的「支笏湖紅葉祭」帶給人們外出欣賞美景的理由。他們也可以在戶外泡溫泉放鬆身心，並看著紅葉在身邊飄落。

日本不是唯一可以欣賞秋色的地方。在德國，漸漸變色的樹木最適合作為萊茵河谷城堡的背景了。甚至連該區的葡萄藤也加入它們特有的金黃色來共襄盛舉。它們為德國著名的「秋日十月節」（又譯作「慕尼黑啤酒節」）構築出一幅美麗的自然裝飾。

雖然多數人會把英國跟雨聯想在一起，英國北部的湖區可是以秋天的美景而聞名。湖區的山丘上布滿一種稱為帚石楠的植物，它在天氣變冷時會變成紅色和黃色。色彩倒映在此區的許多湖泊上，使得景色美麗加倍。

來到美國，佛蒙特州是秋天開車兜風的好地方。有人甚至稱此區為「秋色之都」。開車經過亮黃色和橘色樹木林立的道路，你不會感到失望。此區有廊橋和路邊小販在販售自製蘋果汁，確實提供了一些絕佳的秋日兜風體驗。

十月時節，秋天的色彩正閃閃發光，在眾多可以欣賞美景的地方中，我們只提到幾個而已。也許樹葉就在你身旁換上新裝。發掘美景的不二法門，就是在今秋趁著冬風將秋葉吹走前，到戶外去搜尋自己的秋葉美景吧。

英國湖區（Lake District）秋季時呈現萬紫千紅的景貌。 圖片 / Flickr: Marilynjane

1. **one of + N. . . .** 其中一個……；……之一

此用法用來指稱群體中的其中一個人事物，of 之後接複數名詞，one of + N. 作主詞時要
搭配單數動詞。

複數名詞

- [One of my favorite things to do] is to go running on the beach early in the
morning.

搭配 one，用單數動詞。

我最喜歡做的事情之一就是一大早在沙灘上跑步。

若指稱群體中的其中一些人事物，則用 some of + N.，名詞為複數可數名詞時搭配複數
動詞；為不可數名詞時則搭配單數動詞。

複數可數名詞

- [Some of the boys] are picking up the heavy boxes and moving them to
the door.

複數動詞

其中一些男孩正拿起沉重的箱子並把它們搬到門邊。

不可數名詞

- [Some of the tastiest food] to eat is in Italy.
其中一些最美味的食物在義大利。

單數動詞

2. **put on** 穿戴上；上演；增加（重量）

片語動詞 put on 有好幾個意思，這裡介紹幾個常見的用法。

① 指「穿上；戴上」，後接衣物、飾品等，如文中用法。

- Carol put on a coat and hat before she left the house.
卡蘿出門前穿上外套，並戴上帽子。

② 指「上演；舉辦、安排（表演、展覽）」，如文中用法。

- Every year, the school puts on a play that is written by one of the teachers.
這所學校每年都會演出一場由校內一位老師所編寫的戲劇。

③ 指「增加（重量、體重等）」。

- Ryan put on a few kilograms during his trip to France.
萊恩去法國旅行時增加了好幾公斤。

3. **get in on the act** 參與（活動等）；共襄盛舉

get in on the act 指「參與、加入某活動」，特別是指加入別人發起且已大獲成功的活動，
類似中文所說「湊一腳」的意思。

- When the stock was finally offered to the public, thousands of people wanted to get in on the act.
  這支股票終於上市時，數千名民眾都想要參與。

4. **blow away** 吹走；被風吹散

①指「吹走；被風吹散」，可作及物用，如文中用法，也可作不及物用，如以下例句用法。

- The man's hat blew away, and he couldn't catch it.
  那名男子的帽子被風吹走了，他抓不到。

②指「擊敗；使潰不成軍」，受詞可為人或事物。

- Brad's painting blew away all of the other artwork in the art contest.
  布萊德的畫作擊敗了藝術比賽中的所有其他作品。

③指「使某人印象深刻；使驚訝」，受詞為人。

- The story you wrote really blew me away, and I think your teacher will feel the same.
  你寫的故事太讓我驚豔了，我認為你的老師也會有同感。

Chipping Away at Winter's Gloom[1]

In many parts of the world, the cold, dark weather of winter is something to hide from. People go inside, turn on the heat, and wait for spring. However, a few cities turn the chilly weather into a bright spot[2] by hosting festivals filled with stunning ice and snow sculptures. These events attract visitors from around the world.

The Sapporo Snow Festival on Hokkaido is one of the most well-known of these celebrations.[3] It all began when high school students created six snow statues in Odori Park in 1950. Five years later, a group of soldiers built huge snow sculptures and snow slides for children that the event is now known for. The massive sculptures have had different themes[4] over the years, from dinosaurs to palaces. If there isn't enough snow, thousands of truckloads[5] of it are brought to Sapporo, so the weather doesn't dictate[6] whether the festival takes place or not.

札幌雪祭（The Sapporo Snow Festival）為北海道冬季盛事，於每年二月登場，活動分三個會場，主會場為展示大型雪雕的大通公園（Odori Park，此圖），薄野（Susukino）會場展示冰雕作品並點燈至午夜，社區圓頂（Tsudome）會場則提供各種雪上活動。圖片 / 札幌市

除了雪雕作品，札幌雪祭中亦有日本傳統舞蹈表演。
圖片 / 札幌市

Building the gigantic[7] snow and ice sculptures for the Sapporo festival involves heavy construction[8] machinery[9] that helps to pack snow inside frames made of metal and wood. Part of the frame is then removed, and artists outline the design before beginning to carve it. After the rest of the frame is taken off, the final details are filled in.

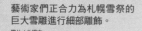

藝術家們正合力為札幌雪祭的
巨大雪雕進行細部雕飾。
圖片 / 札幌市

札幌雪祭除了雪雕，還設
有供孩童遊玩的雪造滑梯
（snow slides）。圖片 / 札幌市

Vocabulary

1. **gloom** [glum] *n.* 陰暗；憂鬱；絕望
2. **bright spot** [braɪt] [spɑt] *n. phr.* （困境中）值得高興的事；亮點
3. **celebration** [ˌsɛləˋbreʃən] *n.* 慶典；慶祝活動
4. **theme** [θim] *n.* 主題
5. **truckload** [ˋtrʌkˌlod] *n.* 卡車的負載量
6. **dictate** [ˋdɪkˌtet] *v.* 影響、支配；決定
7. **gigantic** [dʒaɪˋgæntɪk] *adj.* 龐大的；巨大的
8. **construction** [kənˋstrʌkʃən] *n.* 建造；建築
9. **machinery** [məˋʃinəri] *n.* 機器（總稱）；機械設備

魁北克冬季嘉年華（The Quebec Winter Carnival）
為全球最大型的冬季嘉年華會，活動期間除了以雪為
主題的各種活動外，更有遊行、獨木舟橫越聖羅倫斯
河、音樂會及化裝舞會等活動。
圖片 / Carnival de Québec 加拿大魁北克冬季嘉年華

Of course, ice and snow sculptures aren't limited to northern Japan. The Quebec Winter Carnival[10] welcomes about a million visitors to the history-rich French Canadian city around the beginning of February. In addition to admiring the beautiful carvings, crowds attend night parades, try out ice slides, and watch canoe races on the St. Lawrence River.

In Moscow, two overlapping[11] events—the Russian Winter Festival and the December Nights Festival—pair incredibly detailed[12] ice carvings and snowmen with live classical music performances. In Red Square, an ice rink[13] is set up for people to skate or watch ice hockey[14] matches. It's a great atmosphere for Muscovites[15] ringing in the New Year as the bells toll[16] from the clock tower above.

圖片 / 路透社

莫斯科的俄羅斯冬節（The Russian Winter Festival）於十二月底至一月初舉行，遊客可品嚐傳統美食並觀賞民俗音樂表演。十二月夜節（The December Nights Festival）則在十二月中至一月中舉行，期間有許多古典樂及民俗舞蹈表演。

圖片 / Wikipedia: S Pakhrin

Vocabulary

10. **carnival** [ˋkɑrnəvəl] *n.* 嘉年華會

11. **overlap** [ˌovəˋlæp] *v.* （在時間、主題上）與……部分重疊
    （overlapping 為現在分詞作形容詞用，指「與……部分重疊的」）

12. **detailed** [ˋdiˌteld] *adj.* 精細的；詳細的

13. **rink** [rɪŋk] *n.* 溜冰場

14. **ice hockey** [aɪs] [ˋhɑki] *n.* 冰上曲棍球

15. **Muscovite** [ˋmʌskəˌvaɪt] *n.* 莫斯科人

16. **toll** [tol] *v.* （緩慢持續地）敲（鐘）；（鐘）鳴響

圖片 / Flickr: Steve Langguth

圖片 / Flickr: Rincewind42

哈爾濱國際冰雪節（Harbin International Ice and Snow Festival）由太陽島國際雪雕藝術博覽會、冰雪大世界，以及兆麟公園的冰燈藝術博覽會組成，雕刻師們利用從松花江運來的冰打造一棟棟壯觀的冰雕建築，再以螢光燈打亮來增添魔幻風情。

Harbin, China, held its first Ice and Snow Festival in January 1985. The city experiences freezing temperatures for 190 days per year, so it is the perfect place to celebrate. The event has grown into an extravaganza,[17] complete with sculpting competitions, an ice lantern show, and a film festival. It draws in more than 12 million visitors every year.

Why are these festivals such huge draws? Perhaps it's because they serve as symbols of playfulness[18] in the year's dreariest[19] season. In fact, they just might be the perfect cure for anyone's winter blues.[20]

Vocabulary

17. **extravaganza** [ɪkˌstrævəˈgænzə] *n.* 盛會；盛大的表演或賽事
18. **playfulness** [ˈplefəlnəs] *n.* 活潑有趣；嬉鬧
19. **dreary** [ˈdrɪri] *adj.* 沈悶的；陰鬱的
20. **blues** [bluz] *n.* 憂鬱；沮喪

北國的冬季慶典

在世界上許多地方，寒冷陰暗的冬季讓人避之唯恐不及。人們走進室內、打開暖氣，等待著春天來臨。然而，有些城市透過舉辦令人驚艷的冰雪雕刻慶典將冷冽的天氣化為歡樂。這些活動吸引了來自世界各地的遊客。

這類慶典中其中一個最有名的就是北海道的「札幌雪祭」。雪祭可追溯至一九五〇年，當時有高中生在大通公園創作了六座雪雕像。五年後，一群士兵打造了巨大的雪雕以及供孩童遊玩的雪造滑梯，如今雪祭即以此聞名。過去幾年來，這些大型雪雕每年都有不同的主題，從恐龍到宮殿都有。如果雪量不足，載滿數千輛卡車的雪會被運來札幌，所以天氣並不會對慶典是否舉行構成影響。

建造札幌雪祭上的巨大冰雪雕刻品，得動用重型工程機具來幫忙將雪堆入以金屬和木頭製成的框架中。接著移除部份的框架，然後藝術家會先擬出設計的輪廓再開始進行刻鑿。待剩下的框架取出後，便進行細部雕刻。

當然，冰雕和雪雕並非只有日本北部才有。每年二月初，「魁北克冬季嘉年華會」迎接約一百萬名遊客前來這座歷史悠久的加拿大法語城市。除了欣賞美麗的雕刻作品之外，群眾也會參加夜間遊行、嘗試滑冰滑梯，以及觀賞聖羅倫斯河上的獨木舟比賽。

在莫斯科，時間重疊的兩項活動──「俄羅斯冬節」及「十二月夜節」──用巧奪天工的冰雕及雪人來搭配古典音樂的現場演奏。紅場設有溜冰場供民眾溜冰或觀賞冰上曲棍球比賽。對迎接新年到來的莫斯科人來說，鐘聲從上方鐘塔響起的那種氛圍非常棒。

中國哈爾濱市於一九八五年一月舉辦首屆「冰雪節」。這座城市每年有一百九十天處於冰天雪地之中，因此是舉行冬季慶典的絕佳地點。該活動因有冰雕賽、冰燈籠展以及電影節而發展成一場盛會，每年吸引逾一千兩百萬名遊客。

為什麼這些慶典會如此吸引人？或許是因為在一年中最愁雲慘霧的季節，它們象徵著歡樂喧鬧。事實上，它們或許是治療冬季憂鬱的最佳良方。

1. **chip away at sth** 削減、削弱……

chip 作動詞用，有「削去；鑿落」之意，chip away at 之後可接感覺、想法、制度等名詞，表示「逐漸破壞、漸漸消弱」的意思。chip away at 之後也可接 debt（債務）或金錢數額，表示「逐漸還清（債務）；慢慢減少（金額）」的意思。

- Being defeated in several games in a row has chipped away at the player's self-confidence.
  連續在好幾場比賽中輸球已削弱了那名球員的自信心。
- Kyle tried to chip away at his debt by paying back some money to the bank every month.
  凱爾藉著每個月還銀行一些錢來慢慢清償他的債務。

2. **take place** 舉行；發生

此片語的主詞須為事件或活動，且用主動來表示，意思為「發生；舉行」。

- The festival will take place on Saturday in the park next to my house.
  慶典將於週六在我家隔壁的公園舉行。

補充 hold / host / put on 舉辦；舉行（主詞是人，主詞為事時可用被動）

- The mayor will hold a party for the firefighters.
  市長將為消防隊員們辦場派對。
- A press conference was hosted to promote the director's new movie.
  為了宣傳這導演的新片而舉辦了一場記者會。

3. **fill in sth** 提供（更多資訊）

用法 fill in + N.、fill + N./ 代名詞 + in

fill in 作及物動詞時，除了表「填寫」之意，亦可表「提供更多……」的意思，文中 the final details are filled in 即此義的被動用法。

- Let me tell you about the decision made at the meeting first, and then I'll fill in the details.
  讓我先告訴你會議上做出的決定，然後我再補充細節。

比較 fill sb in (on sth) 提供某人（關於某事的）資訊

- Ted filled his friends in on the basketball game he watched on TV last night.
  泰德向友人說他昨晚收看的籃球比賽經過。

4. **try out** 試用；嘗試

當及物動詞，表示「嘗試；試用」，可接事物或人，指試試看感覺如何、是否有效或適合，如文中用法。

- Before you buy the bike, don't you want to try it out?
  在你買這台腳踏車前不想先試騎看看嗎？

- I'm not sure Dean will be a good fit for our company, but we can try him out for a week.
  我不確定迪恩是適合我們公司的好人選，但我們可以試用他一個星期看看。

比較 try on 試穿（衣物）

- Is there a place where I can try on these clothes to see if they fit?
  有地方可以讓我試穿這些衣服、看看合不合身嗎？

5. **complete with** 具備（特色）

complete 在此作形容詞用，指「完善的；完備的」，complete with 是指「具備、包括（設備、特色等）」。

- They served a full dinner, complete with salad and dessert.
  他們提供一頓豐富的晚餐，沙拉甜點一應俱全。

The Christmas Market in Nuremberg— A Magical[1] Time of Year

It's a cold and snowy winter evening. Golden lights shine in the sky, and the smell of sweet roasted[2] almonds fills the air. In the distance, you can hear people singing a Christmas song, and before you, gifts and food are displayed in brightly lit stalls. Known as the Nuremberg Christmas Market, it's a magical event that everyone looks forward to every year.

Here, handmade wooden toys, tree decorations, and Christmas angels are sold. Among these items is one that the market is particularly known for—prune dolls. Made with dried fruit and nuts, these dolls are meant to be kept inside houses to keep harm away.

紐倫堡擁有全德國最大的聖誕市集 圖片 / Flickr: Uwe Niklas

旅遊達人10大嚴選

旅遊達人私房推薦

旅遊達人季節限定

紐倫堡小檔案

德國作家霍夫曼（E.T.A. Hoffmann）的童話故事《胡桃鉗與老鼠王》就發生在紐倫堡的市政廳，這個故事後來被柴科夫斯基譜寫成芭蕾舞劇《胡桃鉗》（The Nutcracker and the Mouse King）。

紐倫堡舊城區中央的「主市場」在每年聖誕節前幾周就會開始舉辦各種活動，而在紐倫堡的聖誕市集一般被認為是德國歷史最悠久且規模最大的。

李子人玩偶（prune dolls）又稱為 prune people，是由李子乾、堅果做成的擺飾，為紐倫堡傳統藝品。
圖片 / Flickr: Jametiks

Vocabulary

1. **magical** [ˈmædʒɪkəl] *adj.* 神奇、美妙的；充滿魔力的
2. **roast** [rost] *v.* 烤；烘烤（文中用過去分詞 roasted 作形容詞表示「烘烤的」）

331

紐倫堡市政廳旁的美之泉（Schöner Brunnen），金碧輝煌的噴泉上裝飾著四十座雕像。在美泉的圍欄上有個小銅環，據說只要對著美泉許願並且轉銅環三圈，願望就能成真。

【從旅遊看文化】

薑（ginger）在古歐洲是一種昂貴的香料，只有在聖誕節等大節日才會被用來製作點心，因此薑餅（gingerbread cookie）成為聖誕節的代表之一，紐倫堡更有「薑餅之都」的美稱。

聖誕市集販售的東西種類琳瑯滿目，有各式精巧的聖誕禮品，還有陶瓷餐具等生活用品。 圖片 / Flickr: andy liang

Another high point of the market is the food. Gingerbread cookies hang from stalls selling a variety of baked goods. Nuremberg's barbecued sausages[3] are crunchy[4] and aromatic[5] and go deliciously with hot spiced[6] wine served in decorated cups.

The market brings back a time when Christmas meant more than beating the holiday rush[7] to shop for high-tech items in department stores. *With this warm, traditional feeling, it's no surprise that the market is loved by young and old alike.

Vocabulary

3. **sausage** [ˋsɔsɪdʒ] *n.* 香腸；臘腸

4. **crunchy** [ˋkrʌntʃɪ] *adj.* 脆的

5. **aromatic** [͵ærəˋmætɪk] *adj.* 有香味的；芳香的

6. **spice** [spaɪs] *v.* 加香料；加調味品（文中用過去分詞 spiced 作形容詞指「添加香料的」）

7. **rush** [rʌʃ] *n.* 繁忙的活動期

Just around the corner of the market is a special children's area that seems to have come right out of a fairy tale.[8] Here, kids can go for a ride on an old-fashioned[9] merry-go-round[10] or a Ferris wheel[11] and join in Christmas baking and candle making.

An event that children look forward to especially is a visit by the Christ Child, or "Christkind," in German. Every two years, a teenage girl is elected[12] to be the Christkind. Wearing a white robe,[13] a crown,[14] and golden curls,[15] she makes a speech at the opening of the market to welcome everyone. Then, she invites all of the children to go for free rides on the merry-go-round. The Christkind represents the Christmas spirit by bringing hope and joy to children. For this reason, she is also an important symbol[16] of Nuremberg.

Nuremberg's Christmas market begins in late November and lasts all the way until Christmas Eve. Indeed, visiting the market is a marvelous way to get ready for the holiday season. Everyone who goes is sure to leave with a smile and a warm feeling.

紐倫堡聖誕市集每兩年會選出一名當地十六至十九歲的女孩作為開幕式的「童年基督」（Christkind）。
圖片 / Flickr: Marcus Meissner

應景的聖誕裝飾
圖片 / Flickr: charley1965

Vocabulary

8. **fairy tale** [ˋfɛri] [tel] *n.* 童話故事
9. **old-fashioned** [ˋoldˋfæʃənd] *adj.* 舊式的；過時的
10. **merry-go-round** [ˋmɛrigoˏraʊnd] *n.* 旋轉木馬
11. **Ferris wheel** [ˋfɛrəs] [hwil] *n.* 摩天輪
12. **elect** [ɪˋlɛkt] *v.* 選舉
13. **robe** [rob] *n.* 長袍
14. **crown** [kraʊn] *n.* 王冠；（戴在頭上的）冠狀物
15. **curl** [kɝl] *n.* 捲髮
16. **symbol** [ˋsɪmbəl] *n.* 象徵；符號

紐倫堡聖誕市集——年度魔幻時刻

這是個下雪的寒冷冬夜。金色的燈光在天空閃爍，空氣中瀰漫著香甜的烤杏仁味。你可以聽到遠方有人在唱聖誕歌曲，在你眼前的則是禮品和食物陳列在燈火通明的攤位上。這裡就是紐倫堡聖誕市集，是個大家每年都期待的神奇活動。

這裡販售手工木製玩具、聖誕樹裝飾品和聖誕天使。這些商品當中有一樣是這個市集特別出名的：李子人玩偶。這些玩偶是用果乾與堅果製成，置於室內用來保平安。

這個市集另一個最精彩的項目便是食物。販售各式烘焙食物的攤位上掛著薑餅。紐倫堡的烤香腸又香又脆，搭配盛在裝飾杯裡熱騰騰的香料酒，十分美味。

這個市集讓人想起過去那段聖誕節不只是到百貨公司瘋狂搶購高科技產品的日子。因為帶有這種溫暖、傳統的感覺，這個市集受到老老少少喜愛也就不讓人意外了。

市集附近有個特別的兒童區，看起來就像直接從童話故事中搬出來似的。孩子們可以在這裡乘坐復古的旋轉木馬或摩天輪，以及參加聖誕烘焙和蠟燭製作的活動。

孩子們特別期待的一項活動是 Christkind，也就是德文的「童年基督」的來訪。每兩年會有一位少女被選為童年基督。她穿著白袍、戴著皇冠和金黃色的捲髮，在市集開始時發表演說歡迎大家。之後，她會邀請所有孩子去坐免費的旋轉木馬。童年基督代表著帶給孩子們希望和喜悅的聖誕精神。因為這個緣故，她也是紐倫堡的一個重要象徵。

紐倫堡的聖誕市集在十一月底展開，一直持續到聖誕夜。確實，造訪這個市集是為假期做準備的一個超棒方式。每個到訪的人都一定會帶著微笑和暖意離開。

紐倫堡規劃精彩的兒童聖誕市集，讓小朋友搭乘摩天輪、騎乘旋轉木馬，如同遨遊童話樂園。

圖片 / Flickr: Tourismus Nürnberg

1. look forward to 期待；期盼

此片語中的 to 為介系詞，後面須接名詞或 V-ing，表示「期待某事到來或發生」，帶有興奮、渴望之意。

- Everyone in the office is looking forward to the holidays.
  辦公室裡的每個人都期待假期的到來。

- I look forward to seeing you again soon.
  我期待很快再見到你。

比較 動詞 expect 指「預期；預料」，表示預期某事會發生，用法為 expect + N. 或 expect to V.，為較中性的用法。

- Dana is expecting a phone call from her friend.
  黛娜在等她朋友的電話。

- No one expected to see Roger at the beauty salon.
  沒人料到會在美容沙龍見到羅傑。

2. around the corner 在轉角處；在附近不遠處

如字面意思表示「（某事物）在轉角處；在附近不遠處」，要注意的是，此片語須以事物為主詞。

- The bank is right around the corner from my house.
  銀行就在我家附近。

補充 表示「（某事、某日）即將到來、發生」。

- Everyone is busy preparing for the New Year, which is just around the corner.
  每個人都忙著為即將到來的新年做準備。

- Sam could feel success right around the corner.
  山姆可以感覺到成功在望。

延伸學習 on the horizon 以字面意思「在地平線上」引申指類似意思：「（某事）即將發生的；已露端倪的」。

- The company formed just a year ago, and it already has some problems on the horizon.
  這間公司一年前才成立，已經有一些問題露出端倪。

3. **be sure to V.** 一定會做某事、出現某情況

表示某人一定會做某事或確定會發生某事。

- Mark is sure to be pleased with the good news.
  馬克聽到這個好消息一定會很高興。

補充

①Be sure to + V. 一定要做某事（常用於叮嚀別人）

- Be sure to lock the door when you go out.
  出門前一定要鎖門。

②There + be + sure to be + N. 一定有某事物

- There is sure to be a lot of food at the Christmas party.
  聖誕派對上一定會有很多食物。

Sentence Patterns

* **With this warm, traditional feeling, it's no surprise that the market is loved by young and old alike.**

句型 With N. (. . .), S. + V. 因為、有了某條件，（所以）……

- With rising gas prices, many people are now using public transportation.
  因為油價上升，很多人現在都使用大眾運輸工具。

- With both children away, Mr. and Mrs. Smith's home became quiet.
  由於兩個孩子都離家了，史密斯夫婦家裡變得非常安靜。

句型 It's no surprise that S. + V. ……不令人意外

- Amy likes warm weather, so it's no surprise that she chose to go to a beach for vacation.
  愛咪喜歡溫暖的天氣，所以她選擇了去海邊度假並不令人意外。

動手寫寫看 參考答案

Unit 1 規劃旅遊行程

1. Where do you want to go this time?
2. When can you take days off to travel around Bali?
3. Do you want to join a tour group or travel independently?
4. Do you want to enjoy the autumn colors in Kyoto this fall?
5. Let's plan a three-day package tour of Macau.

Unit 2 旅行社英語

1. I'd like two airplane tickets to Guam.
2. How much is it for the cheapest ticket to Singapore, and on which airline is it?
3. We are on a tight/shoestring budget. It's better not to go over 50,000.
4. Are there any double rooms available during the New Year's holiday?
5. I'd like to change my flight.

Unit 3 自助旅行英語

1. The advantage of backpacking is that you can go wherever you like.
2. It's better to rent a car when backpacking in California.
3. Why don't we be more adventurous and take the subway?
4. I plan to stay in San Francisco for three days. Are there any must-sees?
5. Are there any special passes that I can use for traveling around Osaka?

Unit 4 機場英語

1. May I see your passport and boarding pass, please?
2. Your baggage exceeds the weight limit. You'll have to pay an extra charge.
3. Could I have an aisle seat, please?
4. Can I carry this bag into the cabin?
5. We have to wait for two hours. Let's go to the VIP room and sit down for a while.

Unit 5 機上英語

1. Excuse me, is it possible for me to exchange seats with you?
2. Can I use my laptop on the plane?
3. How should I fill out this form?
4. You can press the call button if you need help.
5. Please put the tray table up because we are about to land.

Unit 6 旅館英語

1. I want to stay one more day. Do you still have any vacancies?
2. I've made a reservation online and paid a deposit.
3. Can you add extra beds to the double room?
4. I'd like a wake-up call tomorrow morning at seven o'clock.
5. Can I use wireless Internet here?

Unit 7 住房英語

1. There seems to be something wrong with the air-conditioning in my room.
2. The room you gave me hasn't been cleaned yet. Can I get another room?
3. The people in the room next to mine are so noisy that I can't sleep.
4. I need a detailed list of my room expenses.
5. I probably lost my room key.

Unit 8 購物英語

1. How much are these shoes?
2. Can I try this on?
3. Can you knock the price down a little if I buy two?
4. I'd like to buy this for my friend. Can you gift wrap it for me?
5. Could you ring up these items for me?

Unit 9 餐廳英語

1. I'd like a nonsmoking table, preferably by the window.
2. How large are the portions?
3. What dishes do you suggest/recommend?
   What do you suggest I try?
4. Would you please wrap this dish (up) for me?
5. We'd like to have the bill/check.

Unit 10 問路英語

1. I'm totally lost. Where is the closest subway station?
2. What's the best way to get to the art museum from here?
3. Is the train station down this road?
4. I need to get back to Meridien Hotel. Which direction should I go in?
5. Is there any place for me to park my car?

Unit 11 租車英語

1. Do you have any cars available to rent?
2. How many people/passengers does this car seat?
   How many people/passengers can fit in this car?
3. Do I have to return the car to the same location?
4. How much do you charge if I am an hour late?
5. Please check the tire pressure for me and add air if necessary.

Unit 12 急難救助英語

1. My wallet has been stolen.
2. Where is the lost and found office?
3. I need a copy of the missing item report.
4. My friend is sick. Is there a hospital nearby?
5. Someone is injured. Please call an ambulance.

NOTES

NOTES

LIVẽ PẽN 智慧點讀筆

隨點隨聽 是您最佳的語言學習家教!

　　學習語言時,遇到不會唸的單字或句子,不是問人就是只能拿起翻譯機聽著死板發音,這種學習方式已經落伍了!LiveABC 邀請您一起來體驗嶄新的學習模式!

　　LIVẽ PẽN **智慧點讀筆**,使用高品質的光學感應筆頭,書中的單字、句子、段落都可隨點隨聽,走到哪、讀到哪、聽到哪,不受任何時間地點限制,攜帶方便,外型輕巧時尚,符合現代人講求方便、快速、有效的學習需求,一筆在手,樂趣無窮。

功能說明

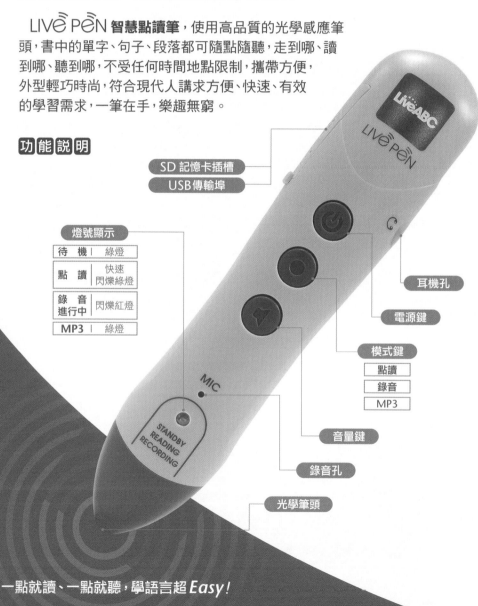

| SD 記憶卡插槽 |
| USB傳輸埠 |

燈號顯示

待　機	綠燈
點　讀	快速閃爍綠燈
錄　音進行中	閃爍紅燈
MP3	綠燈

MIC

STANDBY
READING
RECORDING

耳機孔

電源鍵

模式鍵

| 點讀 |
| 錄音 |
| MP3 |

音量鍵

錄音孔

光學筆頭

一點就讀、一點就聽,學語言超 *Easy*!

使用範例

1. 高品質光學感應筆頭，以筆尖輕觸頁面上的文字或圖片，
   即可進入點讀模式，隨點隨聽，學習零距離。

2. 內建高品質喇叭，可依個人需求外接耳機，打造專屬的語言學習環境。

3. 搭配隨筆附贈之錄音卡與音樂卡，馬上變成錄音筆和MP3播放器，一筆多用。

4. 內建4G大容量記憶體與可擴充SD記憶卡插槽，方便儲存多本書的檔案。

本書範例

點 PLAY ALL 圖示，即播放整頁或整段的發音

各別點選內文句子及單字皆可聆聽發音

＊每本書可實際點讀發音之部分皆不同，依各書所列為準。

產品規格			
尺　寸	14cm×3cm×2.4cm	耳機介面	3.5mm
重　量	38公克(不含電池)	點讀檔案格式	*.ecm
電　源	4號(AAA)電池2顆	USB介面	USB 2.0連接埠/連接線
省電功能	自動關機(約3分鐘)		(USB Cable僅供資料傳輸用途，不具充電功能)
工作時間	約3-4小時(依實際使用功能而定)	按　鍵	電源鍵、模式鍵、音量鍵
揚聲器	內建喇叭	音樂播放格式	MP3 Mode檔案格式支援：*.mp3
電源指示	LED指示燈	記憶卡	4GB (產品內含4GB記憶卡)

訂購資訊

心動了嗎？請立即上 **LiveABC** 官網點讀筆專區訂購：
http://www.liveabc.com/site/Online_Store/livepen/index.html

國家圖書館出版品預行編目資料

看影片學英語 用英語去旅行 / LiveABC 互動英語教學集團編譯.
　初版　臺北市 : 希伯崙公司 , 民 103.06

面；　公分

ISBN 978-986-5776-46-6 (平裝附光碟片)

1. 英語　　2. 旅遊　　2. 讀本

805.18　　　　　　　　　　　103010756

看影片學英語 用英語去旅行 《數位學習版》讀者回函卡

謝謝您購買 LiveABC 互動英語系列產品

如果您願意，請您詳細填寫下列資料，免貼郵票寄回 LiveABC 即可獲贈《CNN 互動英語》、《Live 互動英語》、《每日一句週報》電子學習報 3 個月期（價值：900 元）及 LiveABC 不定期提供的最新出版資訊。

姓名		性別 □ 男 □ 女

您從何處得知本書？
□ 書店　　□ 網站
□ 電子型錄　□ 他人推薦
□ 雜誌
□ 其他 _____

您以何種方式購得此書？
□ 一般書店　□ 連鎖書店
□ 網路　　　□ 郵局劃撥
□ 其他 _____

出生日期	年　月　日	聯絡電話

您對本書的評價

	書名	封面	內容	編排	紙張
很滿意	□	□	□	□	□
還不錯	□	□	□	□	□
普通	□	□	□	□	□
不滿意	□	□	□	□	□
很後悔	□	□	□	□	□

住址	□□□

您覺得本書的價格？
□ 偏低　□ 合理　□ 偏高

E-mail	

您希望我們製作哪些學習主題？

學歷	□ 國中以下　□ 國中　　□ 高中
	□ 大專及大學　□ 研究所

職業	□ 學生　　□ 資訊業　□ 工　　□ 商
	□ 服務業　□ 軍警公教　□ 自由業及專業
	□ 其他 _____

您對我們的建議：

縣 市

市 區

鄉 鎮

村 里

路 街

段

鄰 巷

弄

號

樓

室

希伯崙股份有限公司客戶服務部 收

英語數位學習第一品牌